EPILOGUES

FOR

LOST GODS

CAT RECTOR

First printing November 2022

Edited and Proofread by Ivy L. James
Sensitivity Read by Dal Cecil Runo
Cover Art by Grace Zhu
Cover Text Design by Cat Rector
Interior Formatting and Design by Cat Rector
Manuscript Critique by Erin Kinsella
Viking Era Ornaments by Jonas Lau Markussen

Further contact information for contributors can
be found at the back of the book.

ISBN - 9781778076305 (paperback)
ISBN - 9781778076312 (hardcover)
ISBN - 9781778076329 (ebook)

www.catrector.com

To everyone who read my first book and decided I should write another. Each one of you has had a hand in making this dream of mine come true.

Thank you.

It was at this point that Bilbo stopped. Going on from there was the bravest thing he ever did. The tremendous things that happened afterward were as nothing compared to it. He fought the real battle in the tunnel alone, before he ever saw the vast danger that lay in wait.

— J.R.R. Tolkien, *The Hobbit*

When Cal first clambered into the loft and spied Blackblood glimmering darkly in the corner, he made no comment on it. "Cozy," he said instead. "Be wantin' a bed and dresser, no doubt." "No need," said Viv. "I'm used to sleeping rough." "Used to ain't the same as ought to."

— Travis Baldree, *Legends & Lattes*

TRIGGER WARNINGS

If you've read Book One, you know that this isn't going to be a light book. If you haven't, this is Book 2, what are you doing here? Turn Back.

This book has a primary focus on pain, grief, and healing. If you're not in a position to explore those topics, you may want to put this aside for another time.

The book features scenes of:
Vulgar language
Body horror
Gratuitous violence and torture
Scary run-ins with monstrous things
Physical assault/attempted murder
Trauma-related mental health issues
Mentions of mental, emotional, and verbal abuse
Unhappy situations for LGBTQA+ characters
Mentions of sexual coercion
Discrimination and fantasy slurs
Death

An extensive list of warnings, tropes, and representation can be found on my website, CatRector.com

Don't forget to hydrate.

PREFACE

If you haven't read The Goddess of Nothing At All, you should turn back now. Very little of this book is going to make sense to you.

This book is a bit experimental. It took a while for me to realize what I was truly doing, which was writing a 100k word epilogue to the first book. So if it feels unconventional, it probably is. But so was book one, so perhaps you already know what you're getting into.

So many stories wrap up all their plot threads and attempt to tie things into a perfect little bow for the reader. There's not much left to wonder about, and the experience of the character's life is complete. No more events, no more consequences. While this is satisfying, and often expected, it's not very life-like, is it? What happens to characters after the best and worst moments of their lives?

Epilogues for Lost Gods is the aftermath of Sigyn's story and attempts to deal with all the things that come after loss, hardship, and trauma. You may find my take on this to be rewarding, or you may find it frustrating, but in any case, you've been warned.

Just like with Book One, this is not a faithful retelling of Norse Myth. In fact, there are no myths left to tell. If you want the purest version of the myths, I've included a list of research materials in the back. You can also find recommendations for other works of Norse fiction via my Goodreads lists.

Also, this book has been written and edited in British English. Don't worry, I can spell.

Usually.

Unless we're spelling Psychology. Then it's just chaos.

WHERE WE LEFT OFF...

The Goddess of Nothing At All was a thick book, but let me remind you of some of the key beats.

SIGYN AND LOKI

After falling in love with Loki, Sigyn finds herself dragged through endless amounts of trouble. By the end of the book, she's given birth to two sons and is at odds with Loki. The two are locked in a hot spring together where they're meant to stay until Ragnarok. Once they're able to escape, Loki flies off, determined to get revenge for the death and violence against his children. Sigyn is reunited with Váli and they try to stop the battle from happening, but having failed, Sigyn tries to get her family to safety. Sigyn is the one to ultimately take Loki's life, and she escapes Asgard to hide with her family in Urd's Well. Once the realms are habitable again, she returns to find that not all the gods are dead, and the realms aren't as empty as they seemed.

VÁLI, NARVI, AND HREIDULFR

After growing up in the ranks of the einherjar, Váli isn't a fan of Loki. Once it's clear that the family can no longer live in Asgard, Váli, Hriedulfr, Narvi and Sigyn attempt to make it to Jotunheim by foot. Hreidulfr is left to die, but the others are captured and taken to the hot spring, where Váli is transformed into a wolf. Váli mindlessly murders Narvi, then runs out of the hot spring. At the end of her imprisonment, Sigyn finds Váli in the woods, and they return to Asgard to stop Ragnarok. On the final day before battle, Hreidulfr visits the family's old home, and the lovers are reunited. Váli and Hreidulfr survive the final battle, and go with Sigyn to Urd's Well, later accompanying her to the surface at the end of the book.

ANGRBODA, JORMUNGANDR, FENRIR, AND HEL, SLEIPNIR

After Loki's second family comes banging on Sigyn's door in the middle of the night, they're eventually found and captured by Odin. Sigyn, trying to ensure the safety of her own family, tells her father that Loki brought them to her home against her will and pleads for mercy. Jormungandr is thrown into the sea in Midgard, Fenrir is bound, and Hel is sent to Helheim. Angrboda is imprisoned but escapes and isn't seen again. During Ragnarok, Jormungandr and Thor kill each other. Fenrir kills Odin, but is killed by Vidar. Hel leads her army of the dead to victory and destroys the realms. Sleipnir also perished during Ragnarok after being impaled. He died protecting his family.

HOD AND EYVINDR

Sigyn's brother Hod has been a friend to the family during the book, but falls prey to Loki's bad schemes. While trying to get revenge for his children being thrown across the realms to die, Loki kills Baldur in front of a crowd of people and disappears. Hod is accused of the murder and immediately killed. Eyvindr grieves the loss of his lover, and distances himself from the family after the funeral. After Ragnarok, Hod and Baldur have somehow escaped Helheim and returned to Asgard.

MAGNI, MODI, AND VIDAR

Along with Hod and Baldur, Magni, Modi, and Vidar are the godly survivors of Ragnarok. Magni and Modi are the sons of Thor, and Vidar is the son of Odin, and each has a deep love for Old Asgard.

THE OTHER GODS

The gods not mentioned above were killed during Ragnarok, either in battle or during the aftermath.

PROLOGUE

LOKI

Before

"Screams.
Nothing but screams.
They come for me every night."

— *Ingrid, Volume 10*

Why was everything so fucking cold?

Someone shouldered me, sent me stumbling into someone else. There were so many bodies, all shambling forward.

Mindlessly, almost.

I tried to see their faces but my vision wouldn't focus, not the way it should have. Like I'd been asleep. The edges of everything were hazy. Dreamlike. Something caught my eye and I looked beside me. She—he? Once, maybe. Now they were barely more than a walking corpse, charred and flaking, the smell of cooking flesh in my nose. Frozen in place, I kept staring.

The flesh steamed.

How was this thing still moving?

I lost my balance and lurched forward into another faceless body, pain splintering out from my chest at the impact. I put my hand to the spot and it came away red, blood painting my fingertips.

A hole. A hole had been ripped in my body.

Blood. The wound, my clothing, soaked in slowly drying blood. Not bleeding, not anymore.

I blinked back the fog in my eyes, trying to move with the crowd, the unending sea of bodies. My vision was a little better, but I was no longer sure I wanted to see. The tide of people stretched as far forward as I could see, and just as far behind me. Thousands—maybe hundreds of thousands. Jotun, Human, Elf, Dwarf.

How did I get there?

I couldn't remember.

How could anything have ended with so many walking corpses?

A cry split the air from somewhere in front of me. The crowd was funnelling to the side, moving around an obstruction in the road. I pushed forward, hand clasped to the wound in my chest that didn't bleed enough. Her face was familiar: auburn hair cascading over bloodied armour. Freya. She was trying to fight off a dozen black-armoured soldiers, chains lashed around her middle. A deep gash cut from one of her shoulders and across her chest in the shape of enormous claws. White bone peeked out from between the red.

I'd seen her die. The memory came back in a flash, burning like lightning. She'd gotten too close to Fenrir. And he'd killed her.

If she was dead and all these people were walking pieces of meat, then—

Impossibly tall gates loomed open ahead of the crowd, towering above the shambling bodies passing through them, cold iron hinged on either side of a rock wall. They were too familiar. My insides were coiling, I knew them, I knew them—

No.

Something pressed at the edges of my memory, something sharp and violent and I—

I pushed forward, trying to get through the gates, to know, to get proof that it couldn't be real. That I was making it all up. I had gone mad, finally truly mad.

Please, let me be out of my mind and not—

The crowd followed the path down a winding stone slope on the side of the high cliff. Bursting out of the throng, I nearly stepped off the cliff edge in my hurry.

Below was a city, black and shadowy, sprawling out in the enormous cavern below. Thousands of people poured down the pathway towards it, towards the flickering fluorescent-blue lights that ran along the streets and in the windows of houses, taverns, market stalls. Everything wound toward one point, one sprawling building at the back of the city, carved into the walls, tall spires and looming arches of black stone lit by the flickers of pale green wildfire.

I knew this place. And I knew how I'd gotten there.

I wanted to fall to my knees and weep. It was too much, too much—but the sea of bodies pushed me along, walk or be trampled. And so I flowed with them, following, but I wasn't there, not really.

Epilogues for Lost Gods

I remembered it all.

And the horror of it was enough to shred everything that I was.

Enough to tear my consciousness from me and send it hurtling to where I'd come from.

To the wound in my chest, the place where the knife had been.

The place where he'd stabbed me.

Where she'd pushed it deeper.

I remembered the realms on fire and bleeding and flooding, and everything that I had done.

I saw the moment the world went dim.

The glisten of her tears down her cheeks as I became nothing.

As the world faded away.

I was dead.

They'd brought me to Helheim.

CHAPTER ONE

LOKI

Later

"They promised it would be easy to move on."

— *Kóri, Volume 27*

❝ Just put the knife down. Please."

—couldn't see, couldn't think, breathing—chest hurt, metal against bone, flesh ripping—

the knife I—

"Father, you're safe. You were dreaming."

The voice. It pushed into my consciousness. Past the sea of bodies, the smell of burnt flesh, and the taste of blood. The blur in my vision slowly cleared, like hot breath on a cold window, fading. Narvi was standing in front of me, hand held out. My knuckles were white, a death grip on the knife.

Pointed at him.

How? Where did I—

Blood, flashing, bone white, bruises—

No. Distract yourself. Think of other things. Butterflies. Warm stew. Soft beds and luxurious furs and goose down pillows. The smell of her hair. Count the flowers carved in the wooden wardrobe.

Think of anything but the bodies.

Breathe. Air in the useless lungs, air out of the useless lungs.

Slow down.

Slow.

Epilogues for Lost Gods

The overwhelming panic abated, if only enough to tell friend from foe. Never enough to be fine.

"Narvi." I pulled in a long breath. Sleep still lingered at the edges of my good eye—the bad one was always a cloudy arrangement of lights and shadows, cutting off everything that was too far to the right—and the world seemed so abstract. But I was in my room. The dream was gone, back in the past where it belonged. Hiding just around the corner. Waiting for me to let my guard down again.

I relaxed my grip on the knife and fell back onto the mattress. "I'm sorry. It was the same. It's always the same."

Narvi sat on the edge of the mattress and took the knife from my hand. "I know. It's alright."

His eyes were narrowed in concern. He looked so much like his mother when he did that. His brown eyes were hers and so was that deep frown he wore when things weren't alright at all. Even down to the dark brown of his hair, though he had none of her curls.

I tried to shake off the melancholy that that thought brought to the surface. It was bad enough he had to see me so broken apart; he didn't need to know how much he made me miss his mother as well.

My hand shook as I reached for the bedside table and grabbed the beaten wooden pipe. I lit the still-stuffed end with a snap of my fingers and took short puffs, willing it to burn. A long inhale. Hold. Exhale. Another inhale. Slowly, knowing the borrowed calm would soon creep over my body, I could start to truly breathe again.

I hated feeling so weak, so needy, especially in front of Narvi. My insides curdled, knowing he was there, looking at me, watching how little I was able to keep myself stitched together.

Stitched together, what a joke. I peered down at the hole that was still carved into my chest, raw and open like it was every time the glamour wore off. The long, jagged, ugly slit that had opened me up and taken my life. Still burning and itching even though the blade was long gone.

Narvi was too quiet, staring at the faint fluorescent-blue lamplight reflecting on the surface of the knife in his hand.

"Did I wake you?" I couldn't look him in the eyes.

He shook his head. "I've been up since well before lights."

"Again? Narvi, you need to sleep sometime."

"I'd rather not." He slid a finger against the edge of the knife, then drew it away, looking at the thin slice in his skin that didn't bleed.

The dead don't bleed.

5

The dead don't do anything.

I forced myself to get up and pull a tunic from the wardrobe. "Have you seen your sister yet?"

"She's already working at the table. I think she's waiting for you."

"Right." I went to the mirror and tried to braid back the unruly mess of flame-red hair that hung over my shoulders. I was tempted to stop and stare, but I'd gotten good at tidying up without seeing the mess that I'd become.

I whispered a few runes, the mirror reflecting the seidr glamour that fell over me, returning me to the Loki I wanted to be. Snow-white skin, blood still pumping beneath, no melted-wax scars dripping down one side of my face. The cloudy cornea and scarred tissue of my blind right eye became black and white and emerald green, just like the other. No hole in my chest.

A Loki who was whole and unmarred by all this damnable suffering. But no matter how many glamours I hid myself under, no matter how many empty laughs I choked out, that Loki never really appeared. He was only skin-deep.

"She's not wrong, you know." Narvi's reflection stared up at me. "You need to start doing something more with your time. You're just torturing yourself."

"You're all overreacting." I turned back to Narvi. "There's nothing wrong with the way I spend my time."

"You stay confined to the palace and wander around the halls like you're trying to haunt the place."

"I do not," I huffed. "And if I did, it would be fitting, wouldn't it? I *am* dead." I slipped on my boots and opened the door to my chambers, gesturing for Narvi to leave.

"Just because you're dead doesn't mean you shouldn't live a little. You need to do more than placate the things that haunt you with that pipe. Go out. Go to the tavern. Meet new people."

"Ah yes, then we introduce ourselves. '*Oh yes, my name is Ullr, and you?*' '*I'm Loki. I likely killed you and all your family.*' We'll be best friends in no time."

Narvi let out a long, exasperated breath.

"Haven't found an answer to that one, hmm? Me neither. And besides, I don't see you taking your own valuable advice either."

Narvi shot me a scowl.

The same old tune, the same old dance.

We rounded the corner into the dining hall. Like everything in Helheim, the palace was made of grey-black stone. The walls were adorned with the tapestries of every god of Asgard, gifted to Hel by the Nornir themselves. Each portrayed the lifespan of a particular god, from birth until their demise. And that was what Hel had wanted them for: a collection of gods whose blood was on her hands. Ragnarok, her life's glory on display.

Hel was sitting at the head of the table, paper and books sprawled out around her, picking at her breakfast as she worked. She was still in a long black silk nightgown, her black hair pulled back in a dishevelled bun, all of her face uncovered. Half of her was pale Jotun flesh, the other half blue and mottled and dead, bone peeking out from underneath. She was at once stunningly beautiful and absolutely chilling. More important, she was so dangerously clever. The daughter every father wished for.

Hel looked up as we entered, her fierce emerald eyes catching my gaze. "Good morning."

"Morning, dove. How are things in the realm today?" I pulled out a chair that kept her on my left, where I didn't need to twist around to see her properly. I swept my hand out, pushing making room on the table for me to lean. There were books and parchment everywhere, almost as if she didn't have at least one office to work in.

Funny how the most important women in my life kept themselves surrounded by stacks and stacks of books.

Looking back down, Hel scratched more notes onto her page. "There was an uprising of dwarves last night against a clan of humans, nothing the sentries couldn't handle." She paused, stared at her notes for a moment, then sighed and scratched them out. "But I need someone to double-check my accounting. Keeping these books balanced is an atrocity."

"You could pay someone to do that for you, you know." I stole her cup of coffee and breathed in the deep, earthy smell of it. Eating or drinking anything with a barely functioning body was a recipe for a very messy day, but I never missed the chance to smell someone else's coffee. It was almost enough to fool myself that it was working and that I'd soon be fully awake.

"If I paid someone, they'd still do it wrong." Hel took a bite of honied bread and wiped her fingers on her nightgown, still not looking up. She was alive and most everything about her body worked the way it was supposed to, regardless of the visual imperfections. How I envied her ability just to *eat*. "Are you going out today?"

I took a deep breath. "Wasn't planning on it, no."

"But you'll go to the gatekeeper, yes?"

"Maybe." I didn't know why she bothered to ask. We all knew I would, like every day before this one. One disappointing trip back and forth.

"Then if you're going out, stay out. I don't care what you do, but don't you dare come back before dinner. Your lurking is scaring the staff."

"Lurking. Really?"

"Well—" Narvi cleared his throat. "—I did say that you kind of skulk around."

I took a long drink, glowering at my traitor son. "When did you two start teaming up against me?"

"Always have been," Hel said.

"I'm going to go up to the offices to work later." Narvi was picking at a bread crust he'd never eat. "You could join me there when you're back, if you want."

That finally got Hel to look up. "That's not socializing. You're each as bad as the other. I don't care if you take up social knitting or even pottery but you need to make some fucking friends here. I—"

I pushed my chair back, pushing the coffee toward her. "No, I think that's a splendid idea. Off I go. Be back soon." And I was out of the dining hall before anyone could force me into yet another horrific attempt at *making friends*.

Helheim as a realm was largely a vast, dangerous, unexplored wilderness, but Helheim the city was bustling. I'd once heard a couple of the more modern corpses compare it to "New York but if it were Dee and Dee New York"; however, despite endless hours spent updating my languages, due to being trapped in a cavern for centuries I still had no clue what the *fuck* that meant. The city sprawled on for miles, humble homes tucked into blocks, some stacked on top of each other, market squares set up at convenient distances. Everything was made of stone; a distinct lack of forests down in the dark meant wood was at a premium. Bioluminescent plants crawled up the sides of everything, some allowed to grow wild and some expertly cultivated into shapes and patterns. And the closer you got to the wild edges of the city, the more construction you found.

Hel had tried to prepare her city for Ragnarok as best she could, but who could possibly be ready for an influx of hundreds of thousands of souls? Any Jotun, Dwarf, or Elf that had died would've made its way down there, not to mention any of the humans in Asgard. Free from their mortal or post-mortal coils, they set up shop—some literally—in whatever corner they could etch out for themselves.

But Hel didn't subscribe to hierarchies, no. The same size house for everyone, the same net worth. In return, you provided a service befitting your skills and capabilities, to add to the growth of the city. She'd found something for everyone, it seemed. *"Fucking communist,"* someone had once screamed at her as she passed, and then I'd had to go to the archives and look that up too.

And Hel dared to ask me why I didn't socialise.

By the time I'd trudged my way out of the city and up the cliff path to the gates of Helheim, I'd worked myself back into a relatively foul mood just thinking about…

well, everything. It didn't help that this place where I'd spend the rest of my eternity was also dark and dingy and didn't mix well with my lack of depth perception. I spent every walk summoning and snuffing out wildfire to help me see because no amount of adjustment and adaptation since I'd lost part of my sight had stopped rocks on the ground from appearing out of nowhere to trip me up. Every time I stumbled or fell, it rubbed against my pride.

A lot of things had rubbed against my pride in my life, and I was beginning to see how that was a problem.

Right inside the massive iron gates that separated Helheim from the rest of the realms was a table. Edvin, the gatekeeper and the head of New Soul Intake, was scratching runes into a book. He was sporting a wispy grey beard and a pair of spectacles propped on his nose. He was old, but he was sharp as an axe. And if we're judging friendship by how often you visit someone, Edvin was my best fucking friend in the nine.

He looked up as I got closer. "Loki, how are you today? Any news in the palace?"

I smiled and stuffed my hands into my trouser pockets. "They've kicked me out again, Edvin. Can you believe it? Their own father."

"Well, all the better for me. No one else ever visits and I'd be terribly lonely if you didn't stop by." Edvin smiled and I couldn't be sure what the message behind it was.

I laughed. "You're patronizing me, but I'm going to let it slide." I looked up at the gates. "Nothing again?"

Edvin shook his head. "Not today. You know, if she were to arrive, I'd send word immediately. You can trust me."

"I know." I shook the familiar disappointment from my shoulders. "What can I say? Sitting around doing nothing feels like I'm doing nothing."

"Understandable."

After Ragnarok, after I'd fought through the absolute, inescapable terror of being dead, I'd sat with Edvin for a week straight, waiting for them. If the realms had ended, they would come eventually. But they never did. It meant my family had to be alive somewhere. No other havens were left for our dead. But how anyone could've survived Ragnarok, I wasn't sure. And then slowly a few more souls trickled in with stories of a new city, run by one of the old goddesses.

Edvin marked his page and closed the ledger before reaching below the table and coming back with a wooden box. "Time for a game, then?"

I smirked and pulled out the spare stool he'd started keeping under his table for me. "All I have is time."

He pulled the box open from the centre, revealing a game board with black and

9

white tiles and the variety of carved pieces that came with it. Chess, the newcomers called it. Edvin had learned from the dead before Ragnarok and had spent the last seven years attempting to teach me the intricacies of it. I didn't feel as sharp or as quick as I'd once been, but every once in a while I managed to take a game off him.

"And what story do you have for me today, Silvertongue?" Edvin lined up the black pieces on his side of the board, one by one.

I followed suit with the white pieces and, when the board was ready, made the first move. "Have I told you about the time Thor had to wear a wedding dress?"

Edvin moved his own piece. "You have. I'm in the mood for something closer to home."

There wasn't a soul in Helheim I talked to about my family, save for Edvin and my children. It was no one else's fucking business, something Hel and I had been disagreeing on for a long time. She even tried to get me to go to something called a "therapist." He'd wanted me to share my feelings, tell him all about it. Except who in their right mind would have any sympathy for me? My pain was mine. I wasn't about to go spilling my guts to someone who could never begin to imagine what I'd endured or the reasons I had for what I did.

I scratched my chin, moved a piece. "How about the time Sigyn flooded the kitchen?"

Edvin pushed his glasses back up. "Ah, now that I'd like to hear."

"The boys were still young. Váli was five, I think. Sigyn had been doing the dishes after breakfast and there was this gods-awful shriek from the other room. We rush in and Narvi's hanging headfirst out the window, and Váli's holding on to his leg to keep him from falling. So his mother grabs his other leg and I'm trying to pull him in, but he's wriggling and screaming like someone had lit him on fire. Finally, we get him inside and eventually everyone stops crying. Must have been in there twenty minutes trying to sort out *why* Váli put his brother out a window—trying to sneak out for sweets, as it turned out—and when we head back to the kitchen, the floor is a sea of water. Sigyn had left the tap running. The only reason it stopped was because the barrel was dry. So Sigyn starts losing her mind again and the boys stop crying long enough to go splashing through the water, running circles around the kitchen in their sock feet. And all I can do is laugh because they're such a sight. Sigyn is fuming, screaming, '*Take this seriously, Loki! The floor will warp!*' So she whips up some seidr and manages to lure most of the water out the front door, and the boys and I are crawling around behind her with towels and furs and whatever else picks up water. And Sigyn comes back inside, takes one look at us, wet, on our hands and knees, and just sits down in a puddle and starts laughing." I took a moment, smiling at the image of her in my head, that serious face melting into frustrated joy. "She was always beautiful, but especially when she was laughing."

Edvin nodded, lips pursed in a smile. "That's a very good story. It reminds me of what's most sacred." We'd been playing as I told the story, and he slid the knight forward with a satisfied flick of the wrist. "Checkmate."

"Fuck. You just wanted to keep me talking so you'd win, hmm?"

Edvin croaked a laugh. "Tell yourself what you need to, Trickster. Maybe you're just not good at chess. I hear they play Catan at the Thillows every second week if you need a change of pace."

I swept up my useless king and all the other pieces and put them back in the pocket built into the board, my good mood souring again. "No thanks, old man."

Depositing his own pieces, he snapped the board shut and looked at me intensely. "Loki, if I've told you this once, I've told you a thousand times. You're going to need to forgive yourself before anyone else can."

I glowered back. "I'm responsible for the near extinction of every species that's ever existed in all nine realms, so tell me, how exactly do I do that?"

Edvin actually laughed. "Do you think that your presence alone was the sole catalyst for Ragnarok? Or do you think it's more likely the result of a million choices made by thousands of the most influential beings in the nine? Did you destroy the ecosystems on Midgard and start the Fimbulwinter? Did you attempt to enslave the Dwarves? Did you—"

"We gave in to the prophecy! Angrboda and I made the children. That was us!" Tightness curled in my chest and it was pulling at my brain, badgering me with guilt and shame. The phantom smell of burnt flesh and smoke seared my nose again. "I wanted everyone to suffer with me and they did. I killed *everyone* and when the anger was gone, I—" Tears were welling in my eyes. "You have no idea how heavy that is. To think about each of them, one by one, and imagine their deaths. To see them in the streets and know it was *me*."

My hands were trembling.

"Loki." Edvin stood and walked around the table. He motioned for me to get up, and I followed him to the edge of the cliff that overlooked the city. "Do you know how many of these people I've personally let in? Most of them. We have prisons for the scum in the city, but this is the last bastion of the dead in the nine. There are mothers down there who starved their children, leaders whose knowing neglect led to the avoidable deaths of thousands. I've let in people that I'd rather see thrown into a black abyss." He turned to me. "Ragnarok was put into motion by choices made before you were born. You played a part, like all of us. Yours was bigger than most, granted, but you keep trying to take all the credit for it. They trapped you in a cave and it stopped nothing. Your absence made no difference. They removed you from the picture and made damning choices without you, over and over. Ragnarok came without you."

Part of me wanted to believe that. It would be convenient to throw away my responsibility and go back to a life of blissful, childish rebellion, but it wasn't true. We did this. *I* did this. I gestured to the city. "And them? Do you think they feel that way? They're dead and they blame me."

"What you did, you did out of pain. You avenged your family and yourself. I've heard of worse reasons." Edvin pulled up the sleeve of his sweater, revealing a mottled, long-healed burn that ran from his wrist to his shoulder.

I'd never seen him without sleeves before, but it hadn't occurred to me that he had something to hide. Though I suppose we all had something to hide, somewhere in us.

He ran his fingers down one of the lines of the burn until he came to his wrist. "There was no one to protect me from my father. Every child deserves someone who would kill for them."

The words caught in my throat. I couldn't look up anymore, not at him or his burns. Something twisted in my chest, and it stole away anything I could say. Nothing made sense and I felt so much and so little. All these things in me like steel weights, pulling me down.

Edvin put his arm around my back and walked me back to the path. "Go home, Loki. Spend time with your family. Enjoy what you have and stop focusing on the past. I'll see you again tomorrow, hmm?"

I nodded and started down the winding road to the city, trying to quiet the clamouring voices waging war in my head.

You killed them.
They deserved it.
Not all of them.
It was worth it.

CHAPTER TWO

SIGYN

"It's amazing how little you can live with…
How you can scrape together a life from
nothing but scraps and hope."

— *Dýrfinna, Volume 5*

L ying beneath the rippling mix of jewel-tone and green leaves swaying among the branches, I was easily able to pretend that everything was as it always had been. That I was beneath Yggdrasil, enjoying the sunlight and the warmth, a book curled against my chest. The breeze would whip up the leaves, their soft rustle lulling me to sleep, and for a moment, I could breathe.

Only for a moment.

I was not in Asgard. This tree was not Yggdrasil. And I was no longer the kind of girl who stretched out in the sunlight like a forest cat, relaxed and full of life.

There was a knot in my chest, curled around my heart like a fist. That was the case more often than not, and coming out to the Sister Tree was one of the few ways I had left to lessen the hold of it. If I stayed there, looking only at the sky, I could feign peace for a few moments before the urgency came rushing back.

Curled between two roots felt a little like being held. The branches of Yggdrasil that we had stolen and grafted onto the Sister Tree years ago were dotted with golden apples, waiting to be plucked. The Sister Tree never asked anything of me. It never needed me to sign documents, or make decisions, or save anyone's life. It just was, and it let me just be.

I took a deep breath.

The tapestry of my future had shown me in a crown, ruling over a shining city.

13

And I had done that. Together with half of the last beings in the realms, we had built Fólkheim, a place to begin a new kind of life. Somewhere I could be proud of. It was one of the best things I had ever done and would ever do…

But I was also so desperately tired.

Tired of working endlessly, only to lose more ground than I'd gained. Tired of being woken in the night to deal with one crisis or another. Tired of Asgard and its new gods biting at our heels.

Tired of being responsible for the lives of so many.

Maybe Odin had been right all along. Maybe I wasn't ready. Never had been.

That thought came to me now and again, and it never ceased to curdle my stomach. It was a guilty thought, one that was bound up in emotion, not logic.

I pushed it away, because it was a dangerous thing to let take root in my heart. Too much rode on my ability to be headstrong, even in the moments when I needed to feign it.

I'd needed to feign it too often lately.

I reached into the pocket of my dress and found the scrap of paper I'd tucked there. It had arrived in the early morning. I unrolled it, looking one last time, as if I could change the contents by will.

Asgard is mobilizing. Getting ready for something.

I whispered a rune and destroyed the message with a spark of lavender wildfire so that no one else would see it. I couldn't allow anyone to know who had written it. It was too obvious. One look at the thick paper and deep indents and they'd know.

Asgard was coming for us.

In the years since the realms had been remade, we had built Fólkheim in the hollow husk of Vanaheim, and Asgard had rebuilt upon its own grave. They had done the same thing we had, scouring the realms for anyone who would join them. But Asgard was set on being as strong and controlling as it once was, and gods were greedy. They'd learned well from their fathers how to take. Vidar had risen to take his father's throne, so alike in spirit to Odin himself. Thor's boys, Magni and Modi, were the face of Asgard, playing at diplomacy, asking for meetings that resulted in nothing, proposing treaties that always fell through. And Baldur. Hiding away in Asgard's halls somewhere, too afraid to leave lest someone take his life again.

Swine, all of them.

Except Hod…

The ghostly grip on my heart tightened, thinking of the one brother I still truly loved. Hod would know what to do, what to say, if only I could see him. He was there, in Asgard with the others, but free travel was a thing of the past and visiting Asgard was a dangerous affair.

If he wanted my company at all.

The thought burned me to the core. I had lost so much over the decades. In trying to earn respect from my family, I'd lost every one of them. I'd had my children stolen, my husband killed, my spirit crushed. And with all that, how exactly did I think I could protect an entire city?

There was one thing I could do…one last resort…but no. I couldn't entertain that thought for more than a moment. It was more temptation than I could stomach.

Tears streamed down my cheeks. Trying to be this version of myself was a foolish thing. I hadn't been prepared for what leading a city asked of me. I was tired and scared and hollowed out. It was not how leaders were supposed to feel. I had never known my father to be anything but resolute and cocksure. He had never faltered, not where anyone could see him, and whatever mistakes he had made, he had made them with all the righteousness of a man who owned everything.

Maybe that was the problem. Maybe I thought too much and felt things too deeply to ever be truly effective.

Maybe.

A deep, groaning wail sounded from the distance, tearing me from my self-pity. I sat up, my eyes scanning the horizon. Fólkheim was a collection of ruined, mismatched buildings, constructed out of the broken rubble that had once been Vanaheim. White stone and marble had been glued together with clay and metal and cement, until we had a city that looked like it was made of broken pottery. The only thing that stuck out was the tall piece of machinery that the Modernists—what we'd taken to calling the more recent faction of Midgard's dead—had called a crane.

The beastly moaning stopped a moment and began again, louder than before. Even from a distance, I could see the crane swaying left, then right, and left again.

It had been made from scraps of metal, welded together by the best smiths we had, but—

The crane groaned and listed to the right, toppling down into the horizon with a deafening screech and mighty crash of debris. Dust rose into the sky.

I bolted to my feet and ran, pins and needles bursting through my sleeping legs. My skirts were bunched up in my fists, any semblance of decorum gone. Soon I was off the grass of the Sister Tree's small sanctuary and back on the stone and dirt paths of Fólkheim. I darted around anyone in my path, weaving through streets that would lead me to the crane. Some were running with me, as it should be; we'd built a city on a foundation of unity, and what better moment for unity than a disaster.

Each street felt longer than the last. Vanaheim had been sprawling and vast, and its ruins were just the same. How many would be hurt? How many homes had we lost in our effort to be more efficient? How many lives would we lose this time?

As I got closer, the air became thicker. It was full of dust and debris, choking everyone in the street. I waved my hand in front of my face, trying to bat away the cloud. It was useless. The whisper of a few runes could clear the air but I couldn't stop coughing long enough to speak them.

Someone screamed. I felt my way forward, my hands coming up against more people, against wood and metal as I fumbled towards the sound. I was getting closer, the screaming turning to desperate pleading. My eyes burned, tears trying to wash the grit from them.

A harsh gust of wind picked up, whipping the dust away. I blinked, trying to cry the sand from my eyes. One of the völur was standing on a roof above us, hands out, her lips moving with silent runes, doing the exact thing I had been unable to.

The enormous crane had snapped in half and fallen into a row of our makeshift homes, shattering the roofs. There was blood in the streets and who knew what else in the wreckage.

No one needed to be told to move. Jotun, Human, Elf, it didn't matter. The uninjured were rushing forward to find the damage, rescue the weak, stabilize the homes. The scream rang out again and I followed it to the place where the crane had hit the ground. Lodged beneath it was a young Jotun girl, the metal crushing her ribs.

"Sigyn!"

I turned to see Hreidulfr running towards me, the engineer Alyssa on his heels.

"Help me get this up!" I grabbed one of the smoother edges of the crane and pulled. It was solid, but we had to get it up just enough to pull the girl out. I attempted to lift it. The weight of it made me tremble. A moment later, Hreidulfr had the other side, and the metal started to budge.

"Alyssa, can you pull her free?"

The engineer bent over the crying Jotun—Joanna, if I remembered right—looking for complications, then pulled her by the torso far enough to let us drop the crane again. It hit the ground with a thud and a groan that ran up the entire broken structure.

I fell to my knees beside the Jotun and pulled up her shirt. There was no external bleeding but her skin was purple. "Listen, I need you to breathe, alright?" I pushed her hair back from her eyes. "It's going to be over very soon."

Alyssa dropped to the ground and took the girl's hand, trying to give her something to hold on to.

Palms above her torso, I began to whisper. I knew the runes by heart. Replenished in this new age, the realms offered up their energy willingly; it flowed through me, changing with the runes on my breath, and flowed into the girl's skin. It travelled deep, and she cried out as something in her chest moved, her ribs stitching themselves back together. Slowly, the blood that had pooled under her skin lightened and faded, and the desperation in her voice died out into a muffled, traumatized sob.

She grabbed my hands, her face a mess of dust and relief. "Thank you, Goddess. You saved me."

"Of course. You're too precious to lose." I squeezed her hands and turned to Hreidulfr. "Take her to the infirmary. She needs to rest."

Hreidulfr and I helped her stand, and he offered her a piggyback ride, which she accepted with a tired smile. Once they were gone, I turned to Alyssa.

She was still kneeling in the dirt, staring at the wreckage. "I thought my design was perfect," she said to no one in particular. "What went wrong?"

I fell down next to her to catch my breath and steady my nerves. I stared up at the crane, an enormous patchwork of welded metals and rope. "The same thing that always goes wrong. We're working with what we can get, not what we need."

"Someone might have died. Maybe someone *is* dying." Her grey-blue eyes were glazed over, her fingers holding her sweeping golden-brown hair up at the back of her head, frozen in shock. A length of the bottom of her hair was an electric blue, a magical kind of hair that only the Modernists of Midgard ever had. She turned to me; I'd been staring too long. She had started to cry. "I can't be responsible for someone's death."

And that was one of the differences between the old guard and these Modernist humans who had died in the days of electricity and engines; most of the Modernists had never shed blood, while we were soaked in it.

I reached out and took her hands in mine. "The völur will help everyone who's hurt. We're going to find out what happened and make sure it doesn't happen again. It'll work better next time."

Her breathing slowed and she nodded, lips quivering. Then her eyes caught something behind me. I turned to look.

Váli was padding towards us, calm, but the muzzle of his grey wolf form was speckled with blood. He sat down beside us, his emerald eyes taking us in. His thoughts came to me, sliding into the back of my mind in the old familiar way. "*It only hit three homes, so the casualties are minor. There were four people injured. They've been sent to the infirmary. It wasn't as bad as it could have been.*"

"It's under control then?" I looked over my shoulder at the people scrambling back and forth, pulling away debris. Something pulled at me, desperate to be in the moment with them, but knowing that very soon my work would be behind the scenes: rehousing the families, arranging repairs, and all the other dissatisfying administration a city required.

"*As much as anything ever is,*" Váli said.

"Alright." I stood, pulling Alyssa up with me. I brushed uselessly at my dust-covered skirt. "I'm going to—"

Something caught my eye.

Tucked into a corner of the debris, barely noticeable from the street, was a leg protruding from the rubble.

I ran toward it, panic filling my mind. The house had collapsed and the mess of lumber and rock was piled on top of whoever was in there. A moment later, Alyssa, Váli, and a few others had joined me, trying to dig them out. It was achingly slow, each rock and beam revealing yet another obstacle in our paths until—

Alyssa backed away and retched.

One look was enough to know that there was no saving him.

We had lost someone else. Someone too young, too innocent. Someone who was loved and needed and would never return to us.

Again.

Progress was a dirty, difficult thing, and more often than we wanted to think about, the cost of progress was blood.

I knew this, and it didn't stop the pain of it.

The rage built under my skin until I was forced to turn and walk away. Váli's voice rose in my head, but I didn't want to hear him.

"Find his family."

It was all I could manage to say.

No words would change what had happened here.

We were piecing together a city out of spit and willpower, and it wasn't enough. People were dying because we didn't have the resources to help them thrive. Because we were making mistakes. What would happen when Asgard was on our doorstep? We already had nothing left to spare. A war would take too much from us.

That familiar idea bubbled up in the back of my mind. The one that I had kept secret all these years, because I knew that if I uttered it, if I made it real, I could never turn back. If I spoke the words, I wouldn't be able to tell myself no anymore. Wouldn't be able to let dead bodies lie.

I had come this far and let my loved ones keep their peace, but now Fólkheim needed help. There were no allies left. Not in the living realms.

But there were plenty in Helheim.

CHAPTER THREE

SIGYN

"I wish...I wish I'd spent more time with the people I loved.
So many were gone before I was, and it always seemed too
soon. Life doesn't always give second chances."

— Sigrún, Volume 13

" We're concerned for you is all." Hreidulfr had perched on the edge of my bed, elbows on his knees, staring at the ground. "Almost no one has gone to Helheim alive, let alone come back. We don't know what's waiting for you."

My room was big enough for me, but it felt cramped with three others inside. Váli had laid himself out on the floor in front of my bed, his emerald wolf eyes watching me wherever I went, and Alyssa was leaning against the door. This room, these people, a little slice of the realms that belonged to me. Now every one of them was trying to keep me from doing what I'd planned.

Just as I'd known they would.

"Hreidulfr's right." Alyssa pushed herself off the door and crossed her arms over her chest. "Are you sure it's safe?"

"Nothing in the nine is safe." I pulled a fresh pair of slightly frayed trousers from the wardrobe and set them aside. "We're not safe. We don't have any choice but to ask Helheim to face Asgard with us like they did at Ragnarok."

Alyssa rubbed her temples. "You haven't spoken to them since their deaths. How can you know that they'll agree to help?"

"I can't." I found a tunic and a warm shawl and put them next to the trousers. "But we're not talking about strangers. Hel promised me Narvi was safe with her, and if he is, so is Loki. And Loki may be a lot of things, but he loves his family. I just need

19

them to decide we're worth mustering a small army for."

A growl rose in Váli's throat. *"Loki was insane before he died. He—"*

I slammed my hand down on my desk. The rage was so sudden, so unbidden it surprised me as well. "I know. I do. Who else should we turn to, Váli? The empty realm of Midgard? The collapsed caverns in Svartalfheim? The last of the Elves are here. The Jotnar are here. Half of the realms are here and the other half is in Asgard. Who. Would. You. Ask?"

Váli narrowed his eyes, but he didn't answer.

I kept going. "I've been practising the seidr for months, in case it came to this. The völur taught me to shapeshift so I could be ready for *this*. And I'm going today. I told you about the latest message out of Asgard. If we wait any longer, they might appear on our doorstep before we can even sharpen our axes."

Hreidulfr shifted on the bed. "Ma'am, I don't want to ask this, but how much of this has to do with what the city needs, and how much is about what you need?"

He wasn't wrong. I'd been able to keep up a decent facade when it came to outsiders, but the people close to me knew better. Between the nightmares, and the days they caught me staring out windows with tears on my face, I couldn't hide it. I missed my son, and I missed whatever love was still left between Loki and me. I had been putting the needs of everyone else before mine, and now I was being given an excuse to have both. It seemed foolish not to take it.

Except.

Going to Helheim and stepping foot in my stepdaughter's halls meant facing their deaths in a way I hadn't already, and I wasn't sure if I would ever be ready for that. It would be real in a way that it hadn't been before. Or, if I went there, as tired and threadbare as I was, would I have the strength to look my husband and my son in the eyes and leave again? Would I find myself rooted to the spot, reunited with the other half of my family, ready to let go of all this responsibility?

I wasn't sure.

Alyssa sighed and the hard exterior fell away. "You know I'm just worried about you, right?"

I flashed her a thankful smile. "I appreciate it, but it's not needed. I'm not making a popular choice. I understand that. But I'm doing what must be done for the good of our people."

Váli's voice hit my mind with a distinctive growl. *"What's good for the realms might not be good for you. You moved on, Mother. Why are you so determined to destroy that?"*

I turned and stared him in the eyes. My voice wavered as I pushed back the wave of emotion that threatened to crash into me. "There's a difference between moving forward and moving on. I've been working to keep this city alive, but I have *not* moved on. How could I? There isn't a day that I don't wish your brother was alive, or that I could be with Loki the way I once was. I am *trying*, Váli. But do not mistake my functionality for peace."

I stopped speaking, a tear rolling over my cheek, and the room grew quiet. No one could look at me.

"*Fine*." Váli stretched and stood on his four paws. "*Our opinion clearly doesn't matter to you, so I'm going to get back to training the people who are actually going to be here fighting for their city. After all, we can't all abandon it at once.*"

His words should have burned, but I knew my son too well. That pain was his, and he had a habit of directing it outward to snap at the people he loved most.

I said nothing and waved to the door to let him know he was welcome to go work those feelings out somewhere else.

Váli got up and padded towards the door. But because it was closed, he was forced to stop and look up at Alyssa for help.

"Hard to storm out spitefully when you can't use a doorknob, isn't it?" I smirked.

Alyssa opened it, and as Váli left, I called after him, "Is there anything you want me to tell them?"

Váli stopped but didn't turn around. It was a long moment before the words crept into the back of my mind, tinged with regret and bitterness. "*You already know what to say.*"

And then he left.

Hreidulfr stood. "I suppose I should be a good partner and go after him." He came over and wrapped his enormous arms around me. "Be safe, ma'am. We'd be in a bad way without you." He patted me on the shoulder and left, closing the door behind him.

I let out a breath. I'd hoped they'd have come around by now, but I understood their reasons. There was so much emotion caught up in all of this, and it didn't take divination to know what Váli was thinking.

That his brother would hate him.

That his father would disappoint him.

That he was going to lose me too.

The conflict must have shown on my face. Alyssa put her hand on my shoulder and directed me to the bed. I followed her instinctively. As she settled in against the pillows and pulled me into her arms, my thoughts shifted to the calm she always brought to me.

"You're not alright, are you?" Alyssa said into my hair.

"And how can you tell that?" I breathed her in, the scent of dust, sweat, and metal on her skin. "You're not allowed to use your Midgard psychology on me."

She laughed and the sound brightened my mood just a little. "I don't need psychology to understand why you'd be in pain right now."

I sighed. "Why is it that you can hear me in ways that no one else can?"

Alyssa ruffled my hair. "Because I'm your very best friend and that's different from being someone's family. Children don't always understand that their parents suffer as well. Our relationship isn't built on a long history of temper tantrums and timeouts."

I nodded and let the sentiment linger in the air, saying nothing. It was good to have a friend who could focus on me, whom I didn't need to be strong for. Lying in her arms was another of the few escapes I had. Warmth bubbled in my chest as we laid there, at peace with each other, until I had to quell it with rationality.

She was a wonderful person. An amazing confidante. The best friend a person could ask for.

Anything more than that was a lie. I was on a path, and I'd chosen other things, other people.

It couldn't be anything more than friendship.

It couldn't be.

I needed a distraction.

"Tell me something new," I said, curling my head into the crook of her arm and closing my eyes. "Before I have to go."

"More psychology, I presume?" Alyssa pushed a lock of hair back from my forehead, one of her small, kind gestures that I had to force myself to ignore.

"Since we happen to be on the subject," I said. It was a topic I loved learning about, because it seemed to me like the closest anyone in Midgard had ever really gotten to true magic.

"Alright." She paused for a moment, thinking, then her finger started to turn slow circles on my shoulder. "Many psychologists thought most things wrong with the adult mind could be traced back to something that happened to them as children. If an adult woman was afraid of dogs but didn't know why, it was possible she was attacked by a dog in her childhood, even if she couldn't remember it."

I opened my eyes and looked up at her. "Really?"

"Absolutely. But not just fears. Anger, hope, sadness, courage. The things we become stem from the things we've been taught. A mother teaches her son to fear the world, he grows up to fear the world. A father teaches his daughter that she's worth nothing…" Alyssa trailed off, realizing too late what she'd said.

"She becomes nothing."

"She *thinks* she'll become nothing." Alyssa stole her arm back and leaned on her elbow, suddenly very serious. "Knowing what we've been taught is the key to unlearning it. You're not nothing. Your husband taught you that, and the rest of us will help you remember it."

"And is that part of psychology too? Unlearning?"

Alyssa smiled. "It's the very best part. The whole world opens up to us when we decide for ourselves what's worth keeping and what no longer serves us." She gave me a long look. "Are you ready to go now? You've got a long way to travel."

I nodded, reluctant to move away from her comfort and go back out into the harsh reality of things. In here, curled up with Alyssa, it was warm and soft and loving. A refuge from everything else. Seeing Loki again would be hard, complicated work. With her, I didn't need to worry if seven years had driven a wedge between us, or if I was crossing the realms for nothing, or if she harboured some secret resentment for me. Staying with Alyssa was safe.

Everything outside was raw and scathing.

She pulled me out of bed and kept me company as I changed into friendlier clothes for travelling. She talked about someone named Freud and someone else named Edipus-with-an-O and laughed when I expressed my disgust on the subject of sleeping with your relatives.

"The gods of Greece might disagree," she said.

Alyssa walked me out of my room and into the cavernous hallway. Vanaheim had been built against a cliff, and as part of its defences, all of the city's offices of power were inside the cliffs themselves. In the event of an attack, it would house the people in our city that couldn't fight, but it also served more practical, day-to-day purposes. Its rooms served as council chambers, planning centres, an archive, and dozens of personal bedchambers. Hallways and rooms had been carved out of stone and lit with seidr brasiers that illuminated stunning paintings. Ragnarok had left waterlines along the stone, destroying some of the paintings below, while the tops remained intact, but it was beautiful in its own way. Impermanent and flawed.

I had to find beauty in it where I could. I'd forced myself to. It had taken six months for me to start sleeping in my own bed inside the cliffs instead of whichever uninhabited home I could find. I'd had to learn how to step foot inside without seeing Loki tied to a rock.

We stepped out of the corridors and into the bright sunshine. A pair of waterfalls roared on either side of the entrance, pooling into the basins below before they snaked through the waterways around the streets. For all the things we lacked, fresh water was not one of them, and it had been one of the key reasons we'd chosen Old Vanaheim for our Fólkheim.

Ahead of us was a city square, the ground paved with grey stones. Citizens moved this way and that, most of them in a hurry, on their way somewhere. No one stopped to pay us any mind as we walked halfway across the square and stopped.

"All set?" Alyssa took my hand and squeezed it. My chest was tight, but I couldn't help but smile. She was always making me smile.

"Take care of them while I'm gone?" I spared a look around the open square, taking it in. I'd only be gone a few days, but with the way my life had gone, every farewell felt like goodbye.

"Of course I will. Now go before you get cold feet." Alyssa gave me a hug, and for a moment everything smelled like the raspberry-scented oil she'd made for her hair.

I let her go and took a deep breath. I'd spent months learning to do what Loki had always so easily done. It had been gruelling, painful work to learn how to become something else. Even now, knowing how important it was, how much my city needed me to do this, I dreaded it.

Drawing up the energy, I focused on the runes running off my tongue. They were familiar now. Practised. And as the seidr took hold, I felt it in every muscle, every bone in my body. The twisting, grinding, painful mess of it. The shape of me changing, bending, becoming something else.

And with a searing pop of light, the world became so much bigger. The discomfort faded, and I looked up. Above me was Alyssa, waving down from so high above my little self. The world from the eyes of a falcon.

I stretched my new wings and took flight. I climbed up, wings flapping, trying to keep the right pace until I was looking down over the city in a way few ever would. Below, Alyssa watched me as I circled. And then I veered towards the south. Towards Helheim.

Towards Loki.

CHAPTER FOUR

LOKI

*"He kept things for me. Collected dresses and jewellery, made
a shrine of my new things in his home. When I arrived in
Asgard, he'd already built us a life."*

— *Elena, Volume 4*

Hel gave me a dirty look when I passed her in the hall, but I wasn't in the
mood for that same old father-daughter banter. I headed straight to the back
of the palace, through the blue-illuminated halls, and up to the study where
Narvi spent a large part of his days.

His head was down when I went in, stacks of parchment around him. The sound
roused him from his work, and he stretched back in his chair. "Back already?"

"I can only lose so many games of chess before I have to walk away." I bent over
his desk, peeking at the parchment. "Your sister is keeping you busy."

Narvi ran his hand through his long hair, only to have it fall back in his face. He
sighed. "Who knew there'd be so much work involved with running a realm?"

"Who knew indeed." A notebook sat open on the desk. It was different from the
rest, full of Narvi's rune scratches, and the cover seemed handmade.

I reached for it and Narvi snatched it from under my grasp. He closed the book
and put it in his lap. Even though he stared me in the eyes, neither of us said anything.

Once upon a time, Narvi showed me everything.

Not anymore.

I turned and walked to the window across the room. It was the only one, with all
the other walls covered in shelves of ledgers and history books. The city sprawled out
below us, dozens of people the size of ants walking in the streets, everything dotted in

25

that same bioluminescent blue. A drawer opened and closed somewhere behind me, and a moment later Narvi came to the window next to me, watching with the same melancholy boredom, the notebook gone.

"And did Edvin say…anything new?" His quiet voice broke my heart. He knew I'd say no and it was never what he wanted to hear.

"Not today."

"Father…" Narvi's voice trailed off as I turned my head to him. He kept staring forward. "Do you think we get what we deserve?"

The question hung in the air like a blade, the answer he expected too sharp to do anything but cut.

I put my arm around his back. "No, we don't. Because if we got what we deserved, I'd still be trapped in that cave, spending eternity in excruciating pain, and you'd still be alive."

He looked at me then, a glisten in his eyes. "Haven't you ever thought that you deserve better than that? Maybe I'm the one who deserves worse."

"What? No, absolutely not." I pulled him against my side, holding him tightly. "You were the best person I knew in the nine and now you've worked so hard with your sister to build this city. You have *purpose*. You could be happy here."

He leaned his head on me, looking away. "I'm not happy for the same reasons you aren't."

I let out a long breath. What could I say to that? There was no forgetting that you were dead. Existing as this thing that was just dead enough to feel cold inside and just alive enough to remember every moment of the pain that killed you.

What answers did I have for him when I had none of my own?

So we stood in silence, his head tucked against me. We stayed there so long that my legs hummed to move, but I didn't dare. Staying put was all I could offer him.

After a quiet supper, I went back to my room. It was the only space I'd carved out for myself in the whole of Helheim, and most days it didn't even feel like it was mine. It belonged to a pair of strangers. One who had loved elegant clothes and good books, who had filled the room with soft furs, and who had once lived in this body but didn't anymore. And the other one, who never laughed and woke up screaming, and was new here but didn't want to leave. And so the room looked like both of them. An elegant, comfortable chamber with a side room for a bath, packed with a wardrobe, a bed, a chair, and a hearth, and it was so utterly fucking empty of meaning.

I rummaged through one of the piles of books on the mantle and pulled out a comfortable old favourite. Levaine Theavin. Hel had had enough forethought to have her people raid the realms for books while she'd burned cities to the ground, and I had praised her for it. She'd made an archive for the city with it. But I'd kept the ones I loved most for myself. And the ones Sigyn loved most.

She would want them someday.

I grabbed the pipe from the bedside and lit it. It had become a ritual for me. Smoke a little pot, read a good book, and maybe, just maybe, fall asleep without jarring visions of a dark, dank cave or a knife in my chest. I looked up through the window towards the cliff where the gates were. Sigyn had never liked it when I smoked. She couldn't stand the idea of losing control of anything long enough for it to settle her mind. But she wasn't here and it was the only thing that brought me close enough to who I had been. To the Loki who had slipped through the world easily. Trickster, Sky-Treader, Silvertongue. Not the hollowed husk I'd become.

Narvi had used the words *too much, too often* to describe my habit. But what else was I going to do?

Settling into the chair under the window, I curled my legs up and started from the beginning. A story divided in two, each character trying to make their way back to each other after a devastating war. A true story from Midgard. It even had a happy ending.

Two chapters in, something tapped at the window near my head. I looked up, the calm haze already settled over me. A raven. Odd. There were only a dozen ravens in Helheim and two belonged to Edvin.

Edvin and the gate.

I swung the window open, nearly falling over myself to do it. The raven hopped inside and perched on the back of my chair. A note hung from a piece of twine on its foot.

It was a struggle to stay patient enough to be gentle, not to just rip the fucking thing off its leg, consequences be damned. When I finally had it in my hands, I took a deep breath and unfurled it.

It's her

I dashed towards the wardrobe and tripped over my own feet, my legs half asleep from sitting. I was up again and pulling a tunic over my head a second later. My hand was on the door handle, and then I thought better of it. I shook the fog from my head and tried to focus. Flying was faster.

As I whispered the runes, the change began immediately, that old familiar tingle. The warp and strain of all the nooks and crannies of my body. It had been a long time since I'd needed to fly, but it's not as if you forget how. Tucked into my tiny hawk body, I hopped forward, trying to force myself to adjust to it, and followed the raven up and out of the window.

The flight to the cliffs was short and when I was high enough to see properly, I spotted two shapes near the gates. Small at first, and as I drew closer, I knew without a doubt that it was her. I'd seen her over and over in my dreams, and she was here; she had to be. Unmistakable. The thick brown of her hair, the soft gold of her skin, a ragged travelling cloak draped over her.

Sigyn.

The raven landed first, drawing Sigyn and Edvin's attention to the sky. I flew close to the cliffs and when I was close enough to land, I let the hawk shape drop away. My limbs shrieked and creaked back into place and I stumbled into the ground, rocks digging into my legs and the palms of my hands.

It didn't matter though. Nothing mattered. She was here.

The throbbing and stinging across my skin were strong enough to register in my mind, but I didn't care. I lay there in the tumble I had landed in, holding myself up, staring at her. Sigyn's hands were over her mouth as she looked down. I couldn't read what was on her face, what she was thinking behind those scared eyes. Was she scared *for* me or *of* me? Had I imagined this all wrong for so long?

The last time she'd seen me, I was killing the realms. I'd been a raving madman, burning everything to the ground. She didn't know who I'd become, that I was just a deeply sad, pathetic excuse for a god. That I was lonelier than I'd ever been in my life, that I—

I dropped my gaze to the ground, unable to bear the disappointment she must have felt, seeing me again.

She fell to her knees in front of me and wrapped her arms around my neck. It startled me, and I struggled to keep my balance, holding myself upright on one arm, the other reaching back to her. My face was tucked into her neck and the scent of her was like coming home. The faint smell of feathers and cold and the wilds, and under that, the soft sweetness of her skin.

Sigyn relaxed her grip on me and leaned far enough back to see my face. I blinked, trying to see her through the tears in my eyes. With my free hand, I traced a line down her cheek with one finger. There she was, her skin under my touch, tears streaming down her cheeks, as beautiful as the day I'd first seen her. Her brown eyes glistened; her lips quivered. She was trying to speak through the sobs, but I couldn't make out a word.

"Sigyn, I—"

Her hands went to my cheeks, and she kissed me. Soft and short and over and over, desperate. It was all so much so fast and I had dreamed, begged for this for so long I'd lost count. I'd planned it a million times, everything that I'd say and do. And with her in my arms, I suddenly didn't know where to begin. For the first time in years, I could *feel* something.

"Sigyn." I brushed my hand across her cheek and she looked up at me. The words came slow and hard, like I'd been pushing them down for an eternity. "I love you so much. I wanted to tell you that every single day."

Her breath hitched and she pushed back a deep sob. "I know. I love you too."

"There's so much I want to say."

She pursed her lips, paused, desperation in her eyes. "Is Narvi here?"

I nodded. "He's going to be happy to see you."

Her breath hitched again, a smile on her lips.

"Sig...where's Váli?"

Wiping the tears from her eyes, she sniffed. "He's safe. Keeping watch on the city with Hreidulfr."

They were alive. Safe, but not here. It was the most bittersweet news she could have given me. I wanted them with me, and I wanted them alive. There wasn't a way to have both.

Edvin came to stand over us. "You'd best tell him now, Sigyn. He's been waiting a long time for you and it wouldn't be fair."

All at once, her expression turned guilty and I didn't know what to make of it. She took my hand and held it tightly. "Loki, I'm not dead."

I stared at her, sure I had heard her wrong. All the million scenarios I'd imagined and this hadn't been one of them. For the first time, I noticed how warm her skin was on mine. "How are you here?"

Something proud passed over her eyes. "I flew."

Edvin laughed. "I told her we don't let in the living, but she threatened to set me ablaze if I didn't let her past the gates. You've told me so many stories, I knew right away it was her."

I pressed back a smile and ran my thumb down her cheek. "That does sound right." Her being alive raised so many questions, ones I wasn't sure I wanted the answers to. She wasn't staying. That much I knew without asking, and knowing it threatened to tear me apart. "If you're not dead, why come to Helheim?"

Sigyn's shoulders sagged and a darkness pooled under her eyes, like she hadn't slept soundly for a very long time. "There's a lot I need to tell you, but I need to tell Narvi as well. And Hel."

"What's wrong?" I pushed a lock of her hair behind her ear, unable to stop staring at her, still too sure that I was dreaming.

No, not a dream. Because if she wasn't staying, it was a nightmare.

"We're in trouble, Loki."

My head was so full. I was spinning in too many directions at once. She was here but she wasn't and there would be no happy reunion like I'd imagined. Nothing like what I wanted, nothing like what I needed to save me from this version of myself that I'd become. I blinked, shook my head. Tried to focus on what she'd said. "Alright. Then you're here to see Hel."

Her gaze didn't break from mine. "I have business with Hel, but I've never wanted to see anyone more than I've wanted to see you."

She had so much sincerity in her eyes, but it was hard to believe her. It wasn't fair, not in any manner of the word, but this felt like a betrayal somehow. Like a broken promise that she'd never made, never agreed to.

"Loki." She wrapped her arms around me again and held me close to her. The thump of her heart under her skin made me suddenly aware of how mine refused to beat. "Please, speak to me."

I took a breath and tried to think of her. Of what she needed. I'd made it about me, like I always did. She'd come at last and I was letting it slip away.

"I'm glad you're here," I whispered into her neck, breathing her in. "Whatever's wrong, we'll help you."

She sat up. Sigyn's eyes searched mine for something, and I suddenly felt bare. I didn't know what she expected. I wanted to say so much. That I was who she thought I was. That I wasn't. That I was the same and torn apart and put back together and that I forgave her. But how could I say any of it? So instead, I pulled her against me and kissed her again.

I'd thrown away a lot of second chances in my life. This wouldn't be one of them, no matter how temporary it was.

CHAPTER FIVE

SIGYN

"I loved her more than anything in the nine,
and she lived on without me."

— *Osa, Volume 3*

Helheim was nothing like I'd imagined. I'd seen a version of it so many times in my dreams and nightmares, and yet walking down the cliffs into the heart of the city, I realized how little I'd known. The only thing foreboding about it was the dark, and even that was made bearable by the twinkling blue lights that hung from everything.

Loki's hand bumped mine as we turned a corner, and I looked at him. He'd been staring at me the whole way down, but the moment I turned, his gaze darted to his bare feet.

He hadn't even put on shoes before he'd come.

"What's wrong?" I asked.

Loki didn't look at me. "It's just…If I stop looking at you, I think you'll disappear."

I entwined my fingers with his. "Is that better?"

The corners of his mouth turned up. "Better than anything I've ever felt."

There was something unsettling about those words. "Loki, have you really been waiting all this time for me?"

He looked at me as if he thought me daft. "Of course I have."

The words hurt. He couldn't leave this realm, but I could have come. I wasn't *supposed* to come, because Helheim was not a realm for the living, but I could have.

I stopped walking, pulling him to a stop with me. Reaching to take his other

31

hand, I felt cool metal on his fingers. Our wedding rings, his on his ring finger, mine on his pinky, and it was enough to rip open my heart. While I was up there in the light, building a life and a city, trying to *move on*, he was in the dark, stuck in place.

"I'm sorry that you waited so long." I squeezed his hands and stared into his eyes, the seidr hiding his scars so well done that I almost forgot that he was blind in one eye. "It's complicated, and I'll tell you everything you want to know as soon as we're with the others. Just please, tell me you've been happy here."

The answer came too slow. It took a few beats too long and everything on his face reeked of falsities, like not even his remarkable skill at deception could hide it. "I've been happy."

It was the sloppiest lie he'd ever told.

An edge permeated the space around him, an uncomfortable fear. It felt like approaching a doe at the edge of a forest and knowing that any sudden move would scare it away. Not to mention the musty air around him that told me he'd been spending time with a pipe between his teeth.

I didn't know what it added up to, but he was hiding something important.

There was nothing to say, so I let him put his arm around my shoulder and we walked in silence to the bottom of the cliffs, into the city itself. The air was damp, but also filled with the smells of baking and fermenting and homemade wares. It was a city alive and well in the last bastion of death.

I tried to take it all in, every nook and cranny, but distraction came in the form of Loki's hand gripping my shoulder too tightly. I looked around, trying to spot what was upsetting him. What I'd been overlooking.

People were staring.

A whole group of humans had stopped what they were doing and were whispering amongst themselves. Just ahead, a Jotun walking in our direction scowled. One after the other, the rest of the square looked up to see what the rest were staring at.

Loki's chest heaved in shallow, strained breaths. He was pushing us forward, walking faster, like he knew something was about to happen. My heart was starting to race. Surely this was nothing different than anything we'd endured in Asgard—

Someone spat at our feet.

Loki skidded to a stop and whipped around.

Next to us was a battered old einherjar, scowling with her arms crossed over her chest. "Got your god-killer girlfriend back, eh, murderer? World-ender. Traitor."

I pulled Loki's arm, but he tugged it out of my grip. There was suddenly something absent in his eyes, a snarl on his lips more animal than man. Before he could turn on the einherjar, I stepped in front of him and put my hands on his cheeks.

Epilogues for Lost Gods

"This is *nothing*." I shook his face. "Do you hear me? We've been chained up and torn apart. Our children were taken from us. There's nothing left to do to us. These words mean *nothing*." I stared at him, holding him still until his breathing slowed and the rage bled from his face.

Loki's eyes raised from mine, catching the stares of onlookers around us. It was a long moment before he broke from my grip and stomped off, starting towards the palace without me.

"And you." I turned on the einherjar. With a whisper there was wildfire in my palm. I pushed her up against the closed wall and pressed the fire into her cheek. She cried out, the smell of burnt flesh filling the air. I held it until the skin started to blister and peel, then let her fall to the ground.

She clasped her hands over the burn and sobbed.

I spat at her feet. "Enjoy your fucking day."

When we arrived inside the palace, Loki took me directly to the dining room. Even though it was late, Hel was bent over a pile of papers and books, quill scratching runes into a ledger. Her eyes flashed up and then away again, to see who had come in.

"Father, if you're going to skulk around—" Then she stopped and looked up once again, staring past Loki, directly at me. She put her pen down, pushed back her chair, and walked over to wrap her arms around me. "Stepmother, you've arrived at last."

"I—"

Hel's face twisted as her cheek skimmed mine. She stopped and withdrew, setting her flesh-covered hand on my cheek. "Mmm, but you aren't dead, are you?"

I smiled at her, unsure how she was going to react to my intrusion in her realm. She was Loki's daughter, not mine. She could easily decide to usher me out without a second thought. "I'm not. I'll explain, but I need to see Narvi. Please."

"Of course. Sit down and make yourself at home. I'll go get him." Hel gestured to the table and strode away, black shadows chasing behind her like the train on a dress.

Loki pulled out a seat for me, but I shook my head. My heart was racing. I hadn't let myself think too much about this moment. Seeing Loki was a different thing from seeing the son who'd been ripped from my life. It was everything I wanted, but I didn't know if I could bear it.

Just when I started to wonder how damn far away he could be, the echo of boots came from the hallway. Narvi burst around the corner and came barreling into my open arms. He fell into me like I'd had a Narvi-shaped hole in my chest. He was the same size, the same shape, identical to the moment I'd last seen him. I'd known it would be true; I had. But it was one thing to know, and another to see that they'd ripped his future from him.

I burst into sobs, a tangle of regret and love and pain. His tears were soaking into my shirt and I buried my face in his hair, trying to calm him. A hand cupped my shoulder and Loki stepped in to wrap his arms around us both and for one long moment, I felt almost whole.

Narvi sniffed and wiped his face.

There was so much to say, and there would never be enough time.

I kissed his forehead. "Let's sit down. I have so much to tell you."

Hel had come back and settled into her chair at the head of the table, watching us with cool curiosity. Narvi sat so close he could rest his head on my shoulder, and Loki took the chair on the other side, his hand on mine.

"Where to start?" I licked my lips, thinking. "What do you know about what's happening in the other realms?"

"Very little," Hel answered. "We gather information at intake when someone dies, but there are so few deaths these days. We knew you were alive, but you disappeared from the stories for a long time, until someone came to Helheim speaking of a new city under the rule of an old goddess. How did you survive Ragnarok?"

"The Nornir took us in. We stayed there—Váli, Hreidulfr, and I—until they told us it was safe to go back to Asgard."

Narvi's head popped up. "They're alright?"

"They are. They're part of the reason I'm here, but we're not at that part of the story yet." I stroked his hair as he settled back in to listen. "When we came to the surface, it was different. New. And Baldur and Hod were alive again, somehow."

Hel's face curled up in disdain. "While we were fighting at Ragnarok, Baldur was freeing himself and his brother. I have no idea how they got back to Asgard through all the barren wastelands between here and there, but they did. He even left his wife behind in a cell, like a real hero."

"That's not the only strangeness," I continued. "Magni, Modi, and Vidar all lived. The five of them have spent the last years trying to rebuild a new Asgard that's too much like the old one. It's been two years since we came out of Urd's Well, and before that…I can't say what they were doing in that time. Their methods of running Asgard are in line with Odin's and so our faction has decided to offer an alternative.

"The boys and I have been trying to create a revolution. There were more survivors of Ragnarok than anyone knew. Dwarves trapped inside mountains, Elves and Vanir trying to make lives out of the ruins of Vanaheim. We've offered refuge to as many people as we can. A place to live and work together, to build a city. It's made of wood and scraps and dreams, but it's ours, and Asgard wants to wipe it off the face of the realm. If we offer unity between peoples, Asgard can't rule with an iron fist."

Hel tapped her fingers on the table. "That still doesn't explain why you're here."

"They're coming for us and we're going to lose. We need an ally."

Hel crooked an eyebrow. "What sort of ally?"

"The kind that comes to battle and helps us win a war."

Sitting up, Hel shook her head. "That's just not possible anymore. Ragnarok is over, but it's been part of the tapestry of all lives since the beginning of things. The next measure of history is still being written by the Nornir. They won't allow any more uprisings on that scale, not until another Ragnarok comes into play in the far future. Among other things, it seems it caused an awful lot of complications in the weaving of things."

"You're joking." My mouth was hanging open, the shock feeling an awful lot like someone had thrown iced water on me. "Can't we just borrow part of your army and return them to you?"

Hel calmly took a drink from the cup in front of her. "I'm afraid not. The Nornir have exerted their power and are watching very carefully to ensure the dead stay dead after Baldur's escape. Anyone that wants to travel from Helheim to the other realms needs to make an appeal to them for their life and prove that they've earned a new thread of fate. And they don't come easy."

I leaned my elbows on the table, palms over my face. "How often have they granted a new thread?"

"Four times since Ragnarok." Narvi's voice was sullen, quiet.

"Fuck." I dug my fingers into my scalp. It was my only play. I would return to the city with nothing and when Asgard showed up at our doorstep, we would lose.

"I'm sorry. I truly am." Hel toyed with the handle of her cup. "There's nothing I'd love more than to see those gods stuffed in my cells with the rest, but the Nornir might be the last beings in the nine more powerful than I am."

My mind was spinning, trying to think of other possibilities that would save us. "What about Fenrir and Jormungandr? If we had someone who—"

Loki squeezed my hand. "When they died, there was nowhere down here big enough to put them. It was agreed they'd live out their afterlives in the wastelands of Midgard. There's nothing there to hurt them anymore."

All I could do was nod. They weren't just weapons for me to acquire; I knew that. I couldn't begrudge them their peace. But what were *we* going to do?

"How much force do you need to stand up to Asgard?" Loki asked.

I looked up, trying to do the abstract calculations in my head. "A small army. They've attracted a lot of the refugees who were warriors or smiths, and so many of our people are just people. We're training them but you can't make true einherjar out of labourers and children."

Loki bobbed his head a moment, thinking. "I could be a small army."

Narvi finally sat up. "What do you mean?"

"Come on, I'm not that rusty." Loki actually looked a little indignant.

Hel drummed her fingers on the table impatiently. "It's not about rusty. Are you saying you want to beg the Nornir for another fate? Today I couldn't even get you to go outside for a *walk*."

Loki looked at me, watched the look on my face melt from desperation to confusion. "If you need me, I'm going to try."

Hel let out a long breath. "And what exactly are you going to tell them you did to earn your new fate? I've tried a dozen times to send you to a therapist but you won't go. You sit here stewing in your own misery as if it's your best fucking friend. I don't think you've made *any* headway in the last few years. None."

"Therapist?" I whipped my head to look at Loki.

"I'll explain it later, alright?" Loki crossed his arms over his chest and stared at his daughter. "What else am I going to do? Let Sigyn go back up there to face Asgard with no help?"

Hel shrugged. "You'd finally get your wish because she'd be dead and back down here soon enough."

The comment took me aback. Narvi and Loki both responded with a chorus of disgust.

"Just because it's unkind doesn't mean it's untrue." Hel threw up a hand. "You want me to let you trek across Helheim's untold dangers, past the Nidhogg, and up the root of Yggdrasil to Urd's Well, as if that's just a nice day at the beach. You might die for good, wiped off the realms like you were never here. That's what happens after this, you know that? This is the last stop. The Nornir might not give you your fate and you'll have to turn around and make the journey again, and *that* might kill you *for real*. Why would I be alright with that?"

"She's right, Loki." I sat up, struggling with what I needed in the face of what I might lose. "It's too much to risk and I'm not sure you would make enough difference in this fight to be worth losing your afterlife for."

"What afterlife?" His voice was suddenly raw and angry, not unlike the Loki I'd seen in the market not long ago. "I'm here doing nothing. Isolated from everything because of who I am and what I've done. I have *tried* to make something here for myself, but the fear and the anger stop me at every turn. If the Nornir want someone to prove they're worthy of a new fate, what better story than the beast who tore apart the realms and then came back to save them?"

The room fell quiet. My heart was racing underneath my skin. All these things he had said, these enormous daggers he had driven into my heart. The plan to defeat Asgard fell to the wayside in my mind. He wasn't just unhappy; he was miserable. Every word he had said had rolled off his tongue like it was too familiar to him, too routine. And by the looks on their faces, it was familiar to his children as well. But I'd never, *ever* heard him speak like that. To hear him talk about a life so devoid of meaning, of laughter…who was that man? Even at the worst of things, Loki had still had that sick, dark humour.

I blinked hard. I wasn't going to stain the moment with my tears.

Narvi took a deep breath, slowly and intentionally spreading his fingers along the tabletop. "If you're going, I'm going."

"Ymir's bones, really? You too, Narvi? Are you both insane?" Hel was pinching the bridge of her nose between her fingers. "Do you see what you've done, Father? This is a suicide mission. And not in some hypothetical, storybook way."

"That's why I'm going alone," Loki countered.

Hel rolled her eyes. "No, you're not—"

"I know more about this realm than you do." Narvi drove a finger into the top of the table. "I have more maps, I know more of the people, and I'm a better resource all around. You can't heal yourself, and I'm the only one who knows how to bring you out of your *moments*."

I darted a glance to Loki. Yet another secret. "What moments?"

"It's nothing," he snapped and turned to Hel. "I'm going."

Hel's face was practically pressed against the table, her hands clasped over the crown of her hair. "You know what? You're both idiots, but fine. Fine. But you're taking Mother."

"What?" Narvi turned on Hel, but she still wasn't looking at them. "She's unstable."

"You're all unstable. You *died*. I have told you both, time and again, there are resources to help you with your transition into the afterlife but you refuse to go because you're both as fucking stubborn as the other. Mother is your best bet at making it to the other side, because while you've been bottling it all up, waiting to explode, she's been kicking the shit out of everyone that comes near her. No one's calling that *healthy* but at least she brings brute force to the equation."

"Angrboda died too?" I asked, trying to divert the conversation away from this argument I'd unintentionally started. "Aren't you worried she'll die too?"

"Not really, no." Hel tapped her fingers on the table. "I've seen her fight her way out of unreasonable odds, and she also has a penchant for self-preservation, unlike these two."

"I feel like I should take offence to that," Loki said.

"So." Hel finally raised her head from the table. "Is it settled? Narvi, Father, and Mother will go on this wild goose chase to be resurrected and hope they don't get eaten by something in the wilds on the way."

"This conversation really got away from me…" I looked from one to the other. "It's not fair to ask you to do any of this. You've both done your duties to the living world and you have lives here. I'd rather go back empty-handed than find out that you both died again because of me. I couldn't live with it."

Loki flashed a half-hearted grin. "You have so little faith, Sigyn. We're going to help you burn Asgard to the ground."

"Idiots. All of you." Hel grabbed a half-corked bottle of wine from behind a stack of books and pulled out the cork with a pop.

I pursed my lips. "I have another proposal."

Hel looked at me, incredulous. "Haven't you already asked enough?"

"A trade. When we win, I'll kill Magni, Modi, Vidar, and Baldur so you can add them to your collection. I can't allow you to take Hod; he's on our side. And in return, you arrange for Idunn, Bragi, and Eyvindr to safely plead their cases with the Nornir."

"Eyvindr?" Hel asked.

"Hod's lover," Loki supplied.

"Right." The way Hel stared at me was cold and slightly absent. Like she was running the numbers in her head. "I can't guarantee they'll get new threads; that's entirely their problem. But I'm willing to provide an entourage for a prize like that." She paused again, thinking. "And the next time your friends die, they stay here."

"Agreed."

She stood and offered her skeletal hand. I shook it, careful to withhold the discomfort of the bone and muscle touching my skin.

"Then we have a deal." Hel grinned. "You should've asked for more. You could've asked for the moon and stars, and I'd have paid double to have Baldur back. We have unfinished business."

"If you can't give me an army, there's nothing else I need. As for Baldur, do whatever you want with him. My time as his sister is done."

"So…" Loki said. "What now?"

I gathered all the courage I could find and said the one thing I knew I had to, but wanted least in the world to say. "Show me what you've done with the gods."

CHAPTER SIX

SIGYN

"If they really, truly had given a fuck, they'd have apologized before they died, not after. We did everything for them and it took forty years of death here for them to realize they lived like fucking twats."

— *Anja, Volume 18*

S tanding in front of the cells was like being inside a nightmare. The prison itself was massive, filled with the worst kinds of evil all the realms could come up with. It was cold and dank, carved-stone walls that dripped a wet, minerally liquid. It was hardly somewhere I wanted to spend the next hour, let alone an eternity.

And tucked into the back, behind walls and walls of rune-warded gates, were the gods, each in their own private cell.

They were dressed in the barest of clothes, almost no more than a flour sack. Their faces were worn and tired, like they'd given up a long time ago. Each cell had a bed and a chamber pot, and three stone walls. And that was it.

Just looking at them wasting away in their own little corners reminded me of the cave they'd left us to rot in. Maybe that was the point.

I clutched Loki's hand as we walked down the row of cells, trying not to look anything but collected. Trying to shove down every speck of remorse and doubt and pity. Even the anger. Even the righteous, boiling thing that loved to see them in there. Because I didn't want them to see any more of me than they had the right to.

We passed Heimdall sitting on a cot, his eyes covered with a long, discoloured bandage. Sif, whose enchanted golden hair was gone, and in its place was skin as smooth as an egg. Thor, who stopped his pushups at the sight of us and stared. And

39

Odin. My father, who had covered the walls of his cell with rust-red runes, looked at us now with one panicked eye, the other caved in and raw.

I had so much hate in my heart, boiling under my skin. Each of them owed me something I could never get back. Each of them could have done something to change the road we were all on, and they hadn't, either out of spite or cowardice or vengeance.

Sometimes, when my inner workings were calm and collected, I understood. Sometimes I knew they were all playing a part in a grand scheme, each of us doing the thing that we thought was right and just, living with the path that Odin had set us on.

I did not feel calm. I did not feel collected.

But I would show them calm, that enormous lie, because what else was there for me to do?

After ripping Skadi's guts from her body, I knew exactly how much and how little satisfaction revenge could bring. I knew better, and yet I still wanted so badly in that moment to take the opportunity to show them who I'd become. What I could do to them.

Loki's hand on mine was my only tether to sanity.

A loud thump startled me. One of the gods threw herself against the cell barrier again, smashing her fists against it. Freya. Her dress was torn and there was blood on her knuckles. She was still beautiful, but she was empty. Hollow. Her eyes seethed with rage, but her body had shrunk over time, thinned down and neglected. She was screaming but no sound came through.

She had walked into every room, every day of her life, as if her presence alone was a threat.

Not anymore.

"It's alright," Loki said in a low voice. "She can't get out, and the runes cut off any access to energy through the rock. They're harmless."

I shook my head, not taking my eyes off Freya. "They were never harmless, and they never will be."

Since I'd begun to build the city, I'd barely thought of her at all. For her, all she had was time to think. Watching how desperately she wanted to hurt us was enough to steady me.

That desperation would be the thing that made me smile before I slept each night.

Loki led me to the end of the row, to a set of double doors. He pushed them open, and on the other side was a cascade of sparkling blue lights illuminating a tiny stone cottage, a yard lush with plants of varieties I'd never seen, and a tiny wooden fence around the outside. And there was Idunn, bent over a small plot of mushrooms, her hands filthy with soil.

40

Epilogues for Lost Gods

She stood up when the doors swung shut behind us. Her eyes widened, and she looked like a deer about to run. She was better than the others. Healthier. Her blonde hair was tied in a loose braid, but there were no flowers tangled in it like there had once been. There were shadows under her eyes, and she was all at once the same Idunn I'd known, and someone altogether different.

"Your gardens always thrive, no matter where you are." It was a stupid thing to say, but I had to say something. I couldn't stand the idea of her running into her cottage. If she did, I might never again have the chance to speak to her.

"Cages with gardens are still cages." Idunn wiped the dirt from her hands and dipped them in a bucket of water, cleaning the brown from everywhere but under her fingernails.

Loki's head dipped and he stared at his feet. I left him there and moved closer to her, following the fence, noticing the shimmer of the barrier that truly kept her inside.

"I know." I sighed, the difficulty of the moment at odds with how we'd once been with each other. But that was never coming back. "I've made a bargain with Hel. When my side of it is met, you and Bragi will both be free."

Idunn's face turned instantly to a shade of rage I'd never seen on her before. The kind that comes from the deepest, darkest place. "I don't want anything from either of you. I won't live the rest of my life in debt to monsters."

"You won't. You'll be taken to earn a new fate, and you'll be free to go anywhere in the nine realms. You'll never see us again." I touched my hand to my chest. "I promise."

Tears ran down Idunn's face, dripping down into the soil below her. "Do you have any idea what happened to me? Any at all?"

I swallowed hard and looked her in the eyes, the only courtesy I could give her. "The kinds of things that happen to women who are traded to powerful men like possessions."

Her lip quivered as she stared back at me. "No one understood, not really. That Jotun stole me, put his hands on me. In me. He starved me and kept me filthy and made me feel small. He stole my joy from me, and no one could figure out why I wasn't *happy* anymore." Idunn choked down a sob, wiping her face with the back of her hand. "And you come back here with *this bastard* after all this time. Nothing has changed. How was I supposed to be near you or trust you when the person who betrayed me was always on your hip?"

There were so many things I could've said to defend myself. That I *did* leave Loki after she was taken. That he knew he was wrong. That he was protecting his family. That I missed her anyway. But they were all excuses.

"I know." I could barely see through the tears. "I am sorry, and I know that means nothing. So I'm going to buy your freedom and leave you alone."

Her lips curled over her teeth and she wrapped her arms around herself. "What do you expect? A thank you?"

"No." I didn't expect anything.

Idunn and I stood there for a long while, staring at each other, unmoving. Feelings churned in my gut. I missed her; I loved her; I hated her. I was so angry and guilty, and none of that mattered. I couldn't say any of it because it didn't matter what I wanted. I wasn't the one who had been hurt. I wasn't the one who got to choose.

Breaking the long, paralyzed moment, Idunn spat at the barrier between us. Saliva dripped down the shimmering air, obscuring my view of her. She turned back to the cottage, threw open the door, and let it slam behind her.

And that was that.

With tears threatening to blind me, I turned and strode past Loki, into the other room. I passed the silent, horrific, screaming gods, and the closer I got to the exit, the more I knew I needed to run. Run and never look back. All these people and the things they'd done to me and I'd done to them and we'd all done to each other. The horrors. I could go and disappear into the wilds, and just—

Loki stepped in my way.

"It was the best I could do for Idunn and Bragi. The most I could compromise from Hel. Sigyn, I tried—"

"No." I held a hand up to him, trying to calm down. Trying to catch my breath and come back to my body. "She's right. She's always been right. You and I, we hurt people. Together or alone. We hurt each other too. We've made our beds, all of us. This is what I have to live with. You talked about what you'd do for your penance. This is part of mine."

Loki pressed his forehead to mine, his hands running slowly down the length of my shoulders, down to my elbows. He stayed there with me, silent, holding me in place.

No matter what my body told me, we both knew there was no running from what we'd done.

CHAPTER SEVEN

SIGYN

"I have a life here in Helheim. A good life.
But my daughter was Muslim and I would trade every second
of this afterlife to see her just one more time."

— *Maab, Volume 32*

It was late when we finally wound our way back to Hel's palace. The halls were so quiet, each of them made eerier by the lighting: long corridors lit only by the occasional seafoam-green wildfire candle. Loki walked me down one of the corridors, stopping us in front of a door and reaching for his keys.

I cleared my throat and whispered. "Do you think Narvi will still be awake?"

"He doesn't sleep much. Just enough to keep himself going." Loki pointed to the next door over. "You can see if he's there. Might be in the office though."

I pressed close to him, trying to keep my voice low. "How is he really? What Hel said at the table about you both...it's concerning."

Loki drew in a deep breath. "He gets by. He does his best to stay busy. What he went through...you don't just get over that."

"No, you don't..." I looked at the door. "Will you wait for me? I want to see him alone for a few minutes."

A smile touched Loki's lips. He brushed a finger around the back of my ear. "What's a few minutes more, my love? Come when you're ready."

And with that, he opened the door to his room and slipped away, leaving me alone to stare at Narvi's door.

I tiptoed over, unsure what I was going to do or say. It had been seven years. Who had Narvi become while I was away? I knew what time could do to a person. Knew how experiences could hollow you out and leave room for another version of you. What had death made of my quiet, loving son?

I knocked gently, not wanting to wake him if he did happen to be sleeping. But noise came in return, things moving, the click of a lock. Then the door cracked open, a sliver of Narvi's face appearing.

"Mother! Come in." He opened the door wider and I stepped through.

His room was warm, lit by a modest hearth fire. It was so much like his room at home. A desk covered in wild papers, books stacked on the bedside table, his bedsheets askew. He'd even covered the windowsill with tiny potted plants that looked more like fungi than anything else.

"Still haven't learned to tidy up, have you?" I pulled him into my arms, his face curling into my shoulder.

"I did tidy up. You just can't tell."

I laughed and let him go, brushing his long brown locks away from his face. "Look at you. You can't imagine how much I've missed looking at you."

Narvi smirked, just a hint. "It hasn't changed a bit."

I followed him to sit on his bed. "Tell me about your life. What exciting things do you do? Who are your friends? Is there a special someone? How's your seidr improving? Tell me everything."

Narvi looked down at his bare feet, worrying his sleeping trousers between his fingers. Any semblance of that smile had disappeared. "I don't have a lot to tell you."

I put my hand on his, trying to soothe his fidgeting. "Tell me anything you'd like."

"I'm fine, Mother. I promise."

"People who are fine never *say* they're fine." I turned towards him, angling my head to try to get a glimpse of his eyes under all that hair. "Narvi, I don't want to push you, but tonight is all we get. We don't have time to play games, parry back and forth and leave it until you're ready to talk a week from now. If you need to tell me something, now is what we get."

His grip on my hand tightened and his shoulders tensed. I waited for him to say something, but he didn't. His breathing slowed and he sat up straighter, looked me in the eye. "No, Mother. I don't want to waste my time crying about what we can't change. When all this is done, we'll have time for that."

"Narvi—"

"No, I mean it. I'm not going to waste this. I have nightmares all the time, and I have to stare at my scars in the mirror every day. You're here for a matter of hours and those things will be there after you're gone. I'm not letting the things that haunt me steal anything else from me."

Epilogues for Lost Gods

I pursed my lips, trying to come to terms with all the pain he'd laid out for me. I wanted to know, to drag it out of him against his will. I wanted to *help* him. But he was putting his foot down, and he was right. This moment could be a happy one in a sea of sadness.

"Alright. What would you like to talk about?"

Narvi pushed himself back against the headboard and patted the mattress beside him. "I want to sit with my mother and hear about this city you're building. Maybe you've got some tips for me."

I smiled, forcing down all the ache and anxiety, and moved to sit next to him. I put my arm around his shoulder, letting him settle against me. And then I told him every single thing he wanted to hear, stroking my fingers through his hair while he listened, the hearth fire crackling in the background.

CHAPTER EIGHT

LOKI

"I lie awake at night, and you know what I think about?
How I never had the guts to love him."

— *Lukas, Volume 2*

Hearing Narvi and Sigyn laughing through the wall stirred strange things in me. It was beautiful to hear. There had never been enough laughter in those halls, but it also filled me with this terrible melancholy. I wanted to be laughing with her, with my son. I missed them, missed being happy with them. And even if I'd been invited, I still wasn't sure if I could've laughed. Not like they were. I would've sounded hollow and false, and they'd have known I was playing pretend.

I could've pressed myself against them and still felt leagues away from where they were.

The self-pity welled up a panic in my chest until the laughter felt like an attack, and I curled into myself and sobbed for the person I could no longer find inside.

Were they hiding in there between all my thoughts and squishy bits, all those other Lokis? Or were they truly gone?

I'd cried myself out by the time Sigyn came to the room. She closed the door behind her, unbuttoned her travelling cloak, and hung it from the hook on the wall. Her shoulders sagged and her expression was lost, torn.

"Is there anything I can do?" I got up and took her hand, hoping that she would say yes. "Would you like a bath?"

She sighed in relief and gave a weak smile. "I would love that."

I led her around my bed to the tiny room where the bath was. A few candles later, there was enough light to see by, and a double tap on the seidr piping started the warm water.

Sigyn was already getting undressed when I looked back at her. I froze. She'd been wearing a tunic a second ago, but it was crumpled on the floor.

She caught a glimpse of me and laughed. "We've been married a very long time, Loki. Aren't you used to it by now?"

I shook my head. "Decidedly not."

She pulled down her trousers and her underthings, grinning at me the whole time. And all I could do was swallow hard and try to breathe as she climbed naked into the water.

"Would you pass me the soap?"

The question woke me from my daze and I did as she asked. She took it and dipped her head under the water, coming up for air a moment later. She was staring at me in a way that had always meant a question was coming.

"Tell me about these *moments* you have."

Fuck.

I pulled a stool up to the bath and sat down. "Do you really want to know?"

"You had one in the city, didn't you?"

I nodded, looking away. "I started to. It's different things, Sig. Sometimes it happens after a nightmare. Sometimes someone decides it's a good day to jump me in the street. If I think too hard about the wrong things, or someone scares me…"

A wet finger ran down my knuckle. "I'm listening."

"Sometimes it's blind rage. Panic. Like I'm somewhere else, right back in the middle of it all." I swallowed. "It's terrifying."

She took my hand and waited for me to continue, but I didn't know what to say.

"I used to love sleep. You remember, I'm sure," Sigyn said wistfully. "I *loved* falling asleep after a long day, drifting off into whatever dream was waiting for me. Especially when we went to sleep together. I can't remember the last time I had a good dream, Loki. I don't think I ever will again."

I stared at her fingers entangled with mine. "Sometimes the things in my dreams follow me when I'm awake. I smell burning meat and I see the battlefield again, like I'm standing in the middle of it."

She watched the water ripple with each of her breaths. "If it weren't for an entire city relying on me, I might never get out of bed. Sometimes I think that's why I do it in the first place. Without someone to help, I might just…slip away."

I squeezed her hand, my heart wrenching at the thought. "I'm sorry."

She squeezed my hand back. "Me too."

I let the subject die in the silence. It felt like more than either of us could solve in the span of a night.

"Are you happy sometimes?" I asked after a moment.

"Sometimes. I have people who make me happy. The work is hard, trying to build a city, but I think we're doing something truly good. And I miss you and Narvi so much that some days it almost kills me. But sometimes. Yes."

I worked to push back the quiet, invasive jealousy that was washing over me. "Good. You deserve to finally be happy."

Sigyn looked at me inquisitively. "Loki, you do understand you made me happy too, don't you?"

I let out a breath, so close to a whimper. "In the beginning maybe. Not after that."

She continued running her finger across mine. "You gave me so many years of bliss. You were the only person who really understood me. If you don't acknowledge that, you're putting aside everything that we were."

"And I spent more years than that hurting you."

"Yes, you did. We both did. And it was so much more complicated than that. So much was in our control, and so much wasn't. And whatever all that amounted to, it doesn't matter right now. I don't want it to." Then she put her hand on my chest and tapped the spot where the knife had been. "Show me."

"Sigyn, no."

"I want to see what I did." She reached for the bottom of my tunic, trying to pull it up.

I held her hand in place. "It's only going to hurt you."

"I need to see it." She had tears in her eyes again.

I wasn't sure if I wanted to, or if it was the best thing to do. I really didn't know. But how long could I reasonably hide it from her? It would happen eventually, and it would hurt just the same, no matter when. So I pulled off my tunic and let the glamour drop.

The look on her face was one I'd seen in my nightmares. First it was grief in her eyes, then it turned to sobs. She sat back in the tub, her hands over her face. Shattered.

"No, please don't cry. It's not so bad." I reached for her hands but she didn't budge.

I knew it was worse than bad. Heimdall had driven the dagger into my chest, opened my lung. And when she pushed the knife deeper, it ripped everything open. If you looked hard enough—like I had many times—layers of me were exposed for all to see.

"I did this to you," she sobbed.

"That is absolutely untrue, Sigyn. Of course you didn't. Come here, please."

She shook her head, crying into her hands.

And lacking anything else to do, I got up and climbed into the bath next to her, trousers and all.

She peeked through her hands, a sob caught in her throat. "What are you doing?"

I pulled her to me and held her, careful to keep her away from the hole in my chest. "What else was I supposed to do? You're crying and you won't come out."

The whimper turned to a laugh and she wiped her eyes with her hands. "Loki, you're an idiot."

"Ah, but that's why you love me?" It was supposed to be a fact, but it came out like a question. "Sorry, I…that's not fair."

She looked up at me. "Of course I love you. I just…we didn't get to have something happy. We were never meant to. I wanted our story to have a better ending than we got."

My breath caught. "A better *ending*. Is it over, then?"

She shook her head. "I don't know, Loki. I get this chance with you tonight, to be here, and I don't want to ruin it with talk about the future. About what we *are* to each other now. But no, it's not over tonight."

I drew a breath. It wasn't the answer I wanted, but I knew it was the answer I deserved. Better than, really. "Are you ready to get out of this tub?"

Sigyn nodded, but that tired look was sinking back into her face. I climbed out, dripping water everywhere, and offered her my hand. She took it and stepped out, wrapping her arms around her chest for warmth. I offered her a towel and slipped my trousers off, slinging them into the now-draining tub. Then it was my turn to catch her looking.

Once we were dry, we went back out to the bedroom and sat on the bed next to each other.

"You don't have to sleep here." It was a struggle to say it, and I knew it came out halfhearted.

She looked up at me. "Loki, I know there's a lot that's going to come between us, but can that be tomorrow? Can we just forget everything that's happened and whatever is coming for one night? Pretend to be who we were when we got married?"

I reached out and slipped a finger under her chin, then let the runes slide off my tongue. Let the glamour fall back over me again, like an old habit. A moment later, Sigyn was staring into the eyes of a young, healthy Loki. Whole. Happy.

I could be him for a night. For her.

I leaned in to brush my lips across her throat. A sigh escaped her and I smiled against her skin. "I do love that sound."

She craned her head in answer, waiting for my lips to make their way up her neck, and I was so happy to oblige. Her fingers ran up my back and the thrill of it spread gooseflesh over my body.

No one had touched me like that in so very long.

I urged her further up on the bed and laid her down, running my hands and lips over every inch of her skin, basking in the way her fingers were laced through my hair. Everything about her was glorious, from the arch of her eyebrows when my lips hit the right spot, to the curve of her hips under my fingers. She was so fucking soft and— there were scars that hadn't been there before and I traced them—

She pulled me up and kissed me, pushing me onto my back. "Not tonight, Loki." She slid her tongue into my mouth, and the thought faded away. All that mattered was her.

I moved to settle against the headboard, pulling her with me. Her kisses were wanting, needing, and she straddled my hips. The warmth of her skin against mine was delicious, and I held her tightly against me. She slowed her kisses and lowered herself carefully onto me, sliding me inside her. My head lolled back, breath caught in my throat. Everything about her was warmth and softness and comfort. Her tongue was hot on my skin as she ran it up my neck and nipped at my ear. I pulled her hips tighter to mine as she ground into me, already panting.

It felt too good. Too real after so much nothing.

I pulled her off and laid her down on the bed, holding myself over her. Her body arched up to meet mine.

I leaned into her ear and hushed her, even as her fingers dug rivets in my skin. "Slow down, my love. I want to savour you."

Sigyn stared into my eyes as she bit her lip, all pent-up wanting.

That, I knew what to do with.

I trailed my tongue from her earlobe, down her neck, thriving on the way her body moved under me. My teeth grazed her collarbone and she gasped. I had thought I'd remembered what she sounded like, what she felt like, but it was nothing compared to the real thing.

Her fingers tangled in the wet tips of my hair. "You're teasing me and we both know it."

"We do." I pressed kiss after kiss into her skin, working my way from collarbone to breast to navel. "You used to love being teased."

Her grip was forceful and impatient. "And you used to make sure I got my fill of pleasure every time, so I don't feel like we need to draw this first one out."

I laughed. "Gods, you *are* starved." Rather than see where her wrath would push her, I dipped my face between her thighs. My tongue took one long, languishing lick, and her body relaxed into the mattress, her fingers loosening in my hair. Waiting for me to begin.

Epilogues for Lost Gods

Refusing to disappoint, I gave her all of my attention. I listened to the sounds she made, felt the way she moved under my hands and mouth, trying to hone my skill to exactly what she needed from me. I still remembered, of course. Still knew what worked and what didn't, but it had been a very, very long time. Perhaps her tastes had changed.

But they hadn't, and in a few short minutes, she was bucking into my mouth, crying ecstasy into the rafters.

Ymir's breath, I had spent so much time fantasizing about hearing that sound again.

Sigyn's fists were tight around the bedclothes as the pleasure subsided, her head pressed back into the mattress. I crawled up over her, running one hand up her sweat-sheened skin. Her heart was racing. I laid down next to her, curling into her side.

She let out a little groan and turned to face me, delight written across her features. "Yggdrasil below, I have missed that."

I grinned. "Did you?" I started to get up, feigning indifference. "What a shame that I'm entirely out of *time*. I hate to leave you here like this, but—"

Sigyn sat up to snag the back of my neck with her hand, pulling me back for a deep kiss. Once I'd succumbed and pressed my body back against hers, she pulled away for a breath. "I've never known Loki to leave a job half-finished."

I stared at her, lust in every fibre of my being. "You sounded entirely finished to me."

She forced me onto my back and straddled my hips again. "You know better than that."

Goddess was a lie of a word that men around the realms used to venerate every woman they came across, but I couldn't help it. Sigyn was a goddess, through and through. The cut of her thighs, the silhouette of her body as it curved out for her hips, just slightly in at the torso, and finished with the softness of her chest...she was breathtaking.

Sigyn licked her palm and stroked between my legs. My eyes rolled back into my head at the touch of her fingers, and then at the warmth of her body. I lavished in the feeling, and she pressed her palms into me for leverage as she rode.

When I opened my eyes, my breath caught, panic and bile rising in my throat.

Sigyn, above me—

Blood streaked across her face

—hands on the knife in my chest—

I flipped her onto her back, startling her. I concealed the fear, pushed it down, pressed my hands into her hips like I'd done it on purpose, tucked my face into her neck so she couldn't see, as if I was fueled by lust instead of alarm. As my finger slid down and worked between her legs, her surprise turned to a moan. If I could breathe.

If I could focus on her, perhaps she would never realize I had nearly thrown her off the bed in sheer terror.

I swallowed hard and explored her body, trying to drown myself in it. I touched her, inside and out, until the fear was smaller than the panic, until I was enthralled in her again, the nightmare lost to the warmth of her skin.

I pushed into her and thrust, single-minded in the pursuit of the end. I lost my every thought, touching her, kissing her, careening my hips into hers over and over, her delighted panting in my ear. She let out a passionate gasp and that was it. The sound drove me over the brink. I braced myself on the mattress, overcome with the roiling pleasure as it wracked through my body. An arm gave way and I nearly collapsed on top of her.

I looked up, trying to breathe, and she was grinning from ear to ear. She always did like to see me come undone.

Relaxing on top of her for just a moment, I let my face sink into her neck. "You have always been divine, Sigyn."

She nudged me until I rolled off her, and then she curled up against my chest, batting her eyelashes at me. "Well, I'm going to let you catch your breath, but I think we would both agree divinity requires more worship than just this, hmm?"

What a *minx*.

If she wanted worship, I would give it to her, but I would demand some in kind. I let a familiar string of runes slide off my tongue, and in short order, I had turned my body into something more feminine.

Sigyn's eyes lit up with excitement. She ran the fingers of one hand softly down my newly conjured breasts, incensing every nerve under my skin. "Are you really going to give me such a generous treat as this?"

"Absolutely," I growled, and pushed her down for a kiss.

The dream came back that night. Of course it did.

Sigyn kneeling above me, jamming the dagger into my chest.

Drowning in my own blood.

Feeling my heart stop.

That was always when I woke drenched in sweat. That night was no different. I tried to breathe, tried to get it under control. I was in my bed. I was fine. No one was here to hurt me. Sigyn wasn't the one who'd killed me, not really. She was here, with me. Still loved me, even just a little.

Or maybe not.

Maybe I'd dreamt the whole thing and she was gone.

Epilogues for Lost Gods

But there was a shadow in my bed, a shape lying next to me. A calm settled in and I reached, just to feel her.

Sigyn stirred, sighing as she woke. She rolled over and pressed her skin into mine. "Why aren't you sleeping?"

"It's nothing. Just dreaming of you." It wasn't precisely a lie. "I feel like I should apologize, Sig. That…it was phenomenal, but it wasn't part of the plan."

Sigyn planted a kiss on my lips, firm and reassuring. "It was part of mine." She still sounded sleepy, and her hand came to rest on my waist, her head tucked against my breast. In a moment, she was asleep again, and I was left alone in the dark of my bedroom to force all of these jagged pieces of my existence together.

CHAPTER NINE

SIGYN

*"I put a lot of my life into my job, and the rest into the gods,
and it just didn't matter. I was alone then, and I'm alone for
the rest of eternity. I thought I knew what I was doing."*

— *Lilya, Volume 29*

The next day was peaceful. Loki told her best collection of funny stories over breakfast, which made us all burst at the seams with laughter—even Hel. We went together for a walk into a cave system with Narvi as our guide. He told us everything he'd learned, not hesitating to point out that all the glowing blue lights hanging from the ceilings in Helheim were actually tiny maggots, something I really had no desire to know. Afterward, they had the chef cook their best rendition of my favourite meal, smoked rabbit stew, and we ate lunch curled up on a bench in front of the hearth, quiet but content.

And in every moment was the lingering pain that soon I would need to leave.

Soon.

Soon.

Soon.

Each time the thought rose up, I pushed it back a little further. The realms could wait five more minutes. Maybe an hour. After lunch. After supper.

And I could feel Loki's eyes on me, her soft features concerned and discontent. Waiting for the moment when I would stand up and say I was leaving. It was slow torture, I knew. The certainty of the inevitable; not wanting it to happen, but wishing it were over all the same.

I had to go. I had to.

Epilogues for Lost Gods

And then Narvi laughed at something Hel said, his voice ringing like a bell.

"I'll leave tomorrow."

The table quieted. They were staring at me.

"What did you say, Mother?" Narvi's face was blank, uncommitted to any particular expression.

"I said I'll leave tomorrow." The words spurred a war in my chest. Ecstatic over my choice to be with my family just a little longer, and pained by the sense of duty I was pushing aside.

Loki reached out and put her hand on mine. "Are you sure?"

"I…" I swallowed hard. "I've given everything to everyone else all my life. If the realms burn tonight because I was with my family, then so be it."

When I woke the next morning, I was half convinced it was still the middle of the night. I was rested enough but the room hadn't changed; the only light came from the blue illumination outside the window. And then I remembered where I was and how it all worked. A fist clenched around my heart.

I still had to leave.

Loki's fingers traced the line of my jaw. "Good morning."

Looking up at her, I forced a smile. The glamour was still there, two emerald eyes staring back at me. It would be so easy to pretend we were that pure again, unmarred by time. And there was no reason not to keep pretending, if only for five more minutes. If only while I was wrapped in her arms.

I pressed a kiss against her skin and put my arm around her waist. "I missed this."

She kissed my forehead. "I missed everything about you."

"That's not very likely." But even as I said it, I smiled, tucked away so she couldn't see how flattered I was.

"But it's true." Her fingers intertwined with mine, cold metal brushing against my fingers. The rings.

"I still can't believe you kept them."

"You told me to."

I kept my face hidden in the crook of her arm. "It's been seven years since you died, Loki. I thought you'd have…moved on. Especially after what I did."

"You never did anything that made me stop loving you, Sigyn. Not even at the worst of it."

I took a long breath. "That's not how it feels. We've earned a lot of hatred from each other. It was easy when I hated you. But it's not so simple anymore. We were put in impossible situations over and over again. Sometimes I lie awake and think about the thousand moments that got in our way. If Odin hadn't taken Sleipnir, would we have been happy? If you had never gone to Midgard with him, would I have left you? The gods meddled in our marriage just as much as we did. So it's hard, Loki. Most days I love and hate you all at once, until all of it feels numb."

Loki chuckled. I gave her a look of disbelief but she waved it off. "I realize it's a bit bleak, but all things considered, that's a glowing review. It's a miracle you feel anything good for me at all."

I sat up, the covers falling off my body, and looked at her. "That's not how I mean it."

She sat up as well, kissing the curve below my ear. "I'm not stupid. We're going to get this blink of time together, and you'll go back to your life. You might decide you're finished with me after all. And maybe we'll both live through what's coming. Maybe we won't. Maybe this is all we get."

"Loki, you're going to get a new fate. It won't matter—"

"Yes, if I manage to get across the realm, and if I can sneak past the Nidhogg at Yggdrasil, and *if* I convince the Nornir to give it to me. That's a lot of ifs."

"But—"

She shook her head. Her eyes were misty, and a tear ran down her cheek. "No. We can't lie forever. None of us know what's coming. So just...just kiss me."

I leaned into her, grief clawing a hole in my chest. I pushed it down, tried not to think. I kissed her, just like she asked, slow and meaningful. Pressed my bare chest against her, ran my fingers into her hair. In each brush of our lips, I tried to tell her that I loved her, that it was okay. That we were okay. Because I didn't have the heart to lie to her.

Nothing had been okay for a very long time.

Maybe it never would be again.

I set my mind to leave after breakfast. I couldn't bear to drag it out any longer. So when our plates were cleared and the silence settled in, I knew it was time.

My lip quivered for just a moment before I got it under control. Start with the easiest first.

"Hel, thank you for your hospitality. I know you didn't expect a guest, or so many large requests, but it means the world to me that you've given me this time with my family." I tried to smile, though I was sure it looked rigid and unwelcoming as I tried to hold back tears.

"You're always welcome here, Stepmother. Though don't let the rest of the realms get word of it." Hel smirked, the flesh of the mottled half of her face moving unsettlingly. "We don't want to be a tourist attraction for the living."

"Of course not." I stood and pulled my travelling cloak from the chair beside me. I couldn't look at Loki and Narvi, not yet. "I wish my visit could have been longer. Happier."

Loki stood and came around the table. He took my face in his hands and forced me to look up at him. "These have been the best two days I've had in years." He kissed my forehead. "Let me walk you to the gates."

I nodded somberly. "Narvi?" I looked up. "Do you want to come with us?"

Narvi shook his head. "You should say goodbye alone. And I think…I think I just want to go back to work. I've fallen behind." His face was sunken, shadows under his eyes. Perhaps he hadn't slept at all.

"Alright, come here then." I opened my arms and beckoned for him to join us.

He did, though somewhat reluctantly. He began to sob the moment he settled into my arms, his body shaking against mine. I held him tightly, refusing to cry. He needed to see me strong this time. "We're going to see each other soon. You and your father are going to help me save the realms and we're going to be a family again. You're so strong and I love you so much."

He pulled out of my grip, wiping his face on his sleeve. Then he took something out of his pocket. A small letter. He held it out.

"What's this?"

"I think it works. Maybe it won't. I've had it for years, waiting for a time to give it to him. Father told me that Váli was trapped as…as the wolf. This should turn him back."

My heart burst, overwhelmed. I pulled Narvi back into my arms, holding so tightly that he wriggled. "You are the most intelligent, bravest, most loving person in these nine realms. Your brother will be so proud of you. And so thankful." I kissed his cheek. "He loves you so much, Narvi. He thinks about you all the time, and someday he'll tell you he's sorry, in his own words."

Narvi nodded and backed away again, out of my reach. His arms settled over his chest and he couldn't look at me. There was so much pain in him and I had no time to fix it.

"Let's be on our way, shall we? Let Narvi get to work." Loki ruffled his son's hair, then took my hand to lead me out of the dining hall. I waved to Narvi and Hel as we left, then we turned the corner and were alone.

"He tries." Loki opened the front door of the palace and held it as I passed through, tears running down my cheeks. "Some days are better than others. He wants to forgive Váli. In one sense I think he has. But it's difficult to forgive someone who hasn't said the words yet."

"After all this is over, they'll have their chance." I brushed my hand across my face, trying to blink away the tears.

Loki nodded. "Maybe."

CHAPTER TEN

LOKI

*"I hated going viking. I was terrified of battle, but very good
at pretending. I died doing something I hated because I
couldn't just admit I wanted to be a fucking farmer.
How stupid is that?"*

— Hafsteinn, Volume 15

Walking Sigyn to the gates was one of the hardest things I'd ever done. I'd been scarred beyond recognition, beaten, battered, had my children stolen from me. And giving my wife back to the realms for the *greater good* was right at the top of the list.

It was a quiet walk to the cliffs and up to the gates. I was trying to figure out what to say. How to say it. Nothing felt right. It was too insubstantial. What was I ever going to say that amounted to what I needed to tell her? What I needed to apologize for?

As we approached the gates, Edvin pushed them open, gave us a nod, and excused himself to the far cliff edge. Each step we took forward was heavy, like my boots were full of lead; I didn't want to get closer to losing her again.

Sigyn stopped. She turned to face me, linking her fingers with mine. "Loki, I've spent the last two days trying to be in the moment and enjoy being together, but there's so much left to discuss. And we're out of time. I need you to hear this, whether you believe me or not. There are things I've forgiven you for. You deserve that forgiveness. And the things I can't forgive you for—not yet—I accept. I accept you as you are."

My chest tightened. She was lying to make this sweeter; it was obvious. "You don't have to say that. I know what I am and you don't have to say—"

"I'm not. We both became things we didn't want to be. And you were worse than

I was; I'm not going to pretend otherwise. You did unspeakable things." She shrugged, a slight smirk playing on her lips. "I ripped Skadi's innards out with my bare hands. It's not something I would've been proud of when we met."

"You know, when she got here, she refused to say who did it." I pursed my lips and pulled Sigyn against me. "I don't deserve your forgiveness."

"Maybe not," she said into my shoulder. "But it's better to be a monster with you than a monster alone. So I forgive you, and accept you, and I'm going to miss you every day."

The words felt true this time. Real. And the honesty tore me open. Everyone had so much to say about all these things that I'd done, that I should accept it and move on, because what else was there to do with eternity? But I'd hurt no one as badly as I'd hurt Sigyn. That she had come here, that she could look me in the eyes…How much strength did it take to care about the person who had torn your life apart?

Sigyn held me as I wept, my face pressed into her hair. I tried to commit everything to memory, every curve of her body, the way she smelled, the sound of her breathing. In a minute she would be gone and it would be all I had to hold on to.

"It's time, Loki." She tilted her head up and kissed me, sweet and slow and full of despair. Then she pulled away. "I love you. Take care."

I whispered the words back to her as she turned, her hand threatening to slip out of mine as she took a step away.

Not yet. Please not yet.

I pulled her back into my arms and kissed her desperately. One kiss and twenty and a hundred. Catching our breath in short bursts between each passionate one, stealing more and more. Holding onto each other for another second.

"I love you. Go," I said against her lips. "Go."

She broke my grip and took off through the gates. As she ran, the air around her changed, blurred. Then Sigyn was gone. Wings spread and the faint shape of a bird rose up and out of sight.

The world went dark for a moment. I couldn't remember falling to my knees, or the rocks biting into my hands. Edvin was hovering over me, face awash with concern.

It had been one thing to be empty, knowing she would come back someday, but she was gone again and it was a fresh wound in my chest, one right next to the other. I didn't want to feel this cold fucking agony. This lack of everything.

Seeing her had lit a hope in me that was going to do nothing but burn me to ashes.

CHAPTER ELEVEN

LOKI

*"She never surrounded herself with allies, you know? Nothing
but crooks and thieves. If only someone had been
looking out for her..."*

— *Bromthrun, Volume 41*

When I found Narvi in his study, he was surrounded by maps. They were
rolled out in all directions across his desk. Some were old and torn, others
new. And every one of them charted a detailed, intricate start of Helheim
that slowly petered off into the stark blank parchment beyond.

"Did you find anything?"

Narvi looked up. "Yes and no. Is she...did she make it out alright?"

I nodded. "Your mother's tough as nails. She'll be just fine." I leaned over the desk,
trying to get a closer look. "They don't say much, do they?"

Narvi pulled one across the surface of the desk. "No one goes that far from the
city, not really. This map has the river and up to the stalagmite field. This one—" He
set another map on top of it, stained in rust-red spatter. "—was found outside the
mines. Along with the bodies."

"Well. That's encouraging." I ran a hand through my hair, pushing it back. "What
do you think?"

"I think it's really dangerous. Before the city was carved out, this realm was
nothing but wild things trying to eat the dead. But that doesn't matter, because Mother
needs it and you're not going alone." Narvi pushed the maps aside to reveal a new one
in progress, starting at the edge of the city and unfolding out. "I'm combining them
into one map. I've found things on my walks that aren't on any of these, so I'm adding

them as I go."

"How can I help?"

"You can't. Well, you could, but I want to do this. Keeps my mind busy." He pointed at the chair across the room. It was piled with satchels, knives, cooking gear, and a bedroll. "You could pack. I should have this done by tomorrow, and then we can leave."

"There's still an unknown variable."

"Angrboda?"

I nodded. "Angrboda. I'm not sure which side she's going to swing towards, ecstatic or enraged."

"Do you think she'll agree to come along?" Narvi pressed his palms into the edge of the desk, leaning against it.

"I'm not half as concerned with that as I am with you. Are you going to be able to handle an untold number of days and nights with her?" I tried to make it sound like a joke, but we both knew it was a genuine concern. The two of them weren't exactly fast friends. But where Váli would've been crass about it, Narvi kept discomfort coiled in him until it started leaking out his ears.

"I'm not a child, Father. I've handled worse than Angrboda." He gestured to his stomach.

"Alright, I believe you." But there was something on Narvi's face underneath the cool mask he was trying to put on. He'd never been good enough at lying, always wearing his heart on his sleeve. I cleared my throat. "You know, your old man could use a hug for the road. It's been a hard enough day without having to go down and beg favours."

Narvi cracked a pitying smile and stepped into my arms. I held him tightly, breathing in the musty book smell that always seemed to waft off him, trying to relish this tiny moment of peace. Narvi wouldn't admit to needing help; he never wanted anyone to know. Better an act of charity towards his broken father than to let anyone in.

So I played the part and held him close and wished I could do something, anything, to put him back together.

I heard the chaos before I reached the tavern. The sharp crack of wood, the shattering of glass, and the scream of battle. Just another day at The Three Harbingers.

A chair flew by the moment I opened the door. The room was in a state of disarray. Tables were knocked over, daggers stuck out of seat cushions, and someone was unconscious on the floor. And in the thick of the fight was Angrboda, as wild and beautiful as she had ever been, all Jotun-white skin, muscle, and fury. She threw a punch, hitting a burly man twice her girth square in the jaw. He fell flat on his back. As she turned to strike someone else, her long hair threaded through the air, adorned with all manner of coloured feathers and bone and beads. A full mug of ale hit her in the chest, spilling out over her and drenching her clothes. She growled and drove her fist into her assailant's gut.

Making my way around the chaos, I sat at one of the far tables and put my feet up. It was best to let her get the aggression out; otherwise, she'd just end up turning it on me. It had always been a delight to watch her fight, moving masterfully in the tattered, wild clothing she favoured. She was a fire that couldn't be contained.

A bottle flew too close to my head, crashing against the wall behind me, and my mind became static again, my heart beating too fast. It was too much too close too loud too much out of my line of sight—I leaned forward on my elbows, pressing my palms into my eyes, trying not to see the flashes of blood and bone. The phantom pain was back, ripping my chest open—

Hot summer days. Warm pastry. The smell of fresh books.

Breathe. It's not real. Not anymore.

The smell of Sigyn's skin after her bath. The rise and fall of her chest while she slept. The sound of her breath in my ear.

Focus.

I pushed it down. Angrboda couldn't see me like this. Weak. Sigyn had valued softness in me, but Angrboda couldn't abide it.

I patted my pockets. The pipe was back on my bedside table, forgotten.

A drink. That was what I needed. It would come back to haunt me tonight when my body couldn't use it, but it would be worth it.

I got up, trying to appear composed. I had to walk over debris to get to the grimy bar, but the barkeep seemed unaffected by the ruckus. He was drying off a stack of mugs, watching the tussle as if he were bored. It was only as I leaned on the counter that a look of intrigue crossed his face.

"Mead, if you please." I slid a black coin across the counter, the thing that passed for currency in this gods-forsaken realm. "Something Elven if you've got it."

The barkeep put the mug and cloth down and delicately fished the coin from the wood. "You have elegant taste," he said, looking me over much too slowly to be polite. "I'm afraid I've got only the swill these brutes drink, but—" He reached under the counter and pulled up a dusty old glass bottle with Vana markings on it. "—I'm willing to share a bit of my personal stash. It's not often we have handsome, cultured individuals such as yourself in here."

I drew in a breath, my mind suddenly a blur of confusion. Was he...? I took a moment to look a little closer at the barkeep. He was a young thing really, in his twenties, though only the Nornir knew how long he'd been dead. His hair was blond and his clean-cropped beard cut a sharp figure underneath his chiselled face. And his arms, well. I wasn't quite sure how a man could get a figure like that drying dishes.

"That's very generous of you." It was all I could manage to say. It had been a very long time since I'd played this particular game. It wasn't as if people were lining up to woo the realm breaker, after all. I leaned forward and took the small cup the barkeep held out for me. "It's none of my business, naturally, but shouldn't you put a stop to them? I don't imagine it attracts clientele."

The barkeep snorted as another chair broke over the back wall. He poured a generous helping of sunlight-yellow mead that smelled of lilacs and hemp. "You're joking of course. As if I'm going to put myself in the middle of that. Besides, this is a glorified playground for that woman over there. But you would know that better than I would, Loki Laufeyjarson? Your daughter sends more chairs and drinking horns and it's as if nothing happened. Rinse and repeat every single night. Better in here than out on the streets, I suppose."

I looked over as Angrboda's bicep wrapped around some other woman's throat, then held my cup towards the barkeep. "To senseless violence."

The barkeep tapped his cup against mine and we both took a drink. We were silent for a moment, and then the barkeep leaned in. "Listen…once they're finished, I won't have much left for business. Perhaps you and I…" His long, nimble fingers reached out and touched the outside of my hand.

Ymir help me.

It wasn't every day I got a proposal like that. Not even every year, not since I'd arrived in Helheim. And gods, it was tempting to indulge in a tumble to take away the pain of everything else. But I gently pulled my hand away and touched it to my chest. "I am flattered and it's a very appetizing offer. Really, normally you're just my type, but I'm afraid I made a promise to a lady that I don't intend on breaking again." I wiggled my fingers, the two wedding bands glinting in the dim light.

The barkeep pouted. "More's the pity. I was so hoping…"

I bit my lip and moved back from the bar before I said something very stupid. A romp was a very good distraction; I knew that too well.

I gave the glass a shake. "But still. Thanks for this."

The barkeep waved his hand dismissively and winked. "If you ever change your mind, you know where to find me."

I managed a flirtatious smile before I turned my back on the barkeep, then cursed myself for all manner of reasons, including how suddenly uncomfortable it had become to sit.

If nothing else, the flirting had pulled me out of myself long enough to feel alright again. These *moments* often came in two shapes: paralyzing or violent. And if Angrboda had caught me curled up in a dark corner, I'd never hear the end of it.

I was halfway through my drink when Angrboda separated herself from the fight and came to me. She slammed down a horn of dusky ale and sat down, reclining in her seat. Her boots hit the tabletop next to mine, one foot very deliberately resting against my own. A new cut was open on her cheek, deep enough that it would need stitching later to close it back up. "To what do I owe the pleasure, lover?"

"Can't a man get a drink without being interrogated?"

"You hate this place." She took a long drink, watching me carefully.

"It's not exactly the pinnacle of culture." I lifted my mead to take a sip.

Angrboda rolled her eyes and pointed to the rings on my hand. "You're still wearing that junk?"

I ignored the comment and pressed on. We'd had that argument enough times already. "I need a favour."

Angrboda laughed as if it was the most absurd thing she'd ever heard. "The God of Lies, asking for a favour? What could you possibly need? I haven't got any of your *medicine* left, not for a while yet." She made a gesture with her hand as if she were smoking an invisible pipe and I tried to ignore the mocking tone on her voice.

"Nothing so simple as that. I saw an old friend today, and she needs something done. Something she can't do on her own."

"An old friend?" Angrboda was eyeing me suspiciously. "You're going to need to do better than that."

"I need to go to the Nornir to ask for a new fate."

The cackle that rose from her belly was loud and boisterous. "You're an idiot, Laufeyjarson. People like you and me don't get new threads. We're too much ourselves to change. Who would ask such an insane thing from you? And that you would agree to it? Moronic."

I stared down into my drink and took a deep breath. "Sigyn."

Angrboda narrowed her eyes. "It's finally happened, hasn't it? You've finally lost your fucking mind."

"Most days, yes, but not in this particular instance. She arrived two days ago and left this morning. She's alive and she needs help."

I relayed the story of Sigyn's arrival and the fight against Asgard to Angrboda, keeping the more intimate things to myself. Not that I needed to; Angrboda had always known when I'd gotten too close to Sigyn again, like she could smell it on me.

She listened, pouring her drink down her throat and snapping her fingers for a new one. By the time I was finished talking, she was halfway through that one as well.

"And how exactly do you think I factor into this?" she asked.

"Hel won't let Narvi and me go unless you go with us. I can't even sneak out of the palace without her knowing, so either you come with us, or no one goes."

"You have the biggest, brassiest balls to ask me this, Loki. You want me to do something that might just kill me in order to please your prissy little wife."

"You admitted that you liked her."

"I said a little. I liked her a little. She's still one of the Aesir, and she's still the other woman."

I rolled my eyes. "*You're* the other woman, Bo." I licked my lips and tried another tactic. I leaned toward her, palm on the table. "I need you with me. You and I were unstoppable, once."

Angrboda laughed. "You can't buy me with silky words. Save it for your goddess. That was never us."

Well, apparently some skills *are* actually lost with time.

I leaned back and put my hands up. "You're right. So are you coming or not? I need someone along who can handle themselves. I apparently have no discernible skills left and Narvi's intelligence will only get us so far."

"And if I say no?"

"You get to march up there and tell your daughter to her face."

"No fucking thank you. I may have birthed her but she still scares the pants off me." Angrboda lifted her mug to her lips, staring coldly at me. "When did we stop being in charge?"

I shrugged. "When Odin handed her a realm to rule, I suppose."

CHAPTER TWELVE

SIGYN

"I'd forgiven him 135 years ago and never told him. He still doesn't know, and he never will."

— *Tarathiel, Volume 28*

L oki had always boasted about how freeing it was, being able to fly. I used to believe him. But it turned out it was just another thing we disagreed on. He was always prone to flights of fancy and I had had my feet planted firmly on the ground, which felt quite literal in this case.

After leaving him at the gates of Helheim, I flew until the sun started to disappear over the horizon, and then stopped for the night in a patch of trees in Midgard. I'd built a fire and fallen into a deep sleep, knowing the thoughts that had haunted me all day would be waiting when I woke.

And sure enough.

Passing over Midgard hurt. The water had risen, creating pockmarks of marshy grass in the middle of all that blue, popping up here and there like inverted lakes. Mountains hid beneath the surface, poking through like a gap-toothed maw, bare of snow. Steel and brick broke out of the ocean, the last remnants of ruined cities. An enormous metal ship floated along the surface, rusted and going nowhere. Very little lived on what was left of the land, but now and again I spotted the white spurt of water from the back of a whale or a pod of seals below. All that men had built was lost to the ocean and nature was ready to begin again.

Thinking about all the destruction below, all the calm, eerie peace, was the only thing that kept me from turning around. I had a responsibility to keep this from happening to Fólkheim. I had a son who needed me and a city that needed a future. I'd promised that to them, and to run away now, to let myself be dead to the realms, felt too easy to do. Too tempting.

The Bifrost shimmered in the middle distance. Or what was left of it. The thin sliver of rainbow that had once connected Midgard and the realms of the gods above was shattered. Once able to shimmer in and out of view, it now floated above the realm like a broken stained-glass window, stepping stones suspended in the sky.

Above it would be Asgard. Better a detour than to be shot dead, so I cut straight up, grazing the edge of the Bifrost, and veered away from the city before I could catch a glimpse. I didn't want to see it. Things were hard enough without all those memories.

It took another two hours to reach Fólkheim. My heart clenched as I approached, waiting to see that my neglect had caused the city to burn somehow. But it was still there and nothing seemed amiss. Not from so far out, at least. People the size of ants made their way through the streets, between buildings in all states of disrepair. In the garden, the Sister Tree was reaching her grafted jewel-toned branches towards the sky, the way Yggdrasil had before her.

I made a quick round from overhead, pushing back my exhaustion for a few more minutes. Repairs were wrapping up in the district that had been damaged by the crane. The market was bustling. The construction of new homes was ongoing. All seemed well.

Or as well as it ever was.

I landed back in the square I had left from, letting the form of the falcon melt off me. I tensed against the shifting of bone and muscle and sinew and became myself again, braced against the stone walkway on my hands and knees. Everything in me ached. I wanted a bath and a drink, and to forget everything. To hide and mourn. But I had no time for that. I'd already squandered too many hours as it was.

I peeled myself from the ground and headed into the city, towards the training grounds. There was still plenty of daylight left, and if my son was anywhere, he would be there.

Vanaheim had been dense and sprawling, everything too tightly tucked together for my liking. But the ruins had provided a place to start. Once some of the stone had been broken up and removed, an old hall belonging to one of the wealthy Vanir had become the training grounds. The remnants of the building were a stark contrast to what it was used for, all that gold and crystal and violence. The east and west wings— or what was left of them—served as compact battle arenas, each of them scattered with rubble that served as cover. One section still had its roof, and on the wall was a severely damaged family portrait that stared down at the trainees.

Váli and Hreidulfr were overseeing a group of visibly inexperienced fighters when

I arrived. Most of the Elves and Jotnar they were training were teens at most, but some of the humans were well past their thirties, having never picked up an axe in their lives. A challenge, to be certain, but one that we would overcome.

Hreidulfr was watching over the flock, arms crossed and eyes focused. In the middle of the hall, Váli had gripped a young Elf's pant leg in his muzzle, forcing the boy to adjust his stance. It didn't matter that he couldn't talk to them. He made do with what he had.

Ymir willing, that was almost over.

"Is it a good day for training today, *sir?*" I said, stepping up beside Hreidulfr and drawing out that last word.

He smirked at my little tease. "Every day is a good day for training, *ma'am.*"

Váli's ears perked up and he whirled to look our way. As he trotted over, his voice rang out in my mind. "*Oh, look who finally decided to come home.*" His tone was cutting, but his tail was thumping against the ground.

"I would've stayed away but I missed your soft temperament too much." I bent down and kissed him on the forehead.

Hreidulfr rested a hand on my shoulder. "How was the trip, *ma'am?* Was Helheim as sunny and beautiful as we've heard?"

I chuckled. "It has its charms. I'm ready to sleep for two straight days, but there's a lot to tell. We need to update the council, but not yet. First I need time with you. Is there anything resembling coffee left?"

Hreidulfr stuck his fingers between his lips and gave a sharp whistle.

His apprentice hurried over, her face covered in dust, an enthusiastic grin plastered across it.

"Sigyn needs us. Can you oversee the rest of the session?"

"Absolutely. Wrap up with shield wall practice and a cool-down jog around the district?"

"That's the one. Don't let them step on your toes." Hreidulfr winked at her and sent her back to the fray. He held a hand out, gesturing to the door, and we began to walk. "Is it good news? We could all use some of that."

I gave them the highlights of the adventure as we walked back to my room, saving the more intimate details for when we were behind closed doors. By the time I'd settled onto my bed, I'd tucked my hand into my cloak, Narvi's notes between my fingers.

"But they're alright?" Hreidulfr was leaning against the wall opposite the bed. "They sound alright."

"It's a complicated thing," I said. "They remember dying, and that leaves a mark."

Váli slumped onto the bed, his ears drooping.

Hreidulfr nodded, his mood sober. "That it does. When the people in my village in Midgard talked about going to Valhalla, they only talked about the glory. No one said anything about what it would feel like to die. I didn't know the newly dead sleep in different barracks because all they do is scream in their sleep. No one tells you that."

I reached out to offer comfort to Hreidulfr with a touch. "I'm sorry. I hope…I hope things are better now." Hreidulfr nodded and said nothing, and so I continued. "Loki and Narvi are doing their best to enjoy their afterlives. And they'll be on their way to the Nornir soon, if they're not already. If the Nornir agree, they'll have their new threads."

"*It can't be that simple.*" Váli's tone was full of emotion, but it was hard to pin down which one he felt most deeply.

"It won't be. It'll be very dangerous and if the Nornir don't find them *worthy*, then they have to go back to Helheim and we're alone in this. If they survive, we see them when we die and go to Helheim. If they don't survive the trip, they die for good." A tightness pulled at my insides. I hadn't allowed myself to think too deeply about that potential result and I wasn't about to start.

Hreidulfr scratched at the back of his hand, keeping anything telling from his face. "They're strong. They're going to be alright."

"But—" I cheerfully pulled the note from my pocket and held it toward Váli. "— Narvi sent us a gift. If his work is correct, this should give you your body back."

The room was silent, the words hanging in the air. Then a slow build of noise rose from our link with Váli's mind wasn't anything intelligible, just a deep, desperate pain. Hreidulfr dropped to his knees beside the bed and pulled Váli's curled-up form against his chest, hushing him.

"I've got you. I've got you." Hreidulfr turned his gaze to me. "Are you sure?"

"As sure as I can be. Narvi was always the innovator in the family and he—"

"*I don't deserve it.*"

"None of that now." Hreidulfr stroked his hand down Váli's neck. "We can talk all day and night about what you deserve when you're yourself again, hmm?"

"I've looked at it and it seems viable," I said. "I can do it now, if you're ready. Or we can wait."

"*I killed him. And this is what he does in return? Gives me my life back? What kind of sick joke is this? He has to hate me. He has to—*"

I tapped the space between his eyes with my finger, breaking his train of thought. "Your brother knows it wasn't you. These runes are his forgiveness, in one way or another. You need to forgive yourself, and this is how you start."

"Please." Hreidulfr stared into Váli's eyes. "You know I've been patient and if you need the time, fine. I'd wait forever for you; you know that. But if we have a chance, we have to take it. *We* deserve a chance to be truly happy again."

Váli whimpered. "*What if it doesn't work?*"

"If it doesn't work, we try again. If it never works, we keep searching. No one is giving up on you." I flattened the paper on the bed in front of me, runes open and ready for reading. "Are you ready?"

Váli nodded, but the cower in his body didn't make me very confident.

I pursed my lips, let out a long breath. "I don't have the impression this is going to be simple and painless. If we're reversing what Odin did…" The memory knotted my stomach. Watching my son's bones crack, his body reshaping itself while he screamed. Sometimes the scene played out in my nightmares. One among many that could wake me in a cold sweat. But I couldn't linger on that, not now. "This could be very painful, Váli."

Váli straightened out, wriggling from Hreidulfr's grip. He shook off the outward apprehension and started acting more like the Váli to whom fear was foreign. Pain was something he knew what to do with. He hopped down from the bed and sat on the floor. "*Let's get it over with.*"

"What can I do?" Hreidulfr was wringing his hands, a look of unease written on his face.

"Nothing for now. Be patient, and don't get in the way." I moved to sit in front of Váli, the cold of the stone seeping through my clothes. "No matter how much pain he's in, you have to stay where you are. We can't afford anything going wrong."

Hreidulfr nodded, bracing himself on the bed.

I settled in, crossing my legs. Drawing deep breaths one after the other, I called up energy. Focused on it. Let it warm my skin, familiar and soothing. Váli was still, watching me closely. If I stared at him too long, I would lose my nerve. And so I began to read.

The runes Narvi had concocted were long and winding. Out of necessity and practicality, a lot of seidr was short and easy to use at a moment's notice, but this was not. It was more story than incantation, and I had to get each word right. I read from the paper, the runes a whisper on my tongue.

Halfway through, Váli's muzzle twitched.

Staying steady, I kept reading. Then his ear flicked. His shoulders tensed, the fur standing on edge. Something was happening. Working. I reached the end of the runes and started again. Onwards, steeling myself, because it would only get uglier from there.

A low growl started in his throat and Váli leaned forward, squirming. He scratched at the stone, teeth bared, snarling. His front leg twitched. Snapped. Pulled back of its own accord. A howl broke from his throat, mourning and pained. His body shook, tremors raging through his body. Watching him was a nightmare, worse than any I'd had. Beast and man and neither, all at once.

Fur sloughed off in small tufts, and then in wet pieces of flesh. Cracking resonated in him, his body changing shape, legs twisting, bones setting, muscles retracting and expanding.

And the screams. Through all of it, the screams. Wolf to man and back again.

Through all of this, I kept reading. I had no choice. To falter was to doom him and I wouldn't. I couldn't do that. We had set out to fix him, and I would, no matter how much it tore me apart to do it. I had to bear it with him.

The change in his face was hardest to watch. His jaw snapped a thousand tiny times to hide a muzzle he no longer needed. The fur on his cheek slid off and hit the floor, blood spattering out around the impact. His skin, his real skin, was underneath. My son was still there.

Váli was braced against the ground, sobbing and crying out, but that voice was no longer a wolf. Every muscle, every fibre of him was a man again. Blood and wolf-flesh clung to him, the last bits of a nightmare that was losing its grip on us.

He was back at last.

I stopped whispering and crawled toward him. He barely knew I was there. His chest heaved. He was crying like I'd never seen him cry before.

Hreidulfr scooped Váli into his lap, pressing him against his chest. "It's alright, my love. We're here. We have you."

I pulled the blanket from my bed and wrapped it around Váli, pressing against the other side of him. To keep him warm. Safe. "Welcome home," I whispered in his ear, pushing the matted red curl of hair from his forehead.

As the pain subsided, his cries changed. Gradually it became laced with something else. Laughter. A smile blossomed across his face and he looked up at us, tears still streaming down his cheeks. Like he was seeing us for the first time in a very long time.

There were deep circles under his eyes, and when I wiped the blood from his cheek, the skin below was a sicklier grey than I had remembered him being. A beard had grown in, patchy and long, and streaks of grey ran through his red hair. He was tired, top to bottom, but he was home, and a body was something we could fix.

He opened his mouth to speak, but the words came out more like the whine of a wolf. He grimaced and laughed again, hand over his mouth.

All things in time.

Hreidulfr took Váli to clean up and to rest. It was a sight to see, the two of them walking down the hall slowly, Hreidulfr supporting Váli's new legs. The blanket was still wrapped tightly around him and there were bits of gore everywhere. It wouldn't be long before half the city knew he was back.

I'd made them promise to take the day to themselves, and something about the way they were looking at each other made me think they didn't need to be told twice.

As I was on my hands and knees, tossing pieces of flesh into a bucket and mopping up the blood, I struggled to contain my crashing emotions. This news, this miracle of a moment, was trying to escape me and I had nowhere to put it. I wanted to climb to the top of the cliffs and scream it for the realm to hear. The unbridled joy of it was bubbling under my skin and begging to be let loose.

I managed to contain it until I had the floor and myself cleaned up, then found my feet taking me to a familiar place.

Whenever the smithy was operational, it was common to smell it before you saw it. Smoke poured from the hole in the roof of the large, well-insulated building, tossing the strong odour of coal and soot into the air. Every window was covered with thick fabric and boards to keep the sun out, allowing the Dwarves to work through the day when needed. As I opened the front door, heat burst across my face, stopping me in my tracks for a moment as I caught my breath.

Once I stepped inside and closed the door behind me, the sweat started to bead down my back. Metal only became workable at a very, very high temperature, and yet the inside of the smithy always surprised me. The air was heavy and hard to breathe, and I imagined that standing inside a volcano would feel similar. Inside were three forges, each of them manned by a pair of workers. Everything about the place was overwhelming, and the din of hammers slamming into steel was enough to start a small ache in the back of my head.

This was most certainly her place, not mine.

Alyssa was hunched over a desk, in the middle of a spirited back-and-forth with a tall, well-muscled Jotun woman. They were both wearing sleeveless shirts and protective aprons, covered in dirt and soot and sweat. The two were drawing lines across a large parchment featuring a complicated sketch that looked from a distance to be a crane.

A small pang of jealousy crept into my chest. I wished I could understand blueprints and speak to Alyssa in the language of her heart, the way this woman so obviously could. I deeply admired Alyssa's intelligence and the new and interesting ways that she thought. I had the chance to learn so much from her, and yet I always felt so far behind.

Hmm.

I had felt like that with Loki, once. Straining to know what he knew, enthralled in the excitement of it and, later, what it grew into.

Epilogues for Lost Gods

I pushed the realization away before it could sink its claws into me.

Approaching the desk, I cleared my throat, but it wasn't audible over the loud noise of the smithy. I tried again, but the two were so caught up in their conversation, yelling back and forth about measurements, that I couldn't get their attention. Feeling helpless, I waved somewhat dramatically.

Alyssa looked up with a start and a new smile burst across her face. "Hey!" she called out. "You're back!"

I nodded and returned the smile, not feeling too keen on straining my voice to respond.

Alyssa gave the Jotun woman a pat on the shoulder, rolled up the parchment, and sent her off with it. Then she gestured for me to follow her through a low door, into another room.

Once the door was closed, the small office that Alyssa had set up for herself provided a bit of a reprieve from the noise. Plans and papers and half-empty mugs were strewn across her workspace, with shelves and shelves of half-baked mechanical concepts carved out of wood and metal cluttering up the shelving.

"Oh shit, I have got to tell you, this whole learning-to-work-iron thing, it might be a mistake." Alyssa flexed her arm, the skin glistening over the lean muscle of her bicep. She grimaced. "I'll be lucky if I can hold a spoon tomorrow, let alone do another day of hammering. I *need* to have a better understanding of it so I'm not just creating plans for impossible projects, but I did *not* understand what I was getting into. Solveig tried to warn me, but *phew*. I am *tired*!"

I couldn't help but smile as she rambled on. She always let her passion show when she talked about her work.

"What?" Alyssa flexed again. "Are you not impressed by how fit I'm getting?"

"Of course I am!" My face flushed and I slapped her arm playfully. "Put that away before someone gets hurt."

"The only people getting hurt by these arms are the boys when I steal all their girlfriends." Alyssa kissed her own bicep and a laugh peeled out of me that I wasn't expecting.

Why was she so good at making me laugh?

"Enough about that. How was your trip to Helheim?" She wiggled an eyebrow. "Did you see Loki?"

The words got caught in my throat. The easy answer was yes, but for some reason, I felt compelled to hide the extent to which our reunion had…reunited us. It felt wrong to voice that kind of thing to her.

"I saw him. And Narvi. And a lot of other people, and I'm not entirely sure how to feel about it," I sighed.

I told her an abbreviated version of events, skimming around the things that didn't feel right to say. Alyssa had always been a phenomenal listener, inserting the right comments and expressions in all the right places. When I finally arrived at giving Váli his body back, Alyssa threw her hand up.

"Wait. Are you telling me that right now, Váli is in his original body, somewhere in this city?"

I nodded.

"Sigyn!" she cried out. "That's amazing news!" Alyssa rushed forward and threw her arms around me, squeezing so tight that I couldn't breathe properly.

I curled my arms around her and let myself fall into her. Something about being wrapped up in her was so comfortable, so freeing. I let all the weight on my shoulders slough off for a moment. She still smelled like raspberry oil underneath all the smells of work.

Alyssa pulled away, her arms still holding me tightly around the middle. Her eyes were full of excitement, her face still closer to mine than was generally acceptable. And I didn't mind. Not one bit.

The moment lingered and then she released me, her hands sliding down my arms to slip into my palms. She made space between us but didn't let me go, and I valued that little action so deeply that I couldn't express it. Then her face tightened into a pitying expression as a tear slipped down my cheek.

Alyssa reached up to wipe it away and my skin sparked under her touch.

I looked away. "It's good," I said quickly. "Váli deserves his life back. He and Hreidulfr have waited long enough."

Alyssa gave a sharp nod and moved back to sit on an empty corner of her worktable. "It sounds like your journey was worth it, even if it was hard on the heart."

I wrung my fingers together. It had been.

"Well." The word came out as a sigh. Alyssa reached into her apron and pulled out a small metal case. She flicked it open, pulled something from it, and held it out to me. "I hate to be the bearer of bad news…"

It was a tiny, rolled-up parchment.

"It came by raven yesterday evening," she said. "I haven't looked. I know the rules. I'm flattered that you'd trust me with your messages, but I have to admit it's been weighing on me."

"I apologize. I didn't think—"

Alyssa waved away the end of the sentence. "No, no. I just got a very small taste of what it's like to carry the fate of a city around in my apron, that's all."

Epilogues for Lost Gods

I swallowed, very familiar with that feeling. A note from Asgard had never, ever been good news, and I didn't want to open it. Perhaps if I left it curled up and pitched it directly into one of the forges, whatever was inside would never come to pass.

If only that were possible.

I pulled the tiny string that was tied in a bow around the outside and the paper loosened from its little cocoon. When I opened it, the crisp, etched letters read:

Asgard trains more horses. Land was promised to Dwarves
in exchange for weapons. Arming for war.

"Fuck." I summoned a puff of wildfire and burned the scrap immediately.

"Are they coming for us?" Alyssa stood straight, her arms crossing defensively over her chest.

"Not yet. But we're running out of time." Tension curled back into every muscle in my body. The time for comfort and reverie was over. I had a duty to attend to. "Get your things. It's time to call the council."

"So you've placed our future in the hands of the same man who took it away the first time, and now we need to brace for attack from Asgard. Is that about the gist of it?" Niklas' knuckles were white from gripping the table edge.

"That's not fair." Alyssa jabbed her finger into the book laid out in front of her. "We've been over this. Everyone in this room knows what *really* happened. Not what Odin said, not what the stories said. You told me your brother killed you over a deer during Fimbulwinter, Niklas. You know what Midgard became before the end, even with Loki and Sigyn trapped in a cave."

"My lack of faith in humanity doesn't restore my faith in a trickster god," Niklas snapped. I tended not to let men scare me anymore, but even so, his anger made my skin crawl. He may have only been the city legislator, but he was built like a tree, tall and tough, and was hard to budge in both mindset and body.

I stood up and pressed my hands into the tabletop, staring out at the faces around me. We'd called the council and they'd come, ten of them packed around a worn old table. It should have been twelve, but Hreidulfr's and Váli's seats were empty. Alyssa was in hers as head Modernist Engineer, alongside the other positions that made our city livable each and every day.

I took a deep breath and tried to summon the easy confidence that I'd always watched my father use when discussing business. "First of all, few of you are old enough to have actually met Loki. You've only heard the stories. And yes, I understand that the majority of you don't care for my husband. I understand why, and I have often cared for him far less than you do, given that he did those things to *me*, not you. We're going to do everything we can to ensure that Fólkheim can survive without the help of Loki, Narvi, and Angrboda. And they will—"

"Angrboda?" Oda put her head in her hands, pulling her silver Elven hair back from her face. Her fingers massaged lines across her deep brown skin, like she was trying to stave off a headache. She was a worrier, and it made her a meticulous city treasurer. "Yggdrasil above, we're all dead, aren't we?"

"Have I ever given you any reason not to believe in me?" The room stilled as I let the question settle. "I chose you all to be part of this council because I knew you'd excel at your jobs. Some of you are here *specifically* because I knew you'd challenge my opinions. I wanted you to give me a reason to second guess myself because this work has to be for the people, not for anyone's ego. But this time I'm asking you to have a little faith in me. I deeply believe that they're going to come through for us, because I have seen how strong they are. I know how resilient and determined they are." I paused and gave a small, compromising wave of my hand. "Still, something down there may eat them all and we'll never hear from them again. We will plan to stand alone, in case help never comes. But I'm not ready to give up on them yet."

A few heads nodded, and the surlier of the group stayed quiet.

"If war is coming, what needs to be prepared?" I asked.

"I normally don't presume to speak for Hreidulfr in his absence, but based on what he's said in the past, I can say with all certainty that our best shot is to stay within the city and use it to our advantage." Oda flipped through her ledger. "Arm our people. Fortify the streets. Nothing about that has changed. But how close are we to reaching that goal?"

"Not close enough." Alyssa flipped to another page in her book. "According to the ledger, we should have a stock of seventy-three pikes, thirty-five hand-axes, fifty shields, and around two dozen blockade walls. Does that sound correct to you, Oda?"

Oda ran her fingers across several pages and at length gave a nod.

"Good." Alyssa snapped the ledger shut. "We'll be working day and night to increase the number of blockades and ammunition, but I'm not sure how many we'll be able to produce. We'll need more supplies faster than usual, and more bodies if anyone has labour to spare."

"Merel, can we put any of the older children to work at something?" I asked. "Delivering food and water to the workers, feeding animals, anything?"

Merel scratched her beard and adjusted her stout Dwarven body on her chair. "The short answer is yes. We've had more than two dozen older children getting ready to transition into new homes, and another two dozen can be put to some soft labour jobs. Either case should provide basic support for the city and free up more capable bodies for harder tasks." She paused. "I don't like it though, and I want that understood."

"Neither do I." I pursed my lips. We'd known it was a possibility for a while, and one that we had avoided capitalizing on. Children deserved freedom to play and grow, but none of these children were carefree. They already knew what it was to lose, and they were growing up with the weight of that on their shoulders. Once this fighting was over, we could give them a better life than this, but for now...

"You have the list of families," I sighed. "Contact them and pair them with children ready to handle the responsibility. Make sure the transitions are smooth, and any child that can't handle it goes back to the caretakers. I won't have anyone further traumatized over this."

"Right away." Merel scratched notes into her book.

Alyssa's disapproval was evident on her face. "Is there really no one else we can ask for help?"

I shook my head. "It frees the adult labour you need. I'm sorry. I wish we could do better."

The meeting went on and on. Food, weapons, training, structural stability. Every single detail that could be thought of. And all the while, my body and mind crept closer to exhaustion. I still hadn't slept since I'd come back. With all that had happened between, Helheim suddenly felt like it was weeks ago. And at long last, the questions stopped, and the room grew quiet with the weight of everything that had to be done.

"If you have apprentices who can begin the direst items tonight, take advantage of that. Get some sleep, everyone. It's going to be a long week, if we're lucky enough to get that long." I shuffled all of my things together and made sure I was the first person out the door. I was moments away from collapsing in on myself and I'd prefer that happened in my own room.

I'd just managed to get my dress off and was walking around in my underskirts when a knock came at the door. I peeked it open to find Alyssa with a tray of food and a jug of water.

"You can let me in or I can force my way in." She tilted her head, a sly pout on her lips. "I know you haven't eaten."

I sighed and let her in. "Have you started reading minds now?"

"No, I just know *you*. Always putting everything else first." She set the goods on the bed. She was also dressed down to a slip and a robe she'd cobbled together from old fabric furs. "Eat and tell me absolutely nothing. Once you're done, it's time to sleep."

I slid down onto the bed and curled up near the food, popping a chunk of bread into my mouth. "And you'll stay?"

I knew I shouldn't open doors that way, but I was too tired and too in need of comfort to care anymore.

"If you want." Alyssa brushed my hair back behind my ear and lay down across from me. Expecting nothing. Just being near me.

I nodded and kept eating. The silence was a good one, a comfortable one. I ate everything she had brought me, my hunger making itself apparent after the first bite, and finished off the water. And all the while she was just there. Smiling that half smile, watching me delight in the small moments: the taste of the cheese, the simple luxury of berries. I felt blessed beyond words to have found a friend that cared so deeply for me. And once the food was gone, she blew out the candle, tucked us into bed, and held my hand as I fell asleep.

CHAPTER THIRTEEN

LOKI

"The Christians would say that 'the sins of the father are to be laid upon the children.' I took every one of my father's sins and did worse. "

— *Clifford, Volume 81*

Angrboda had never been on time to a thing in her life, and just because we were heading out into the realms to save a city and possibly die, well, that didn't change a damned thing.

"I'm sure she'll be here soon," Narvi said, looking up from his book. He'd perched himself on the top of a crate of gods-knew-what and was biding his time in the way he always did.

Hel let out a long sigh as the bells rang out over the city, indicating the time was just before midday. She tapped her foot for a bit, then switched legs to tap the other. Finally, she threw her hands up. "I can't wait all day for her. I have things to do." She reached out to Narvi and gave him a long hug. "Make sure they don't do anything stupid, alright? But if they throw themselves into a pit, you leave them there and come home. There's always a place for you here."

When she stood, a small tear fell down Hel's living cheek. She blinked the rest away and looked at me.

"I promise not to jump into any pits, if that helps." I tried to smile, but the grief of leaving was sitting under my skin, so close to the surface it threatened to drown me.

"It does, but not very much." She reached out for me and I pulled her into my arms.

My darling girl, my little dove. She smelled of lilac and earth, and I wanted to hold her so tightly no one would ever be able to pry my arms from her. But certain parts of her body had always been somewhat fragile, and I forced myself to be careful.

I had chosen this. I had decided to leave, to make use of myself. Still, it felt too familiar. It felt like being ripped away from my children again, and I couldn't afford to fall into that despair. She was grown and it was me leaving the nest, not her.

I was fine.

I was fine.

I breathed in the sweet scent of her hair, trying to keep this moment fresh so that later I could look back and know exactly who she was, my precious daughter.

But small moments always ended too soon, and she was pulling away from my arms, her eyes full of mist. "Be careful, Father. I'm proud of you."

The words were like another knife to my chest. Proud. I wanted it to be true. I wanted her to believe it, and more than that, to believe it myself. I was choking on everything I could say to her, all of it lost beneath the weight of *proud*. I kissed her forehead. "I love you, dove."

"I love you too." She squeezed my hand, pried herself from my grip, and was back inside the palace walls before I could find my words.

Narvi was watching me, concern on his face.

"What?" I asked.

"Nothing, nothing." He turned his attention back to the book in his hands.

"I'm not going to implode every time something stressful happens."

"Of course not," he said, in the realm's most pacifying voice.

"I should hope you won't," came a voice from the street. "It would make it awfully difficult for you to visit me."

Edvin had come down from the gates. It wasn't a thing that happened very often, but—a sudden pang of guilt washed over me.

"Edvin, I'm sorry, I—"

"You were just going to rush off chasing your wife across the realms and not even say goodbye." He waggled a finger at me. "Don't try to deny it; I know it perfectly well. A little birdie told me."

"I was in a hurry." I looked down at my boots, a knot curling in my chest. "Besides, I wouldn't think you'd be that eager to hear from the person who spent every single day harassing you about a woman who was never coming."

Edvin put his arm around my shoulder and nudged me into a walk. He led me slowly towards the street, not seeming to be heading anywhere in particular. "Only you think of it that way. Your visits were a balm on my tired soul, Loki. That gate is my burden, and there weren't many others who thought to visit an old man. Your company has been a blessing."

Epilogues for Lost Gods

I knew that already, just a little. He'd been a friend to me, and I hoped I had been one in return. But it was easier to accuse myself of being a burden than to admit I was sad to leave him. I'd never loved goodbyes, especially not so many at once. The finality of them. The feeling of trying to hold in your insides as every word, kind or not, tore you open and left you bleeding.

I'd had too many for one life.

"I know it's a long trip to come visit an old man, but if you spare me a moment's thought, send a letter by raven." Edvin took each of my shoulders in his palms, forcing me to look him in the eyes. "I want to know how you are, and if she was worth all this waiting."

A smile crept onto my face. "She will be."

That was the only thing I knew for sure.

"Good," he said with a smirk, leading me back toward Narvi. "Because I'm going to need to train a new chess opponent and I hold your wife personally responsible for that."

Angrboda arrived late, looking like she'd had a fight with a bag of rocks. After some heckling and a few choice curse words, we set off toward our first stop.

Helheim had grown since I'd arrived and would keep growing for the foreseeable future. It took most of the first day of walking just to get out of the city. Narvi had suggested we hire a handcart so we could save time, but Angrboda had said she'd die again before she let some overmuscled man pull her around. And so, hours later, we'd found ourselves at the edge of civilization, surrounded by half-constructed buildings as far as the eye could see and one lonely little inn at the edge of acres and acres of seidr-lit farmland.

Eating wasn't a thing that most anyone in Helheim did, so whatever we grew was for the very few lucky ones still living among us—like Hel, who had been thrust into the realm without dying—or for the dead who just wanted to feel something again. That second version never ended well, so most people avoided it altogether, but the fields were at least still pretty to look at. I'd heard about the varieties of plants out there, but from a distance, all I could see was a sea of green, yellow, and brown. There must have been tomato and wheat and barley under the overly bright false suns hanging above, among other things. And it made me oddly jealous, knowing what was there that I could never enjoy, things I'd taken for granted. That jealousy made me glad I couldn't see what I was missing, even if this would be the closest I'd ever get to being aboveground again.

The inn was quaint, but it was warm and had the feel of being very broken in. Everything felt worn and old, even down to the hunched-over clientele. I wondered if every other building within sight had popped up around this one, and it may not have been that far from the truth.

Narvi paid for a room for the three of us and we settled into a dark corner of the inn with our last comforts before we hit the wilds. Angrboda hated herself enough to order ale, and each of us got the usual Menu of the Dead: a cup of hot water to warm the hands and a hot towel to match. There weren't many comforts left to someone who couldn't eat pound cake or drink down stew, but warmth, that was something a man could hang on to.

After the water cooled and Angrboda had ordered her second ale, Narvi unfurled his map across the table.

"We're here, obviously." He pointed at the city edge on the scroll. "I've been as far as here, and only via this path." He traced his finger over what might have been the expanse of farmland, then to a pair of lines that indicated a river, past a forest, and to the stalagmite fields.

"No sense in going this way—" Angrboda pointed to a blank space to the right of the path Narvi had marked. "It's lousy with plants that'll make your skin crawl off your bones, possibly literally. And here, that's a dead end. This river you want to cross, though, something lives in it."

Narvi sketched in the new additions on the map. "I know. Don't worry about that. I have a way across for us." He tapped a section past the stalagmite fields. "There are some records of a mine shaft here that cuts through the cliff into another section of Helheim, but I've never actually met anyone who's seen it. The Nidhogg and Yggdrasil's root are definitely on the other side. That's just about the only thing I know for sure."

"How can no one know?" I leaned closer, trying to make out all the details that the others were seeing so clearly.

"The realms had no sense of order before Hel arrived," Narvi said. "The majority of souls here were from Midgard and written history wasn't something they were concerned about. It was more urgent to survive in the wilds against whatever beasts were out there. We have some oral sources, passed down over the years, but many people just disappeared into the wilds with all the information they'd gathered, and there was no getting it back. Building the city made it easier to collect information and protect it, but it was already too late for some things."

I sighed. "What a lovely bedtime story. Can't wait to think about all the dying and disappearing I'm about to do."

"Still time to turn back." Angrboda emptied her ale in one long drink. "We wouldn't be out here if it weren't for your lovestruck agreement to get ourselves fucking killed."

I leaned over the table, a wolfish grin on my lips. "Admit it. You're itching for a little adventure."

Epilogues for Lost Gods

"Not for her, I'm not. All that has nothing to do with me, and the fact you're that pussy-whipped is something you should be *deeply* ashamed of—"

"Excuse me." Narvi folded his hands on the table, looking intently at Angrboda. "If we're going to be travelling together, I'm going to have to insist you refrain from using phrases like 'pussy-whipped' in relation to my mother. I understand your history with Father makes this complicated, but I'm just not going to listen to it."

Angrboda's eyebrow rose as she stared at Narvi. "I'll speak however the fuck I please, pup. You're like a twig. What are you going to do about it?"

"Intelligent people don't need strength, Angrboda. They just need the right ingredient to slip in the ale late one night—something that tastes strangely like nothing at all—and then no one wakes up in the morning." He said it so cooly and emotionlessly that a chill ran down my spine.

Angrboda flexed a hand, her face altering to a look of wary uncertainty. Then she got up without a word and went to the bar.

I leaned over to Narvi. "Are you alright? What was that?"

"Negotiating and begging never got me anywhere before, Father. People don't want to be reasoned with. So I said exactly the kind of thing she'd respond to." Narvi held his cup of fading heat, not looking me in the eyes.

And here I'd been worried that *Váli* was going to turn out too much like me.

Narvi went up to the bedroom first, never having been much for crowds. I stuck it out for a while longer, watching from our table as Angrboda played pinfinger with three labourers and a very sharp knife. And it was almost a guarantee that she'd get into a bar fight before the evening was up. I couldn't be bothered to stay any longer. Let her solve her own problems.

I wrapped my hands around my newest cup of heat as the last of the warmth was fading. Warm for a little while, but never in the places that counted. I'd stay a moment longer. And just one more. And then the cup was as cool as I was, so I got up and made my way across the room. The rooms were upstairs and to the back of the inn, so I made my way up the stone stairs, then down the long corridor to the room at the far end. The second-to-last room they'd had.

Pressing my ear to the door, I listened for movement. If Narvi was asleep, I wasn't going to be the one to wake him. Gods knew he slept too little already. I heard nothing, so I cracked it open just enough to see by.

Narvi was standing next to the far wall, his back to the door, staring into a long mirror. Shirtless and missing the corset-like device that kept his insides in place, he was watching himself. The glamour was gone, and looking back at him was a young man torn to shreds. There was a gaping wound in his throat, bone and muscle exposed. Part of his arm was raw and patched up in jagged lines. And his stomach. The flesh was torn open, black around the edges, and some organs were there, yes. But his intestines were gone, and everything had just…caved in. A mess of his pieces, none of them where they were supposed to be.

When we had arrived in Helheim, they'd offered to stitch me up to cover the wound and I'd declined. For Narvi, there'd been nothing they could do.

The worst of it was his face. How hollow and unmoving his expression was as he slid a finger into the pit of his stomach and felt his insides.

It was a horrible, ghastly thing to do, something I had done to myself often enough. That anyone dead who had stared too long, too hard, had done. Because with no consequences and nothing but time, what's to stop you?

Something was bubbling in me. A well of horrific emotions pressing against my insides and trying to escape. I had to breathe deep to keep the memory of his evisceration from engulfing me, swallowing me whole. It flashed before my eyes—the wolf, the guts, the light leaving his eyes—and it felt a little like drowning.

I closed the door and leaned against it.

Mother's soft voice.

Chasing frogs in a stream.

Mint tea on a cold night.

Ten. Nine. Eight…

After a while, the urgency of it subsided. I straightened up, smoothed my clothing, and knocked on the door. It would give him a chance to hide his pain, as was the habit. And when I opened the door, Narvi was himself, sitting at the edge of his bed. No holes, just him, the glamour back in place and the corset around his middle.

"Finished for the night?" he asked, looking up from taking off his boot, as if he hadn't just had that hand in his guts.

"Have to be, I think. I want to enjoy this bed a little." I gave the bedpost next to his a pat.

The room wasn't much, but nothing was much in Helheim. Phosphorescent lamps stood on stone tables next to each bed, illuminating everything in that eerie blue. Three single-person beds lined one wall, and at the end of the long room was a window that looked out on the dimming false sunlight of the enormous seidr lanterns over the fields.

I kicked off my boots and undressed down to my underpants, then crawled into bed. It was harder than my bed by a lot, but softer than the ground, so who was I to complain.

I turned to face Narvi. "Anything you want to talk about while we have a minute alone? Going to be a long walk with Angrboda and I don't think we'll have this again, not for a while."

Narvi stared at his feet for a moment, unmoving. Then he shook his head. "No, I'm alright. Just thinking about Mother."

He may have been learning to bluff, but Narvi still couldn't lie.

"Me too. I'll be glad to see her again. To do this for her." I stifled a yawn, trying not to give Narvi another reason to shut me out.

"Do you think it'll work? Really, truly think so?"

"Of course," I lied. "It has to."

Narvi nodded, then got under the covers. "Good night, Father."

"Good night."

I watched him for a while, looking for the rise and fall of a sleeping chest, but it never came. And in the watching, the silence, I fell asleep myself.

Something woke me later, though I didn't know how long it had been. A quiet murmur. When I opened my eyes, two shadowy figures were at the window. It was open and Narvi was sitting on the sill, legs hanging outside. Angrboda was standing next to him, leaning against the wall.

"It's not that..." Narvi said under his breath, so quietly I almost couldn't hear. "It's the nightmares. I'd rather not have them."

"Why do you think I spend my nights at taverns, pup?" She put a hand on his shoulder, little more than shadows in the darkness. "No one sleeps down here."

CHAPTER FOURTEEN

SIGYN

"When you kill to survive, you can't think about that too much, you know? But all I have here is time to think. I killed a lot of people, and hurt a lot more."

—*Juris, Volume 21*

"Are you sure you're feeling fine?" I asked, checking the back of his neck, the square of his shoulders, and a dozen other details. Maybe his armpit had grown back together wrong. Maybe he was sporting a secret tail. Anything was possible with such complex seidr.

"I'm sure, Mother." Váli's voice rose in my mind. He was perched on the edge of his and Hreidulfr's bed, newly clean-shaven, and shirtless for my forced examination. He cleared his throat as I lifted his arm and checked his side. When he opened his mouth, it was almost a croak. "I'm fine."

"Well, sure, but your darling already had a chance to dote on you and I haven't. What if your leg snapped back into place wrong or something? I'd never forgive myself."

Váli gestured to his legs. "There's nothing—" His voice cracked and he shifted back to the link in our minds again. *"There's nothing wrong as far as I can tell. Walking is easier today, and my voice is coming back to me. I ate and slept, and other than some strange digestion, nothing is the matter."*

"Strange digestion?" I squatted in front of him and started probing at his stomach with my fingers. "What do you mean?"

"Mother. My last meal was raw rabbit. How well do you think that went over in my newly human stomach?" He rolled his eyes at me in that way all children knew how to do to their mothers.

I let out a long breath. "Maybe you're right. Maybe I'm just worrying. But I think I'm allowed some worry." I stood up and hugged him against me. "I'm very good at waiting for the other shoe to drop, as it were."

"I know."

The door to his chamber burst open and a Valkyrie stood there, panting and sweaty, trying to catch her breath.

Váli looked at me. "I guess that's the shoe."

Mist was the last known Valkyrie in the nine realms. Her enormous swan wings were lying flat against her back, a stark contrast to her dark skin. She was already dressed in light armour, and her black hair was windblown, likely from flying her patrol route.

"Shoe?" Mist asked between breaths. "What shoe? Did someone—? No, there's no time for that. Magni's here."

"What about Magni?" I asked, all concern over Váli dismissed for the moment.

Mist took two long, deep breaths. "Magni is at the border of the city. He wants an audience with you."

"Why?" Everything in me grew rigid, every ounce of compassion I'd had toward Váli hardening into steel.

Mist shook her head. "When I asked, he said he wanted to talk about a trade agreement, but I think we all know that's birdshit. I only saw two others with him, so it's possible he's not looking for a fight."

I took an annoyed breath. "Fine. Get Gylli and the three of us will handle this."

Mist nodded. "See you down there." And then she was gone.

"Fucking Magni," I swore as I grabbed my healing kit and started toward the door. "I'll be back later to—"

But Váli was up and had a tunic pulled over his head before I could get the words out. He reached for an axe on the side table and hooked it into his belt.

"You are not coming." I crossed my arms over my chest and glared at him.

"I am," he croaked, then cleared his throat. "I'm reborn, not a toddler."

After an eternity spent fighting against Váli's stubborn nature, I knew that my choices were to accept that he was coming or knock him out cold. Though I felt a little like smacking him in the head, I opted to give up instead.

He passed me a dagger and gave me a sly, shit-eating grin. "Love you."

"Oh, shut up." I flicked him on the ear and hurried him out the door.

Pulling the strap tight along the side of my armour, I took a deep breath to test the fit. Váli and I had stopped at the armoury along the way, just in case. Magni wanted to talk, but anyone who knew the kin of Odin knew what *talk* really meant.

A rush of wind rose up beside us. Váli and I moved to the side to make room as Mist sank gently from the sky, her sturdy hands carrying a large Jotun axeman by his armpits. Gylli dropped gently to the ground, clinging white-knuckled to Mist's arms.

"I fucking hate when you make me fly. It's not natural and I don't want to do it." Gylli backed away from Mist, his face screwed up in a cantankerous fashion.

"Haven't I told you before? I don't really care." Mist's wings expanded to their full, beautiful girth, shook, and then flattened against her back once again. "You walk as slow as a troll and we have places to be."

"Dead. You're dead to me," Gylli spat.

That was about the twentieth time I'd heard the very same conversation between them, and by tomorrow they'd be fast friends again.

"Listen up," I interrupted. "We don't know what Magni wants. He wouldn't come here just for fun, and it's not impossible that he came for a fight. I want you with me and ready to break skulls, but I hope it's just undue precaution."

"Speak for yourself." Mist pulled her hair into a voluminous high ponytail. "I haven't broken anyone's spine in a long time."

"You were in a fight *yesterday*." Gylli shifted his weight to the other foot, a smirk on his lips. "You really need to see someone about that short-term memory of yours."

Mist's wings ruffled in response and she gave him a playful push. "My memory is more accurate than your aim."

"Well, if I'm useless, at least we have a mighty *ulfhédnar* on our side." Gylli slapped Váli on the back. "Someone who can really let the beast out—"

"No." Váli's body went rigid, his breathing changing. He shrugged the Jotun's hand off his shoulder. His voice had changed from a croak to a rasp. "I won't. I just got my life back and no one can make me go back in there. No one."

Hands in the air defensively, Gylli took a step back. "Alright, godling, no harm meant. An axe is as sharp as a tooth anyhow."

The low whinny of a horse drew our attention back out to the open land ahead.

At the far border of our territory was farmland, small fields of vegetables and seas of wheat that made it feel so much more peaceful than the ruins and homes of the city. With the sun shining down on it, I could remember simpler times. A day spent lying in a meadow with a book until the sun melted over the horizon.

But not today, because at the border were three idling figures on horseback: Magni and two of Asgard's soldiers.

Magni was erring on the side of caution. To strut past the borders of our territory in front of our eyes was bolder than their typical tactics. It would be a provocation, and while we were very nearly at war—and would be at a moment's notice—I didn't get the feeling they were looking for that today.

The gods of Asgard wouldn't come quietly in the night, no. They would make sure we saw them in all their proud, boisterous vanity.

"Alright, let's get this over with." I strode out in front of the others.

I knew what we looked like, walking down the worn dirt road between two wheat fields, under-armoured and horseless. Fólkheim had only managed to capture a few healthy horses, and they were kept safe, away from prying eyes. So we went by foot, Magni and his entourage towering over us as we approached. If it did end with a fight today, I'd be taking their mounts home with me.

When we were close enough, I stopped and stared up at Magni, hands on my hips. "I'd hoped Vidar would bring the news himself."

"What news, Auntie?" The smug look on Magni's face made me want to punch it off.

"That the realms will finally be at peace and that Asgard has given up its need to rule everything."

A laugh burst from him and he slapped his hand on his thigh. "Oh, you are funny. Surtr could burn the realms again and they would still belong to us by right."

I smirked. "I would *love* to see a contract that states that Asgard has claim to the nine. It would really put an end to all this, you know?"

"There isn't one because there doesn't need to be one. Everything belongs to the Allfather, and in his absence, it belongs to us." Magni watched me with a dark storminess in his eyes that made me curious. He looked so much like his father. He had Thor's thick frame, his red-blonde hair, his booming laugh. The rage in him was of a different flavour, though. Not one of pride and righteousness, but a rage made of all the things that had been taken from him. Made of everything he thought he deserved.

"So what dirty work has Master Vidar asked you to do then, little pup?"

Magni's face soured further, his composure threatening to crack at the corners. "You understand nothing." He took a deep breath, squaring his shoulders. "Vidar wants to propose an alliance of sorts. Diplomacy in the form of trade."

"As if we would want anything to do with you after everything you've done in the last two years," Váli snapped, edging up behind me.

I held out a hand towards him. Váli had always been too harsh and didn't know how to talk sweetly enough to open doors. It hadn't mattered when no one could hear him, but now… "Vidar hasn't given any impression that he tolerates us at all. You've been stealing bits of our territory constantly and your soldiers don't hesitate to kill our people when they find them. So what's changed?"

Shrugging, Magni looked towards his comrades. "I can't help what they do when we're not around. Soldiers are wild, Auntie. Like wolves." He flashed a grin at Váli.

"Consider it a first step into reintegration. We don't want to destroy you, just for you to come back into the fold. Let everything go back to the way it was. Asgard in control, as it's meant to be."

"More than half the realms were free of Odin's control. Svartalfheim, Jotunheim, Alfheim. They weren't beholden to him—"

The cackling cut me off, drawing a snarling scowl out of me. The look on Magni's face was insolent, like he was speaking to a worm. "You know that's a fucking lie. If it looked like that to anyone, it was an illusion. Who do you think the Elven matriarchs asked for more supplies when they were fighting with Vanaheim for territory? Who do you think kept Svartalfheim's market so packed with commerce? Everything belonged to Odin and it always will. Someday our army will be large enough to storm Helheim and bring him back, and we will. Baldur knows how to do it. We're going to restore everything." His eyes narrowed, a sharp grin splitting his face in half. "Grandfather will be so very proud."

Bring back Odin. Yggdrasil below.

It had been a thought. A possibility. But none of them had said it before now; none had confirmed it. Gathering the power to storm and conquer Helheim would take a hel of a lot more soldiers than the nine realms had now, but if they took Fólkheim, there'd be no one to oppose them. Just a long, slow, inevitable journey towards freeing all the gods that had corrupted these realms in the first place.

I waved a hand dismissively at him. "There's no deal to be made here. Not now and not ever. You either come to me with peace treaties or you cede Asgard to us. There is no other option. Go back to your master and let him know he can tighten your leash again."

"My leash?" Magni's face was turning scarlet. "Awfully bold of you, considering this is the patchwork city of mutts."

And then he whistled.

The tall wheat to our left burst into frantic waves of motion as half a dozen soldiers leapt from hiding and ran towards us at breakneck speed. Swords, axes, shields. Ymir's body, how had we missed them?

My allies sprang to life around me, drawing their weapons. Mist took flight, her enormous swan wings tossing dirt into the air as she flew skyward.

The rage left my throat as a scream. I drew the energy up into my body as quickly as I could, but they were on us before I could think of the right runes. Gylli leapt in front of me, twisting his axe into the gut of a woman who had charged directly for me. He pulled upwards and out, ripping her stomach open like it was a hot knife through butter. She collapsed to the ground with a wet slap.

Eight.

Epilogues for Lost Gods

The horses. Kill the riders, collect the horses later. I summoned up a handful of wildfire and lobbed it towards the face of one rider and then the next. The first hit and the soldier wailed, falling from his saddle. The second missed, but the horse spooked. With a whinny and a kick, it bucked the rider off. They hit the ground and struggled to get up. Dodging past my son, I threw my weight onto the soldier and drove my dagger into their neck. Hot blood spurted over my hand, onto my clothes.

Seven.

Magni wasn't in the fight. He'd already backed his horse to a safe distance, waiting to see if he needed to celebrate or run. I pulled myself off the body and turned towards Magni, only to be blocked by a towering woman. Before I could react, she drove her flat palm into my chest. The breath rushed from my lungs. I fell back, landing in the dirt, gasping for air.

"We're supposed to take you alive." Her voice had the cadence of a Modernist and she was built like a brick wall. Her shortsword flashed in the sunlight. "Doesn't mean I can't hurt you first."

Runes. I needed runes. But I could hardly breathe. Whatever she had done, my chest felt bruised, tight. The others were still fighting and I couldn't scream. "Help—" The wheeze pulled at my insides and I winced.

The woman slammed her boot into my chest, pinning me to the ground, her heel coming to rest on my neck. I tried to push her off but it was so hard to breathe. I needed her off. Off. Now now now—

The tip of her blade touched my jawline. She pushed it into my skin and ripped my cheek open, a gaping wound into my mouth.

"Mother!" Váli charged toward me and was blocked by a pair of axemen. One swing and a miss, and then they had him on the ground.

I tried to scream but it came as a ragged wheeze, my throat raw. Blood seeped onto my tongue and down my face, the air burning the wound. Please, gods—

A cry of rage pierced through my pain, and then a howl. The weight on my chest disappeared. I drew as deep a breath as I could, my lungs shuddering, and turned to push myself off the ground.

Váli had tackled the woman off me. Not Váli—the wolf. He was snapping at her face. It was a mess of blood and sinew and bone, and when she put her hands on him, he tore the flesh from her throat.

Six.

When I managed to stand, Mist dove down from the sky and grabbed one of the soldiers by the arms, hoisting him back up with her. Her enormous wings propelled them upwards until she was small in my sight. Then she dropped him. The scream got louder as he drew closer and when he hit the ground, pieces of his body splattered into everything in sight, covering the ground with gore.

Five.

The soldier I'd burned was stumbling around, as damaged as I was. He dove for me, axe ready, but he was too eager. I sidestepped him, his momentum pulling him forward. One kick, one short, manageable rune for lightning, and he was convulsing on the ground. Beside him, another body fell, Gylli's axe buried in his side.

Three.

They were starting to get nervous. Two soldiers and one god on horseback. Except when one of them turned to look, hoping for a call of retreat, Magni was already gone. The small speck of a horse galloped in the distance, running like a rat from a ship.

"You have two choices," I wheezed, trying to stand like my head wasn't spinning from the loss of blood and the pain of speaking. "Die for your god, or do time in my jail." Another deep breath. "This is the city of second chances."

One dropped to his knees immediately. The second hesitated, her pride clear on her face. Then she drove her sword into the dirt in frustration. "What a fucking coward!" she screamed after Magni.

Gylli laughed.

The air stirred around us as Mist landed. "You alright?" she asked, spotting the open window into my mouth.

I bobbed my head noncommittally, not wanting to speak too much. "I need a völva, please."

Váli came up beside me, stark naked except for the waistband of his trousers that had survived his shapeshift. Concern and anger were written across his face. "Let's go."

I took a look back. Mist and Gylli were tying the remaining soldiers' hands. They could handle themselves, and I was woozier than I wanted to admit, the world starting to twist and list around me. I didn't want them to notice any weakness, so I only leaned on Váli a little. This close to him, he smelled like blood and dirt and fur.

"Váli, I'm sorry. You didn't have to—"

"Shut up." He put his arm around my back, nudging me towards the city. "I didn't want to. I...don't know if I'll get stuck again, someday. But I...I won't lose you because I'm afraid. It needed doing. But no one ever gets to ask me to."

He looked down at me, that little bit of extra height he had on his poor mother.

I pressed a light kiss to his cheek, though it hurt to do it. Or to breathe or speak. And I said the only thing there was to say.

"Thank you."

92

CHAPTER FIFTEEN

LOKI

"I never took a lover and to this day I don't regret it. I just wished that everyone else had believed me when I said it never mattered."

— *Gauti, Volume 35*

The first half of the first day was uneventful. The expansion of the city had pushed a lot of the creatures and dark things farther away, past the rows and rows of strange Helheim vegetation and blazing seidr lanterns. Sometimes something would scurry underfoot, flitting in and out of sight: pale lizards that were nearly translucent; bats fluttering and swooping above us; long, thick centipedes that were all limbs and antennae.

I wasn't afraid of much, but I'd die again before I woke up with one of those on my face.

I felt a change of self a few hours into the walk, and slipped into a more feminine physical form. It made the tunic a little tighter around the bosom, but these were not the places to wear pretty, loose things that I'd have liked. For now, I'd have to make do with letting my hair down and dreaming of the feathers and furs that waited for me above.

There wasn't much conversation either, which made for a dull, tiresome walk. As eager as I was to pass the time *somehow*, what were we going to talk about? How blissfully happy our lives had become? How we were probably marching off to our deaths? Unlikely.

The river was our first obstacle. We'd all been out this far for one reason or another, but neither Angrboda nor I had crossed it. The current was too strong to attempt to wade across, especially when we didn't know how deep it went. At one end

93

of the river was an enormous lake that the water stemmed from, but downstream was a tight cavern that would likely swallow up anyone who fell in. And besides—

"Aren't there sjörå in that lake?" Angrboda crossed her arms over her chest, leaning towards the river bank but not daring to step too close.

"There are." Narvi pulled his bag off his back and began fishing inside it. "It's nothing to worry about."

"I love your optimism, Son, but sjörå have a reputation for a reason." I scanned the waters, looking for any sign of shadows moving below the surface, but it was too tumultuous to see anything.

"The *neck* have a reputation." Narvi looked up, his arm still in his bag, and his gaze went from me to Angrboda. He sighed. "Neck are river spirits who lure in victims with beautiful music, usually so they can drown them. The *sjörå* are women who *might* drown you if you're cruel to them." He paused. "Or if they're hungry."

"Well, then!" Angrboda threw up her hands impatiently. "Nothing to worry about. We just need to make sure we come after supper."

Narvi pulled out a small bundle of cloth that jingled and a second, larger bag. "You're a very angry person, you know that?"

I snickered.

"What?" Angrboda turned on me, eyes narrow.

Pushing the grin down, I shook my head. "Nothing, nothing."

"And I suppose you know all about this, Sir Smarty Pants?" Angrboda watched Narvi as he put his bag safely aside and sank to his knees at the river's edge.

"Have a little faith, Bo." I struggled to keep my voice steadier than I felt. Narvi was deeply intelligent, but he'd always been naive. Kind. I'd always worried it would get him killed, and it was always within the realm of possibility that this was the moment.

Again.

Narvi picked up a pebble and used it to tap a rhythm on a larger rock on the river's edge. His face was over the water, too close and vulnerable for my liking. And immediately after the tapping stopped, a shadow moved.

Everything in me wanted to dart forward and grab Narvi. Pull him away before this creature could pull him under. It was too easy to imagine him struggling against the current, gasping for air. Kicking, screaming, drowning—

The surface of the water broke and a woman's head emerged, a wide, knife-tooth smile on her face. "You're back!"

The coil in my throat unwound and I drew a long, steadying breath.

Her hair was a tar-slick black, woven through with lake weeds, a brass flower pinned behind her ear. There was no white in her eyes, just the mud-yellow and black of a toad, large and wet. As Narvi sat back, the sjörå emerged further from the water, her elbows and bare breasts resting on her riverbank. Her skin was grey and slightly translucent, slick with all manner of things that grow at the bottom of lakes.

She was stunning. Not in a typical way, certainly, but I longed to touch her. To run my fingers along her skin, to whisper sweet things in her ear as we languished in the water. Everything in me twisted with wanting. I really did know better. I knew the tricks of creatures, the way they could play havoc with hearts and loins, but...maybe she was just beautiful.

Gods, she was like nothing I'd ever seen.

When I looked at Angrboda, her face told the whole story. She was practically drooling on her boots, her features soft in a way I'd only seen on her when she'd adopted a new puppy.

Fuck. Maybe the sjörå wasn't simply beautiful, then.

"I missed you!" The sjörå leaned forward and pressed her nose against Narvi's. "Did you bring me a present?"

"I did." Narvi held up the two bags, one in each hand. "You can have both, but you need to choose one first."

The sjörå looked up at me, as if just noticing I was there. She recoiled and hissed, her long legs splashing out of the water for a moment. "Who are you?"

Narvi waited a moment, but my tongue had frozen to the top of my mouth, so he spoke for me. "Ceri of the river Doom, this is my father, Loki, and my..." He turned to glance at Angrboda. The thoughts were churning behind his eyes. "My stepmother, I suppose." Narvi turned back to Ceri. "They're safe. These gifts are from them as well."

Ceri considered us for a moment, sniffing the air as she glared. Her eyes went back to Narvi. "Are they good gifts?"

"Pick one and see."

The sjörå hesitated for a moment. She poked at one bag and listened to it jingle, then smelled them both. "This one first."

Narvi put the large, quiet bag in her open hands and we all watched as she untied it with claw-like fingers. Inside was an entire fresh rabbit, a rarity he must've stolen from the breeding cages in the palace. Its neck flopped at a lazy angle, entirely intact but very dead. Even from a few paces away, it was starting to smell.

Ceri gasped, her eyes wide and enthralled. "I love it. I've never seen a creature like this. Is it to eat?"

Narvi nodded.

She ripped the hind leg off without a second of hesitation and stuffed the foot in her mouth.

How beautiful she was, chewing the—

No. No, no. Use your brain, you fucking halfwit.

I focused on the crunching of bone between her teeth until the violence of it turned my stomach.

"It's *sooooo* good." Ceri's food muffled her voice. "You always bring me the best things."

Angrboda sidestepped towards me and leaned in to whisper, "This…this isn't your son's *girlfriend*, is it?"

"No." I shook my head. "I don't…I don't think it is. Why, are you interested in a tumble with her?"

Angrboda looked at me sideways. "What if I might be?"

"Then we might both be under her influence, I think. Or do you always find yourself attracted to monsters?"

She furrowed her eyebrows. "I fucked you for years, didn't I?"

Checkmate.

Ceri offered Narvi a bite of the rabbit leg, but he declined.

"Can I have the other present?" She pawed at it with a bloody hand, making its contents shake.

Narvi set the bag on the riverbank and opened it up for her. Inside were coins of all types. Some with the mark of Odin, some of old Vanaheim, some I'd never seen. Copper, bronze, silver, black. And at the centre was a gold ring.

The rabbit was immediately discarded, though I didn't get the impression that a little dirt would deter the sjörå from finishing her meal. Ceri fished through the coins, holding them up one after the other. When she got to the ring, she examined it carefully, then slipped it onto her finger.

"The others are going to think I'm a goddess because of you." She pressed her hand against her face to show the ring off, then fiddled with the bronze flower in her hair. "It's so beautiful! You're the very best man and the very best friend." She touched her nose to his again before sliding her fingers through the coins one more. "You could be my prince, you know. Join me in the lake forever. I could be yours." She paused, looking forlorn. "Why do you never want me?"

Her prince. I could be her prince. Or princess. I could do that and everything in between. I was flexible and I *knew* things, if only—

Angrboda nudged me in the side. Gods help me, this was not a good look for any of us, pretending not to be attracted to a water spirit who so clearly was going to eat us the second we climbed in that lake.

"Oh, Ceri, it's a wonderful offer." Narvi smiled as he brushed a hair from her cheek. "You're amazing, but I've never wanted anyone. I'm just not built that way. I'd make a very bad prince for you. I'd much rather be your friend who loves you and brings you presents. Is that alright?"

Ceri tilted her head, considering him. Then she went back to her coins. "Alright. Friend love is good love too. I have lots of lovers on the lake bottom, but no friends."

A shiver ran down my spine, the remnants of her influence being overshadowed by common sense and self-preservation. Time to *go*.

Angrboda knelt next to Narvi and took Ceri's hand. She placed a kiss on the sjörå's knuckles and her lips came away slimy. "If Narvi won't have you, perhaps you'll consider someone else?"

Narvi cleared his throat with a pointed aggressiveness. "Angrboda is needed elsewhere, Ceri. She doesn't have time to stay right now. Maybe later."

Angrboda glared at Narvi, clearly upset that he was getting in the way of her conquest. "I hate to—"

"Narvi is right. Angrboda will have to join you in the river another day." I sank to a squat and hovered over the shoulders of Narvi and Angrboda. It drew scorn from Ceri, but she allowed it. "Ceri, we're going on a very important journey, but the three of us need to cross your river to get there. Will you help us cross safely?"

Ceri peeled off a piece of rabbit fur and swallowed it whole. "Yeah, alright."

She kept eating, but after a moment, the river calmed noticeably. The size of the crests became smaller and the roar of the water stilled. Soon the surface was as still as glass.

"Better?" she asked.

"Well, fuck a duck." Angrboda placed her hands on her hips, looking out over the water with something like awe on her face.

"That's incredible, Ceri. Thank you." Narvi put a hand on her shoulder.

"You should be careful of wolves." She swallowed hard. "There've been more drinking at the river lately. We eat some of them, but there are still more. Too many, maybe."

"Thank you for everything." Narvi pressed his nose against hers and rose to his feet. "I'll be gone for a while, but I'll come back when I can. River hold you, Ceri."

"River hold you, friend." She smiled back, her teeth red and full of scraps of fur. She ripped another strip of rabbit off, paying little mind to us as we climbed down into the calm, chest-high water.

Something in my chest hurt as we left her sight, but I was fairly certain I wouldn't regret it. When you've lived as long as many of us have, you've walked away from a long list of seductive monsters.

The water was cold and the bottom was hard to walk on, all jagged edges and smooth, slippery rocks. In the light of day, we might have been able to see what we were walking on, but in the dark of Helheim, the water didn't betray much of what was down there. I took my time, feeling out the path from rock to rock. Steady, steady, until I put my foot down again, and something cracked and collapsed under my weight.

I froze.

Someone's skull had fractured under my boot. Something long and black and slithering pushed its way out, its home destroyed.

Nope. No, I was done.

I picked up the pace, pushing past Angrboda and hauling myself out of the water, using the bank as leverage. My clothes were dripping and my threshold for nonsense had significantly lowered, but at least if I was going to die, it wouldn't be in the maw of a frog person.

I waited under a large black tree for the others to climb out. As we shook off the water and tried to squeeze the worst of it from our clothes, a rustle drew my attention. Above us, nearly invisible in the edge of the lantern light, was a raven. It was carefully perched, its head twitching periodically, its eyes on me.

An uneasy feeling settled in my stomach. Once upon a time, a raven had meant Odin was keeping an eye on me. Not always, but often enough. But Odin was locked away and his ravens were long dead. So who was this?

I turned to Narvi. "Are there wild ravens in Helheim?"

"Only the ones in the city, for messages. Why?"

I pointed up to the tree, but when I looked back, it was gone. "Hmm. Maybe I'm going blind in my second eye." It was hardly the first time I'd seen a shadow that was nothing. Since my right eye had gone cloudy, I'd started to see all manner of things that weren't there.

"Not before this fucking quest of yours is over, dimwit." Angrboda adjusted her pack and trotted away from the riverbank.

We walked for a few more uneventful hours, drying off in the not uncomfortable climate of Helheim. But we were beginning to droop, unable to keep up the tempo we'd previously had. It was time to find shelter for the night.

We weren't very inclined to stay out in the open, so when a treeline appeared underneath a sparkling of blue luminescence, we turned toward it without hesitation.

"Not too far in," Narvi said, scouting between the trees with his lantern. "We don't want to lose sight of the edge of the forest. The map doesn't say where it leads."

"Fair enough." Angrboda tossed her pack down. She brought out a small bundle of kindling and unhooked the hatchet from her belt. "Time for a fire. My skivvies are still wet and it's beginning to chafe."

I pursed my lips and gave her a look. "You are the pinnacle of refinement, Angrboda."

Epilogues for Lost Gods

"And your father was a dappled sow. Shut the fuck up, Loki."

But I'd stopped listening before she'd finished speaking. I watched the distance for a moment. Something was creeping under my skin. There was no reason for it, not really. But something wasn't quite what it seemed.

The thick plunk of Angrboda's hatchet startled me out of my thoughts. She passed me a thin branch and told me to get to work, so I did. In a few minutes, we had a minuscule fire to sit around, and Narvi was passing out cups of hot water.

By the time the cups had cooled to lukewarm, the song started.

Low and crooning and sweet. It came from the depths of the trees, somewhere so far away that it was almost hard to hear. It sounded like something familiar. Like a song my mother used to sing when I was a child. An old Jotun lullaby that I hadn't heard for ages.

"You fucking hear that, right?" Angrboda was up on her feet, staring into the trees. "Someone's playing a jig back there. Right?"

"No..." Narvi looked up at her from his seat at the fire, and then to me. "I hear music, but it's that song you sang to me at bedtime when I was a boy, about the dancing sheep."

None of us were hearing the same tune.

"Alright, time to leave, right now. Let's go." I grabbed up our things and packed them away as quickly as I could. We hadn't taken much out of our bags, and we were back on our feet and out of the forest in moments, leaving the fire crackling.

If we were lucky, the whole fucking thing would burn.

CHAPTER SIXTEEN

SIGYN

"He didn't need to tell me. I wish I didn't know."

— *Laurissa, Volume 76*

By the time we got to the infirmary, the heat of battle had worn off and the only thing left was the stomach-churning, agonizing pain in the side of my face. Váli helped me over to one of the empty cots and made me sit. Blood was streaming down my face. I grabbed one of the clean pieces of cloth that sat on the bedside table and pressed it to my cheek. I hissed, and the edges of my vision went black.

"Mother—" Váli batted my hand away and held it himself. His face was a mix of concern and anger. "Stay awake."

I had every intention of doing exactly that, but lacking the concentration to heal myself with seidr, I'd lost enough blood to make me groggy and disoriented. I wanted to sleep, but the pain was keeping me awake.

Váli whipped his head around, scanning the room. "A little help here?" he called out.

A heavyset man with a thick beard craned his head to look our way, and after a moment, his eyes popped open with recognition. He tossed away the towels he'd been folding and darted in our direction.

"Don't scare the völva, Váli," I chided him. Speaking sent another burst of pain spiderwebbing up my face and I tightened my grip on the bedsheets. The recent battle and this *blistering fucking ache* were stealing all of my patience.

"Didn't mean to keep you waiting," the völva said, nudging Váli out of the way. "Sorry, Goddess."

Epilogues for Lost Gods

I gestured for him not to worry about it and hoped he would get the point without my having to open my mouth.

"Got into a fight, did we?" The man gently peeled back the cloth that was now sticking to my skin. The cloth had already turned very red. "Oh yes, let's get this cleaned and healed, why don't we? Sorry, I'm Gregory, Goddess. We already met before but I'm sure you know a lot of people. No, no need to speak. Lie down for me, please."

I did as I was told and lay back on the pillow, my injured cheek turned toward him. Váli started pacing at the end of the cot, as if there were any actual danger to my life, which there wasn't.

Gregory's large hands were surprisingly nimble as he used tweezers and a damp cloth to clean the wound. It didn't burn any less when things came out, but at least his touch was light. I didn't want to know how much dust and dirt had found its way in during the fight.

"It'll be fine, though, right?" Váli stopped pacing long enough to glower at Gregory.

I snapped my fingers and pointed at him in a way that I hoped implied that I'd like him to quiet down. A fresh rush of pain rose in my cheek and my vision burned white for a moment, all the light in the room intensifying. It was all I could do not to scream as he pulled a pebble from my flesh.

"She'll be right as rain very soon," Gregory replied without stopping his work.

Váli took two more steps and stopped, looking back. "Do you want me to get someone? Alyssa maybe?"

Gregory moved to get something off the bedside table and I shook my head vehemently. Váli was concerned, yes, but I couldn't handle all these *questions* right now.

"I think she'd want to know." Váli was barely paying attention to me, and there was a strange tone in his voice, like he wasn't entirely present. "I can get her."

"*No,*" I growled between clenched teeth, trying not to move as Gregory put his fingertips around my wound and began a whispered chant of runes. Bless him, he was more patient with Váli's worrying than I had the capacity for.

I wanted to say more, but the crawling sensation of healing skin took over, churning my stomach. It was a good thing, but feeling your skin grow back and your muscle tissue weave itself together was not always something that helped keep your lunch down. As I focused on the strangeness and the pain in my body, Váli kept talking, his nervous chatter grinding against me even as the actual words slipped past my consciousness without my hearing a single one.

"All finished," Gregory said at last. "There's a little scar, but it only adds to your fierceness, if you don't mind my saying."

I stretched my jaw and made a conscious effort to be kind to Gregory, despite my completely depleted soul. "Thank you for this. It feels much, much better."

"You're gonna need to rest tonight, Goddess. You lost a lot of blood and there's only so much I can do about that. Eat well, drink a lot of water, and *sleep*," Gregory insisted.

"I'll do my best. Would you mind giving me a moment with my son?"

"Of course." Gregory stood. "Anything you need, I'm right over there." And with that, he went back to his folding.

"Váli," I hissed. "I'm going to need you to get a hold of yourself."

My son returned to his spot next to the cot and squatted down. "You're better?"

"Yes, I'm better. I know seidr isn't your strong suit, but you know how this works. I can't have you in a panic over nothing. I'm simply too tired."

Váli's expression fell. "It's not nothing. You're hurt. Were hurt. I just…"

I pinched the bridge of my nose. My stomach was burning with hunger, my muscles were aching, and I just wanted to rest. "I know, Váli. I swear I do. But no one needs to panic. We don't need to go around telling anyone. I just need to rest."

Váli looked at me curiously. "Not even Alyssa? If it were Hreidulfr, I'd want to know. I'd be furious if he didn't tell me he was hurt."

"Because you're a couple," I sighed.

Váli gave a frustrated gesture. "And so are you and Alyssa."

"Excuse me?" I sat up and stared at him in disbelief. "That is *not* true. Where are you getting something like that?"

His face paled. "I—The way you two are with each other, I just thought—"

"What? That we were running around together in secret?" It was a struggle to keep my voice low and not cause a scene. All of the worries I'd been harbouring had somehow surfaced in my son, and if he believed it, I could never hope to quash it in myself. I had to stop this. "Do you think that I'd see someone romantically and not tell you? That I'd run around behind your father's back? What exactly do you think of me?"

"I *thought* that you were happy for the first time since I was a child!" The chided sadness was fading from Váli's expression and he was meeting my rising anger. "Honestly, fuck Loki. He's dead, and he wasn't a great husband when he was alive. You're allowed to move on!"

"Well, I haven't!" A tear ran down my face. The frustration was boiling over. I felt like I'd been hit by a boulder and my son wouldn't leave me be. "Alyssa and I are not together and frankly it's insulting you'd think I would behave that way!"

My father's words resurfaced from the place I kept them buried, festering and debilitating.

Goddess of Fidelity.

Why did it always come back to that? To him?

Epilogues for Lost Gods

"Alright, Mother." Váli stood up, his fists white-knuckled. "If that's the way you want to live your life, do it. Together or not, Alyssa deserved to know, because she obviously cares about you." He turned and walked away, but before he left the infirmary, he sent his parting words along the link between our minds. "*You're so focused on the past that you're going to drive away everyone who loves you* now."

And then he was gone.

I threw myself back onto the cot and let out a frustrated sigh. I wasn't taking anyone for granted! I wasn't *doing* anything! What an accusation. What made him decide things like that? He was making things up. No one else felt like that, surely, and certainly not about Alyssa and me.

I pressed my palms into my eyes until the black turned into a strange pattern of swimming lights behind my eyelids.

I'd never said anything to anyone that would lead them to think that, had I?

Memories cascaded through my mind, one after the other. Late nights spent planning and strategizing. Days spent poring over books. Long walks, good conversation, deep glasses of wine. I respected her. We were good friends. Wasn't that what those moments would tell the onlookers?

Except I couldn't fool *myself*, could I?

I knew the guilt that so often came with thinking about her. The little tinge of sadness and regret I had to bury beneath denial. She was so *easy* to think about. To get lost in.

When I lay awake at night, thinking of Loki was a complicated, messy thing. Loki came to me in dreams all the time, but so many of them were drenched in fear and pain. I loved him, to be sure. But sometimes it was easier not to think of him. To put him out of mind. Because I could only get so far into a daydream about being in his arms before someone pushed a knife into his chest.

It wasn't fair.

I wanted a love that was easy, and instead, what fate had given me was a tangled, disastrous thing that cut me each time I got too close.

I'd fallen asleep on the cot. For how long, I didn't know. Hours, certainly. No one but Váli had known where I was, and Gregory had let me sleep. Blessedly, I had dreamt nothing but blackness, and that suited me just fine.

I was groggy when I sat up. A bowl of cooled soup and a large cup of water sat on the bedside table. My stomach growled at the sight of it, and I made quick work of it until my stomach was like a balloon inside me. It felt good to be satiated, at least for the moment.

After a while, I felt more awake, more conscious. And of course, with that came regret. I would need to find Váli and apologize. He had just been worried and he didn't deserve any of the venom I had given him.

But I knew myself and my son well enough to know it was too soon. He would still be fuming, and I needed some strength back before I could have that conversation without growing frustrated and having it slide back into a disagreement.

The ache was still in my body, and after begging for a pain reduction tea from Gregory, I went back to the cliffs for a bath.

So much of the infrastructure of old Vanaheim had been destroyed during Ragnarok, and we hadn't had the time or resources to restore the water systems in the city. We had, however, restored the public baths.

Tucked into the back of the cliffs, the two large stone pools were kept warm by the constant flow of water from the underground hot springs tucked somewhere beneath the city. Once, the pools had been separated by gender, but since things like that were becoming less and less useful to us, people tended to peek their heads inside and decide which selection of people they could stand bathing beside the most.

Being that it was midday and most people were still deeply entrenched in their work, neither bath was very busy. I stepped inside and the heat enveloped me in an instant, already pulling a little of the tension from my body. The air smelled of sweat and sulphur and soap. I went to the hooks along the wall, untied my dressing gown, and hung it up.

As I walked naked along the far edge of the old, worn tiles, nodding in greeting at three older women as I passed, I marvelled at how different this moment would have been from the same one in my youth. I'd visited Vanaheim in my youth, and every public bath had been deeply uncomfortable. I used to cower under my robe until the last moment, then practically dive under the water the second I took it off.

Things change.

Now I hated the public baths because sometimes the sulphur smell took me back to my own horrors. Dropped me back inside that cave until I was shivering in the corner, trapped inside a thought.

Not often. Not anymore. But there were still days…

I sat on one of the short stools off to the side of the pool and washed the worst of the dirt from me. The buckets of rising water reflected my face back to me, tired and worn. As I lathered the soap into my arms, dirt from the battle trickled down to the floor with the used water, toward the holes in the floor that drained out of the room, off to who-knew-where.

The room was hot but the rinse water was cool, and I shivered as I tossed it on my body, washing the last of the dirt away. It was the worst part, and I did it quickly and made my way to the pool, shivering.

I stepped down into the pool and sighed as the water caressed the tops of my feet. A soft, satisfying burn ran up my calves, my thighs, my stomach, as I walked deeper and deeper into the pool. Slowly, I walked to the far side of the water and sank down, sitting on the tile bench that ran along the perimeter. I let my head loll back and let out a deep breath, trying to release the day from my bones.

It wouldn't work, but I could try.

It wouldn't work because I knew all the feelings would come back for me once I left, and because I had become—maybe I had always been—the kind of person who sits where she can see all the doors. Never truly relaxed, never truly at home anywhere.

My thoughts wandered as the heat took hold of my body. They slipped over and through and past me one by one. What to eat for dinner. What I would say to Váli. How I'd been planning to mend one of my dresses for months but had never gotten around to it. That I missed reading, and that someday, when I was done saving everyone, I would start collecting books again. If there were any left to collect.

I vaguely noticed that the ladies in the pool had started climbing out. I heard the rustle of clothing and the slapping of wet feet on tile. Their voices faded away and I was left alone.

I might have fallen asleep again. Apparently, it was the kind of day for napping. It was a light sleep, if it was one, coming back and forth between dream and reality, surreal and ethereal.

When I woke, I woke up choking.

Hands were holding me underwater. I scratched for purchase on the tiles, but I was being pushed away from the edge of the pool. Everything was slippery. There was nothing to grip, nothing but the body pushing me to the bottom of the pool. I couldn't see past the ripple of the water, couldn't see who it was. Their legs moved over me. Straddled my hips. I kicked and flailed, but they were stronger.

As they reached for my hands, I swiped one out of the water and clawed at their face. They screamed, the sound muffled by the water, and a tiny spattering of red dropped into the pool. Their balance changed and I kicked myself out from underneath them.

The first breath of air burned like wildfire. I coughed up sulfurous water as I pulled myself towards the edge of the pool. There was a splash behind me and when I turned to look, a furious man was snarling at me.

I'd managed to strike him across the cheek, and deep rivulets of blood were running down to his chin, disappearing into the pool. He was a Jotun; that was obvious by his nearly translucent skin and the blue tattoos running up his neck.

"Get back here, you bitch," he growled, lunging toward me.

I hacked up another mouthful of water and forced myself up over the edge of the tile. It was slippery and I couldn't gain purchase as I stood. I slipped and crashed to one knee, my bones vibrating under my skin.

He grabbed my ankle and pulled, taking out any last semblance of my balance. I landed on my hip and kicked him square in the jaw. His neck swivelled and he grunted.

Free again, I ignored the ache in my body, shimmying as quickly as I could across the wet tile. Runes. I needed something more deadly than this body I owned. I started to whisper, but it only brought forth another coughing fit. This time, I threw all my force into it and hacked up the last of the water.

He was coming toward me, crawling out of the pool in a drenched tunic and trousers, his long brown hair matted to his head. He was going to kill me if I didn't act.

Runes whipped across my tongue. I was so ill-equipped for this moment, too wet for wildfire or lightning. So much of what I knew would be useless, but—

The attacker slowed and wobbled. His eyes rolled back into his head, and he toppled to the side, back into the pool, not unlike the belly flop of an enormous sea lion.

He sank to the bottom, asleep.

And dead soon, if I wasn't quick.

I scrambled to the door, whipped it open, and screamed for help. Everyone in the hall ground to a stop and looked at me, stark naked and dripping wet, but it was hardly the largest worry I was carrying at that moment. I dashed back inside, jumped back into the pool, and tried to haul the man's head out of the water.

Dead men tell no tales, and I needed to know who wanted me dead.

"Ymir's breath!" A lanky young person stuck their head inside the door and immediately dropped all their possessions to come to my aid. A middle-aged woman joined us, and between the three of us, we managed to drag my assailant's heavy body out of the pool.

The youth straddled the man's torso and started pressing their open palms into his chest in a steady rhythm, trying to push the water from his lungs. I'd seen it before from some of the Modernists, but it was on a long list of skills I hadn't picked up since being trapped in a cave for eternity.

The woman brought over my robe and tucked it around my shoulders. "Are you alright, Goddess?"

"I've had much better days in my life, but I'm alive." I pulled the robe on, the water soaking through it, but at least I was covered. "Do you recognise him?"

She looked at the man, squinting with determination, but she shook her head. "Never seen him before. His face is kind of messed up, though."

"He tried to kill me just now."

The youth stopped their chest compressions and stared at me. "Tried to kill you? Well, why the fuck am I giving him CPR?"

"Keep going, please." I waved for them to continue. "I'm eager to hear what was worth killing me for."

After being deemed far too connected to my own attempted assassination to be allowed to interrogate the man, I joined the rest of the council around the meeting table to wait. Food, drink, and fresh clothes were brought for me, and I told them all what had happened. As I spoke, the room filled with a roiling set of emotions: Oda tried to hide that she was crying; Váli clasped his head in his hands; Niklas had a cool air of revenge about him.

It was strangely comforting to be among such intensity. I couldn't afford to have this throw me off my guard, but I was grateful to feel safe and cared for among my peers.

"I shouldn't have left you alone." Váli didn't look up, just leaned his elbows on the table and massaged his temples.

"I've lived through worse." I still owed him an apology, but this wasn't the right audience for it. "Besides, it may give us some insight into the coming war. If he's from Asgard and has a loose tongue, we may gain an advantage from his sloppy assassination attempt."

Niklas adjusted himself in his chair. "We need to put an emphasis on security. Not for you, not specifically. If we can spare a few more guards for the cliffs, we could ensure the safety of the council, the guild heads, and whoever else might be a target."

"That can be arranged," Hreidulfr said. "I'll pull a few of the stronger trainees from their exercises and put them at the entrance with a war horn. Should help."

"Is there anything I can do?" Alyssa stopped scratching nervous ink swirls into her ledger long enough to ask the question. "Barricades, machinery, whatever. I can divert—"

I held up a hand. "No, I don't think that's wise. It could be exactly what Asgard wants from us. Split our efforts between preparation and defending our leaders, and weaken us from inside. If—"

A knock came at the door.

Several voices beckoned them in at once, all of us eager for news.

The door opened and an intimidating Elven woman stepped inside. Ethana had been a professional in *wet work* before the fall of the realms. While her services weren't often used, she was happy to lend a hand in extenuating circumstances. She was still wiping her hands with an old rag, transferring lines of blood from her dark skin onto the fabric.

"He's not from Asgard." Ethana's voice was gruff, and when she spoke, the long claw mark scars on her face stretched and moved. "Not officially, at least. He had enough willpower to stand up to the questions, but after a few encouragement cuts, he told me so many things that I didn't want to know about him."

I squinted at her. "Such as?"

"He doesn't much care for the way you're doing things around here." She picked some dirt from under a long nail. "Equality and male völur and open acceptance. I guess he assumed if he cut off the head of the snake, the city would suddenly change its ways." Her voice grew cold and sarcastic. "I mean, I know my wife would've switched sides *so quickly* if it weren't for your *personal* encouragement to be queer."

The comment drew a wry laugh from myself and a few others, and I appreciated the moment of levity.

I sighed. "That's a shame. I was really hoping for some insider information about the enemy."

"He gave up the names of some of his like-minded friends. I'd love to show them the error of their ways, but I already know what you'll say."

"Reform or exile," Niklas scoffed.

"I know you don't agree with that, Niklas, but that was the majority vote," I said. "He and his friends get their reeducation inside the detention barracks, and if they can't come around to a peaceful coexistence, they can leave."

"And they'll go right to Asgard." Váli sat back in his chair, arms crossed over his chest.

I shrugged, growing increasingly tired now that the threat was tapering off. "That's the risk we take. We wanted to do things differently here, and part of that is being prepared for others to push back."

"Anything else we should know, Ethana?" Niklas asked.

She shook her head. "We'll get him fixed up and ready for transport. If that's everything...?"

"It is." I yawned. "I'll be going back to my bed for a few hours, if we're ready to conclude."

"Go rest," Oda said. "A few of us have more to prepare, but we'll see you when you're better."

I nodded and got up, the attention of the table dissipating to clusters of conversation. I turned to Váli. "I'm sorry about today."

He shook his head. "We were both in a bad place. There's nothing to be sorry about."

"There is. I wasn't prepared for a conversation like that, and I felt cornered. You paid the price for it. I should've acted more like a mother."

Váli gave me a weary smirk. "So you acted like a person for once. I'm not going to hold that against you." He pulled me in for a hug, his chin resting on my shoulder. "I was out of line and so were you, and that makes us even." He let me go and gestured toward the door. "Now go get some sleep. The city will still run without you."

I gave him a kiss on the cheek, which was followed by an involuntary yawn. "I'm not even tempted to argue with you. Good night, Son. I love you."

"Love you too." He flashed me a smile and urged me to leave once more.

As I turned away from him, I could feel the last of my willpower seeping out of my pores.

I opened the door to leave and my entire body stopped pretending. It slumped down, dragging itself forward. I could prop myself up in front of everyone else because that was part of the work, but I wasn't as good at fooling myself. Two near-deaths in one day was too much. I was falling apart.

I glanced back at the table. Half of the council had started packing up their things, while the others were bent over one corner of the table, comparing notes and looking for solutions.

No matter how tired I was, it was hard to delegate and walk away. To let go of control. But that had been the point of a council of dissenting voices, so I had learned how over the years.

Mostly.

As I tried to close the door behind me, a hand pushed it back open.

Alyssa gave me a bemused smirk. "As if I was going to leave you to your own devices after today. Please. I've seen how you take care of yourself. You just leave it to me."

The heat of the fire-warmed stones calmed me the moment Alyssa tucked them into the foot of my bed. I let out a luxurious sigh. It felt strange to be sliding into comfort, to let down my guard after a day of danger and violence, but I made an effort. The muscles of my shoulders refused to relax, but at the spots where the warmth touched my skin, those places were considering it.

Alyssa crawled under the covers next to me, curled up on her side. She reached out and turned my head with her finger, taking another look at the scar. "You've had a hard day."

I nodded, and for a moment, I could feel my attacker holding me underwater again. My breath caught in my throat, like my body was trying to keep me from drowning again.

Alyssa squeezed my hand. "You're safe here. Do you want to tell me about it?"

I wiped a tear from my cheek. "No, not today. I don't want to keep living in it. I need something else before I sleep."

She propped herself up on one elbow. "What do you need?"

My lip quivered. "It just feels like so much right now."

Alyssa pressed herself into me, holding me close as I broke into a sobbing, messy cry. I was too tired to hold it in anymore, and Alyssa always made me feel so safe. Like I could tell her anything. I didn't *want* to need it. I didn't *want* to ever feel weak and incapable and like I couldn't do this on my own.

But that was foolish thinking.

If I had to be weak with someone, it would be her.

When was the last time I'd felt safe with someone else? Someone who it wasn't my job to protect? My son, his spouse, the people I worked alongside; they were all my responsibility. Who was the last…

Loki.

For a moment, I imagined that the arm around me was hers. The long hair at the edge of my face was hers, flaming red and meticulously braided. The beat of her heart, the feel of her skin. She had made me feel safe for so many years. Heard and valued and respected. And for a moment, I imagined that I had that back.

Loki wasn't there when I opened my eyes.

But Alyssa with her electric blue-tipped hair and her worried brow, she felt so much the same. Not alike, but adjacent. Akin to.

I missed so many things.

So many.

My tears slowed. I let them fall down my skin and said nothing. I felt too much to know what to say.

"What you're trying to do, it's overwhelming." Alyssa's voice was soft, her head next to mine. "You don't have to say anything. I know it's not the same, but I know a thing or two about being overwhelmed."

I relaxed against her and listened to her heartbeat as she spoke, hoping that it would soothe the turmoil living in my skin.

"When I was living as a mortal, and the doctors told me I was dying, everything came crashing down around me. I was supposed to have time—" Alyssa drew in a sharp breath and didn't speak for a moment. "All of a sudden my plans for the future were gone. I didn't have a woman that I loved. I didn't have children, or a home of my own, or a dog. I'd never been to see the pyramids. And now I was never going to."

The sadness on Alyssa's face was a deep wound that had been torn open. She'd told me about this before, vaguely, but it wasn't something she spoke about freely or easily.

There was nothing fitting to say, and *I'm sorry* was never going to be enough, so I just let her speak.

She bit her lip, drew a breath, and continued. "It was a lot. I had a big family and each of them wanted chunks of me to keep before I died, something to carry with them. So between all the tests and chemotherapy, and the vomiting and the sleeping, I went to theme parks and zoos and birthday parties. I built the electric toy train I had promised to my nephew. I made so much time for everyone else, right up until I had to stay in the hospital for the last time. It was so much." She wiped her cheek with the back of her hand. "They tore chunks off me to keep, and I understood why, but each one took something from me. Sometimes I forgot I was supposed to be the one enjoying *my* last days."

Alyssa sighed and composed herself. "I don't mean to burden you with that. All I hope is that you know I understand what it's like doing things for others and putting yourself last. I know there's no one here looking out for you with their whole selves, especially not you yourself. So while you're busy saving the realms, neglecting what you need, I'm going to be here saving you. Alright?"

Especially not yourself.

Some truths are so sharp.

I wished it wasn't true, but it was. It felt a little like I'd betrayed myself. Like this body and this mind were something that were simply along for the ride, and if I didn't feed and water and nurture them, too bad for them. I'd put my family first, this city first, and fuck everything else.

If I tried to recall where the majority of my basic needs had come from in the last while, it was her. When I had been too enthralled in work, staying up all night and dragging myself through the day, she had orchestrated food and drink and delegation. Sometimes I had noticed, but sometimes things had just...appeared. And nearly every time, it was her.

"I should do better," I breathed. "You shouldn't be carrying me around on your back like that."

"Don't apologize." Alyssa scrunched up her face in offence. "I don't want to hear that. You're doing everything you can to keep Asgard from wiping us off the face of the realm. If I have to force a few suppers down your throat to help you get it done, well, at least I was on the right side of history."

The guilt in my chest made way for appreciation, and in that moment, as bone-tired as I was, I nearly kissed her.

In my mind, I saw myself do it. Saw what it would be like, felt the thrill of it on my lips.

But I didn't.

I was still not tired and weak enough to betray him.

Instead, I looked away and found something else to grasp onto. "I guess I don't know how to do things another way."

She nodded. "That makes sense."

"I feel like I have so much to make up for." I wiped the wetness from my cheeks. "The things my son and his partner went through. What happened to Loki. The things my father and my family did to the realms. Our part in Ragnarok." My chest hurt. "There's too much to atone for."

"You're only one person, Sigyn. The weight of the realms doesn't fall on your shoulders."

I looked her in the eyes. "But what if it does?"

Alyssa sighed. "No one will be able to change your mind except for you, but I promise you that no one person is responsible for the fate of the realms. There are no armies without the individual choices of thousands of people to pick up a sword and get in line."

The sentiment rang true, but it did nothing to deflate my guilt.

Alyssa put her hand on my cheek and made me look at her. "You are not your father. You are not your family. You have done the best you can for a lot of people. Whether Fólkheim falls or not, that will still be true."

My lip started to quiver again. I leaned into Alyssa and cried softly until the irresistible lull of sleep pulled me under.

CHAPTER SEVENTEEN

LOKI

"I looked for her. No one knows where she went. It's like the realm ate her up and never bothered to spit out the bones."

— *Loki, Volume 61*

Far in the distance, almost farther than I could see, was a crack in the ceiling of the realm. Light poured in, bursting into the darkness. It would have illuminated everything around it if there had been anything to see. But from here, it was just a rare, unfamiliar sight to break up the shadows of our dark lives.

Between us and that light, however, was a wide field of fallen rock.

Whatever had happened aboveground, it had made the ceiling there fragile. Some of the rocks that had fallen were nearly the size of horses, while others were no bigger than a pebble. They were littered everywhere, lying haphazardly. No rhyme, reason, or pattern. And as we stared at it, a chunk the size of a head crashed to the ground, raining debris in its wake.

As I looked up at the ceiling of the cavern that made up the realm, thinking about the fact that it would only get more dangerous from there, it occurred to me that we could just turn back and forget this whole thing.

"What causes something like this?"

Narvi hushed me. "I don't know," he whispered. "It could be anything. I'd guess that the roof of the realm is thin here. It's on old maps, so it's not new. Must've been getting worse for decades."

"Any suggestions then?" Angrboda's voice was low as well, her arms over her chest. She didn't take her eyes off the ceiling.

"I think we just have to go forward. The map here only shows fog." Narvi held it out. After the end of the rockfall, there was nothing. Like the realm dropped away and returned again on the other side.

"If we get to the other side of the rocks, we could fly out of here," Angrboda offered, gesturing to the hole.

"Did you learn how to fly?" I asked, sure that the answer was no.

"Of course not. But you can. You could surely come up with a plan that'll bypass this whole adventure." She shrugged. "Isn't that your whole reputation in Asgard? Being the weirdo that finds a way out of everything?"

It *had* been my reputation, yes. But I hadn't felt that sharp in years. Something about being mortally wounded, dying, and being inside a waking nightmare. "I can try. Hel already spelled out what happens if we leave this realm with our dead bodies. They'll start to decay and there'll be nothing left in a week or two."

"That may be true, but what if we could skip this whole wasteland and fly directly to Yggdrasil? Go to Urd's Well from there?" Angrboda kept her eyes on the hole in the realm while she gnawed off one of her fingernails.

"It's not a half-bad idea." Narvi had a look on his face like he was calculating possibilities in his mind. "If it's possible, it would be safer."

"Can we worry about this part *after* we worm our way through the falling rocks?" All of this planning was giving me a crawling under my skin that I didn't much appreciate. There were too many *what ifs* happening and not enough certainties.

Gods, I was starting to sound like Sigyn.

Was this what it was like in her organized, chaos-free mind? I had a feeling I was getting half the experience, all downsides and none of the benefits. It was too easy to focus on the worry. To remember how the whole realm was really a giant cave, and that the rock field in front of us made everything feel more compact and closed in.

Unfortunately for me, I'd grown a deep dislike of caves over the years.

Can't imagine why.

"What are the odds that the whole top comes crashing down?" I asked.

Scratching the back of his head, Narvi pursed his lips. "It would be incredibly bad luck if the whole ceiling waited until we arrived to collapse, but we still need to stay quiet. Loud noises cause reverberation, like when there's an avalanche on a mountain. No seidr, no fighting, no yelling. We just get across it and keep going."

"Who wants to go first?" Angrboda pulled her pack off and put it on top of her head, holding it there. When no one spoke up, she sighed. "Wow, such brave men and women here. Fine." She went in first.

Narvi followed and I trailed behind him, trying carefully to avoid the rocks on the ground. Our boots crunched with every step, the ground covered in sand and stone. We must've looked like quite the sight, three idiots creeping along in the near dark with travel sacks as hats.

The rockfall field was wide, and we moved slowly, intentionally. Every small sound, every rain of dust from above tightened the knot in my chest. But it was a cycle, an unwinnable battle. This…this spiral of the same thought over and over. *Don't think about being trapped in a cave under a rockfall.* Which, of course, is thinking about being trapped in a cave under a rockfall, just in a sideways manner.

Every second that we weren't on the other side of it was another second for the terror to build in my chest. It was pulling at me. At my thoughts, at my rationality. The memories were creeping up in the corner of my mind. Shadows played in my murky eye, keeping my head on a swivel, trying to watch for things coming out from the dark, when in reality, nothing was there. Was it my eye? My memory? Which pulverized piece of me was trying to get my attention? It kept latching on, biting, pulling, panic in my chest like a scream. Sigyn. The cave. The venom. Trapped, trapped, trapped—

The soft clink of pebbles on dirt, right next to my boot.

Angrboda's hand was over my mouth before I could react, pulling me backward. She must have seen it, must have recognized the terror on my face.

Something creaked above, off to the side, and a large piece of ceiling cracked away and smashed into the ground, rolling and kicking up dust.

No one breathed. No one moved.

And nothing else happened.

After the longest wait, Angrboda let out a breath. Hand still clasped over my mouth, she leaned in so close that her lips touched my earlobe. "You take a deep fucking breath, Loki. Get. Over. It."

As if it were so easy.

I prayed that my will to live would overpower the panic. That the shaking would stop. I did all the things that had worked before. Focusing on the smells and sounds, counting my breaths. I thought about the way the sheets had lain across Sigyn's hips as she slept, about the weight of Narvi in my arms when he was a little boy. Tried to be anywhere but where I was.

Angrboda was watching me carefully, those angry eyes scanning my face until she must've seen what she was looking for and let me go.

My shoulders sagged. Would I have screamed? Would I have lost control and run, putting us all in harm's way? Probably. I couldn't be sure. The things I'd done in the past when the terror came on…there were a lot of things I wasn't proud of.

Narvi waved a hand to follow him. To keep moving.

There were no other close calls.

Narvi reached the edge first. He stopped. Before Angrboda and I could see what lay ahead, we knew. The way his shoulders slumped said enough.

Standing there was like looking over the edge of the realm.

There was nothing below but a sea of fog, so thick and grey it looked almost solid, if not for the way it roiled and churned. The crack in the ceiling was just past the fog, and the light that poured through it illuminated something green beneath it. The kind of green that meant life.

"Well, I really don't want to go down there." Angrboda's gaze went from the fog to the hole in the ceiling above it. It was still not quite overhead, still no warmth of sunshine on us, but it was within wing's reach.

I took off my pack and put it at Narvi's feet.

"Are you sure you're well enough?" Narvi's brow was furrowed in that way that had left worry lines between his brows.

I stretched my neck and listened for the crack of muscle, trying to loosen up my cold insides before the transformation. It would be easier if I slipped back into my original form first, but it felt like it was too soon, like I still needed this body. "I'd never describe myself as *well*, but I'll manage."

As I began to whisper runes, Narvi and Angrboda backed away, giving me space to work. It was slower than the last time. Harder to concentrate, to push past the panic that had tried to overtake me. I tripped over the runes more than once, but in the end, it worked. My body creaked and groaned into a new shape, and I pushed off the ground as a bird, taking flight.

I pressed toward the gap in the ceiling, flapping hard. Sometimes there were bats and I had no desire to find myself tangled up with a group of them. It wasn't that far after all, and I could be there and back quickly, as long as something on the other side of the sunlight didn't eat me alive.

The hole grew closer. Below, the fog roiled like a cloud of thick smoke, even though there was no wind. On the other side of it, a tree grew next to a small lake, grass sprouting under the sunbeam. If we were lucky, we wouldn't find ourselves visiting either of them, because we'd already be flying halfway to Urd's Well by then.

How we'd all fly would be another problem. I could work enough seidr to keep this form, and enough to create an option for someone else, but three bodies was too much. Perhaps Narvi could—

The air tightened around me, thick and porous, like trying to push through mud. I pressed higher, working my wings harder, but even still, my movements grew too slow.

I hit something solid and was propelled back downward, toward the ground.

Epilogues for Lost Gods

The realm spun as I careened towards the mess of fog. I flapped my wings but I'd already started spinning out of control. I fought against gravity and whatever had pushed me back down, fighting for control.

Now. I needed to straighten out *now*.

I expanded both wings at once in a desperate bid to stop the spin, to regain some traction on the air. The spinning slowed almost at once, but my vision was blurred, dizzy from the freefall. My wingspan carried me forward, helping me glide as I gained my composure.

The realm came to a slow stop around me, and I realized I was gliding away from Narvi and Angrboda. I started to change course, careful not to move too quickly and upset the delicate balance I had on my trajectory. I could do nothing but take my time, lazily making my way toward the rock field once again.

When I landed, I let the shape of the bird slip off, collapsing onto my back. My head hurt, like I'd been swirled around inside a whirlpool and spat back out.

"Are you alright?" Narvi leaned over me, his fingers searching my body for wounds. "Did you fall? What happened?"

"I couldn't get out." I pressed my palm into my good eye, peeking through my fingers to ease the spinning in my vision. "There's something blocking the exit. Some kind of seidr maybe. I don't know, but we're not leaving that way."

"Can't you try again?" Angrboda was still standing, hands on her hips, annoyed.

"You can fucking try again, how about that?" I snapped. "It bounced me back with a kick harder than an unbroken stallion, so if you want to get on that ride, be my guest." I was not flying anywhere else, no fucking way.

Angrboda let out an exasperated sigh. "Sometimes I regret not learning to shapeshift, the same as I regret getting involved with you."

"That's fine. Only seers have no regrets," I barked back.

"*Only seers have no regrets,*" she mimicked in a sour tone. "Ugh. Down we go then, I guess."

Angrboda knelt, looking straight down the edge of the rock. The slope was sharp, the kind of thing we could slide down but would have difficulty climbing back up. She picked up a pebble and tossed it. It click-clacked along the slope, into the fog, and disappeared, the noise coming to what seemed like a natural stop.

Nothing happened.

She looked up at us as if to ask if we were sure.

Sadly, I was.

Feeling as good as I was likely to feel, I sat up and went over the edge first. I had the impression that scooting down on my ass was my safest bet, but I was unwilling to lower myself to anything like that. The moment I put my feet on the ground and started my descent, the angle forced me into a run to keep my balance. A short moment later, I was enveloped in the fog, unable to see anything but the thick, grey cloud. The air had a strange, sour smell, a bit like sulphur or maybe rotten food. Something about it left my mouth dry and sticky.

Rocks scrabbled behind me. Narvi pierced through, nearly running into me. We moved back a step, and Angrboda quickly followed, skidding to a stop on her boots.

It was just us and the fog.

"Stay together." Angrboda walked around us, taking up the lead. "Who knows what's hiding in here. If we get split up, we might never find each other again."

"What are the odds we're walking in a straight line towards that tree?" Keeping up with Angrboda was a task in itself. She was far more confident in her steps than I was, and the lack of a second eye didn't make it easier on me.

"I don't know…" Narvi seemed hesitant, turning slowly as he tried to peer through the fog.

Something moved in the corner of my vision.

Stopping, I looked around to see what it was. A shadow maybe? Real or imagined? There was no way to know, not in this place. It was gone as fast as it had come, and there was too much space between myself and the others. Hurrying to close the distance, I misstepped and nearly lost my balance.

There, again. Something in the fog. I turned.

Nothing.

When I looked back, Narvi was almost out of sight.

I ran forward and collided with something, falling back onto my ass.

My head throbbed from the impact. I looked up. It was a large, wooden door. There was no way it had been there a moment ago. I blinked. The door was still there. Narvi had just gone that way, how could—wait. I knew that door. I'd gone in and out of it a hundred thousand times.

My door.

Ours.

The door to Sigyn's hall, where we had lived in Asgard.

Home.

Every thought was swimming, trying to make sense of it. Had I fallen asleep somehow? It had to be a dream. But when I reached up, the door handle was cool and hard under my hand. I turned it. The latch clicked open, and light flooded out into the fog.

The savoury scent of rabbit cooking over the fire filled my nose. The kitchen was the way it had always been: herbs drying from hooks on the walls, books scattered across the disused end of the dining table. And at the end of the long room were the boys, playing with wooden horses, making them prance across the floor.

I squeezed my eyes shut, but they were still there. Váli couldn't have been more than seven years old…but I had just seen Narvi, he was a young man—wasn't he?

Váli raised his head, catching me standing in the doorway. "Father's home!"

Without another word, they were up off the floor and diving toward me at breakneck speed. Overcome, I dropped to my knees and pulled them into my arms, my face nuzzled into Narvi's shoulder. They smelled like children do: dirt and outdoors and a bit of goat milk soap somewhere underneath. I could barely make out what they were saying, each of them clamouring to tell me what had happened while I had been gone.

Gods, I'd missed them so much.

"Don't cry, Father." Narvi reached a small hand up and brushed the tear from my cheek. "Mother won't want you to be sad."

"I'm not sad." I pressed my lips to his forehead. "I'm very, very happy."

"Happy to see me as well, I hope."

Sigyn was standing in front of the door to our room, dripping with Vanir silk that hung from the curves of her like a waterfall. Her hair was down, flowing over her shoulders, her eyes hungry.

When I looked down, the boys were gone, already back to their games. How had they gotten out of my arms—

"You wouldn't keep me waiting, would you?" She shifted her weight to her other foot, her bare leg peeking out from underneath the silk. Kohl lined her eyes, dark and regal. That look. I had missed that look.

I went to her, taking her face in my hands. Her breath hitched as I pressed her back against the door, feeling the solidity of her body against mine. The warmth of her. All of her, everything. She was my everything.

Was. Why did that word feel so sad?

Her lips met mine, pulling me away from my strange, scattered thoughts. I'd missed it so much, the way she could make me feel with just a kiss. I'd been away from home too long, but gods, how I cherished the returns. Blood rushing, I ran my hands over her skin, thrilling at the feel of her curves in my palms. I let my body shift back to its masculine form, wanting to do very specific things with her. To her. Sigyn, who was so intelligent, so kind, so beautiful. Everything I ever wanted, wrapped up in one woman, one lover who saved me over and over, from myself and everyone else. And maybe that was selfish, but there would be time to ask those questions later. When we were finished with each other, curled in bed and—

Sigyn's hand went to the door handle and twisted it open. I stumbled with her as it swung into the room. She pushed, sending me tumbling forward, into the darkness. The door slammed shut again, taking the light with it.

She was gone.

The darkness lingered as I sat splayed on the ground, chest heaving and terrified. The space lit up slowly, the room revealing itself to be...something else. Not ours. But I knew it all the same. It was sparse and there was a pungent smell of slow decay. Of sweat and infection and withering. The smell that lingers from bloody chamber pots and vomit, no matter how often you clean it up.

Hadn't I buried this twenty lifetimes ago?

A familiar bed. Large and long and built for two, but only ever with one in it. She was curled up on her side, the furs pulled up to her face. Cold. Mother had been so cold.

I peeled myself off the floor and went to her. On the bedside table was a clean bowl of water and a cloth. Her skin was clammy, perspiration on her forehead. Her fiery hair was matted against her skin, the emerald in her eyes dull, her cheeks sallow. There wasn't much time left; anyone could see that. Squeezing the water from the cloth, I ran it over her forehead as gently as I could. But even that was enough to wake her.

She never slept very well, not at the end.

"Loki, I'm so glad you're here." Her voice was a rasp, like she was raw all the way through.

"I'll never go far, Mother." My voice sounded too young, like the centuries had bled out of me at the sight of her. I sat down at her side, the mattress creaking under me. I felt small next to her. Weak. Helpless.

There had been nothing I could do. No matter how much she ate or drank, she just got frailer. Poisoned food would do that—but I didn't know that yet. Not now, not until it's too late.

"Did you have a good day?" She took my hand and squeezed, all the tiny bones so prominent under her skin. "I saw it was sunny. Did you play outside?"

"I practised seidr, like you said. I can change a rock into an acorn now. Do you want to see?" Even as the words poured out of my mouth, they sounded childish. Something from a lifetime ago, and so much hope in every one of them.

"Show me, darling."

But there was something wrong. Her face. The skin was getting sharper, like tightening the skin on a drum. It drew back around her bones, dark pits sinking around her eyes. Her hand was loose and lifeless in mine. And her jaw was still moving, but no sound came out. The vivid colour of her eyes dulling, her hair falling out onto her pillow, decomposing under my hands. Dying in front of me like she had but not like this, not so vivid, not like a hundred years in the ground—

I closed my eyes, pushing it away—

I'm not here I'm not here I'm not here—

A howl.

The clamour of battle erupted around me. Steel striking steel, screaming, dying. I opened my eyes and the world was on fire. Jotnar fighting einherjar, Hel's dead army crashing into Valkyries, chaos everywhere. Panic rose in my chest. Too close to home, too familiar.

I ran. Tried to escape. Tried to reach the edge of the battlefield, somewhere safe. There had been no such thing as safe that day; I knew that. Ragnarok would take everything I loved. Would take me before it was done. But that wasn't yet; that wasn't now. I could still live if I ran fast enough.

Another howl, so loud and piercing that my insides curdled. At the far end of the battlefield, Fenrir's head tipped back, his bottom jaw tearing off his skull and crashing to the ground. Blood poured out of the wound, gushing down over his fur, and he careened to the ground, crushing everything in his way.

Dead.

Bodies everywhere.

The numbing ripping tightening of my chest stole my breath. I fell to my knees between the clatter of swords and axes. He was dead and I was already dead—certainly inside—and I couldn't breathe couldn't breathe—

Jormungandr's body slack, curled around the mountains of Jotunheim.

Hel, pierced by dozens of arrows, falling from the sky like a bird

—not how it happened—

My name. Someone screaming for me. Heart hammering in my chest, I looked up. Sigyn. Hreidulfr and Váli and Narvi. I crawled forward, trying to reach them as they ran towards me. Not fast enough. An enormous hand reached out of the throng and grabbed Váli by the neck, twisting. He fell limp into the mud and didn't get back up. A hammer to Hreidulfr's skull. Narvi, eviscerated by an axe. All dead, all at once. Everything in my life, gone.

Sigyn fell last, the tip of a golden spear ripping through her front and propping her body up from the ground. Odin was behind her, marching towards her body to take back his spear.

"Sigyn." The word choked out. I wanted to scream, but it was caught in me, buried in my stomach, regret and pain in the way of its escape. Crawling to her, I took Sigyn's face in my hands. Kissed her. Begged her to stay. "Please, my love. I need you. I've always needed you."

121

Sigyn's hand brushed my cheek, her eyes fluttering. Her blood was on my hands, sickeningly warm and sticky. I wanted to give her more time. She deserved more, deserved a quiet life with her books and her herbs and her sons. All the things I'd ensured she didn't have. Instead, she was in my hands, bleeding out into the dirt, becoming cold. Dying.

And then she was gone.

It was too late for all the things I should have given her. She'd been torn from me. I pressed my face into her chest, the cry muffled by her limp body, blood seeping over me. I'd thought she lived through Ragnarok but I was wrong. She'd been alive, I'd sworn that, but she wasn't. She wasn't. We've all been dead, all of us. I screamed into her skin, into the corpse of her until my throat turned raw, and longer after that. Couldn't live like that, won't live—

Something collided with my chest and the scream died as I rolled onto the ground. My head bumped into a rock and my vision blurred. Everything was quiet. The noise, the smell of fire and blood—where had the battle gone?

"Get up!"

Angrboda stood above me, hands on her hips. Angry wasn't the word for what she was. Livid. Furious.

"What...what happened?" I curled up around the pain in my chest that had certainly been caused by her boot.

"The fucking fog. Or—I don't know. Something in the fog." She pressed her hair back with her palm, exasperated. "We got separated. I saw visions. I only found you because you wouldn't stop fucking screaming."

I let my head loll back into the dirt. Visions. Yggdrasil below.

"Wait, where's Narvi?" I pushed myself off the ground, ignoring what was surely going to be a bruise.

Angrboda shook her head. "I don't know."

"Fuck. Narvi!" I turned out of habit, as if there were any way for me to see him out in the fog.

As I took a step away, Angrboda grabbed my arm. "I don't think so. You fucking hold on to me or we're going to lose each other again. Probably fucking die out here..." She positioned herself on my blind side and hooked her arm in mine.

We alternated calling and listening. The fog seemed to dampen our voices and I couldn't be sure how far they were carrying. I felt insane, seeing things in the fog that weren't there, still stuck in a reality that wasn't *there*. It was hard to say how long we walked. Too long. My legs were weak and if it weren't for the fact that Narvi was vulnerable and alone somewhere, I'd probably have collapsed into a deep sleep among the dirt.

And then we heard the sobs from somewhere nearby.

We made our way carefully towards the sound. I wanted to call out but it occurred to me that it might *not* be him. There was always a chance something else was in the fog with us. Something worse.

But it was him. One foot forward and then another, and his shape appeared in the grey. Tears slicked his face and he was crawling around on all fours, dirt covering his pants and the palms of his hands.

"Stop," he whined between sobs. "Stop growling, please! Every day it's the same! You kill me every day, but I'm already dead!" He reached to pick something up, something invisible, then pressed his hand to his stomach before reaching again. Like he was trying to put something back.

My poor boy.

I dropped to my knees next to Narvi and held out my hands. "Son, it's me. I'm here. Come back to us. None of it is real, I promise."

If he heard me, he didn't show it. Instead, he reached for something else, his voice cracking as he mumbled to himself.

Wanting to free him of the delusions, I grabbed his shoulders.

"No!" Narvi flailed against my grasp, trying to push me off. "Brother, no!"

My heart shattering, I slapped him on the cheek hard enough to burn my hand.

Narvi blinked, confused. Stretching his jaw, he looked around. Only fog and dirt and broken people. When his eyes settled on mine, the composure broke and he collapsed against my chest, gasping between every sob.

"I've got you, Son. I know." I wrapped him in my arms, threading my fingers into the hair at his scalp. He shook against me, crying so mournfully it was more like a howl, the deepest despair.

"He took me apart." Narvi's choked words were fumbling, crackling. "Váli pulled out my insides and made me put them back, over and over. Why can't I just *forget?*"

"It's over now—"

"It's never over!" Narvi sucked in a deep, trembling breath. "Every night. He kills me every night, in every dream. I can't make it stop!"

No, of course he couldn't. And neither could I. The two of us, lost to our nightmares, pieces of us shredding off, one sleep at a time. Like father, like son.

At a loss for words, I looked up at Angrboda. She was looking elsewhere, watching the fog, tears trailing down her cheek.

CHAPTER EIGHTEEN

SIGYN

*"My regrets? You know them already, darling.
I regret ever letting you out of my sight."*

— *Eyvindr, Volume 1*

Waking next to the softness of a body, to the in and out of sleepy breath, nearly startled me. I wasn't sure where I was at first. What part of my life I was in. When I slowly opened my eyes, pushing back sleep, and saw Alyssa curled on her side next to me, I let out a sigh of relief. That made sense, at least. More than any of the confusion that lived in my dreams and often leaked out into the morning. Fear, anxiety, regret. Alyssa was none of that.

Alyssa was comfort.

Her breath came slowly. Long inhales, long exhales. The electric blue of her hair was like some magical waterfall, crashing down over her shoulders as she rested beneath it. Yesterday's kohl around her eyes, her hand tucked under her cheek. She looked light. Unburdened.

Beautiful.

She was sleeping so deeply. I couldn't remember what that was like. Even when I was exhausted, I usually woke at least once in the night, and if I was very unlucky, I would stay awake.

Not her though. So full of the naive confidence of being young—young as compared to a goddess that lived an eternity in a dank cave at least—and of someone whose actions hadn't contributed, however indirectly, to the end of nearly every life in the realms.

Epilogues for Lost Gods

I caught myself as I was reaching out to tuck a piece of hair behind her ear. My face flushed. These emotions were slipping out of the cracks of the seemingly well-crafted wall I'd made, and that couldn't be allowed.

I felt something for Alyssa. Something more affectionate than I wanted to admit to, and it was getting harder and harder to keep it down.

A bitterness soured my stomach, a sudden anger that drowned out everything else. What a spineless, fickle whore I was. Hadn't I just gone to Helheim to ask Loki to risk his afterlife to help me, dangling my affection like a carrot for a horse? Hadn't I *just* lain in his bed spouting maybes and possibilities? And here I was, contemplating my affection for someone else.

What kind of person did something like that? Led someone on like that?

But was that the right phrase? It had been honest, what I'd said to him. That I loved him and resented him and forgave him. That there was a future for us, in some capacity. So how was I now lying next to someone else whom my heart yearned for and asking these kinds of questions?

Everything about it felt like a betrayal.

Wasn't my loyalty who I was?

I had too many thoughts to consider all at once. He had betrayed me first, and he had done much worse than this. He had run off with Angrboda and sired three children by her. And if he had done that, was I justified in wanting someone else? Could I live with the look on his face when we met again and he discovered that I'd tricked him? Was it a trick if I had barely known it myself?

If I cared for someone else, did that mean I didn't love him at all?

People all over the realms ran circles around their spouses, from one bed to the next. Why was this so easy for them and so unthinkable for me?

Fidelity.

The word filled my mind, bringing all the loathing with it. My title, my curse. The final gift that my father had given me. Was that it? Was I so loyal that I had no right to any love but Loki's, no matter how broken and damaged it was?

My mind thrummed with all those thoughts and more, stirring a faint headache in my temple. I didn't want to face any of it. There were too many difficult questions, too many unknowns. I could hardly rely on the facts, because only one thing was clear to me: I didn't *not* love either of them.

Fuck.

A sharp knock came at the door, startling me from my thoughts and Alyssa from her sleep.

"Jesus Christ—" Alyssa threw her palms over her eyes in tired frustration, stretching out her limbs.

"Yes?" I sat up, pushing my hair back in an attempt to look presentable.

Hreidulfr opened the door and slid inside, looking a bit nervous to intrude. "Another raven, ma'am—Sigyn." He came around to my side of the bed and handed me a tiny, rolled-up note. I took it from his hand and unrolled it.

Vidar furious about retaliation. Attack imminent. Prepare.

My stomach curdled. Of course. Leave it to a coward to run home and tell his brother about how mean the other faction was.

"What is it?" Alyssa rubbed the sleep from her eyes, yawning like a cat.

"Asgard is coming for us. But this isn't enough information." I lit the paper with wildfire and crushed the ashes in my hand. "I have to find them."

"Find who?" Hreidulfr moved out of my way as I pushed the furs back and got out of bed.

"Our informant. I haven't wanted to risk their life by going in person but we can't fight what we can't see coming." I started to strip off my sleeping clothes, too hurried to care who was watching me change. I pulled a pair of trousers and a tunic from the wardrobe. "And if Asgard is coming, I need to get our informant out safely. Bring them home."

"How will you do it?" Hreidulfr had turned his gaze away, the sweetheart.

"I'll fly there, but I'm going to need help getting them out of the city. You collected the horses from yesterday?"

"We did, both of them."

"You and Mist take the horses. I can get the informant to Yggdrasil, and from there you'll need to get them back here."

"Right. We can do that. But..." He scratched his beard, worry on his face. "We're risking an awful lot so close to their attack. I need to know why. I value loyalty; I do. But one life isn't worth risking the entire city, is it?"

"Normally it isn't, no." I turned to them, unsure if I should be telling them at all. But time was already up. "We're risking everything because the informant is Hod."

Trying to fly undetected over Asgard was a curious thing. I didn't want to look like I was flying too straight, because birds don't tend to be that purposeful, but I also didn't want to linger on any one place long enough to draw attention.

From above, Asgard had similarities to Fólkheim. It was the remnants of a scattered city, so much of it built back from the rubble. The places I'd loved most, like

126

Epilogues for Lost Gods

Idunn's woods, the market, and the archives were gone. At a glance, survival had taken precedence: fields and animals and tanneries, smithies and forges, and more functioning training grounds than could reasonably be necessary. Where we'd done our best to make room for bits of culture and family, Asgard had seemingly prioritized battle.

I shouldn't have been surprised.

In the distance, Odin's halls weren't quite as tall and shining as they had once been. Pieces had broken away, and entire chunks were missing. Greenery had tried to lay claim to it, crawling up its sides and in through the cracks.

And where our home had once been, they'd erected a statue of Odin stepping on the neck of another man.

How lovely.

Having taken in all I could stomach, I landed on a roof or two and pecked pointlessly at some twigs. Slowly, I made my way towards a gathering of ravens perched on a small balcony, part of the remnants of Valaskjálf. The birds scattered as I sank towards them and landed at a run on the stone.

In Odin's day, the rookery had been used by his staff to send messages across the nine realms by raven. Now it was sparser. They kept fewer birds, and by the look of things, they were far less tended to than before. No devoted keepers, no young apprentices to keep things tidy, which meant watching where I stepped.

The doors on the balcony were thrown wide open. It was lit only by the sunlight from outside, enough to show me the cages, some with open doors and others with ravens sealed tight inside. One spotted me, craned its neck, and squawked. The room stank of feathers and bird shit. Off in one corner was a writing desk, where one of the ravens was perched like a guard.

I hopped safely inside and let the seidr fall off me. The stretch and grind of my body unsettled me as I became myself again, reminding me how little I wanted shape-changing to be part of my everyday life. Every single time I swore never again, knowing it probably wouldn't be the last time.

I breathed deep and shook the feeling off. I had no time to dwell on it.

The raven preened itself as I approached, unperturbed by my transformation or my presence. The desk was littered with scraps of paper, many of them blank or bearing the deeply etched runes that Hod used.

There wasn't much of note. Most of the scraps were mistakes, discarded partway through writing them. An apology to someone, a list of wares, a threat. Dozens of pieces of information with no context to place them together and no time to do so.

The mess bothered me. It was uncharacteristic of Hod. I'd always known him to be precise and careful. Meticulous in anything that had to do with the archives. Perhaps he had fallen into the trap that so many of us had; too much had changed. Too much was gone, and prime among them was the man he'd loved.

When your insides are torn up, it shows up in the world in the most tangible ways.

I pressed my ear to the door at the far side of the room, listening for anyone who might be passing. I heard nothing. From my very sparse visits over the years, I knew that Hod's room was close by, more by his choice than anyone else's. He'd told me no one else had wanted to be near the rookery with all the noise and smell, and that suited the privacy of our cause well enough. Let them sleep in their lavish beds, away from the plotting of their undoing.

The hall was empty, but I still moved quickly. His door was only around the corner, and when I knocked, I did so in a quick pattern, something from when we were both younger. A game we'd played in more innocent times, when I was a child and he was simply a brother who had taken an interest.

The door flew open. Hod was clearly on edge, his brows furrowed in fear. He looked ready to pounce and protect. "Get inside. Come on." He ushered me in, his head poking out into the hall. Though he was blind, I knew he was listening in case someone else had spotted me.

Once he was satisfied, he closed the door behind him and leaned against it. "Sigyn, what are you doing here?"

He seemed harried but healthy; his chestnut hair had grown out to his ears and needed a trim, and a bit of stubble had popped out along his cheeks. A walking staff was gripped in his white-knuckled hands and he was wearing at least one knitted sweater too many. I wanted to stare at him forever, to make up for all the time I had missed my brother dearly, but the furrow of his brow and the look in his cloudy blue eyes told me he was worried.

"I got your note," I said. "Is it as bad as you made it sound?"

Hod nodded grimly.

"Then you're leaving with me. If this is the end, then I want you with us, where you belong."

Hod's shoulders softened and sagged, a look of relief falling over him. "Well, it's about time."

I laughed at the clear display of exhaustion. "Don't look so eager."

"Eager? That doesn't begin to describe how desperate I am to leave this place." Hod moved away from the door, guiding himself around the room by memory and with the tips of his fingers. He found a travel sack and started to fill it as he spoke. "Not only am I tired of playing spymaster for you, I'm also tired of putting up with this horrible family. It was one thing when there were more of them and I could choose which of them to spend time with, but now it's like having three slightly different Thors at dinner every night. If I have to listen to one more joke about sucking cock, I'm going to throw myself from the rookery window."

A mix of guilt and amusement ran through me. I reached out to warn him with a touch, and then pulled him in for a hug. "I've missed you so much. I know it's been hard. You've done the realms a service we can't repay you for, and now you're coming home to retire."

"Retire? Hardly. I haven't been collecting stories since before Ragnarok and most of the ones I'd written down were destroyed in the floods. I've got work to do." Hod ruffled my hair and paused for a moment. "Did you speak to her? About…him?"

I took Hod's face in my hands, wanting to see his expression as I told him. "If we give these gods to Hel, she's going to help Eyvindr ask for a new thread." I explained in short detail the new way of things, and what had transpired in Helheim.

A sob caught in Hod's throat, grief and joy crashing into him. He pressed a palm over mine, tears falling onto his cheeks. "Finally. I just want to start living again. There are so many things I need to do differently. Thank you, Sigyn."

"Don't thank me. I probably helped kill him in the first place. All I did was ask."

Hod's shoulders rose and fell slowly with a long, steadying breath. "No one else asked. No one else cared."

It took everything in me to keep myself together as he said that, the words like a stab in the gut. Because I had done this for him, yes. But I'd also let him stay in Asgard alone, for the cause.

It had been the right thing, the needed thing.

I had so much unkindness to make up for.

"Alright, there's time for all this once we're safe at home," I said. "Gather your things. We're going to meet Hreidulfr and Mist outside the city and they're going to take you home by horseback."

"How exactly are we getting out of the city?"

"We're going to walk right out the front door."

After Hod had packed his things—nearly all of them were loose papers, except for one very thick book—I pulled a few pieces of his clothing on over mine, smudged some ink around my eyes like kohl, and we exited his room arm in arm. I'd pulled up the hood of his old cloak to hide the curls of my hair, and with any luck, most of my face. It wouldn't be like any of our kin to look too closely at someone beneath them anyway.

Hod leaned toward my ear and whispered. "To the end of the hall. Open the door and take a right and you'll be back in Valaskjálf proper. You'll remember the way from there. What's left of it, anyway."

I followed his instructions and found the way to be as straightforward as he'd said. The inside of Valaskjálf was worn and battered, with pieces of the halls chipped and broken away. Water lines on the walls told the story of Ragnarok's flooding, and layers of mould and rot ate at the wooden features. The plants I'd seen from outside had managed to infiltrate the stone, creeping and crawling over whatever they could reach, and some of them had been hacked away where they'd grown too large.

I'd walked those halls and rooms most of my life, and seeing them in such a state of utter destruction churned emotion in me. If I lingered, I knew I would have a memory to match every corner of these buildings. Some were good; I'd chased my sons down that hall, and I'd fallen in love for the first time in that alcove, and I'd stolen away with Loki for secret trysts in those rooms. Other places were full of tears and distrust. Knives in my back.

Maybe it was spiteful to enjoy seeing Odin's halls of gold tarnished.

Oh, well.

I had a lot to be spiteful for.

We were halfway out of Valaskjálf when we ran across someone for the first time. A washerwoman scurried past us with linens piled high to her chest, not giving us a first glance, let alone a second. Still, my heart was in my throat. I'd never exactly been built to be sneaky and sly. That was my husband's job.

Only a set of stairs and two winding hallways stood between us and the outdoors. After slowing down so Hod could descend the stairs safely, it became difficult to keep a moderate pace and look casual. We were so close to the end. If I obeyed the thudding of my heart, I'd have thrown Hod over my shoulder and run for Yggdrasil, but not only was I not capable, but it wasn't particularly smart either.

One more hallway.

A voice boomed somewhere out of sight. Two sets of heavy footsteps marched towards us as the voice got clearer. "I want every one of them properly outfitted. I don't care if you have to dress some of them in bed furs, they'll go to battle with more than the skin on their backs."

I kept my head down as they came into view. One was dressed head to toe in fighting gear, but I didn't recognize his face. The other was Vidar.

Vidar had been born to Odin too late to be of any consequence to me. Our father had paraded him into Valhalla one Yule and announced him as Fenrir's future killer before his entire army. Vidar had been born with a violent purpose, an important fate. And yet I had rarely run across him in the halls, let alone known him. I'd be surprised if he'd even known my name before Ragnarok.

Would he know my face now?

Epilogues for Lost Gods

It was hard to get a proper look at him while keeping myself hidden, but he was the same as I'd remembered: tall and pale and so much Jotun in his blood. His face was thick and stoney. Smooth, like he'd never smiled even once in his life. He'd grown a beard since I'd seen him last, and it did very little to soften his edges. Someone had tattooed a valknut into the closely shaved line of his scalp, Odin's symbolic triad of interlaced triangles.

We kept walking, but Vidar did not.

"Hod."

We stopped at the sound and Hod turned without hesitation. I attempted to look pious and humble, staring at my feet so my hood would cover my eyes.

"Good day, little brother. Is the planning going well?" Hod settled both hands onto the top of his walking stick.

"It is. Where are you off to?" Vidar was looking Hod over with a critical eye.

"Not far. My assistant is taking me to the shops for some last-minute supplies. I'm out of ink, I'm afraid. Makes the job difficult."

Vidar nodded. "Since you're already going out, you can join us. I still haven't settled on my victory speech, and that's the kind of dull thing you'd enjoy, I'm sure."

The casual insult almost caused my eyes to roll back into my head.

Hod cleared his throat. "I'm sure I can come up with something when I return—"

"No, I want it settled now. We're going to assess if the soldiers are battle-ready, and you're never going to get a feel for anything that rushes the blood if you're sitting in your musty little room." Vidar started walking towards the front doors, his lackey following behind him like a dog. He called over his shoulder, "Hurry up. I've got things to do."

"Fuck," I spat under my breath.

"Play along. His attention span is short. We'll be alright." Hod gave my arm a pat and started forward, dragging me with him.

This was exactly the kind of thing I hated about sneaking. I'd always gotten the feeling that Loki enjoyed the thrill of nearly being caught, but I couldn't understand what was so amazing about nearly having a heart attack before being caught, tortured, and murdered.

I was many things, but I was not that kind of masochist.

I steered us in the direction of Vidar, having no idea where we were truly headed. It was in the opposite direction of the new sprout of Yggdrasil, however, and that wasn't exactly positive.

After a few minutes, we stopped next to one of the many training areas I'd glimpsed on my flight into the city. Dozens of soldiers were sparring across a bare stretch of dirt. Some had real, battle-worn weapons, but others had ones made of wood. A few looked completely incompetent, but for each of those, there were another four seasoned warriors that sent a feeling of dread down my spine.

Fólkheim was not like this city of soldiers, and that frightened me.

"You can hear it, can't you?" Vidar's hands were on the fence, curled white-knuckled around the board. "The battle is in the air, and these men are hungry for glory. It's inspiring."

Hod gave a curt nod. "It is. I'm sure this will make for great material."

"I want the people to know we're always going to win." Vidar wasn't watching us. His eyes were on the soldiers. Talking near us more than to us. "As the bloodline of Odin, nothing can stop us. No one can take our lineage from us. We were destined for great things, Hod, great things."

It was clear to me that he didn't care who was listening, and that he believed himself wholeheartedly. He kept on without waiting for Hod to answer.

"The realms don't know what's *good* for them. How should they? Most of them are commoners, labourers. How can they have the good sense to step outside their lot in life? We'll take care of them. The gods will make sure that everyone in the realm knows their place, that they have hard work and purpose in this life. The gods will provide."

Listening to him was making me sick to my stomach. I wanted to shout at him, to argue each point he made. Once again, I was not meant to be sneaky. But I held my tongue.

The war I was planning to win wasn't going to be fought with words.

"And you want all this in the speech, yes?" Hod was cool and calm, as if he'd heard this a hundred times before. Likely he had.

"Yes, all of it." Vidar turned to Hod at last. "It's good, I think. Rousing. Everyone is looking for their fate, aren't they?"

He looked at me.

I froze, not daring to take a single breath.

"Do you have faith in the gods?" Vidar's head tilted just a little, examining me as he waited for my answer.

"She's mute, brother." Hod forced a smile, tightening his arm around mine. "Hasn't spoken since Ragnarok. We make a fine pair. Purpose, as you say. Being of service to the cause gives her purpose."

I nodded slowly, trying to keep my composure. Trying not to think about the comments Hod was making at his own expense, knowing what kinds of brutes would be pleased to hear them.

"Good." Vidar shifted his gaze away from me, his attention back to his army. "Write something that will make everyone believe. I'd hate to have to kill too many dissidents."

Epilogues for Lost Gods

My blood ran cold.

I wanted to leave. I wanted to run so far and so fast the words couldn't follow me. Asgard and the realms would fall in line or perish.

As small a force as we were, Fólkheim had to win. The alternative was too terrible to allow.

Hod motioned for me to back away. Vidar's attention had shifted and we had been dismissed. I tried to step lightly, wishing to simply levitate away without notice. One step at a time, we edged away from them and from the training ground.

Once we were far enough away, I let the tension out of my body with a deep exhale. We weren't out of the city yet, but being that close to Vidar had been a repulsive experience. I felt it in every bone and muscle in my body, how they'd tightened and withdrawn, trying to take up as little space in the realm as possible.

Hod muttered something under his breath.

"Sorry, what did you say?"

Hod leaned in close to my ear. "I called him a fucking moron. Do you understand now what I've been dealing with?"

I sighed. "I wish I didn't."

No one was looking at us in the common areas. People were too concerned with their own lives, their own hardships. As we walked at an inconspicuous clip toward Yggdrasil, I tried to take notice of everything.

I'd heard things, both from Hod and from spies we'd sent into the city, but seeing Asgard for myself was another thing altogether. Being in the middle of the bandaged wreckage of what had always been my home…it was impossible not to get swallowed up by emotion.

The city no longer had Odin's gold and centuries of good trade and diplomatic relations to rely on. Bustling markets and children playing in the streets had once been part of the charm of Asgard. Now I saw only work in every direction. Rebuilding, crafting, sewing, growing. Some of the people—who seemed to come from all corners of the nine realms—carried themselves with a pride that spoke volumes, while others had a darkness coiled around them that was just as loud.

If anyone had looked at our city from the outside, maybe they'd have seen the same. Except…

"Please. Do you have anything to spare?" A young man was sitting against what had once been a linen store. He was dressed in rags and his skin was filthy. His left leg was covered in scars. What was left of the muscles had healed but he would never walk again as he was, not without a cane, which seemed conspicuously missing.

Even in Odin's day, no one would've been left to suffer like that. We'd had an infirmary, and we had taken care of the sick. We'd worked hard to make good lives for those with disabilities.

I pulled Hod to a stop, my blood raging in my veins. I had brought nothing with me, and Hod had packed nothing to eat, but I knelt down close to the man, close enough for our conversation to be private.

"What is your name?"

"Artur," he croaked, blinking back tears.

"Artur, I don't have anything I can give you today, but I promise I will come back to help you. Does anything hurt? I don't think I can fix your leg, not alone, but if you're in pain, I can help."

Artur's eyes wandered, taking in my face. It was a risk. He might recognize me and betray us. But if he did know me, he made no mention of it. "I cough every day. I sleep outside and I...I think it's in my lungs. Dust maybe. I don't know."

"Just give me a moment, alright?" I reached out and placed my fingertips on his chest. Even without knowing what it was, without a diagnosis that I didn't have the time for, some generic healing runes would be better than nothing. I whispered them, watching him as he watched me, sadness and hope in his eyes. And then it was done.

Artur took a deep breath and exhaled slowly. A laugh bubbled in his throat, a smile bursting forth. "You're a miracle. Thank you."

"Be patient, friend. Stay safe and try to stay out of everyone's way for a few days. Then I'm coming back for you, alright? I promise."

He nodded. "I can. I will. Thank you, Goddess."

I put a finger to my lips and shushed him. "I'll see you soon."

I stood, pulling Hod forward before I did something rash. It was better than giving in to the rage coiling inside me. There was far too large a temptation to give up the charade and burn the city down around me. It was a better fate than it deserved.

"That was risky, Sigyn. What if he tells someone?"

I gave Hod a sideways glance. Concern was written across his face. "No one else has helped him for a very long time. If he sells me out to Asgard, he dooms himself to that fate." I paused, gathering my bearings on the street, finding the monstrously tall sapling that had once been Yggdrasil in the distance. "How many others are there like him, Hod?"

His shoulders drooped, a deep sadness settling over him. "Too many. Far too many."

Hreidulfr and Mist were waiting when we arrived, grazing the horses and keeping a stoic watch, not a word exchanged between them. Hreidulfr rose from his perch on one of Yggdrasil's dead roots as soon as he saw us.

Epilogues for Lost Gods

The ground was unsteady so far out of the city. So much of the rubble and nature had been spread across the ground, and it was difficult for Hod to traverse. But Hreidulfr was nothing if not observant, and he brought one of the horses to us.

"Glad you made it in one piece," Hreiduflr said. "It's good to meet you, sir. I've heard so many good things."

Hod held out a hand, and Hreidulfr clasped it. "Nothing too adventurous about an archivist, but I do make a good cup of tea. Do I hear a horse?"

"Astrid's her name. You'll be riding her home. Why don't you get acquainted?" Hreidulfr helped Hod up onto the horse and ensured he was settled in.

Mist approached, her wings folded tightly behind her. A grave look was on her face. "Is it bad in there?"

I nodded. "It's bad. And it's time. I'm done letting the realms rot."

"You're sure you want to fly back?" Mist asked. "You look like shit. You can take the horse. I didn't get these for no reason." She pointed at her wings.

"And if they spot the last Valkyrie, they'll shoot you out of the sky." I gave her the same scowl I always did when the matter came up.

"I know, I know." She looked skyward, longing on her face. "I just miss it, you know?"

Frankly, I did not empathize at all with the feeling, but I nodded anyway. Someday she could have the sky again, and fate willing, I would never be in it again.

I didn't linger any longer. There was too much to do, too much to set into motion. Bracing myself for the feeling of the transformation, I shifted into a hawk again, hating every moment, and rose back into the sky, towards the city.

CHAPTER NINETEEN

LOKI

"I should've told them I was proud."

— Angie, Volume 82

t had taken some time, but we eventually made it to the space underneath the crack in the realm. The fog seemed unwilling to tread there, though it was hard to say why. Maybe, like so many things down in Helheim, it was afraid of the light.

Tired and distraught, we settled in the chunk of land under the tree, next to the small lake. Wherever the light was coming from, it was night there, and the sliver of moonlight had given us enough light to cobble together a fire close to the water's edge. It should have been an opportune time to rest, but that wasn't going to happen for any of us.

Angrboda was working out some of her feelings on the lowest branches of the tree, swinging her hatchet again and again with a force that was going to leave her sore come morning. But either way, she was away from the fire and from us.

She'd refused to say what had broken her from the grip of the fog. It was personal, she'd said, tears in her eyes. Even when she'd once told me about the deaths of her parents and the humiliation she'd suffered at the hands of her sister, she'd never cried. I had no idea what would cause her that kind of pain, and it made me wonder if I knew her at all.

A raven sat in the branches of the tree above her, somehow unperturbed by her outburst. Was it the same raven as before? It seemed too strange to be a coincidence, but there wasn't a single shred of me that had the energy to care. If it was a trap, or if it

136

was Odin himself perched in that tree waiting to kill me in my sleep, let them come.

I felt hollowed out. The trip down memory lane had taken every last bit of feeling from me. As long as there were waking hours and distractions, I'd always been able to escape my nightmares, but this? This had been every last one of them coming for me all at once. The things I kept buried, some of them for centuries, and all of them trying to eat me alive. How much longer did I need to be reminded of what I'd lost? Of the mother who'd wasted away, of the family I'd betrayed, the children who had died—

The spiral would've tightened around me and choked me if it wasn't for the sound of a sharp inhale that interrupted my thoughts.

Despite the heat wafting off the fire, Narvi was sitting dangerously close to the flame, curled up with his arms around his knees. His shoulders were shaking and he was staring into the flame with a look that wavered between terror and emptiness.

I took a deep breath.

Summer wildflowers.

A hot bath in winter.

Fingers running through my hair.

A safe bed.

I methodically took in my surroundings. Long blades of grass around the lake. The heat wafting off the campfire. The bumpy texture of the ground I was sitting on. Staying in the present.

I couldn't afford to slide into one of my moments, not with Narvi in so much pain.

Not for the first time, I tried to get his attention. "Narvi. It's over, Son. You don't have to be afraid anymore." But when I reached out a hand, he leaned away from the touch.

His gaze never moved from the flame, and he said nothing.

We'd gotten through the time since our deaths with an unspoken agreement, he and I. That what happened in our heads was ours to keep to ourselves. That there was a type of camaraderie to knowing that we both suffered things no one else would possibly understand, but that they were our secrets. I'd arrived in Helheim far too late; he'd already shut his feelings away behind a brick wall by the time I'd died, living in Helheim for an eternity with everything he'd suffered. And it was no kindness for me to push my own suffering on him. He didn't deserve that. But we'd kept each other company at a distance for far too long.

This *arrangement* had to end.

I moved to sit next to Narvi and did the one thing I could think of. I threw my arms around him and held him as tightly as I could.

Narvi stiffened at the touch, rigid in my grip. For a long moment, I expected him to fight me off. But that was always more Váli's style. Instead, he froze, barely breathing, waiting for the next thing to happen.

I stroked the top of his head, keeping him close to me, and just waited.

Slowly, the rigidity in his shoulders softened. He started to tremble, and then he melted against me, all tears and gasps, curled against my chest like when he was a child.

"After this," I whispered into his hair. "We're going to see about one of those therapists you and your sister have been on about. And I don't know what I'm doing but I've made a bad example for you, letting us both suffer like this. I don't want you to be in pain anymore, not ever again. And I should've asked, should've pressed you. I wanted to give you the space you needed, but maybe that was never what you needed at all." I kissed his head and squeezed him tighter. "You deserve to finally be happy, and I'm not going to let you do it alone."

Narvi's sobs drowned out anything he was trying to say, but he nodded, his face still pressed into my tunic. He cried for a long time. I wanted to ask so many things, but I didn't know how, not yet. This was a beginning, after all, and sometimes beginnings take a long time to get started.

By the time Narvi cried himself to sleep, Angrboda had finished mutilating the tree and had dropped the wood next to the fire. She glanced at me for a moment, took in Narvi's sleeping form slumped against me, and quietly set her hatchet down. Her hair and skin were slick with sweat and she was breathing deeply, finally succumbing to her exhaustion.

Without a word, she started stripping out of her clothing.

It was strange how routine it felt. I hadn't seen her naked since long before I'd been strapped up in that cave, but there was still something so common about it. She set her belt down carefully, so as not to jangle any of the metal, then pulled her tunic over her head. A thick strip of cloth was wound around her chest a few times, keeping everything in place. One pin removed and that was gone too, leaving her bare-chested. The long open gash in her belly was no surprise; she'd told me how she'd died. But it was when she turned her back to me that my breath hitched.

Tattooed from shoulder to hip were a wolf, a serpent, and a half-dead woman. Our children.

It had never been there before. She must've gotten it done after we'd separated, or perhaps after she'd died. I tried to take in every detail, but in the time I'd been looking, she'd stripped down to her underwear and was walking away from the fire, towards the lake.

As carefully as I was able, I lowered Narvi onto the ground. He stirred a little, but he was sleeping in that deep way that fighting for your life will force on you. A tuft of hair was lying across his face. I took a moment to move it back into place, staring at how magnificent he was. My boy. So brave and broken and beloved.

Certain a bath was the right idea, I set my clothing next to Angrboda's and followed her down to the water. She'd summoned up a small seidr lantern to see by. Looking up in the middle of rinsing her face off, she paused, then continued like I wasn't there. She'd never been shy and wasn't about to start now.

The water was cool when I dipped my toes in. Not quite cold enough to shrivel a person's balls, but not far off either. I'd been cautious of the water when we'd first arrived, but Angrboda had done some stomping and rock-throwing and yelling, and nothing had come out to kill us. I tried to remember that as I waded in up to my hips, close enough to Angrboda to talk without waking Narvi.

"Feeling better?" I splashed water onto my arms, watching the grime roll away.

"Nothing a little hard work won't fix." Angrboda gave me a sidelong look. "And the boy?"

I glanced back to the fire. He was still sleeping. "I don't think he's been okay for a very long time." I took a long breath and debated if I should say it at all. "What kind of father am I to just let that happen?"

"That's what parents do, Loki." She sat down, the water reaching the tops of her shoulders, and began to delicately clean the dust from her bauble-covered hair. "We can choose to do nothing and let things happen as they may, or we can run ourselves ragged trying to prevent them. Fate doesn't need our permission. It all just happens anyway."

I sat down across from her, a chill wracking through me. "You say that like we were ever normal parents, doing things for the right reasons."

"We ended the Aesir's reign over the nine realms. What better reason could there be?"

I leaned back, letting the water seep into my hair, into my ears. Despite the glamour, the water trickled into the edges of the wound in my chest, and I straightened. We were all dead; it wouldn't kill us, but sometimes it got trapped and the smell of rehydrated corpse wasn't one you wanted to have following you around. "It's not that simple and you know it. What we did destroyed most of the nine and killed nearly everyone in it."

"Then so be it. That's the price of starting again." Her face was so full of quiet conviction it unnerved me.

"I don't understand how you can carry it so easily, Bo." I looked away. It was more comforting to watch my fingers making ripples in the lake. "I don't have the same rage that I used to and now every fucking face I see on the street is a life I ended. How do you live with that?"

Angrboda scoffed. "Because all you see is the loss. I'm focused on the glory, the

139

change that happened because of us. I honour the sacrifices my children made to avenge the people the Aesir fucked over for centuries. I'm not going to make their deaths worthless with my guilt."

I stopped making ripples and looked up. "But you have it? Guilt?"

Anger welled up in her face. "There's nothing for me to feel guilty for. We gave birth to a revolution, you and I. Revolution requires sacrifice, and blood is the only price anyone ever considers *enough* to change for. Why can't you just move on from these things? Why do you have to carry all this melancholy around in your heart like it's your birthright?"

"Because maybe it is." I strained the water from my hair, my chest clenching as the words formed in my mind. "Because nothing has been light for me, nothing. Except Sigyn, and I—"

Angrboda sighed and ran her hands down her face, then craned her neck sharply until it cracked. "You talk about her like she's a fucking perfect example of existence. You want to talk about all this darkness in you but I'm the one who saw that darkness and loved you anyways. Because of it."

It was a struggle to keep my voice tempered enough to let Narvi sleep. "You keep saying that, but do you hear the hypocrisy, Bo? You talk about how she can't accept my darkness, but it's the *only* thing you want! If I show a modicum of weakness, you berate me for it. You'd have me force all this grief down until I can't remember it anymore but *it hasn't worked.* I've *tried.*"

"You should be able to accept what you are." She shook her head in disbelief. "It's not that fucking complicated, Loki."

"It's not who I am!" I brushed my hair back, growing more exasperated by the moment. "I'm not proud of that darkness like you are. I fucked up my own life and followed my hatred until it led to you. And I loved you, Angrboda; I did. You're important to me in a hundred ways, but you're not good for me. You bring out things in me I can't afford to nourish. You want me to be the man you met, but I don't. I won't, not again." I pointed up to the shore, at Narvi. "My son needs a better father. A better example."

Angrboda scoffed. "Ah, yes, like the example you're setting on this fool's quest."

"We're helping save a realm."

"You're helping your wife destroy a city."

The words startled me. "She wants to save her people."

"And what do you think that costs?" Angrboda tilted her head, eyeing me as if trying to understand me. "Asgard won't go home quietly. She'll have to kill them to end it. And that's no skin off my back; let them die. But in order to defend her people, she needs to murder the rest."

I took a step forward, rage brewing in my chest. I wouldn't let her cast Sigyn in that kind of light. "That's semantics and you know it. You've toyed with the context."

Angrboda scoffed. "You? Talking to me about changing the context? That's all justification is. Every side of every battle thinks it's doing the right thing, so how can that be true for everyone at once? When you talk about Sigyn and this mighty quest, you use words like *save* and *protect*. But in the end, you're killing more people and to the victor go the spoils, just like anyone else. Is that making amends for Ragnarok? Sending more corpses to Hel's door? How is that any better than what you and I did together?"

The words took the wind from me. I knew these things. I'd always known these things. That war was never so simple. You had to learn it if you were part of Odin's court, watching him play god with the lives of mortals. I'd been so focused on earning a new thread by whatever means necessary that it hadn't occurred to me that I might fall into the same trap.

I swallowed. "It's not like that. It won't be."

Angrboda jabbed her finger into my chest, just above the place where my wound would be. "Have you already forgotten when she lied to save herself and her children? Threw us all at the mercy of her father by crying reptile tears? I respect the move, sure, but it wasn't something a good, honest girl would do. Mark my words, Loki. Someday you're going to look up and find that she looks an awful lot like Odin."

"Fuck you." The words were out before I could think. She'd gone too far. "You're wrong."

She shrugged. "I guess we'll see."

Before I could muster a response, she turned and waded back out of the water. I stood, dumbfounded, and let the words sink as deep into my bones as the cold.

CHAPTER TWENTY

SIGYN

"The holidays were always best. We didn't always agree,
but our family had a lot of love. Not many of us came to
Helheim, but we hold a seat for each of them at the table.
And we miss them."

— *Rowan, Volume 56*

I t was hard to say when Asgard would come for us.

Soon. It would take at least a day to march that many horseless soldiers across the realms to our doorstep, and they hadn't been nearly prepared to leave when we were in the city. We had a few days. More if we were lucky.

We were so rarely lucky.

As soon as I landed, I sent word around the city for the council to gather in the chambers. When I arrived, two of the apprentices were bent over a spread of papers, working diligently. Wrong place, wrong time. "Up, now, both of you. Find every council member you can and send them here at once. Don't walk; run."

With a fear in their eyes like my father used to inspire, they leapt from their seats and ran out. The hurried pace of their boots echoed until they were out of earshot.

My head was throbbing. We'd planned on more time, more resources, more everything. But nothing ever goes to plan. Ever.

Where the fuck was Loki?

I sat down, trying to catch my breath. It might be the last quiet moment, the last chance to think. There was so much to lose. My son. His partner. My city, my colleagues, friends—Alyssa. If we lost, they would kill or capture every last one of us and I would never get to see what the future was supposed to hold for the people I cherished.

Epilogues for Lost Gods

What I would've given in that moment for a glimpse of what came after. The fate on my tapestry had shown me only a woman in a crown and a city behind her. Nothing else. I'd used it to guide me towards this community, this city we'd built together, but now I felt adrift. Failure could come in so many ways.

I was tired of the uncertainty. Of feeling like I needed to hold everything up. Things had been so wrong for as long as I could remember, and even though I'd grabbed this opportunity with both hands, I was ready for it to be over.

If we survived this, I was going to chase something other than misery. I had to.

I propped my elbows on the table and leaned on my hands, pressing my palms into my eyes. One moment of weakness, one sob, one tear. I gave my grief that long. Because doubt had no place in this room. I couldn't allow it.

Boots drew near and I got up, turning my back to the door and composing myself.

"Mother?" Váli practically crashed through the door. "What's happening?"

"The others are on their way back from Asgard." I let my hair fall in front of my face to hide whatever emotion was left on it and turned towards him. "Hod is safe but Asgard is readying for war. They're coming."

"Fuck." Váli pushed his hair back, settling both palms on the back of his head. He strode a couple of steps in one direction, a couple back. "We're not ready."

"Yes, we are, and you'll tell that to anyone who says anything to the contrary," I said, slipping back into the Sigyn that the situation demanded. "We're going to need morale on our side. You know the plan; you know what to do. You've been working on this for years. Fólkheim's army is yours to command."

He stopped his pacing and gave me a look of desperation.

I strode across the room and put my hands on his shoulders. "You have worked so hard for this day. We will live by the hands of the people you and Hreidulfr trained or we'll drag our enemies to Helheim with us. If we die, we go to Hel's table to be with our family. There are worse things in these nine realms, Váli. Fear can't rule you if death is nothing to be afraid of."

More boots came from the hall.

"Go." I nodded my head towards the door. "I love you."

"Love you too." He pressed a stubbly kiss to my cheek and burst out the door just before a pair of council members arrived.

They came in a steady rush after that. I repeated the same thing again and again— *it's time, they're coming*—and sent them off to prepare for war. Anyone who couldn't fight or help with the preparations would be brought into the stronghold of the mountain to shield them from the battle. Anyone who could use their mind or body to contribute would be put to work. There were barricades to be raised, Modernist

143

machines to be put in place, people to evacuate, food to distribute and protect.

So many things and not enough *time*.

"You're the last one, yes?" I asked the head of the Dwarven construction guild.

"You'd know better than I would, Goddess." He hefted a heavy bag back over his shoulder. "You know they're not as ready as I'd like, don't you?"

"They're as ready as they are, and that's what counts. Walk with me." I headed out the door, aiming for the exit to the city. "Weapons distribution is going to need a hand and without some of your people, they'll fall short. Once that's done, have them gear up. If you see anyone without a task, give them one. Today the hive works together or it's all for nothing."

"That, it does." He followed me out of the cliffside and into the inner square. Already the city was teeming with people running to and fro. The sound of hammers and shouting, the collective chaos…it was almost heartwarming to see. They had practised for this and maybe, just maybe, it would be enough.

"Goddess, I don't mean to cast doubt, but your husband…" He trailed off, wringing one hand in the other.

"I know. It was a long shot that they would make it in time. We're just going to have to figure this out on our own."

He just nodded and walked into the bustle of the city.

The question stirred up a storm of thoughts I'd been trying to hide from. Were Loki and Narvi on their way? Were they already dead, wiped from these realms forever? If they never came and we won anyway, how many years would I need to live without them?

How long could I bear that?

The tears welled in my eyes, blurring out the city, and I pushed the emotion back down.

So much still needed to be done, and my future would have to wait.

I took a drink of water and tried to focus. My candle had nearly burned itself out, only a tiny chunk of it left to see by. I'd been bent over lists and figures and maps for hours. It was always hard to say how late it was inside the cliffs, and when it got quiet, when the late hour stopped the boots and whispers, it felt like a cave.

Like a trap.

Crawling. It always started with a tightening of muscle in my chest that felt like something was crawling up from my stomach, through my abdomen, into my throat. It made it hard to breathe, dried out my mouth. And sometimes when I let it go on, when I couldn't fight back the memory, I could hear him screaming. Screaming for forgiveness and release and death.

Epilogues for Lost Gods

That wasn't what came, though. This time, in the real space outside my head, I heard something else. The quiet mirth of familiar voices.

I looked up and a second later, Hreidulfr and Hod were in the doorway of the council chamber, arms interlocked.

"Are we interrupting anything?" Hreidulfr nodded his head toward Hod. "This one wouldn't go to his room without meeting with you first."

"I'm not a *child*," Hod said, laughing. "I would have snuck off without you but I'm not familiar with the grounds, and you'd probably have found me lost in a storage closet a week later."

"Sit down, please." I ran my hands down my face and stretched. Something in my back snapped in a very satisfying manner and the blood rushed back to my face. "I could use a break."

"Well, I need a bath and some sleep, so I'll leave you two alone." Hreidulfr brought Hod toward the table and waited for him to sit. "Don't get into any trouble."

I gave him a tired smile as he turned and left the room, then asked Hod, "Did you enjoy the ride back?"

"Did I relish riding a horse against a muscular man's back at three times the speed that I normally get around? Why, yes, I did." He laughed. "It was bumpy. It's been a long time since I was on a horse. But for the first time in years, I felt like I was on my way towards something better."

"You are, I hope." I meant to say more, but I found that I didn't know how to strengthen that wording. Anything more promising than that felt like a lie.

Hod edged towards the table, leaning his elbows on it. His brow was furrowed. "You don't sound well, sister."

I gave him my best impression of someone carefree. "I'm *fine*. Really."

"You're *such* a liar and a bad one at that. If I had money to bet, I'd say you're wearing week-old clothes, you've got shadows under your eyes, and you're malnourished."

I caught a glimpse of myself in the surface of the metal water pitcher in front of me and made a face. "You can't possibly know that."

"I know some people don't change and you've never been that good at taking care of yourself. Now try it again without the lies. Are you alright?"

Sighing deeply, I leaned back in my chair. "I'm the organizing factor in a city that's about to trample or be trampled *by* another city. I have a morally decrepit husband in Helheim trying to change his and our son's fate to help us survive this. My other son just turned back into a person for the first time in an eternity, which means walking by him and his partner and picking up nothing but sexual tension. And I might die in a couple of days but I'm not even that mad about it." I paused for a breath. "Is that honest enough for you?"

Hod was smiling. *Smiling.*

"What's so funny?"

"Most of that, really." He tapped his fingers on the table, the metal of a thin gold ring clicking against the wood. "Yours is going to make an amazing story someday."

"You're not starting your new collection of stories with mine. Find someone with the energy to tell it."

"Alright, whatever you say. But eventually, you'll tell me." Hod sat back, relaxing into the wooden chair. "What can I do to help with all this impending doom?"

I shook my head, resisting the urge to press my forehead into the tabletop. "I don't know. I really don't. I'm too tired to think anymore. I can't even get my head on straight."

"Well, there's never been anything straight about either of us, has there."

I stared at him in silent irritation.

"What?" Hod asked. "Do you not get the joke? You know, like the Modernists use the word *straight*, like—"

"I know what *straight* means. I have caught up on *some* of the phrases since I was locked in a cave."

Despite my laugh, Hod's face fell into a quick, deep sorrow.

I stopped. "Oh no, don't do that. Don't make it strange."

Hod drew a long breath. "I just wish there was something I could've done."

"You were dead. Something we had a hand in and you—"

"Our father killed me." Hod's fingers were digging into the arms of his chair, a scowl on his lips. "I heard what part Loki had in it. He shouldn't have. But no one made Odin do what he did. No one made him chain up Loki's children or keep you in the dark about your fate. No one put a spear in his hands and forced him to plunge it into my chest. My own father chose that. Someday I'd like to know that he paid the price for all those choices."

I scooted my chair closer to his, letting the wood scrape on the ground. I set my hand on his. "When I saw Loki, I made him take me to the prison where they keep the gods. They live in tiny cells, apart from each other. Their lives are small and tedious, and their freedom is gone. Odin won't hurt you again."

Hod nodded slowly, lips pursed. "And Eyvindr?"

"I didn't see him. Loki told me that he lives in the city and keeps to himself. I don't imagine that he finds Loki to be the best reminder of good times." I gave his hand a squeeze, trying to be reassuring. "Whatever comes next, you'll see him again."

He nodded again and screwed up his face as he stifled a yawn.

"That's enough melancholy for one night." I stood and gave him an insistent tap

146

on the shoulder. "Let me show you to your room so you can get some rest. Tomorrow I'll have someone tour you around so you can get the lay of the land."

"Fine, fine." Hod stood and took the arm that I offered him. "But later I want to hear more about this place and everything that's happened since I've been gone. Hreidulfr tells me you have a pretty woman now."

I slapped his arm, the blood rushing to my face. "I do not!"

"The lady doth protest too much, methinks."

I bristled. "What? What does that even mean? Who speaks that way? Hod!"

But Hod only laughed.

CHAPTER TWENTY-ONE

LOKI

"It was preventable and we learned nothing. Absolutely nothing."

— Estelle, Volume 20

❝ Well," Narvi said, staring up, "I welcome this obstruction. At least it's a change of scenery. I swear, if someone wrote a saga about our journey, it would just be a story about some people walking across a realm for twelve hundred pages."

I had to laugh because at this point the only other option was to lie down and cry.

Angrboda huffed, holding up the map again, even though there was nothing on it that could tell us more than we already knew. She lowered it and glared. "What the fuck are we supposed to do now?"

The realm had opened up into an uneventful plain a full day ago and we'd been trekking across it ever since. The majority of the scenery had consisted of bare shrubs and disgusting bugs and a haphazardly located stream or two, but that was it. Now we'd come to this impasse, this wall of rock ahead of us that stretched from ground to ceiling all across the cavern. It was like we'd reached the end of the realm entirely, which couldn't be true because the root of Yggdrasil was supposed to be on the other side.

"Go through the mines, I suppose," answered Narvi.

Angrboda pointed to something in the distance. It looked like a set of old buildings but it was hard to tell anything about them from so far away. "That's got to be it."

She started towards it without another word and we followed, trekking over stone and odd bits of brush. The closer we came to the buildings, the more debris was strewn around. Wooden beams, forged iron pieces, and a lot of scattered raw ore.

Epilogues for Lost Gods

Four structures stood in varying degrees of bad health: one so old and decrepit it was in pieces on the ground, and three others still standing but covered in rust and rot. And most disconcerting by far was the undisturbed skeleton of a person, lying halfway out of one of the open doors.

A shiver ran up my spine as I looked around. "Don't you feel welcome here?" I asked, spotting more bones scattered around the mining site, a few here, a few there. "I feel very much at home, I think. Nothing at all amiss, no."

"Shut up, Loki." Angrboda walked straight up to the door with the body and stepped over it. She gazed around the inside, then stepped back out. "At least twenty bodies."

"Shocking, I'm shocked."

She made a face at me.

Narvi pulled a string of leather from around his wrist and tied up his hair into a rough ponytail. "There was mention of this place in a book once, but no more than a mention. It didn't say anything beyond the day-to-day operations and especially not that everyone had just…died."

"*Died* is a generous word. I'd personally lean towards *murdered*." I knelt down to push the bones with a finger, looking them over.

"Mines can have gas deposits that suffocate miners," Narvi answered. "They could've hit something and it either escaped into the open or it had a delayed effect on them."

"Does gas have claws?" Angrboda held up a femur that was striped through with deep gashes.

"Maybe they found something else down there."

"Whatever happened, they've been dead a long time." Narvi started walking around the mining site, making his way towards the wall of the cavern. "How likely is it that whatever killed them is still alive?"

Angrboda raised an eyebrow. "If we're still alive after all this, it could be too."

I shrugged. "I mean, we're tentatively alive at best."

Angrboda did not like that joke either.

We finished looking the site over and went to look for the mine entrance in the stone. It wasn't immediately visible, hidden behind a pile of wood and debris and furniture. The kinds of things you'd pile against a door if you wanted to keep something inside. The barricade was still perfectly intact, however, which didn't do anything to explain why everyone had died very bloody deaths.

"Well, I don't love that." I took a deep breath and let it out. "Alright. There's got to be a map or a journal or something around here. Narvi, see if you can start a fire and heat up some water. I feel like it's going to be a long walk through that mine, if there's even a way to the other side."

149

While Narvi settled down to make a fire, I went to one of the remaining buildings and tried to open the door. It was stuck, probably half-rotten from the years of neglect. I drove a shoulder into it and the door budged. Again, and it came loose, swinging open and toppling off its hinges.

The inside was dark. I summoned up a lantern of my own and the room's dingy, dusty interior revealed itself. The sleeping quarters. Beds lined the walls, some of them scattered into the middle of the floor. One was turned up like a barricade. While there weren't a lot of bones inside—certainly not as many as out there—half a dozen people had died fighting *something* inside.

Angrboda appeared behind me and I nearly let out a scream. "Fuck! If you could perhaps not sneak around in a mass grave, that would be lovely."

"Wimp." Angrboda elbowed past me. While she was very capable of a friendly ribbing, it was obvious there was nothing friendly about it.

"Still not over our conversation, hmm?" I made my way to the opposite side of the room from Angrboda, and started to rifle through old personal belongings, dust churning through the air. Clothes, sketchbooks, dice, smallclothes, but nothing helpful.

"Oh, I've been over everything about you for a long time. You're not as special as you give yourself credit for." She kept her back to me as she spoke. She'd never been able to look me in the eyes when she was truly hurt. Too bold for anything that vulnerable.

Fine. Two could play at that game, even if I did feel a little out of practice. "I hope that level of denial is comforting. I'll believe you when you're not quite so touchy about the subject."

Angrboda whipped around to face me. "I am *not* touchy and if you say it again, my boot is going to touch your face."

"Alright, alright!" I held my hands up, grinning from ear to ear. "You seem entirely unaffected by murdering the realms, my apologies."

Rage radiated off her in waves. She was like an ox in a room full of mirrors, ransacking every drawer and chest she came across, tossing all the old belongings onto the floor with the bones they had once belonged to. I knew better than to prod her any further, though the temptation was certainly there.

Something caught my eye. A *hnefatafl* board that was nearly identical to the one I used to play with the boys when they were young. I picked it up, and a roll of worn, coal-smudged parchment fell into view. Abandoning the board, I carefully pulled out the parchment, wiped the dust from it, and unrolled it on the closest bed.

After squinting at the parchment for a moment, I realized with a start that it was a map of the mine shafts.

"Bo," I called over my shoulder.

Epilogues for Lost Gods

The rattling stopped and she grunted a response.

"I've got it."

As soon as we left the musty building, the smell of burning wood filled the air. Narvi had boiled some water in his little travelling pot and had set out our mugs to warm our hands by. As we sat down, he looked over the map.

"These two pieces are the same map." He pointed to two different sections, separated down the middle. "This one is a top-down view, while this one is from the side. It's a bit convoluted, honestly, but I think I can match them."

"I mean, we're only looking for a straight passage through, aren't we?" I wrapped my hands around my mug and let the warmth seep back into my skin.

"It doesn't look like there *is* a straight path to the other side." He pointed out a series of forked paths that turned into more forked paths. "This one leads to the other side, but none of the rest do. And these lead down, not out."

Left, second right, left, left, first right, left. That was the series of passages leading out. Easy enough. I'd memorized much worse for less important reasons, like the exact location of particular bottles in Odin's wine cellar.

"I've spent more than enough time drinking with Dwarves to know how dangerous the mines can be." Angrboda spoke as she let the steam waft out of her mug and into her face. "Stuff can live down there. And even if it doesn't, if you get lost, you'll never find your way out."

Narvi made an incredulous face. "How hard can it be? Just follow the walls."

Angrboda shook her head. "You ever stand in the pitch dark? Not the dark of your room with all those glowing maggots outside. I mean *pitch* dark. So absent of light, there's nothing but black. When you're in that kind of darkness, you can guide yourself with the wall, sure, but there's no way to tell which direction is up and which is down. Miners that end up without a lantern, they think they're going up. A week later their friends find their body at the deepest part of the mine, deeper than anyone ought to have gone."

"Lovely," I muttered.

"Alright, so we stick together and make sure we each have a seidr lantern." Narvi tapped his fingers on his cup anxiously. "And hope that whatever was down there isn't anymore."

The mineshaft was wider than I'd expected. There was enough room for two side by side, someone trailing along in the back, and the fact that Angrboda's head didn't hit the ceiling told us it hadn't been Dwarves that had carved it out. It smelled old and wet, like dirt and mould and metal. It was both too similar to my own cave and also not at all alike.

I focused on the things that weren't the same. I couldn't get trapped in my own head, not in here.

Each of us had summoned a seidr lantern to hold in our palms. Angrboda had the map, and Narvi was keeping an eye on it, not quite trusting her to guide us. Which was fair enough, since she wasn't the most rational, thoughtful person in the realms, and tended to think with her fists.

Actually, if I thought about it too hard, she was a little bit like Thor, and that made me suddenly concerned about my taste in lovers.

A strange sensation rose on the back of my neck. I turned to look behind me, the seidr lantern in my palm illuminating the tunnel. No one was there. The others kept moving forward, the sound of their boots slowly moving away from me. I had to catch up, but the second I turned my back, that feeling returned. Like someone was watching us.

The first junction wasn't far from the entrance of the mine. The eerie quiet made it difficult to tell how long we had been walking. The air was stale and gritty. Bones littered the ground. Bones that had most certainly belonged to people.

I wished someone would speak. I couldn't think of anything to say, and it wasn't as if anyone was in a conversational mood, but the walls were closing in on me, metaphorically speaking. The space was cold and dank, and I couldn't see more than a few paces in any direction. The seidr lantern wasn't that strong, and the dark was infinite.

Something moved behind me, rocks falling along with it. I turned, but I saw nothing in the dim light.

It could've been anything. A lizard, a mouse, a bat. There was no reason for it to be vicious. Vicious. Venomous. A snake.

I saw it so clearly for just a moment. The underside of the snake's jaw, soft and vulnerable, and the tiny points of its sharp, venomous teeth dangling above. Little droplets collecting and falling and searing.

A cave. Damp and mould and sulphur and excruciating pain.

My lantern was flickering and Angrboda had started to sneer at me.

I counted the things I could see. One, two, three belts. Eleven pieces of bone ravelled into Angrboda's hair. Five working eyes. Six shoes.

Seven tunnels spread out ahead of us.

We stopped and Angrboda opened up the map. She looked up, a scowl on her lips, then back at the map, then up again. "There's too many."

"What?" I leaned forward to look around her shoulder.

Angrboda huffed. "The map has six tunnels."

"We need the one on the left." I pointed to the correct one on the map.

"Sure," said Narvi, looking over the map carefully. "But did they add the 7th tunnel next to it? On the opposite side completely? We have no way of knowing which is the newest one."

I stepped forward and held the seidr lantern into one of the thin tunnels, looking down as far as the light would go. I went to the next, and the next. "They all look the fucking same."

"Did you think there'd be a giant sign that said *exit this way*?" Angrboda scoffed.

I gave an emphatic shrug. "I don't know, maybe. Better than standing here and doing nothing."

"You know what they say: stick to what you're good at." Angrboda's grin wasn't playful; it was downright cruel.

"Ah yes, I'm good at doing nothing. I've always just stood back and done *nothing*."

"Hey!" Narvi snapped his fingers. "Can we please focus? Being stuck in here isn't going to be any better with you two bickering."

"Bickering is a great word for what your father does." Angrboda shoved the map into Narvi's arms, practically balling it up in the process. "He hasn't had any *fight* left in him since the realms burned."

"Really?" I crossed my arms over my chest and leaned on one leg. "This is what you're stuck on? That I'm not big and bad enough for you anymore? Move on, Bo. We're all just trying to *move on*."

"That's rich, coming from you. Always pining away in your castle for Little Miss Aesir." Her voice was getting louder. A flush of anger rose in her cheeks. "You drag me into this fucking adventure, into these fucking mines, and spend half the trip throwing all my work and my sacrifices in my face and what? Expect me to be grateful?"

"No one is saying any of that!" I snapped.

"You are." She drove a finger into my chest, her snarling teeth too close for comfort. "You don't have any respect for me or for what your children did, you—"

A high-pitched whine built in the air, coming from nowhere. It filled the space, echoing in the tunnels, impossible to track to an origin.

"Did you both forget the fucking *mass murder* outside?" Narvi snapped.

A little, yes.

That sense of being watched was stronger than ever. My gaze darted from tunnel to tunnel, trying to find whatever had found us. I still couldn't see anything, but it was here; I had no doubt about that.

Every hair on my body stood up. Something was beside me, something that hadn't been there a second ago. I turned my head slowly.

If ever there was a moment to piss my pants like a little boy, this was it. Above me was the shade of a woman, her eyes sunken and her long dress in tatters. She stood almost against me, her metal lantern hanging in her boney hand. She floated off the ground, her bare toes not touching the dirt, and what skin was visible was flaking off her like birch bark.

A wraith—a gruvrå.

"Oh gods," I breathed.

Her eyes turned to me and a grating voice burst in my head.

Desecrators. Trespassers. Despoilers.

I grabbed Narvi's arm and pulled him into motion, aiming for the second tunnel on the left. "*Run!*"

The mine spirit screamed, the sound shaking dust from the ceilings of the tunnels as we ran, Angrboda taking up the rear. I had no idea if we were in the correct tunnel, but we couldn't just wait for the fucking gruvrå to skin us alive.

The air was too hard to breathe, the floor uneven and slippery. The lantern followed above us, rapidly flickering in and out as I struggled to focus enough to keep it alive. It bobbed and ducked, throwing confusing shadows. Light, dark, light, dark, over and over. I prayed, begging the fates to just *please let this passage be the right one*, until we burst from the tunnel into a wider room. But all the passages went down, not straight through the wall.

We'd taken the wrong path.

"Fuck!" Angrboda bent over to catch her breath. The gruvrå was getting closer, far too close for my liking.

"We have to go back." Narvi looked around frantically. "Can we kill it?"

I shook my head. "I don't think so. I could see through it; I don't think there's anything to injure. We just need to wait until it's here and get around it—"

Narvi screamed as the gruvrå appeared out of thin air beside him and swiped a clawed hand at him. Angrboda was quick, moving in front of Narvi to attempt to rebuff the blow. The claws left a searing mark on Angrboda's skin, but the gruvrå's arm passed right through her body.

Incorporeal *and* deadly, great.

"Back out! Right now, go!" I ran back to the tunnel we'd come out of, trying to ignore the burning in my legs and lungs. We had to make it back out of this tunnel, pick the correct one, and keep going.

"The mine map! I dropped it!" Narvi called back, still running.

"Second right, left, left, first right, left!" If I'd ever learned anything, it was always to expect the worst. Memorizing a path was the smallest of preparations. Now as long as the gruvrå didn't pop out in front of us before we reached the junction…

She didn't.

"This one!" I pointed down the next path, urging them along.

Angrboda ran first, her boots a dull thud as she sped forward. The tunnel ended quickly, into a junction of two new paths. Left. Down another tunnel. Left again. But we were slowing, each of us panting. We couldn't run forever. How thick was this fucking mine?

The gruvrå appeared again, sliding out of the stone with her lantern held out. She shrieked and lunged at me, forcing me to jump back. Trying to slow my breathing, I drew up energy and let a short spurt of runes slip off my tongue before the next breath. A palmful of teal wildfire appeared and I lobbed it at the gruvrå. She covered her face, but the fire slipped right through her, bouncing against the mine wall and disappearing.

"Fuck."

No respect. The gruvrå's voice echoed in our minds. *Return my silence.*

"Gladly! Let us leave!"

But she pressed towards us, blocking the way we were headed, forcing us back.

"Gotta go through her," Angrboda whispered.

"But—"

"No other way. Three. Two—"

Angrboda dove forward, curling into a roll as she came out the other side of the gruvrå and got to her feet, covered in dirt.

Alright.

I shoved Narvi forward, throwing him off balance. Angrboda reached out and pulled him up as his body passed through the mine spirit. It hissed and clawed, catching Angrboda on the elbow again, leaving another mark and the smell of burnt skin.

Then it was my turn. But she was focused on me, claws out and ready. She wasn't going to miss this time.

I took a deep breath, steadying myself. Then I spat a string of runes as I dove, praying to make it to the other side.

Bones crunched and moved and everything about my body rearranged until I was something new, something harder to hit. Her claws nearly clipped my wing as I glided past, swooping around Angrboda and out into the tunnel. Their boots followed, and even though I'd lost my seidr lantern, I could see the passages ahead with the clear, crisp vision of a hawk. In one eye, at least.

"You'd better know where you're going, Loki!" Angrboda called behind me.

Lucky for all of us, I did.

They followed me as we escaped the passage and took the next. Every second I feared the gruvrå was going to burst out of the wall and eat me whole.

Narvi screamed.

I stopped short and turned back to find that Narvi had fallen. Angrboda had already sped past me, and nothing stood between the spirit's claws and my son.

She raised her hand above her head, pulling back to strike. *Defiler. Fortune seeker. My home. My grave. Mine.*

I flew through her midsection and into her face.

The gruvrå startled and backed away, trying to get my bird shape out of her line of sight. I kept pressing into her, flapping my wings, darting back and forth. She was hard to hit, in part because she wasn't solid, and in part because my ability to hit a moving object wasn't what it once had been. She swiped at me and I dove through her, and back into her face again.

Narvi hadn't moved.

I let out a shriek, the only thing I could do to tell him to get the fuck up and run.

The sound was enough to stir him and he crawled toward Angrboda, whose hand was outstretched and ready to grab him.

I dodged another claw, this one nearly hitting the mark.

With the others safe, I dove through her midsection again and flew toward safety, down the tunnel and into the next junction. One last tunnel, if I'd done it correctly.

Fresh air, at last. Light. Not true light, of course, but more than this pitch black. I had no voice to tell them to move faster but they didn't need telling. They ran hard toward the exit of the mines, nearly catching up with the beating of my wings, and then all at once, we were outside, free of the confines of the tunnel. Narvi took three extra steps and collapsed onto the fresh earth, holding his stomach with both hands. His corset had moved in the fray and his insides were trying to become outsides again.

Angrboda stayed standing and ready, not far from the mine's exit. I let the shape of the hawk slip away, trying to be ready to fight alongside her, no matter how exhausted I was. And the gruvrå did appear.

She screamed, her voice carrying into the cavern around us. She didn't leave, though. She just dug her claws into the stone above her and tore. The rock pulled free, falling to the ground in front of her. She tore again and again until the wall began to crack. A rumble sounded and the wall became a shattering crumble of rock, spilling into the exit of the mine and sealing it up.

Her haunting, eerie voice travelled through the layer of stone.

STAY. OUT.

That was fine. I didn't feel like going back in there anyways.

The space we had emptied out into was enormous. The ceiling was littered with hanging blue maggot-lights, higher than any building I'd seen. An enormous tree root crawled through it, bending down the walls of the room and tapering out into a thousand small roots. At the base of the roots, where there should have been an enormous wyrm, was…nothing. The Nidhogg had always been there, or at least that was what all the legends said. For the cavern to be empty…that was disconcerting.

"Where is it?" Angrboda collapsed beside me, pulling the waterskin from her belt.

"Maybe we've finally caught a break?" asked Narvi.

I scoffed. "Have you ever known anything to be that easy?"

CHAPTER TWENTY-TWO

SIGYN

*"When it came down to it, I turned my back on them, for
her. And I've never regretted it a day in my life. I'd have
fought the sun for her."*

— *An, Volume 19*

Three days was what Asgard had given us.

Mist had returned from her scouting trip to report that an army was heading our way. They'd be on our doorstep by midday tomorrow, depending on how long they slept.

One final night in this realm. That was all that was guaranteed.

"—and next I knew, Váli was barrellin' down the hill, screamin' bloody murder, stark naked with a herd of goats on his tail!" Hreidulfr laughed, bent over in his chair. "I never saw a thing as funny as that all my life."

The story—as much of it as I'd heard through my melancholy thoughts—drew a smile to my face. This was why I'd asked them to my room and told them to bring the wine. If it was to be my last night before the end, I wanted it to be with the people I loved most.

Váli was sitting on the bed next to Hod, staring at the floor with embarrassment on his face. "It wasn't my fault! I wish you didn't remember it."

"Oh, I'm really glad he does." Alyssa was perched on the top of the dresser, drink in hand. "It's exactly what I needed to hear."

"It's alright," Hod nudged Váli with his shoulder. "I've heard a lot more mortifying stories than that. A *lot*."

Váli managed a smirk and looked up at me. His smile faded. "You alright?"

I waved the comment away. "I'm fine. Just listening."

In truth, I'd been thinking of many things. My life before Ragnarok. My life after this. I was thinking of Loki and his *moments* and wondering if he was alright, down there in the dark. I was wondering if down there in the dark was so bad, in the long run.

At least it had pretty shimmering blue maggot lights.

Hreidulfr was watching me too. "As if none of us have seen that look on your face before, ma'am. What's got under your skin?"

I sighed and took a long drink. "I'm distracted. It's not as if a war's about to start or anything."

"You need more wine." Hreidulfr took one of the bottles from the bedside table and leaned over to fill my cup.

Váli held out a hand, gesturing to stop. "Maybe take it easy. There's a lot at stake tomorrow and we should all be sober by morning."

I scoffed, already feeling the warmth of the wine in my blood. "Part of me doesn't care what happens tomorrow. Just a little part, but it's there. After everything that's happened, I feel disconnected from it somehow. Like I've seen all this before and I know how it ends. It makes me tired, inside and out…I'm tired of fighting for my life."

The room grew quiet, everyone staring into their cups. I'd gone and made everyone depressed. Well done, Sigyn.

"I didn't want to say anything," Alyssa said, dipping a finger into her wine and swirling it around. "But I'm terrified. I've never been a fighter, only a thinker. I've never been in a battle, not once."

Váli rolled his eyes. "You've already done more than your share—"

"It's not about that." She pursed her lips, weighing whether or not to say what she needed to. "When Ragnarok came, it was entirely luck that I was already in Vanaheim. It was luck that I got inside the cliffs, that I hid in a room that didn't flood or collapse. That was how I fought for my life, by running. And I saw what the end looked like when it came. Fire and blood and darkness. Everything smelled like copper and meat. The people I hid with, we were alone for days and I—" A sob caught in her throat.

I set down my cup and went to her, wrapping her in my arms. She clung to me, her face on my shoulder as she let out a soft, controlled cry. The kind when you know it's too late to go unnoticed, but there are people around. When she sat straight, she wiped away a stray tear and nodded. I moved to the side but kept my hand on hers.

"Sorry. I don't want to spoil the evening. I just…I have to get ready for this too. And I'm scared. I'm not sure how I'm supposed to go out there tomorrow and pretend I'm not."

Váli laughed. "Listen, Modernist, everyone in this city is scared shitless. Every single one. Except maybe her—" He pointed at me. "—and the only way most of us can be honest about it is with a few glasses of wine and a few close friends who won't tell a soul."

"No one is born brave," Hod said, a comforting smile on his face. "It's something we practice and earn. You have to choose the hard path more often than not."

"And have a good reason to live." Váli locked eyes with Hreidulfr. "We may be going to battle tomorrow, but I just got my life back. Do you know how many years I've waited to be with these people *properly*, as a *person*?" He gestured to the room and then looked back at Alyssa. "Not sitting on the floor like someone's dog? If I die now, what was the point of waiting for that long? I've got too much to do." He paused. "And there's something we haven't told you yet."

I cocked my head. "Is there?"

"Are you getting married?" Alyssa's enthusiasm for the idea was evident.

Váli rolled his eyes. "No! I mean, probably we will, but that's not it. We spoke with the family organizer and when this is all over, Hreidulfr and I will be adopting one of the kids that are waiting for a family."

His words took a moment to register through the wine haze. Tears welled in my eyes and my lip quivered. I opened my arms and Váli stood up and stepped into them so I could weep on his shoulder. I tried to say something intelligible, but all I could manage were squeaks.

"Come on now." Hreidulfr wrapped his arms around the both of us. "We've already got a special little kid picked out. Met them and everything. You're gonna love them."

"I know I will." When they released me, I dried my cheeks and picked up my cup. "I'm going to be a grandmother."

Hod held up his cup in a toast. "Congratulations. It's wonderful news!"

"Congratulations to you, great-uncle!" Hreidulfr gave him a pat on the shoulder before settling onto the bed next to him. "This is what we have to survive for. If I die tomorrow, Váli would be very upset being a single parent."

Alyssa was leaning on her knees, hugging them to her chest. "You make it sound easy to *decide* to be brave. There must be more to it than that."

"There is. I have more now than I expected to when I came to Asgard." Hreidulfr grew somber. "When I was alive, I was told I'd have to die in battle to *be* anything. No one else knew what parts of myself I was hiding, but I did, and I thought the gods would know it too. I thought the best I could hope for was to be an einherjar and serve Odin, and use that to hide my shame. But now that part of my life is over. Instead, I have an amazing partner. We're going to start a family. I'm happy. I'm useful and valued and fulfilled. I have a lot to be proud of." He paused, looked down.

"I hope my father would've been proud."

"He'd be a fool not to be." Hod wrapped an arm around Hreidulfr's shoulder. "It's not hard to figure out you're a good man. I barely know you and already that's obvious."

Hreidulfr sniffed and nodded. "I appreciate that. But it's your turn. What do you have to live for?"

Hod thought for a moment, and we waited. "I've spent all my life gathering stories and keeping them safe. Which I failed to do, in the end, since most of them burned with the realms. But I've been so focused on making sure everyone else's were told that I never told anyone my own. The love of my whole life is going to be returned to me soon and the first thing I'm going to do is write down our entire lives. It's going to sit on a shelf with all the others, because I'm never going to love him from the shadows again."

The words stung me, though I knew he didn't mean them to. It felt like a personal failure, somehow. I could've done more. I reached out to take his hand. "I'm sorry, Brother. I always understood why you stayed quiet, but I wished for better for you. You should've had everything you'd dreamed of." I looked around the room. "That's why I'm going to live tomorrow. Because you all deserve a better world."

"Skål," Váli said, lifting his cup, and the rest of the room did the same.

Hreidulfr began speaking with Hod and soon Váli leaned in. I used it as my moment to check on Alyssa, who was still curled up on her perch.

"Did those rousing speeches help?" I pushed a hair back from her face.

"A little." She looked up at me, wine-blush in her cheeks. "I'm still not sure where it leaves me, but I guess I'd better try hard not to die."

"You can't die tomorrow because I'd be lost without you." The words were out before I could properly think them over.

My throat immediately closed up, and I was left staring into her beautiful, hopeful eyes, wondering what brand of idiot I was. I was saying too much, making it too obvious. I cared about her, thought about her when I shouldn't, *loved* her more than I should, and if she knew, it would only cause heartbreak. The rest of my family was coming home, and I owed them a chance at a life uncomplicated by my own lack of loyalty.

I cleared my throat and tried to look composed. "You're essential to this city and you've been the best friend I could ask for. You're part of the family."

She smiled at me with the sweetest gaze and my heart fluttered.

Fuck.

"Alright, that's enough being sentimental," Hreidulfr said. The bedside table scraped as he pulled it closer to the centre of things. "We've got dice and nothing to lose, so you're all going to gamble with us."

And that was that for at least an hour. Throwing dice, making bets, winning, losing, losing some more. The loser was forced to tell an embarrassing tale, and it became a riotous event. Gods help anyone in the rooms near us who were hoping to rest, but I had the feeling that the city was full of people just like us, too full of being alive to sleep.

After a while, Váli's hands started lingering on Hreidulfr's knee, and a look in his eyes spoke volumes to anyone who happened to notice. He was as timeless as the rest of us now, but part of him was still a teenager at heart.

"I think it's time we get some rest," Váli said as he stood, setting his empty cup on the little table. "Can't go to war drunk and tired."

"Absolutely not." I smirked at him and he rolled his eyes. "Couldn't have that."

I walked him the two steps to the bedroom door and opened it. Hreidulfr bid the room goodnight and ducked out first. Váli lingered a moment.

"Everything's going to be alright tomorrow. You know that, don't you?" he asked.

I nodded. "I know."

His eyes shot past me to where Alyssa was sitting on the bed, chatting with Hod. "And you know it's not too late to move on and be happy, right?"

I flicked his arm with my finger. "You mind your business. I'm *fine* the way I am, thank you."

"Whatever you say." He gave me a knowing look as he walked backward into the hall, smirking at me in exactly that way his father used to.

I started to close the door but Hod spoke up. "I should be going too. I've been tired for a while but didn't have the heart to leave before the lovebirds and admit how old I am."

"They're pretty obvious, aren't they?" Alyssa laughed.

I shrugged. "I'm happy that they're happy, but we're going to need to start keeping buckets of ice water next to them for emergencies."

Hod took up his walking stick from where it leaned against the wall and made his way to the door.

"You're confident you know the place well enough to go alone?" I asked.

"Of course. It's been days and I've had plenty of practice." He reached out a hand and gave mine a squeeze when he found it. "Sleep well, Sister. Big day coming."

"You too." I pressed a kiss to his cheek, watched him leave, and closed the door after him.

And then it was just Alyssa and me.

"What a wonderful evening!" The dice and the stories had eventually pulled her out of her thoughts, and now Alyssa was throwing herself backwards on the mattress, spreading her limbs out. "I don't know if it's going to last, but I am so relaxed. Wine really is the best medicine."

I laughed and went to stand over her. "I'm glad you found a way to unwind. I don't like seeing you sad."

Alyssa gave me a sideways grin and reached for my hand. I gave it to her and she pulled me down at an awkward angle. I fell halfway across her, my chest pressed against her and my face far too close to hers.

I lingered too long. Wondered for too long what it would be like to kiss her.

She pressed her lips to my forehead. "Do you want to stay up all night talking?"

I grinned at her. "Yes, yes I do."

CHAPTER TWENTY-THREE

SIGYN

"I never told Da' how I felt. He was a mean fucker sometimes, you know? But life was hard and he really loved me. I never said it, and it breaks ma fuckin' heart."

— *Oddlaug, Volume 28*

The only noise in the bedroom was Alyssa's quiet, long breaths. Staying up all night had been a lofty goal. I'd been in the middle of telling her about a trip to Midgard from my youth, and when I'd looked back at her, she was fast asleep.

She deserved it. As kind as she was being, sitting up with me, it would be better for her if she was rested for battle. Focused. It was in my blood to hold vigil when it might be the last night of my life. She'd never grown up with that kind of desperation in her veins. She'd lived a life without armies at her back, without bloody swords and body counts. In the days before she'd gotten sick, before she'd slowly died, had she ever stayed awake and wondered if she'd live to see daybreak?

What *if* she died tomorrow?

Things could turn out a million ways. So many possibilities for who would live and who would fall. As naive as it probably was, I wasn't worried about Hreidulfr or Váli. They'd seen their share of battles and survived so much. They were ready. But was Alyssa?

She was lying there so innocently, tucked under the blanket I'd covered her with, that electric blue–tipped hair fanned out on her pillow, her navy tunic and beige trousers saying so much about her disposition. She was so practical, so innovative, and so kind. And, most likely, so unprepared. We were bringing her into a bloodbath and I wasn't sure I could forgive myself for it.

What would happen to me if she were killed?

164

Epilogues for Lost Gods

Gods, I should've insisted she had more combat training. Should have made Váli do it himself so she'd be the best. And now it was too late and I was going to lose her.

Feeling was welling in my chest. Feeling I didn't want, that I needed, that I didn't know what to do with. I had lost *so much*. I'd never been allowed to just love someone. Each time I'd fallen for someone, it had been a crime I was trying to get away with, to see how far we could run before reality caught up with us. Even my children, whom I'd loved with all my heart, had been torn from me. Maybe I would get both of them back now, maybe. But I could remember so clearly the pain of thinking them dead for an endless forever. I hadn't known Váli was out there waiting. I hadn't known Narvi would get a second chance at life.

I was a person that people took from. I wasn't allowed to *have*.

All I felt was this swelling, growing, burning affection I would never be allowed to keep. Because if a miracle happened and she survived, Alyssa still wasn't mine.

I kept staring at her. The slope of her nose, the length of her eyelashes. The tiny speck of soot on her temple. The slender curve of her fingers, curled loosely on the blanket. I wanted so badly to reach out and take her hand. To wake her up. To make those feelings manifest in every touch.

So many lovers would be grasping for one last moment of passion tonight, just in case. Reaching for one more chance, skin on skin, to be alive. And I could see it. I could see exactly what it would look like as I peeled away Alyssa's tunic and kissed the curve of her stomach. The arch of her back, the hitch of her breath.

If I did, I would probably get away with it. Even though I was already married, even though I'd just lured my husband back from Helheim. He'd probably forgive me a tryst with a lover on the eve of battle, especially for all his own faults. He might even ask me about the details, lurid as he could be. He'd told me worse stories than that about his youth.

But could *I* live with it?

What kind of person asks for such temporary love, knowing that it's doomed from the start? I'd done many horrible things but I'd had my heart too thoroughly shattered to ever inflict it onto someone else.

Maybe if I'd realized what this was before I'd gone to Helheim and asked Loki back into my life…if I'd taken stock of myself before I'd promised him a chance. Because it would be *reasonable* to say, "Ah, yes, I'm sorry, Loki, while you were gone I fell in love with someone else. Couldn't be helped. You were dead, remember?" That's logical. Understandable.

Sleeping with Alyssa now would be a deliberate choice. A specific betrayal.

If she even wanted to, let's not forget that small factor.

I let out a silent sigh and ran my hands over my face. I was acting like I had when I was practically a child. Fifteen years old and lying next to a girl I wasn't supposed to like in that way, wondering what in the world I was thinking. Telling myself no because what I was feeling wasn't the way of things. It was pulling a knot in my stomach that I'd forgotten I'd been carrying around.

Shame. Guilt. Disappointment. Dishonesty.

A dark thought sprung unbidden into my mind. The kind the young Sigyn wouldn't have had.

Maybe none of this moral debate would matter at all, because maybe in a couple of hours we'd all be dead.

CHAPTER TWENTY-FOUR

LOKI

"I was trapped in the dark for a long time, inside myself. I never want to feel helpless again."

— *Narvi, Volume 11*

As we sat on the stone trying to catch our breath, I strained to see past the seidr lantern light. Despite the twinkling maggots hanging from above, a good portion of the chamber was cast in shadow. The large, hollow root ran out from the darkness above, its end open and ready for travellers. Thousands of other tendrils of root ran around it, mounds of them spreading out from the wall, carpeting the floor with things for someone with a lack of depth perception to trip on.

It had been foolish, perhaps, to think the Nidhogg would be here. I'd seen it at Ragnarok, killing its way across the battlefield. If the realms had burned and regrown again, why would an enormous, indestructible creature like that go back to hiding in a hole in the ground? How long had it spent trapped in a stone cage with nothing to do but gnaw away at the tree that bound the realms?

As a child, when my mother had told me the story of the Nidnogg and Yggdrasil, I'd wondered why anyone would be so spiteful as to try to destroy all those realms, all those lives.

I'd since come to a deeper understanding of the subject.

As I drew closer to the Yggdrasil's root, something fluttered above me. I had to squint to see it, black on black. A raven.

Why didn't that feel quite right?

When is a raven not a raven?

Worry curdled my insides.

The bird cawed and dove from its perch to land a few steps away from me. "Still alive, *crawwwwwwwwwwwwk.*"

I hated being right.

"Oh, no. No, I deeply object to this." I turned around to check on Angrboda and Narvi, but they were in conversation and hadn't yet noticed the talking animal. When I turned back, the raven was closer than it had been. I backed up. Some things feel wrong even before you have a chance to understand them, and this raven felt like doom.

"Almost, though. Very nearly dead again." Its voice was raw and dark, scratchy, like wood being sanded.

"This feels very much like a hallucination."

It twitched its head, blinking its beady black eyes.

Narvi turned his attention to me. "What does?"

I pointed towards the bird while pressing another finger to my lips.

It let out another squawk and crooked its head. "Ah, where are my manners?" It ruffled its wings and the feathers detached, floating up onto the air like a breeze had plucked them off and was carrying them away. They swirled around the raven and the air shimmered in a manner that made it hard to look at, a manner I was too familiar with.

A shapeshifter.

Angrboda started to say something, but I hushed her. This stranger felt important. Pivotal. Like I was a box of matches and the raven was a vat of oil and one twitch too far would set the cavern ablaze.

When the flurry stopped, the feathers settled onto the shoulders of a man and became a sleek feathered cape. He was wiry in frame, like he hadn't eaten well for a long time, and he was dressed in dark scraps of fabric that made him look more like a scarecrow than a person. His nose cut out from his face like a beak and his eyes were dark pits. On top of his head of tangled black hair was a crown of tiny bones.

The shapeshifter bowed deeply and looked back up at me with a sharp grin. "It's an honour, God of Lies."

"And who exactly are you that you know me by sight?" Uncomfortable wasn't even close to how I felt. Cornered, more like. Threatened.

"A fan." His neck jerked disturbingly far to one side, like the bones weren't attached quite right. "A devotee. An admirer. Call me Valravn."

Shit.

Valravn was a thing of legend, nearly as famous as the Nidhogg. Stories said he had once been a raven, but he had eaten the heart of a battle-slain king and it had given him a human body. I'd heard about him appearing after a slaughter like his carrion kin, growing stronger with each heart, but I'd never *seen* him.

Very few got close to him and lived to tell the tale.

I pressed my palm into Narvi's body, gently urging him back. "You're looking a little worse for wear, King Eater. Ragnarok must have made things very difficult for you."

"Mmm, yes, that's true." One leg eased forward and stepped down onto one of the tangling roots. "No more enemies. No more battles. No more dead kings with dead hearts to eat."

Angrboda scoffed. "That's very sad, you creepy old—"

Valravn's head twisted in her direction with a sickening snap and she ate her words. "Rude. Very rude. Not enough respect. I have a hundred kings in my veins and you *will* bow to them."

I scrunched up my face, trying to feign sympathy. "She doesn't mean it. She's not very bright; you can see that. All fire and no thinking, if you understand me." Angrboda shot me a glare and I hissed *shut up* under my breath.

Valravn took another shuddering step forward. Like his body was fighting to stay in its form. "I'm very hungry, God of Lies. No more kings in Midgard, no more kings anywhere. And with no more kings, what can I do but eat god?"

Black mist burst forth from Valravn, borne on a gust of wind. The force of it knocked me to my knees and sent Angrboda and Narvi flying toward the back wall. The wind died as quickly as it had come and I scrambled to my feet.

Pieces of me ached from the fall. Every sinew of my body was telling me to run to them, to make sure they were okay, but I needed to keep Valravn away from them.

When I turned to face the King Eater, he was gone. Another breath and all the light in the room went out, shrouding everything in pitch black. No sight. No noise. Only the scent of decay and damp to keep me grounded in my body.

I turned on my heel, trying to see him before he struck. I couldn't find anything. It was like Angrboda had said about the mines; the darkness was so deep it was disorienting. I could barely tell up from down, left from right. Couldn't see my hands, couldn't see the blue maggots that had been above. Nothing. All sense of direction disappeared.

Focus.

A burst of rage rose up from my stomach. I had things to do and he was taking up far too much of my time. "Come out, you ugly pile of feathers! I thought you wanted to eat me, not play hide-and-fucking-seek!"

Something smashed into my chest and threw me onto my ass. The shock reverberated up my spine and I hissed, trying to shake it off and get back to my feet. Something sharp flashed next to my face, slicing a thin, burning line into my cheek.

I tried to summon a lantern, but it barely flickered. Wildfire fizzled the second it appeared.

Faster, got to move faster.

One more try. Runes slipped off my tongue and electricity crackled in my hands. The thrill of success rushed through me. A chance to make it out. I let the runes flow off my tongue and let the lightning bounce into the corners of the cave above.

Valravn squealed, giving away his location.

"Come and get me, you overgrown fucking chicken!" I went back to the runes, and sure enough, Valravn dove after me again, his shape just above my head. I reached up and the tips of my fingers connected, jolting the King Eater and throwing him off course. He hit the ground with a thump and a grunt, the sound the only thing to guide me to him, but by the time I got there, he was gone.

"You play dirty." His voice was bodiless, moving in the dark. "Dirty, dirty. Your insides are filthy too. All guilt and horror and violence."

"That's rich, coming from someone who literally feasts on the corpses of dead soldiers. Have you ever even *fought* the kings you eat? Carrion feaster. Coward." I needed to keep him talking, but if I stopped whispering the runes too long, I opened myself up for attack. And the room…was it constricting? Why did it feel like I was suffocating?

A scream. Faint and warbling at first but then so very clear.

"Narvi!" Where was it coming from? I couldn't fucking *see* and my son, my son—

Valravn laughed, croaking and strained. "Is he dying-dying-dead?"

The scream again, the same, exactly the same.

"Or is it all in your *head?*"

Something curled in my gut. It was too easy for the dark to look like the insides of my eyelids, for me to dream up something in front of me. To see a cave and a hot spring and a wolf and a wife, and to *smell* sulphur.

"Is it your boy's scream? Or yours, Liesmith? Lying always, lying to yourself."

No, it's not real.

"It's real." Valravn was closer now. "Real for forever before, forever now. Maybe you never left."

"Horseshit!" I screamed. I put my hands over my face but the feeling was phantom. I couldn't see my hands. Did I still have hands?

The voice was behind me. "Poor God of Lies. So empty inside. So ready to die."

And just the slightest part of me was. The voice in the very back of my head that was tired. That had learned suffering as a boy and had grown into suffering, worn it like a badge of honour. Like armour. Turned into a man—a woman—a being—who had been betrayed and mocked and tortured. I was hollow, had been hollow so long. It hurt to try. It hurt to strive day after day to be a better person, to prove everyone wrong. What redemption was there for this husk?

And the darkness seeped in. It started from my shoulder, the slightest touch. It permeated everything, soaking into my muscles, my stomach, my heart. The weight was too heavy. I sank to my knees, collapsing under impenetrable desperation.

Valravn's voice over my shoulder was rasping, tempting. "You are finished. All done. Come and gone and no one will miss you. Come into the darkness with me instead." The touch on my shoulder slid up, craning my neck to one side. Rank breath filled the air next to my ear. Something slick—his tongue—ran up my neck to taste the bottom of my ear. "You'll taste so good, Silvertongue. Like metal and spite and wishes."

And it all meant nothing. Who was I to fight the end?

Hadn't I done enough?

"Father!"

My son.

Disgust rippled through me, running along my skin like gooseflesh.

What the fuck was I thinking? I was *this* close to Urd's well and a new fate. In half a day I'd be hugging Váli and eating fresh fruit and, gods willing, fucking my wife again. Why in the nine was I listening to a fucking seagull?

I pulled the knife from my belt and stabbed it backwards into Valravn's gut. He shrieked and dropped back from me. The darkness flickered, the old seidr lanterns and the phosphorescence above coming back to life. And I could fucking see him.

Angrboda and Narvi raced forward as the darkness faded, toward Valravn. Angrboda had a dagger in her fist, ready to go for the kill. Narvi stopped short, his lips moving in a rush of runes. A shimmering shield appeared around Angrboda, and she barreled into the King Eater headfirst.

The momentum of her body sent him flying back, rolling across the ground. The air shimmered and he was gone again, his raven shape soaring across the room, in and out of the light. I lost track of him, looking between the blue and seidr lights, in between the real shadows and the ones in my right eye. Was my sight so terrible that—

Feathers darted past my face. I whipped around to follow them, runes on my breath and—

Narvi.

I let the whisper die, the wildfire in my palm snuffing out.

Valravn had Narvi by the throat, suspended high above the ground. His claws were carefully placed against his skin, pressing in, but not slicing through. Narvi was trying to pry them off with his fingers but Valravn was stronger.

His black void eyes were on me, his head crooked. Waiting for my next move.

"Put him down." I raised my hands, took a step forward. "You already said I'd make a good meal for you. You don't want him; you want me."

Valravn's grin grew wide on his face, his skin taut like leather. Too many teeth. "Everyone loves an appetizer, God of Lies." He leaned in to sniff Narvi. "So much like you. The same notes. Pain. Grief. All that bottled-up regret. Your son's is refined. Bold. Delectable."

"If you hurt him—"

I moved closer, one step at a time, until I was in his reach. "Narvi will *never* have the same depth of flavour that I have. You know that. Take me."

Valravn's other hand darted out. His claws dug into the top of my neck, piercing the skin along my jaw. The pain seared through my neck, spiderwebbing up my face. He hauled me into the air, my feet dangling below me.

"Stupid silvertongue liesmith god. Both is better." Valravn hung his head back and laughed.

I pulled my leg back and swiftly kicked Valravn in the crotch.

The giant chicken-man dropped us. His claws skimmed my face as I fell, narrowly missing my good eye. Narvi and I collapsed onto the ground. As Narvi crawled back, clutching his throat, I scrambled to get to my feet, but Angrboda had already taken the opening. Her fist collided with Valravn's skull and he squawked with the impact.

Standing over him, I wound back my boot, hoping to kick him while he was down, but he had his claws wrapped around my leg before I could swing. Valravn pulled and I went down again, the bruises on my ass multiplying each time I crashed to the stone.

Angrboda swung at him again. He blocked her blow and pressed his palm into Angrboda's skin. Something black travelled between his body to hers, a thick mist that smelled putrid even from a distance.

She froze, her eyes rolling back into her head. Her body shook, and I knew I needed to be quick. I kicked him in the ribs once and then twice. Something cracked and he screamed, breaking his grip on Angrboda. She dropped to the ground and the black mist rose out of her skin like steam, disappearing into the air.

Valravn climbed back to his feet, his winged cape around his arms like he was stuck between man and bird, clutching his side. Black blood seeped from his middle where I'd cut him before, his hand trying to keep it in, and the grin on his face looked blood-crazed. "Still fighting. Tastes better that way."

I couldn't give him time to get in my head again. It would be too easy; I was too good a target. I threw myself at him and pinned him to the ground at the shoulder. Valravn screamed and thrashed, feathers moulting out of his arms. One precise stab should kill him, but it didn't *feel* like enough. He had hurt my boy. So *many* people thought they had the *right* to lay hands on my family.

I wanted his death to last.

I thrust my blade into his chest and pulled it out again. Stabbed him again, his cries of agony echoing in the cavern. Over and over. Kill him; kill the doubt. Empty all this rage and guilt and anger into him and let it be *gone*. Another wound. Another. I needed a new fate. I couldn't keep hanging on to the past. To the things that I had done and that had been done to me.

It was time to stop looking back.

His body had long stilled by the time the muscle in my arms cried out to rest. My skin was covered in spatters of black blood up to the elbows and Valravn was a mess beneath me. The rush ran out from under my skin and finally, I felt fine.

For a moment.

Then it all came throttling back, all the hate and fear and grief. Overwhelming. My senses were full, everything humming and blinding, more than I could take. And as quickly as it started, it began to fade, letting reality back in. Leaving me steady again.

My skin burned where the blood had settled on it, searing into me. I tried to wipe it off, but it was sinking in, staining me. Dry and black and part of me.

Fuck.

CHAPTER TWENTY-FIVE

LOKI

"You'd think getting an afterlife and then another one would mean you could start over, but you can't. What I wouldn't give to wipe the slate clean."

— *eViola, Volume 73*

Surely this wouldn't amount to anything disastrous. *Surely.*

I stared down at my newly pitch-black skin. The markings were inconsistent, rough around the edges. Like I'd neglected to wash my arms after dipping them in a vat of ink.

Or, you know, the blood of a dead raven king.

It didn't hurt anymore. One would think it would, but it was just there. I scrubbed my fingers into each other, scraping the skin until the wedding rings on my hands dug into my skin. Nothing came off. I spat in my hand and scrubbed. Nothing.

Underneath me, Valravn was turning bone-white, like a sun-bleached tree washed up on the shore of a beach.

Narvi dropped to his knees beside me. "Are you alright?"

I just sat motionlessly, hands held out, looking at the mess I'd made.

Narvi looked above me. "I think he's catatonic."

"I'm not catatonic." I looked up at Angrboda. She was conscious, holding her head and groaning. "However, I'm pretty sure I've made an error."

"Wash that off, you animal. That's disgusting." Angrboda gestured weakly to my hands. "That's not even blood. Smells like muck from a pigpen."

"That's definitely the corpse, Bo." I stood up and tried to rub the black away again, to show them. "It's not coming off."

174

Epilogues for Lost Gods

Narvi poked a finger into my skin, assessing the situation. Then he was whispering runes. My skin warmed under his touch, but nothing changed. He whispered more. Nothing. "Well, you're not sick with anything."

"I don't feel sick." It was suspiciously…fine.

"Leave it to you to finish off this adventure by taunting an ancient nature spirit into a fight, nearly get yourself killed, and then get tainted by some kind of ooze." Angrboda slowly hauled herself off the ground, looking genuinely annoyed.

"Oh, I'm sorry, did my newest near-death experience inconvenience you? I'm sick of this." I turned on her. Battle-wounded or not, I was done. With all the dramatics, our argument from the mine had gone unfinished and it wasn't difficult to dredge up that anger again. I gestured to my body with a sweeping arm. "This is what I am now, alright? You're annoyed by how weak and frail I've become but I'm not *being* anything! I'm just existing. I'm just me. And for the moment, I happen to be a fucking mess up here—" I pointed to my head. "—and I haven't got a single clue what to do about it. And because I've spent the last seven years worried about what everyone else would think of *little broken Loki*, I've done nothing to improve the situation. To take the first fucking step, and then maybe help make my *son* better. *You* are part of the problem and—"

I stopped yelling at Angrboda the second I saw the deep, pitch-black darkness encroaching around us, closing in like a trap. I looked down. Valravn was still a white, mushy corpse beneath our feet.

I took a deep breath and the light seeped back into being.

"You've said a lot of shit that I'm not just going to let slide, but that—" Angrboda narrowed her eyes. "Are you Valravn now?"

"No!" I crossed my black-stained arms across my chest. "No."

Was I? Stranger things had happened in the nine realms.

I held out my hand and tested a theory. After a moment of focus, the black under my skin seeped out towards my palm and settled in my hand as a swirl of dark fog. It expanded, pooling outwards until it enveloped us in darkness.

Narvi's disembodied voice came out from the void. "Well, if you're not Valravn now, I don't know what else this is."

"I don't feel particularly compelled to eat hearts." I let the focus in my mind fade and the darkness did as well, sliding into place under my skin. It was something old, something more primal than seidr. And it seemed to whisper, this background hum that gave me gooseflesh. It *wanted*, and I could take a wild guess at what.

"So what do we do?" Narvi wasn't looking very comfortable with this new acquisition.

"We go up the root, I guess. Maybe the Nornir will have something to say."

"Ah yes, my favourite plan." Angrboda stomped towards the root, very unimpressed. "Ignore it until it goes away."

"Well, it worked on me, didn't it!" I called after her.

Narvi put a hand on my arm. He had that look on his face he usually reserved for talking me out of one of my *moments*. "Are you sure you're alright?"

I pushed down the reaction to brush him off and slide back into myself like I'd been doing for years. Being honest was harder than I wanted to admit. "Mostly. For now. We need to finish this for your mother's sake and when we're done, you and I will figure out how to get past all this, yeah?"

Narvi shook his head incredulously, the smallest satisfied smile on his lips. "If you say so."

I nudged him forward and we both headed towards Yggdrasil's root. Angrboda had already disappeared inside. It was just tall enough that I could keep from smacking my head on the wood above us, but I had to bend to avoid the occasional branch or growth. The smell was like a wet forest: mossy and damp, thick with petrichor.

The root sloped uphill, and the climb was uncomfortable. I'd only used Yggdrasil to travel twice before, and neither root had sloped at as high an angle as this one. We kept our footing with the grooves of root in the floor, but there were points where it curved further and we were forced to crawl on our hands and knees.

What I wouldn't give to travel literally anywhere by horseback under an open sky.

The journey took too long. We even considered stopping to sleep for just a little while. Narvi and I began to fall behind, while Angrboda trudged on ahead. I tried never to let her get out of my sight, but my body didn't feel as spry as it once had.

Ahead of us, Angrboda whistled.

When we caught up with her, she was standing next to a tunnel blown into the wall. It was rough and made of new foliage. And a good thing it was there, because our current trajectory led us to a dead end.

"Must've caved in after the realms fell," I muttered. "On we go?"

"On we go." Angrboda stepped in.

Nothing about this tunnel was different, not really. But as we neared the end of it, the smell hit me. Salty, fresh air poured into the mouth of the root, confusing me at first. I knew the smell, I knew I did, but it had been an eternity—the ocean. That briny seaweed smell, that scent of life—it filled me with an indescribable joy. How long had it been since I'd smelled anything *fresh*?

Then the sound of crashing waves filled my ears. And light. So much light.

I covered my eyes, trying to let only a little in at a time. I hadn't seen the sun since it had been eaten at Ragnarok. As I stepped out into the light, my skin warmed like I was standing next to a fire. I couldn't see a thing but I could feel *everything*.

Epilogues for Lost Gods

Stumbling blind towards the sound of the water, I kicked off my boots and kept walking until the water seeped between my toes, cold and spectacular. I dropped to my knees and let it wash over my skin. So crisp, so indescribably *missed*. My kingdom for the feel of ocean water.

I cupped my hands and splashed the water over my face, still unable to open my eyes. I shuddered at the cold and licked my lips just to taste the salt. It occurred to me that I must look like a fool, but that only the Nornir could see me anyway.

I hoped they'd still grant new fates to fools.

Slowly, I peeked open my good eye. It still burned, but it was tolerable. Narvi was standing within arm's reach, face held up to the sun. I reached for his hand and he wrapped his fingers around mine.

"This is what being alive is like," he whispered.

Yes, it was.

Angrboda was waiting for us, hands clasped over her eyes, looking out from the smallest slit between her fingers. "Are you two *done yet?*"

"Not really, but we should probably hurry it up." I looked around. The Nornir weren't waiting for us at all. Instead, they were gathered around a fire, not paying us any mind.

We approached them softly, not wanting to risk anything with an air of disrespect.

The three women were perched on old log benches. Their hands were busy working thread and it was easy to imagine them as three spiders, weaving a web between them. Following the thread to its source, each line came from the inside of a wicker basket, unrolling out of sight.

If I looked inside, would I find balls of thread, or would I find incomprehensible seidr? One was more likely than the other.

Though I'd never made a habit of visiting the Nornir, I knew them. Skuld, the youngest, had dominion over the future, and took the form of a young maid, of an age to be married, her whole life ahead of her. Verdandi knew the happenings of the present moment, and she was a woman in the prime of her life, experienced but not yet bearing the lines on her face of a long life. And Urd, who knew what had come before, she looked a bit like my grandmother had: wise and strong, with deep smile lines around her mouth and eyes.

Skuld looked up from her weaving. Like her sisters, she was wearing simple clothes made from simple fabrics. Skuld's was a copper linen dress that draped loosely over one shoulder, cinched at the middle with a belt of gilded leather. Her arms were dripping with wooden bangles. Each of the women had adorned themselves in bone and antler and carved stone. Runic tattoos ran across their fingers as they wove.

"So pleased you could join us," Skuld said. "We don't get many visitors anymore. I hope your enjoyment of the sun has made up for the long journey."

"Your home is beautiful." Narvi gestured to two swans bobbing up and down on the swell of the ocean. "I don't think I'd ever tire of this view."

"You would not, child." Skuld carefully set down her weaving. "Many would, but not you. Your heart could live in peace for an eternity and never wish for adventure."

Urd and Verdandi gently set aside their work as well. When the thread was tucked safely away, Urd motioned for us to sit. "Join us. We have a lot to talk about."

We sat down on the log across from them. Angrboda was giving off an air of deep discomfort, but Narvi seemed calm. I was somewhere in between.

Verdandi leaned forward and spoke, her voice kind and collected. "Narvi Lokason, you wish to have a new fate. Why?"

Narvi sat straighter. He took a long breath before he spoke. "There are more reasons than one. The simple one is to help my mother and the realms. She told us you foresaw her future and encouraged her to chase it, so I assume you know why it's important that I help her keep her city alive."

Verdandi nodded, but didn't interrupt.

"The rest isn't simple. I'm not who I was when I died. I don't know who I was meant to be and I'll never know. I'll never know what I could have accomplished as a young man with a soft, unburdened heart. I'd dreamed of saving the realms. Of finding new ways to use seidr that weren't about death and destruction. I used to imagine it was hubris to think I was smarter than many, but maybe it's not. Because I *was* intelligent. I still am. And I'd have used it to better the realms when everyone else is intent on pulling them apart. I want a new fate so I can live and so I can keep so many others from dying."

"And you think the people will just listen to your will?" Verdandi asked.

Narvi shrugged. "Maybe not. I used to think that people couldn't see the evils they were doing, but I know that's not always true. The realms are new now and order is still being established. What better chance will I get than this?"

Tears fogged my vision. So many people deserved what they got in life, but Narvi wasn't one of them. My son had been cheated. By Odin, by his family, by the people in Asgard, and by *me*.

Urd nodded. "And if everything falls apart? What will you do in a realm that takes you for granted again?"

"I'll do it anyway." Narvi's face had hardened with his resolve. "No one is going to alter my course again. If history repeats itself and the realms are corrupt at their core, at least I will have fought against it. Done something."

Epilogues for Lost Gods

The sisters looked at each other for a long moment. Skuld turned back to Narvi. "We have no more questions. We will decide."

As if the speech had taken more out of him than I could fathom, Narvi slumped over with a sob, his face in his hands.

I pulled him into my arms and shook him, speaking into his hair. "It's alright. No one deserves this more than you."

He held me in return for a moment, then nudged me off, drying his tears. Composing himself.

Urd turned her attention elsewhere. "Angrboda—"

"No." Angrboda shook her head, a casual look of disinterest on her face. "I don't want a new fate. I'm just here because my daughter could have me exiled and fed to a giant lizard if I didn't help these two."

Urd's head tilted just slightly. "I see. And you're sure?"

"Very sure." She brushed some dirt from her trousers. "I did what I was put in these realms to do. I'm happy with my contribution to history and I'm proud of what my kids became. You may not approve and *you* may not approve—" She pointed at me. "—but I'm proud and I'm done. I don't give a single flying fuck what anyone else thinks of my choices. The realms needed a revolution and I helped give it to them."

She was correct that I didn't approve. I hated what we'd done together. But there was something else to it. Something admirable about what she was saying. She knew who she was and what she wanted.

I hadn't felt that way in a long time.

Verdandi smiled. "Good. Not many have the courage to accept their fate. You'll be free to return to Helheim and resume your path."

I blinked. "Wait, that's going to be one hel of a walk back."

Angrboda shrugged. "I'm dead. What else am I going to do with my time?"

"The tunnel collapsed, Bo. How do you plan to get back?"

She stared me dead in the eyes, not missing a beat. "Well, if you want to get technical about it, I plan to move the rocks and then run until I get to the other side of the mine. Is that a detailed enough idea for you?"

I blinked.

Well, at least it was a straightforward, uncomplicated plan.

"Loki." Skuld turned her warm smile on me, stealing away my attention. "Why do you deserve a new fate?"

Deserve.

It wasn't that I hadn't thought about what I was going to say. I had. But nothing seemed good enough anymore. Every excuse, every explanation felt pathetic.

"I'm not sure I do deserve a new fate."

Everyone was watching me. Narvi and Angrboda were looking at me like they thought I'd properly lost my mind.

Urd picked up a hot cup of water that was sitting close to the fire and passed it across to me. I cupped my hands around the warmth of it, letting it soak into my skin. "Go on," she said.

"Narvi deserves a second chance because he always did the right thing. I did some things right, but not enough. And not enough to outweigh my contribution to Ragnarok. I may never be able to atone for all that, but…but I know I can't atone for anything if I'm in Helheim. Sigyn's asked me to help her protect a city, and that's a start. That's something I can do. After that, I don't know. I might wind up back in Helheim in a few hours, newly skewered. But if not…"

I took a breath. Let it all bubble to the surface. All the things that hurt.

"If I live, I could see Váli again. I could try to be a better father to him. I could give Sigyn something good to wake up to every day, something she deserves. I'd learn to fix whatever is going on inside this broken head of mine and start doing things I'd be proud of. Don't ask me what that looks like. I can't see past tomorrow. I want the chance to make better choices, to tear all the pain from my heart, and to do better." I looked at the ground between my legs, tears streaking down my face. "I just want to do better."

Urd nodded and gestured to my arms. "And what do you plan to do with your newfound power?"

I shrugged. "I barely know what this power *is*. If you have any insights, I'm happy to hear them."

The witnesses to my confession were silent, the question hanging in the air, ignored. The breeze rustled the leaves above us, and the waves crashed against the jutting cliff at our backs. The Nornir were consulting each other in their strange, silent way, looking from one to the other and yet saying nothing.

Finally, after what seemed like far too long a debate, Skuld rose. "Loki, Narvi, come with me."

We rose and followed her away from the others. I stayed close to Narvi, my hand resting on his shoulder, though it was as much for my comfort as it was for his. Skuld led us to a small, dark pool, sat down on the grass beside it, and patted the ground. "Sit."

After we were settled, she rolled up the sleeve of her dress and reached into the water. She fished around without looking into the pool, her face hard with concentration. Then she pulled something out and shook it off. A piece of tapestry.

Skuld unrolled it. It was long, and most of it was stitched in the dark colours of Helheim. But closer to the bottom were brighter images. Some of the detail was lost to my partial vision, but I could make out enough of it. Narvi learning seidr. Narvi studying with Hod and Eyvindr in the archives. Narvi at a pub with Gersemi and Váli. He and I playing in the mud when he was only small. Narvi crying as I left. All of these small, enormous moments that had shaped him.

"This is the tapestry of your life, Narvi. Everything you have ever done or ever will." She rolled it back up and held it out to him. "And now it's yours."

Narvi took it tentatively. "Do you mean…?"

Skuld snapped her fingers and a new tapestry fell out of thin air, into her hand. "This is your new fate. It begins now. Your old tapestry is your past and it remains so, and what you do with it is your decision to make. Some choose to carry it with them. Others choose to tuck it away and never think of it again. And some choose to give it great respect, then burn it and never look back."

Narvi hugged the tapestry against his chest, watching as Skuld dipped the new tapestry into the pool, and tucked it away. "Thank you," he said. "I won't waste this."

Skuld's smile was bright and genuine. "We know you won't." She turned her attention to me. "You were a harder case to decide."

I nodded somberly. What other answer could I expect?

"My sisters and I are not exactly in agreement. You have so much pain in you and so many people choose to hold that pain close instead of letting it go. Do you truly think you can live a life where your pain doesn't rule your every action as it has in the past?"

"I…" The answer needed to be honest. An easy *yes* would do me no good. "I will make mistakes. I know I will. But I'm ready to be more than what others made me, than what I turned myself into. I'm going to try."

Skuld nodded slowly. "Then you have won my vote, and your fate."

Relief washed over me. "Really?"

"You make an honest, compelling argument, Loki." Skuld dipped her arm into the pool. "Others who have made the journey here have boasted about how they'd change their lives, what they could do for themselves, and how simple it would all be. Change is not simple, Loki. It's hard-won by the most imperceptible moments, by the smallest degrees. By choosing it even when it's hard." She pulled a tapestry out—my tapestry— and placed it in my hand. "I think you know that."

My fate was so light in my hand. It was wound tightly and seemed to be far too long. I knew what would be inside without looking, good and bad and in-between. Having my entire past in my hand felt monumental, but I didn't know what it meant, not yet.

Skuld snapped her fingers again and another tapestry appeared. "And you understand this isn't a blank slate?"

181

I nodded.

"Good. No one will have forgotten you or any of the things you've done. This is only a chance to atone, as you've asked." Skuld tucked it into the pool, shook the water from her arm, and let her dress sleeve fall again. She looked me dead in the eyes. "It's the only chance you'll get."

CHAPTER TWENTY-SIX

SIGYN

"It took me thirty-five years to get honest with myself. A
smarter man would've been quicker."

— *Danko, Volume 96*

"There's not much time left. Run us through it again."

Váli pushed the tiny carved soldiers to the side of the map of the city. The wind pulled at its sides, the parchment held on the flimsy wooden table by stones at its corners. As we huddled around a street near the edge of Fólkheim, moments from Asgard's invasion, everything felt surreal. It was a moment we had planned for a long time, but that was always just out of sight.

"The city's been walled off to funnel Asgard's soldiers into these two trajectories." Váli ran his finger down one path and then the other. "Each continues from the edge of the city, all the way to the cliffs. Here, here, and here, we have machinery posted to help blow the fuckers to Helheim."

Alyssa placed tiny wooden cannons in the places Váli had pointed. "Each one is fitted with ammo and people trained to use them. There's also Modernist weaponry hidden in these key locations, in case extra power is needed." Another set of markers on the map.

"The first wave will fire from here." Hreidulfr tapped the front section of the city. "They'll regroup past the first barricades, keeping out of harm's way until there's no other choice."

"We'll keep pushing them into small spaces where we have the advantage, and tear them down one by one." Váli crossed his arms over his chest. "You know we've been over this ten times this morning."

"I know." The whole song and dance was more about shaking off my own nerves than it was for anyone else's benefit. "Is everyone ready?"

Váli gave my hand a squeeze. "We have to go. Be safe, Mother." He turned and left without looking back. He'd always been the strongest of us.

Hreidulfr looked at him, then back at me. "They'll come, ma'am."

I shook my head at him. "How much gold will it cost to get you to stop calling me that?"

"There's not enough gold in all the nine." He smirked at me before turning to follow his partner. "See you soon!"

I took a breath. Alyssa was the last one at the table. She'd started sweating again. "Are you—?"

She held up a hand. She wasn't looking at me, her face pulled into a tight ball of stress. "I need to say something and I'm out of time to say it."

My breath hitched. What she wanted to say could be any one of a hundred—a hundred thousand—things and still, I knew what it would be.

Her hand reached up to cover mine. "If I die today, I need you to know that I love you. I've loved you for a long time, and not just as a friend. Every moment that we spent together made me happy and I'm grateful to be in your life. To get to serve the city next to you and to help you stand in the face of all this. And I know it's not fair that I'm telling you this. It's not right. But I'm not strong or full of magic, and if this is the last time we speak, I wanted you to know that I'll die loving you."

My lips hung open. I couldn't catch my breath. In any other moment of any other life, this was the part of the story where I could sweep her into my arms and confess that I loved her too, that I was *so sure* she was the kind of woman I needed in my life. But this was not another life, and I was married and—

For fuck's sake, nothing was concrete. Nothing! Loki could be gone forever and I might never know. Alyssa could die thinking I didn't love her back, and I didn't think I could live with that—I *couldn't* live with that.

"Alyssa, I—"

A horn, loud and deep, sounded in the distance. They were here. Asgard had come.

She looked up, the new flurry of movement around us making everything more urgent. "I have to go." She rubbed her thumb against the back of my hand. "And it's alright that you don't love me that way. I know you have a family and if Loki shows up to save the day, your life is with him. I just...I just didn't want the last thing I do in these realms to be a lie."

"No, I—"

184

Epilogues for Lost Gods

But she wasn't listening. With tears running down her face, she squeezed my hand, pressed her lips to my cheek, and then ran off into the city.

I wanted to scream. It wasn't fair. It wasn't fucking fair.

I forced it down. To think too hard about what she'd said would mean making mistakes. Missteps and distractions got you killed, and suddenly I *really* didn't feel like dying.

When this was all over, I had to be alive, and so did she.

I took a breath and allowed the details to wash over me.

A quiet that was out of place had fallen over the city. It wasn't the normal bustle of midmorning, with people doing errands, children laughing in the streets, or the din of construction. No. This was whispers and huddling in corners and waiting to kill or be killed. This was the sound of an army getting closer, the wind carrying the smallest sounds.

This was the silence before the war.

I whispered a string of runes and pressed my palm to the map on the table. It burst into lavender flames, quickly engulfing the old, splintered wood. Let it burn. There was no turning back.

A ladder was propped against a house nearby, giving access to the roof. I climbed up one rung at a time, dreading what I might see on the horizon. A hand reached down to help me. I took it, letting the woman pull me up. Three other völur stood on the roof with me, and more scattered across the roofs at our sides. Behind us was half the city, sloping up towards the cliffs, and before us was the other half, dipping slowly towards the fields outside the city proper. At its edge was a sea of movement. Gold and white and red. Hundreds of soldiers at least. A mere speck compared to what Asgard had been, but now it was home to half the inhabitants of the nine realms.

And we would be what remained.

We waited as the army drew closer. One by one, the völur's mouths began to move, silent runes slipping from their tongues. Each palm held a flicker of wildfire, in violet and coral and ruby and gold. Each moment, each heartbeat took too long. An eternity passed as we chanted in silence, waiting, Asgard drawing slowly closer.

They were at the edges of the fields, close enough to see. They had soldiers from every realm. Some were tall enough to be Jotnar and stout enough to be Dwarven. Others were hard to identify with all their armour. And bringing up the rear was a troll. Where had they managed to find a *troll?*

Every day since I'd come back from Helheim, I'd wished a hundred times that our own secret weapons would appear. That Loki and Narvi—*gods,* even Angrboda—would burst through the door and announce that they had come to save us. That for what little extra it would really do, they had come to use their seidr and wits and fists to help drive us towards victory. And maybe it had been folly to think they were that special, that they could make the difference. But it didn't matter because they had not come and we were alone, and I had no way to know if they were alive or dead or—

No. I had no time to let myself dip into that despair.

Asgard had come, and Loki had not.

The horn rang out again.

I summoned up a burst of wildfire. All around me, the flames shot into the sky, arcing in colourful trails and coming down on the heads of the encroaching army. The first scream rose and the völur readied another round. We'd already picked the fields dry of food, but what chaff was left started to burn around the army as they marched through it, breaking their formation. A few of them had caught fire themselves, and they raced and rolled to put it out. But most were still standing, still approaching.

Another round of flame flew towards them. It would never be enough to deter them, was never meant to be. It was only the beginning.

They were pressing into the city now, working their way towards the streets. A sharp whistle sounded and so much happened in quick succession. Barrels of water were pushed from the roofs above the army, soaking Asgard's front line and putting a barrier between the city and the fire. The völur summoned up lightning and shot it into soaked soldiers in the crowd below. The smell of charred bodies would soon be on the wind.

Arrows flew towards us, a quick response to our attacks, heading for our frontline völur. Our retreat was swift, as it was meant to be. We would spend the battle letting them push us further and further into our own city, hoping to use our home to our advantage. But the day was just beginning.

Opposing wildfire rained down over the roofs we were positioned on, slamming into the face of one of the women next to me. She dropped to the ground, flailing to put the fire out, and I fell onto her, smothering it with my cloak. The others were already making their way down the ladder as I pulled her to her knees.

"Take her!" I crouched next to the roof's edge as our comrades helped her down, then followed on my own. "Behind the next barricade, go!"

The sound of sharpened steel was getting closer.

We hadn't made a dent.

CHAPTER TWENTY-SEVEN

LOKI

"Moving forward is the only thing I want to do. I can't keep looking at what brought me here."

— *Sigyn, Volume 32*

"Are you certain about going back, Bo?" I dug the toe of my boot into the sand. "Do you even know *how* you're going to get back?"

"Do *you* know how *you're* getting to Fólkheim? No, you fucking don't. So don't look at me like I'm the only one without a plan."

Fair enough.

Narvi was playing diplomat with the Nornir, something we all thought would be best left to him. A bit strange to think the adults would be the ones standing off to the side, but gods know Angrboda and I were hardly the most trusted or most level-headed negotiators.

"So what will you do with your new life, hmm?" Angrboda didn't meet my eye.

I pushed a hand through my hair, tipping my head up to feel the sun on my face again. "I don't really know. If I don't wind up back in Helheim in two days, I might get the chance to think it over. Why? Are you going to miss me?"

It had been meant as a taunt, but something about it had clearly pierced the skin. She looked up, staring at me with more sincerity than I'd seen since we'd originally fallen into each other. "Loki, I've missed you for a very long time."

I let out a long breath. "Angrboda...I *am* sorry. If I could tear myself down the middle and let the Loki you loved follow you home, I would."

"I think you would. You're soft like that." She pursed her lips and shrugged, the moment already passing. "It was good while it lasted, but we're both past such things now."

"We are." I wanted to reach out and touch her, but I knew she'd never allow that. "I'm sure there's someone in Helheim that's waiting for a fire as bright as yours."

Angrboda smirked, her sharp teeth showing. "Maybe. If they survive being set alight, I might even keep them."

"Father!" Narvi waved for us to return to the fireside. "We've discussed our next moves."

"And?" Angrboda crossed her arms over her chest. "I want to get out of here. All this sun is giving me a headache."

Skuld stepped towards me. "First things first. Loki, your hand please."

I set my hand in Skuld's. Her skin was soft, new, the way Narvi's had been when he was still a baby.

"Your body is not ready to rejoin the living. As you are, you would go above this realm and you would begin to crumble. It would take days, maybe weeks, but no more than that." Skuld ran her other hand over my knuckles, scarred and marred as they were. "I can give you back the fullness of your body. Repair the hole in your chest. And I can repair everything else as well, if you wish it."

I stiffened. "Everything? My sight, my lips, *everything*?"

She nodded, a gentle smile on her face.

All these scars. The battles I'd won and lost, the humiliations I'd suffered. The long eternity that my face had burned for. The unending darkness of my dead eye. She could take all of it away.

And then what? If everything was so easily fixed, so easily removed, what did any of it mean? Would I remember these things even if the scars were gone, or would it make it that much easier to slip back into old habits? To think it was all a dream? No consequences for any of it.

I cleared my throat. "Give me my sight and my health, but leave the rest."

"Are you sure?" Narvi stepped forward. "Father, you could—"

"No. I want to remember. I can serve my own vanity with glamours if I choose. I want to see the scars in full clarity."

Skuld nodded. "A wise choice."

"And what about this?" I held my hands up, the black mist swirling under the skin around my forearms.

"I can't fix that for you." She took my hands and examined them. "Valravn isn't of the body. It's a manifestation of the mind. Someday, you may be able to rid yourself of it. Many have failed to do so since the dawn of the realms. It feeds on the darkness in you, and if you're not careful, it will swallow you whole. As far as its purpose, not all things have one. Some things just happen and we learn to live with them."

My mouth felt as dry as Musphelheim. "So it's up to me. Good, good. Just another problem to add to the pile."

The smile on Skuld's face was laced with pity. "I have faith you'll manage. Now please open your shirt."

I blinked. "Wait—what?"

She snapped her fingers and a needle and thread appeared above her hand. "How else are we going to close that wound? Sit down."

I looked at Narvi. He had paled significantly, but Urd was already closing in on him as well.

Angrboda cackled. "Oh, I am suddenly so glad I didn't say yes to any of this."

Skuld pushed me onto the log behind me, then settled onto her knees between my legs. It very much occurred to me to crack a joke or say something wholly inappropriate, but my words were caught in my throat.

"It's alright." Skuld pulled my tunic over my head and set it on the log. "No one really enjoys this part." She inhaled deeply and blew out my glamour like a candle. Suddenly my chest was wide open again, all of my scars visible for the realms to see.

"You understand that I don't much care for needles anymore." I pointed to the scars that ran into the flesh of my lips. "Having my mouth sewn shut was more than enough."

"No other way, darling. Can't repair something that's torn open. Stay still." Skuld took a piece of my torn flesh between two fingers, leaning too close to me for comfort.

Not that *any* of it was comfortable.

I only watched for a moment, long enough to see the needle slip under the dead skin. She pulled it up, piercing my flesh and dragging the thread through the hole, then pushed down into the skin on the other side of the wound and pulled it taut. It seared and I tried not to scream. Her fingers were under my skin, pushing thread and needle into my wounds, and none of this was *normal*. But the colour of the skin was changing from a faded, mottled grey to something alive again. All that with one stitch.

Each push and pull and tightening spread a new wave of pain across my body. I grasped the wood below me, digging my fingers into the grain and knowing I was driving splinters under my skin. I couldn't breathe. Couldn't stand to be awake and feeling this horror. I stared up at the sky, tears rolling down my face, trying to ignore the young lady tucked between my thighs, sewing my skin back together. Everything had gotten so warm. Beads of sweat dripped down my back. The sky was turning black. Was it night all of a sudden—?

Skuld slapped me.

"Wake up. Nearly there."

Blinking hard, I tried to stay upright. But it hurt. It hurt it hurt it hurt it—it had to stop.

The pain was turning to panic and the swirling dark ink in the skin of my arms was working its way up, writhing. I stared at my hand, dizzy and disoriented. If I hurt her—

"Butterflies," Skuld said. "The smell of her hair. Fresh cinnamon. Cold, salty ocean waves on your ankles. Your mother's stew."

How did she know?

They know everything, idiot.

I focused on the words. On the memories they brought up. I focused on the last one. Warm in my home as a child, in the long night of winter, as my mother taught me how to boil rabbit stew, adding spices that would sear the tongues of the toughest men. I'd sniffed each one and learned their names, and tried hard to remember how much of each. The smell of potatoes and parsnip and onion and fresh-baked bread all around me. The sweet, proud smile on her lips.

And I breathed.

The pain was still there, throbbing and burning, but I could breathe.

Skuld pulled on her thread, twisted it into a knot, and cut it. The sewing was done, my chest closed for the first time since Ragnarok. She placed her hands on my chest and closed her eyes, whispering runes under her breath.

I wanted it to work. I wanted to be healed so badly that I couldn't put any faith in her skill. If for some reason it didn't work, if I didn't come back to life, it would destroy me all at once. If it—

Something fluttered in my chest.

Thump.

Thump.

Tha-thump.

My heart.

I put my hand on my chest, my body and ears suddenly full of this noise that had been missing for so many years. A whooshing of blood as everything began again, pumping into my extremities.

How had I ever taken my life for granted for a single moment?

"All finished." Skuld used a gentle hand to pull my head back down. She took a second to wipe one of my tears away, then covered my good eye with her palm. "What do you see?"

I blinked to clear my sight and paid attention. It was hard to focus with all of these *things* happening inside my body, but I managed. There was something very faintly different, almost like I was imagining it, but it was there. Less cloud and more blurs that might be trees and fire and people.

"It won't come back all at once. Your body has to make all these connections again. It needs to learn to see. But you'll see again in brilliant colour one day." Skuld gave my wound a pat with the tips of her fingers, then rose to her feet.

All that was left of the hole that had killed me was a long line and some stitches.

Narvi's wounds took longer. He suffered through the closing of his stomach with more grace than I ever could have. He was only a quarter of the way through when mine was finished, and once I regained my footing, I went to him. I sat behind him and held him against me. He pressed his back into me like he wanted to crawl away, to get up and run. His fingers dug into the meat of my calves, and I was thankful I could take that pain from him. And all the while, Urd sewed.

The skin would only be the beginning of it. When Odin had murdered him, he'd bound me with Narvi's entrails. He would need new organs, a thing I couldn't imagine seidr doing, but that the Nornir managed to do all the same.

All that pain. It refused to sink into my consciousness. How could I begin to fathom what my son was feeling, deep under his skin?

I whispered memories in his ear and hoped it helped. I told him about how I'd held him for the first time, and the day he'd first come to the woods with me. I told him every silly, pointless moment I could think of, and hoped it did *something*.

Maybe he never heard a word of it.

It didn't matter.

After it was done, we rested, just for a little while. I knew that each moment we lingered was a moment we were costing Sigyn and her city. But as much as they needed me, Narvi needed me more. So I held him until he stirred and made it clear that he was ready.

The Nornir made us our first meal as living, breathing people again. It was simple, but even the experience of eating an apple was revolutionary. I had taken a thousand things for granted every day, and an apple was just the beginning.

After we had eaten and learned to tolerate the rush of blood in our veins, we gathered our wits and made to leave.

"Take the root up to Asgard. The path that veers right will take Angrboda back to Helheim." Skuld walked the last few steps with us to the mouth of the root. "And good luck to each of you."

"Thank you." I reached out a hand to shake hers and saw my skin again, writhing black halfway up my forearms.

"We're grateful, truly." Narvi still had a weariness on his face that didn't thrill me.

"Perhaps we'll see you again soon."

Skuld waved as we stepped into the root and followed it up. I expected it to take longer to find the fork in the road, but it was only a matter of minutes.

The three of us stood awkwardly in the seidr lantern light. Angrboda had never been much for goodbyes, but I had a feeling it would be a long time before I saw her again. Guilt roiled in my stomach for all the things I felt I was leaving unsaid.

Or maybe it was indigestion. I hadn't missed that.

Narvi threw his arms around Angrboda, surprising both of us. It was a hard, short-lived hug, and when he was done, he gave her arms a pat. "I know we're not exactly friends, but I appreciate the help you gave me. Please tell Hel I'll visit."

Angrboda's face settled into an amused grin. "I will. Don't get killed out there."

He returned the smile. "I won't."

Angrboda looked in my direction.

I wasn't sure what to say. "Don't forget to write."

"Oh, shut up." She rolled her eyes and moved to start down the root to Helheim.

"No, really," I called after her. "I feel like we'd be very good correspondence friends. I'll be so lonely!"

She gave me the finger without looking back and rounded a bend, out of sight.

It was a tiny bit easier to handle the light of the realms above than it had been in Urd's Well. It still took longer than I'd have liked for my sight to return in the glaring sun—my foggy bad eye notwithstanding—but we were soon staring at a field of sprouting trees where Idunn's woods once were, and the winding baby Yggdrasil that was growing from the wreckage of the old one.

There was so much I wanted to cherish: the bright, vibrant colours of trees and flowers and birds; the smells, fragrant and alive; the *air*. Crisp, fresh air that I hadn't even known I missed.

"You know what this calls for, don't you?" I asked.

Narvi sighed, his shoulder drooping. "Acorn Ride?"

"Don't look so offended." I peeled my bag off my shoulders and set it down. We wouldn't be needing them anymore. "You used to love Acorn Ride."

Narvi set his down as well. "*Váli* loved Acorn Ride."

"Well, we've got no other choice, so you'd better start liking it quickly."

Narvi stretched himself out, arms first, then legs, then closed his eyes. "Ready."

I let a few runes slip off my tongue. I hadn't used them in an age, but it was hard to forget something that had been such a staple of the early years of the family. A moment later there was a shimmer of air, an undoing of reality, and a pop.

Epilogues for Lost Gods

A tiny acorn fell to the ground where Narvi had just been standing.

When I had whispered the runes and settled into the shape of a hawk, I grabbed the acorn in my talons and took flight towards Fólkheim.

It took far too long to fly across the realms. Each wing beat felt like it took forever, my heart hammering in my little chest. Even from a distance, smoke was visible from the direction of what had once been Vanaheim. Something was happening, and it was hard to think about anything other than how late we were. Had Asgard marched out to battle yet? Was the fight over? Had we already lost, and all of our efforts had been for nothing?

I picked up speed.

The closer we got, the more of the clamour I could hear. Steel and screaming, arrows whistling through the air.

It wasn't over. There was still time for us to turn the tide.

I landed on top of a farm roof at the edge of the city and put the acorn down gently next to me. Three hops and I was far enough away to shift back to my body again. Once the world reorientated itself, I whispered the runes to bring Narvi back. He reappeared with a shimmer of air and a pop, and lurched over.

"Careful." I held him steady. "It's not much fun until you get used to it."

Narvi held his palm over his mouth, looking nauseated. "You can get used to *this*?"

"We were just dead for several years. A person can get used to anything." I scanned the scene before us, giving Narvi a moment to gather himself. The fields were charred and so was a portion of the city. All the trademarks of battle were there: the blood, bone, and bodies. And all that horrible noise.

The familiar tightness started in my chest. This battle blended with all the others that lived in my mind. I could see the sun disappearing from the sky, smell the realms burning. Ragnarok. It was all around me. Had never left me.

My skin was cold.

I looked down at my arms. The black that had settled there, whatever piece of Valravn it was, was swirling up my arms, under my tunic sleeves. Growing.

"Father, whatever you're doing, you need to stop!"

I took a deep breath. If this thing in me thrived on my pain, I had to starve it out. Or...

I tried to focus. To take all the swimming visions of Ragnarok and make them something else. Something new. The black continued to churn under my skin, but I could force it out, let it pool in my hands again, leaving my body.

A soldier was cowering behind a wall not far from us. I lobbed the black *thing* at him, hoping I had decent enough aim. It hit the leg of his trousers and exploded into a cloud of black mist.

The soldier screamed like he was being eviscerated and fell to the ground. He tore off his helmet and started pulling out his hair by the handful. There were no wounds, at least not any he wasn't making himself.

And for what it was worth, I could see clearly again. The panic was fading.

"This could work." I shrugged.

"Isn't that a little cruel? He probably didn't deserve it." Narvi didn't seem as impressed as he should have been.

"Maybe not." I stood up and looked back at him. "Ready?"

He nodded and slid off the roof into a pile of hay below.

I jumped because it was more fun and just in case anyone was watching.

The majority of Asgard's forces were already deep inside the city, but a line of archers were posted on the top of a stable. I gestured to Narvi to keep quiet as we approached. I let the battle around me sink in, let the sounds creep under my skin just enough. And when I thought it would overtake me, I pushed it back out for the archers to have.

My throw was off and the living darkness missed them, but it snaked up their boots and through their clothes until they were breathing it in. They fell into its grasp slowly, their bows dropping to the ground as they twitched and writhed and tried to get away from whatever was bubbling up inside their vision.

Oh, the screaming.

It was easy to see how this would work. Feed the darkness over and over, with myself and with the pain of others, and it would keep me powerful and hungry forever. How long had Valravn been gorging on pain and the hearts of kings to become as twisted as he was? How many years before he couldn't control it anymore? How long before *I* couldn't?

"Shit." Narvi was gaping at me with a mixture of horror and awe. "I think we're going to win."

I took a breath. "Narvi."

"Hmm?"

I swallowed, fear creeping into every piece of my body. "You stay near me and do not leave my sight. You're what's going to keep me in my own skin, alright?"

He nodded, and I knew it wasn't fair to ask this of him. I knew he shouldn't be taking care of me, keeping me from becoming something else. But I asked all the same.

"Come on. Time to find your mother." I pulled him along, the two of us running at a measured clip through the nearly empty blood-soaked streets. We needed to catch up to the battle.

Epilogues for Lost Gods

I breathed deep as I ran. I'd felt it before plenty of times, but never like this. The war hunger was on me, darkness coiling in my gut.

The remnants of a barricade lay broken on the ground, shattered among the bodies. It was obvious who fought for whom; one side was fitted with scraps and makeshift weapons and recycled steel, while the other wore armour that was painted gold and blood red.

As we pressed further into the city, a half-dozen warriors clamoured towards us, weapons already soaked in blood.

A series of runes flitted on my breath and the lot of them were engulfed in wildfire, tearing into the sky in streaks of teal.

Pain ripped into my arm, metal scraping against bone. An arrow was lodged in my flesh. "Motherfucker!"

I lashed out, sweeping my hand in the direction it had come from. Black smoke tore through the air and enveloped another archer. The scream began and ended just as abruptly.

"Stay still." Narvi took hold of my arm. He snapped the end off the arrow and pulled it out, pain tearing through my limbs. Black steamed from the wound, dissipating in the air. His hands settled around my bicep and he whispered runes, the kind his mother had taught him. The skin and muscle sewed themselves back together, leaving a silver scar, almost like the wound had never been there.

Love and pride for my magnificent son surged through me and once again the swirling black under my skin receded.

"Another very impressive scar for the collection." I ruffled his hair. "Thank you."

Narvi nodded and looked around. No one else was around, which meant we still weren't close enough to where the fighting was happening. They'd made it too far into the city.

Narvi kept us under cover of a seidr shield as we pushed further, taking out every soldier of Asgard that got in our way. It had been too easy and it wouldn't stay that way. Most of the battle seemed to be to the west, so we kept to the east, hoping to get into friendly territory.

The theory paid off as we found the first standing barricade. A conglomeration of beings from across the realms were poised behind it, ready to fight.

"Wait!" I held up a hand. "We're on your side! We're here for Sigyn!"

A Dwarf leaned towards a Jotun, whispering. Someone else pushed towards the front, an Elf I was almost sure I recognized from a lifetime ago. He rolled his eyes, which made me a little concerned he was yet another enemy I'd long forgotten about.

"That's Loki. Let him in."

A chorus of loud chatter rose up among the defenders, my name on their voices. And then they began to nod, one after the other. And the barricade moved.

"Where's Sigyn?"

The Elf shook his head. "Could be anywhere by now."

Narvi wiped the bottom of his shirt on his face, clearing away some of the dirt that had gathered there. "Send her a signal?"

I narrowed my eyes. "You're too smart to have been our child." I whispered a string of runes and summoned up wildfire. With a hard swing, I lobbed it into the air, an explosive burst of teal she would know anywhere.

If she was here. If she was outside and turned the right way. If she was still alive. Too many ifs.

We waited. My breath was caught in my throat.

Lavender flame burst into the sky.

She was fucking alive.

The way towards her signal was easier. Barricades moved out of our way one after the other as we sprinted through the streets, past machines and contraptions I'd never seen before and the people who manned them. The city was in tatters, but its people were ready to keep it at any cost. And with us, maybe they stood more of a fighting chance.

Then the rocks began to rain from the sky.

They crashed one after the other into the houses around us, ripping them to shreds. Each one was bigger than a head and they tore through everything in their paths. Whatever was launching them into the sky, they had to be stopped; otherwise, the barricades would amount to nothing.

"You!" a voice called out, unfamiliar but commanding. "Come help me!"

A woman with a brown ponytail tipped in electric blue waved us toward the roof she was perched on top of. Next to her was an odd device, large, long, and metallic, pointed out towards the fight.

"What are you waiting for?" she called again.

"Keep guard. Watch my back," I said to Narvi. I ran around the building and climbed up the ladder that was propped against it. From on top of the house, I had a better view of the city and the wooden machines that were being loaded up with rock.

"Catapults," the woman muttered. "Amateurs. Help me get this in the tip of the cannon."

"The what?"

"This. Help me get this big rock—" She pointed to a pile of rocks. "—into this thing."

I did as I was told, working with her to heft the rock into the tip of the cannon. She angled the barrel of the thing towards one of the catapults and stepped back.

Epilogues for Lost Gods

"Hopefully this works. Get back here. You don't want to get hit by recoil." She knelt down in the back with flint and rock and beckoned me to kneel beside her.

"Fire?"

She nodded.

I whispered a rune and snapped a finger for the showmanship, a spark of wildfire lighting my fingertip.

Her eyes shot up to mine. She looked too hard, too long. "You're Loki."

"Last time I checked."

Her eyes went wide. "Holy fuck."

I nodded to the cannon. "Should I light it?"

She nodded, excitement in her eyes. She passed me a small torch and covered her ears. "Do it."

I lit the torch and covered my ears as best I could with one hand and one shoulder before pressing the torch to the small hole in the back of the cannon. An explosion ripped from the metal and the rock shot through the air, tearing a straight line through everything in front of it, including a pair of soldiers. The shot left a ringing in my ears, and the cold darkness in my skin coiled. Too loud, too sudden.

"Missed." She stood and went to the rock pile again, nodding for me to help. We put another rock in. "A little to the left."

One of the catapults let loose and a rain of rocks came down close to us, one of them tearing a hole in the roof.

"They lack accuracy. Just watch." She stuffed black powder into the cannon, jammed another rock inside, and lit it again. The shot decimated one of the catapults, the wood and metal tearing to shreds under its brute force. The woman shouted and threw a fist into the air. "Yes!"

"Who *are* you?" I asked, more than a little impressed.

She held out a hand to shake mine. "Alyssa. Head Modernist Engineer for the city. Sigyn's friend."

"I need to get to her—"

"I'll go with you. I know where she'll be."

I nodded. "You need to be here though, don't you?"

She waved the comment off. "Nah. I just didn't want to be useless, so I stole someone else's job." She looked up, past my shoulders. "Besides, I think this is about to be lost ground."

A wave of völur were headed towards us, lightning crackling on their fingers, shooting out around them at anyone who came too close.

Alyssa took a red tube from her pocket, propped it on the pile of rocks, and lit the string coming out of the bottom. The string burned quickly, disappearing into the tube, and another explosion sounded, smaller than the cannon. A burst of smoke flew skyward and after a moment, burst into a thousand tiny glowing stars.

She tossed the torch off the roof and onto a patch of bare stone. "They'll know we're retreating. Time to go, city saviour."

CHAPTER TWENTY-EIGHT

SIGYN

*"There was more I could've done with my time.
I'd hoped Asgard was real, but I didn't really know. So why
didn't I do more with the days I had?"*

— Roque, Volume 77

I brushed my hand along the newly healed skin of a Jotun woman. "Ready to go back out?"

She nodded, hauled herself up, and headed back towards the fray with a gait that said someone was about to pay for having almost dismembered her.

All around me were other völur who had remained in the back line to heal our troops. We were never going to beat Asgard by sheer strength or with our numbers, but we had more seidr than them by far. Without anyone to shame them for wanting to learn, people of all kinds had stepped forward to learn the craft, and now we had a tiny fleet of amateur healers to bolster our forces.

With no one in line waiting to be pieced together, I took the moment to pry the waterskin from my belt and take a long drink. It was then, with my head craned back, that the sky filled with teal flame.

A Dwarf with a gash across his ribs jumped. "What the fuck was that?"

"Hope," I whispered, watching the flame curve and dip towards the houses before sputtering out.

They had come.

I secured the water back to my hip, grinning. I stood and let the runes wash across my tongue, trying for the biggest, brightest wildfire I could summon. A pillar of lavender burst from my palms and burned towards the clouds.

Come find me.

My heart sang. My tiny reprieve from the battle was over. Things needed doing. Perhaps a few more völur were not enough to turn the tides, but I knew my family. It had been the legends of Loki's power that had brought me to him in the first place so many years ago, and Narvi had been proving himself more capable than we were since he could walk. If any two people in the nine broken realms could save us, it was them.

Asgard had pressed us back behind the halfway point of the city, the market. It had been cleared out days ago, all the wares and irreplaceable goods stored in a safer place. All that was left were a few old ramshackle market stalls we'd scattered around the open space. We'd barricaded the streets just before the empty square with piles of debris and makeshift fences, but the soldiers manning them were on the retreat. We'd spent months stamping into them that staying alive was worth more than ground, and it was keeping us in this fight.

The first of the barricades fell and dozens of Asgard's soldiers flooded through, all banking on this one entrance as the way to finally get past our defences. Too bad for them that we'd been waiting for just that kind of enthusiasm.

The loud flap of wings came from overhead. Mist, our last living Valkyrie, soared above us with a keg held fast in her arms. She raced from one end of the market to the other, spilling clear, slick lard oil over the soldiers as she went. The group let out a chorus of annoyed, disgusted screams, and a few of them lost their footing.

The archers who had been hiding in our merchant stalls stood, their arrows alight, and fired.

Flame caught the oil in three places, blazing across the ground and over the armour of the soldiers. The few who had stumbled far enough to keep away from the fire were staring slack-jawed.

All except one, who was whispering runes under her tongue, water beginning to swirl between her palms.

Was she an idiot? It was *grease*. She was going to spread the fire further and burn down half the city.

Perhaps that was the plan.

She was too far for me to accurately throw an element at, so I ran forward and ducked down behind one of the merchant stalls next to a bewildered archer. "Quickly, the one in the back line!"

He glanced around the edge of the stall, then stood, pulled back, and let the arrow fly. It soared through the air and pierced the völva in the stomach just as she launched a wave of water towards her burning comrades.

She dropped to the ground, but the grease had spread across the market square, catching on empty stalls and what little greenery had taken root there.

I stretched my neck. Seidr of the variety I needed would take more energy than I'd like, but an uncontrolled fire in the city wasn't a mistake we could afford. I chanted a string of runes for some long-disused wind seidr, peeking around the merchant stall to see how quickly it would work.

It began in the centre of the burning soldiers. A bit of fire dying in a puff of smoke. The space expanded as I whispered, the air pushing itself away from that point and starving out the flame. The nearest soldier gasped and clawed at her throat. Then another, and another. As the flames died, the people caught in the airless vortex suffocated, one by one.

It was hard to think of a worse way to find your way to Helheim than to be burned and *then* suffocated, but I'd have time to feel guilty about that later.

Probably.

With the flames extinguished, I let the chant fade. The air rushed back into the space all at once, ruffling the clothes of so many dead Asgardian people.

A high-pitched whistle caught my attention. I looked skyward, and an explosion rained tiny shimmering stars over the city. Alyssa's fireworks. She wasn't far. I answered with another burst of wildfire. Hopefully one of them, any of them, would find me soon.

Something smashed around the corner of the broken barricade and staggered out into the market. The fucking troll.

The enormous thing was barely clothed and had the deepest scowl on its long, bulbous face. Its skin was already five different colours, blood and soot and who knew what else on top of its normal grey complexion.

"Get back!" I screamed, pushing the archer next to me to move. We ran towards the back of the market, trying to make it to better cover and more comrades before the troll could catch up.

I looked in time to see it pick up one of the stalls, heft it over its head, and toss it. It careened towards one of the other archers and crushed them against the ground. I nearly tripped over my feet as I tried to decide if I should help, but no. There was no coming back from that particular injury.

Back inside the city streets, the closest barricade moved to let us through, then slammed shut behind us.

"Troll!" I tried to catch my breath, pointing back towards the market. Soldiers moved around me as I staggered towards the back line and leaned against a wall.

This was too long a day.

"Mother?"

My head shot up at the sound of that voice. Narvi was there, a few paces away. He was battle-worn but healthy, looking at me as if trying to decide if I was real.

I closed the distance in a breath and pulled him into a hug, pressing my face into his hair. He smelled of dirt and sweat, but he also smelled like my baby boy. I sobbed, choking on all the feelings I'd been pushing down.

They'd come. They'd really come.

"See, I told you I'd find her."

I looked up to see Alyssa standing next to Loki, and my stomach dropped. My husband standing next to the woman who'd just confessed to loving me. It was one thing to know that these things were coming, and another to be faced with it before I had a chance to catch my breath.

Something on Alyssa's face looked pained, or possibly awkward, but Loki was oblivious. His soft, doting smile riddled me with guilt as he set his hand on my shoulder.

"I hope we're not too late." Tears filled his eyes.

Pushing down the guilt, I reached up a hand and cupped his cheek. "You're not. In fact—" I caught sight of his arm, of his hand on my shoulder. It was black as night, something swirling under his skin. "Loki, what the hel is this?"

Loki grimaced. "It's a long, complicated story and I—"

The barricade behind me shattered. Debris flew through the air, some of it lodging in bodies that stood too close. A dozen of our people dropped to the ground, screaming out. The troll swung its arm again, smashing the path wide enough to step through.

I turned to Alyssa. "Special weapons?"

"Follow me!" Alyssa waved a hand and ran in the opposite direction of the troll.

I pulled myself away from Narvi and Loki, looking at them with desperation.

"We'll be fine. Go!" Loki pushed Narvi behind him just as a seidr shield rose around them, runes pouring from Narvi's mouth.

I prayed it wouldn't be the last time I saw them alive.

Thankfully, I'd only fallen a few paces behind Alyssa. She'd guided me through several streets and down an alley, where an inconspicuous box was waiting. From it, she pulled what she had once called *Daddy's 12-gauge*. She strung a pouch of ammunition to her belt and gripped the forged scrap-metal shotgun in both hands. "Let's go."

But by the time we were out of the alley, the battle had spread to us. I could hear the troll, but it was lost somewhere between the buildings and the enemy soldiers. A sword swung too close to my face and I pulled the dagger from my belt, spinning back around to press it into the woman's throat. She grasped at her neck, struggling to breathe, and dropped to her knees. A crack of mechanical thunder sounded and a pair of soldiers in front of Alyssa fell, their armour sprayed with short-range destruction. Her eyes were wide with horror, but she pumped the barrel of her homemade death machine again, pressing on with all the courage she could muster.

Not a warrior indeed.

I summoned up a fistful of lightning and pressed it one after the other against any enemy who came too close. Their flesh shook and burned under my touch, leaving bodies in my wake that flopped like dying fish. The skin on my palm started to peel, exposed for too long, and I shook the electricity free. Another clap of mechanical thunder, another soldier falling.

I had enough time to take a deep breath. To feel the bone-deep exhaustion of the runes. If I was lucky enough to make it out of this, I'd be useless for days. Was probably about to be useless for the rest of the battle.

Flame burst out above us in unnatural colours.

I ducked, the heat coming too close. Enemy völur were scattered on the roofs of the homes and ruins around us, and they were raining wildfire over everything.

"Disperse!" I cried out. "Don't get near them!"

But the street was too cramped. Too many people, too many long weapons. And the enemy wasn't giving us the opportunity to run.

Alyssa fired another point-blank shot into someone in front of us, emptied the gun, and started fishing in her pouch for more ammunition.

Tears ran down her face, her jaw clenched as she dealt out death after death.

"Reposition!" I cried out again, but almost no one heard me. I pressed back, trying to give us more room as flesh burned all around us. We were too closed in.

"Fuck!" Alyssa had dropped the shells she had been holding. Her face was turning red with desperation, her hand shaking, and above her, one of the enemy völva pointed her hands in our direction.

I tackled Alyssa to the ground, slamming her down onto the stone. Violet flame burst out where we'd just been standing. The heat of it pierced my boots and I tried to shimmy further out of the way. People were stepping over us. A boot connected with my ribs and I groaned, trying to breathe through the pain. We'd be trampled if we didn't get out of the way. Alyssa scrambled backwards, finding her way behind a piece of ruined wall. I followed.

"Are you alright?" I crouched behind the fractured piece of wall with her.

She stared out over the stone and into the battle. Her eyes were full of panic and the rush of battle, and she wasn't answering.

I put my hand on hers. "Alyssa?"

She looked back at me and took a long, controlled breath. "You saved my life."

I started to answer, but she leaned forward and kissed me. It took me aback, and I nearly lost my balance. Her lips lingered, brushing against mine with such deep want and gratitude. My reservation melted under her kiss and I cupped her face in my hands. She tasted like debris and gunpowder and sweat. Her fingers laced into my hair, and hidden from the violence around us just for a moment, she made me feel beautifully, effortlessly loved.

CHAPTER TWENTY-NINE

LOKI

"Everything.
I'd take back everything.
It should have been my life he took."

— *Clemens, Volume 92*

Everything crashed to a stop. The screaming, the blood, the crack of bone and wood and steel. It all deafened in my ears. Nothing in the nine could have torn me out of the world as fully, as successfully, as watching my wife kiss someone else.

They were crouched behind a broken wall, hiding from the throng. Nearly out of sight. Not enough though. Not hidden well enough.

Alyssa. The woman I had helped.

What colossal fucking joke was this?

Sigyn had kissed me, slept with me. All but promised me. While I was lying next to her, dreaming about coming back to her, had it been a lie? While I was racing across Helheim for her? Risking my life and her son's life to save her and her *fucking* city?

Every question churned more rage inside me. How long? Why? How could she? Whispers of past pains curled inside my blood, a whisper in the back of my mind.

No one really loves you.

Never will.

They all use you in the end.

Tricked you, like all the others.

An axe cut through the air on my right side, gliding too close to my stomach, and the battle came rushing back. Too fast, too real. I twisted, my seething anger pouring out of me in runes and flame and darkness. I lashed out, pressing the wildfire against someone's skin, not caring who they were. Another and another, armour and leather and metal seeping into the corners of my eye, and I painted them with blood and brands.

Between each distraction, each body before it fell, I watched. Watched Sigyn and Alyssa as their lips parted, their hands trembling, the look on their faces.

They were worried.

Good.

They should be.

Mine. She was *mine*. I had done everything right. I had earned her back. Sigyn had asked me to walk the depths of Helheim for her and I *had*. What good was *anything* if doing the right thing amounted to this bullshit? If all I got was her in the arms of someone else?

This was not the new fate that I had agreed to.

Black was spilling out from under my skin, trailing from my hands without my summoning it. I was full to the brim and it was leaking out. All the things that had ever happened to me, all the fears I had ever had, curling into this one moment.

Taken from me. She was being *taken*.

Taken like your children.

Taken like your childhood.

Nothing is ever yours to keep.

A mortal. A weak, fragile, powerless woman. No seidr in her, no godhood. She didn't have centuries of pain to tie her to Sigyn like I did. Love and loss and a history so long and beautiful and sordid that it burned to look at it too long.

What could she *possibly* ever offer?

I pressed further through the fight, putting the fear of gods into every völva and knife-wielder that got in my way. Pushing through them had made a great distance out of a few meters, but I was close.

A great roar sounded. The house next to me shattered and the force of it threw me to the ground, along with everyone else nearby. My head cracked against the stone hard enough to make the realm spin around me. I tried to see through the haze.

The fucking troll.

It had an enormous piece of lumber in its hand, a makeshift club, and it had demolished that home in one swing. Dust rose in a thick cloud, choking everyone around it, but the troll just kept moving.

Towards Sigyn.

I tried to push myself off the ground but stumbled, still spinning. Sigyn had gotten up, standing between Alyssa and the troll. Trying to protect her, like an idiot.

Epilogues for Lost Gods

A thunderous boom sounded from that *secret weapon* Alyssa was brandishing, but whatever it was, it only scraped the skin of the troll in dozens of places.

Sigyn's lips were moving, and a burst of wildfire shot out at the troll. Just like Alyssa's weapon, the wildfire did nothing but distract the troll for a moment. Sigyn pivoted to lightning, but its spark was small and pitiful in her palm. It wouldn't be enough. And I still couldn't do anything but crawl towards her.

"Mother!" Narvi's voice came from somewhere above me. The air around Sigyn and Alyssa shimmered and solidified, a shield forming around them. It would be enough to buy me time. Enough to bring back my focus for runes or the rage that had been knocked out of me.

I sat up, trying to clamber to my feet like the others who had been too close. Something flew through the air and Narvi screamed.

An arrow was lodged in his shoulder.

The shield fell.

I shook my head, trying to focus. I was summoning up the energy but it wasn't *there,* it wasn't happening, and she was in trouble, I needed to—

The troll picked Sigyn up with its empty hand, and before she could do anything to stop it, threw her into the shattered remains of the house.

Sigyn's scream tore through me. She had landed on the jagged, broken frame of a loom. She hung, her body curved back over the wooden frame that jutted out of her chest. Impaled. Unmoving.

I stopped breathing. Waited for her to move, for her to get up and be alright and this whole thing to be some fucking hallucination. I had been so angry with her, so stricken with grief, and now she was hanging there like a ragdoll, blood spilling from her wounds.

No, I had *not* come this far to watch her die.

Rage ignited in my veins. I could see every moment ahead of me, every empty day, every lonely night. The thought of Sigyn betraying me was *minuscule* compared to the idea of her not existing in these realms. It was wholly unacceptable, *unlivable* for her to die. I had survived so many things, but I would not survive this. I let the sorrow consume me until nothing was left but the seething, whispering hate that Valravn had gifted to me. Darkness filled the air, clouded out the sun, and I stepped forward.

No one stood in the dark void but the troll and me. Everything else, every*one* else was outside, trapped in the false night, their distant clamour and confusion secondary to the destruction I was about to unleash.

The troll growled and swung at me, its makeshift club just missing as I leapt back. "You think a piece of wood is what's going to take me back to Helheim? Take her?

That our legacy ends with a fucking troll?" I shook my head. "No."

It swung again, missed again.

I leapt inside its guard, too close for it to hit me, and pressed my hands to its stomach, feeling nothing but grief and fury. Black mist poured from my hands as I closed the distance and slammed my palm onto its skin. It looked at me, confused and annoyed at first. Then it convulsed, the black seeping under its skin.

"I did *not* crawl back from the dead and change my fate so that some *fucking troll* could kill the love of my entire existence!" I screamed my throat raw. "You have no *fucking clue* what real pain is, you brainless fucking toad!"

The troll's knees buckled, its head craned back to the sky. The roiling mist was crawling up into its body and it began to tear at its own head. Skin ripped and it groaned, but it didn't stop. Just kept tearing at itself like it was trying to dig its minuscule brain out.

Good.

Something took hold of me. An idea that wasn't mine, that came from somewhere else. My hand on the hilt of my dagger, my arm reaching up to plunge it into the troll's chest. I pushed, straining to break its skin, and it gave way with a visceral rip. Blood oozed out, a midnight purple.

Reach inside.

I did.

Warmth enveloped my hand, my wrist, my arm as I pushed under its skin.

The heart. Take the heart.

First trolls. Then kings.

I stopped. Blinked. Realized I was elbow deep in the chest cavity of a troll whose guts smelled like week-old meat, and promptly gagged.

This Valravn thing was not a gift and it was *not* something I wanted to keep doing.

I pulled my arm out of the now-corpse and backed away. The black under my clean arm was fading, retreating down to my fingers as if I'd dipped them in ink, but leaving the rest of me a blood-soaked Jotun-white. The darkness around me was fading, the sun poking through.

Gods, what horrors lived under my skin.

As my head cleared, the voices around me caught my attention.

"Narvi, you're ready?"

Sigyn was still unconscious, still hanging from the loom, surrounded by people trying to help her. Váli, wherever he had come from, was covered in blood spatter. He was behind his mother, his hands under her arms. Alyssa was guiding a pair of soldiers who had her legs. Someone had cut off the end of the loom frame, and made it easier to...

Gods, they were—

"Lift!"

Sigyn snapped to life as her body was heaved off the post that had just been jutting from her chest. Her scream was so loud, so deep and full of desperation that it nearly brought me to my knees.

They laid her out next to Narvi and tore open her clothing. The wound was too big, too deadly. Narvi was good, but this was moments from being permanent.

I dropped to my knees next to Narvi, grabbed his hand, and pushed every last ounce of energy I had left into him.

He had to save her. He had to.

CHAPTER THIRTY

LOKI

*"I think it was the stupidest thing I've ever done, and I once
got into a bar fight over the lineage of a Lord of the Rings
character, you know?"*

— *Alyssa, Volume 3*

S itting on the roof of a boarded-up shop, I looked down over the city, arms on
my knees. It had been three days since the battle and they were still washing
blood from the streets. According to the council, 481 citizens from the
2,000-something who had lived in the city were dead or missing. And there were more
than 1,000 bodies from Asgard.

If a person were to do the math, pressing up those numbers against how many
people were left living in the nine realms, it would be a bleak picture indeed.

So many dead because a few people in charge wanted more than they had.

A nicer version of myself would be down there, helping. I'd found the courage for
two days to be in the thick of things. Dragging bodies to the pyres, finding places for
displaced families to sleep, bringing lost family members to the reunification council.
That last one killed me every time. Watching the emotionless acceptance in the eyes of
a broken child who knew their foster family wasn't coming back.

Two days I had scraped myself out of the cot they'd set up for me in what had
probably once been a closet. Two days I had done what needed doing because it was *the
right thing*. I was trying to deserve my new thread, to have earned this fate.

I couldn't anymore.

I needed to step away from the grim work, but not just from that. Under the
blood and gore, the city knew it was over. Vidar had been found beheaded among the

bodies, and Magni and Modi were captured and put to death unceremoniously after the fight, sent to Hel's halls where they'd been promised. Baldur had never shown his cowardly face in battle, but they would find him and send him to his keeper. Asgard wasn't a threat anymore.

People could start moving on.

Must be nice.

I knew I should be grateful for all the other things I had. Sunrises and fresh bread and the other people in my family. But I'd spent so long waiting for the day when Sigyn and I would meet again. Days when we would maybe be able to move past things, maybe not. I'd expected her to shut me out from the start, but I'd never thought I'd get so close only to end up here.

The ladder on the side of the roof shook, boots stomping up its length. Váli's haphazardly bound red waves of hair appeared over the edge of the building.

"Someone said you were up here, slacking," he joked.

"Did they? I wasn't aware that anyone gave a fuck."

Váli gave me a sour look as he pulled himself up onto the roof and sat down nearby. "That's sullen, even for you."

I kept staring out over the city, barely taking in the bustle. "People change. I've been sullen for years. Death takes a lot of the pep from one's step."

Váli nodded, letting my words hang there for a moment. "Shouldn't you at least be a little happy to be here?"

"How can you—?" I stopped myself before I could say something cruel. Took a breath. "I'm sorry. It's complicated, Váli."

"I can agree with that." His voice was careful, tempered. He shifted, looking over at me. "You covered your arms."

I glanced down at the long-sleeved tunic and the riding gloves I'd pulled from some ruined shop. "It's easier if I don't have to look at it. Everyone else has started using it to measure if I'm approachable or not, and I don't quite like it."

Váli nodded. "Narvi told me what happened with Valravn. Explained how he thinks it works. He also told me what you told the Nornir to earn a new fate."

I didn't say anything back. I didn't know what I *could* say.

He sighed. "Look, I know things have never really been good between us. And there's a lot we need to talk about. A lot. But I also know I spent a lot of time thinking about what I'd have done differently, if I had a chance. I mean, I thought you were dead while you were in that cave, and then you really did just *die*. I had this chance stolen from me before. So if you're going to put in the effort, I'd like to figure out what it is we are to each other."

The speech took me off guard. It was so open, so…full of opportunity. He was offering me a way forward, even after all those years, all those mistakes. I had hoped for a chance like this, someday, but never imagined I'd ever get it. And here he was, asking me to try.

"Yes. Of course I will." I tried to pull the enthusiasm into my voice, though I still felt more empty than full. Like it was too good to be true. "But if I'm being honest, I don't know where to start."

Váli cleared his throat. "I'm going to get married after the city is back in order. You could start by being there."

"Married?" My first son, my daring soldier who had always had an unquenchable, stubborn fire, was getting married. A thing that hadn't been possible not that long ago. I blinked back the tears. "I will. That's good news, very good news."

I wanted to hug him, but was it something he would allow? He'd never let me get that close before.

I decided not to push my luck.

"Are you ready to go see Mother now?"

"Is she awake?"

He shook his head.

"Then no. Let's wait a little longer. She won't miss us just yet." I sniffed and blinked back the tears that were welling up. I had to change the subject if I was going to stall. "What food do you miss the most?"

Váli looked at me, puzzled and suspicious.

"Come on." I waved a hand dismissively. "We used to feast in Valhalla every night. Meat and mead and the best fruit the Valkyrie could find. Then your mother's cooking, after things went to hel. Now breakfast is whatever we're lucky enough to find. You must miss something."

He smirked. "Caverndeep Ale. The Dwarven folk know how to brew, I'll give them that."

I nodded. "Ale was never to my taste, but I'd trade my left leg for another bottle of Elven wine. Something light and breezy. I'm not picky."

"Freshly caught pan-fried breaded cod with lemon," Váli countered.

"Venison stew, as hot and spicy as your grandmother used to make it."

"Apple pastry fresh from the market."

"Oranges."

"A thick steak slathered in gravy."

And on it went, one delicious memory after the other, until things weren't so jagged between us anymore. It was simple. Seemingly inconsequential. But it was more than I'd seen him smile…maybe ever. There was too much to say and not enough room to even begin to say it. This…this was a start.

In all the years Sigyn and I had been married, I had rarely had cause to sit by her bedside, despite how she had spent an eternity sitting by mine. She had only been ill a handful of times, and aside from the birth of the boys, I'd only seen her hurt once in a way she couldn't immediately have mended. She'd broken her ankle in the middle of the woods and she was in too much pain to fix it herself. I'd been useless as she'd cried and screamed, so I'd used runes to put her to sleep and carried her out of the woods on my back. It had broken my heart to see her like that.

This? This was so much worse.

Sitting by her bed and watching her shallow breaths, one after the other, was agony. The völur in the city had done what they could, Narvi included, but everyone was tired. The city had needed so much after the battle was over, and they'd given every ounce of their energy to mend everyone in their power. As they'd cleaned her up, they had found bruises under the dirt, scorches under the clothing. She'd been battered long before she'd been impaled. Even with the hole in her chest healed, she still hadn't woken up.

They'd done what they could. The rest was up to her.

How many nights would I need to spend staring at the woman I loved and hoping she'd open her eyes and…

And what? Tell me that she loved me most? That I had been raving mad on dark thoughts and she hadn't actually kissed Alyssa? This wasn't some romance novel where everything turned out fine in the end because it had been plotted that way the entire time.

This was the woman who maybe didn't love me anymore.

And who could blame her?

The door to Sigyn's room creaked open and a face peeked through. Alyssa startled at the sight of me. "I'm sorry. I can come back later."

"It's fine." I stayed where I was, not bothering to look at her for long. "I haven't had anyone to silently judge me since Váli left."

"I'm not going to judge you. If you want me to leave—"

"No. I'm sure she'd want you to stay."

Alyssa lingered in the door a moment, as if making the choice to stay or run. Finally, she stepped inside and closed the door. With one hand worrying at her other arm, she sat down at the foot of the bed. "Has anything changed?"

I shook my head.

She stared at Sigyn, remorse written all over her face. I'd always been good at reading people, and this woman was an open book. Just being comfortable to sit on her bed, like she belonged there, that told me more than I wanted to know. But the hitch of her breath, the way she sat like she was going to curl into herself...

"I know you're angry at her. At us," she whispered.

It had been too warm inside for riding gloves. I stared at my hands, the black lingering around my nailbeds. Not that angry, it seemed.

She cleared her throat and started again, a little stronger that time. "Sigyn can't speak for herself, so you'll have to trust me when I say that she never did anything wrong. She was my closest friend for years, and in that moment, I couldn't help it. She was kind, and passionate, and sincere. Surely you know what it's like to be in a room with her. She has this pull, and I was just a moon in her orbit."

I squinted. "Orbit?"

Alyssa sighed. "The concept falls apart when you live in a realm where celestial bodies are pulled through the sky by gods..." She pursed her lips and tried again. "I just mean to say that she...Sigyn drew me in. It wasn't her fault I fell in love with her, and I hope you'll forgive her for what *I* did."

Leaning forward in my chair, I put my face in my hands. "I don't know what any of this amounts to. I thought that the hard part would be behind me when the battle was over."

"I'm sorry." Alyssa picked at the skin around her fingernail. "I know she'll choose you. She has no reason not to."

I sat up and stared at Sigyn, so at peace while we were having this uncomfortable conversation. Oblivious and dreaming and so far away from all this pain. "That's where you're very wrong, darling. She has *every* reason not to."

CHAPTER THIRTY-ONE

SIGYN

*"I stayed quiet too long.
By the time I was brave enough, the moment had passed.
Gods, I need another chance."*

— *Daly, Volume 88*

Sometimes dreaming feels like an eternity. I'd had nights where I felt like I'd lived a whole other life between sunset and sunup, and others where I'd just blinked and it was morning again.

This sleep was different.

It was deep and real, and lacked the abstract things that tended to take place in my dreams. And nothing of note happened in it. Not a thing. It was just a series of normal days and normal nights, set in the backdrop of life in Asgard, back when things were easy. My old hall, sometimes full of joyful laughter and other times, quiet and content. Loki, Váli, and Narvi were there, and people there who didn't belong in that time. Mist, several members of council, Alyssa. People who loved or, at the least, respected me. And each day that went by was one that made me happy, devoid of the doom and dread that had ruled over us for so long.

Waking from that dream was not something I was all that pleased to do.

Every muscle in my body was stiff. Some were bruised, and my head throbbed like I hadn't had anything to drink for a year. I tried to sit up, but my torso ached.

"Mother, stay put. Don't try to get up."

I squinted, trying to focus on who was there through my heavy eyelids. Narvi. He slid down from a chair next to my bed and knelt on the floor beside me.

"Do you feel alright? Do you need something?"

215

"Water." My throat was dry and the sound was more croak than voice.

Narvi quickly filled a cup from the pitcher on the bedside table and helped me sit up. It was difficult, not painful, but something told me it was the remnants of something much worse.

My hand trembled as I tried to cup the water, and Narvi kept it in his firm grip, refusing to let me try to drink alone. The water came slowly, a balm across my tongue, a caress down my raw throat.

When the cup was empty, he set it down and took my hand. "How do you feel?"

"Like hel." I cleared my throat, trying to find my voice. "How long have I been asleep?"

"This is day four. It's past noon now." He ran a thumb over the back of my hand. "We were worried."

My head was so foggy, so full of all those false happy days. "I remember being in the battle, but then…then nothing. And I'm guessing we won because we're not dead." I looked at him, paused. "We're not dead, are we?"

A smirk touched his lips. "We're not dead. You got hurt. The troll…it impaled you."

I set a hand on the part of my chest that felt wrong. Someone had dressed me in a gown that parted in the front. I pushed one side far enough to still hide my breast, and there it was. New, silver-tinged skin the size of a fist, sitting just right of centre.

It came back to me in flashes. I could remember looking down, seeing the wood jagged and bloody in the middle of my chest. The pain. The bursting of flesh, the snapping of bone. It had been worse than any—no. It had been *just* as bad as the burn of snake venom on my skin. I stared at my fingers, at the melted-wax welts that had been scarred into them. Small wonder my mind had tried to protect me from yet another horror.

"We did our best, but we didn't have enough energy for seidr after the battle. You had broken bones, torn organs, the skin was missing—" He looked away, took a breath. "We did what we could. We still are. But a lot of other people needed saving too."

I reached up to tangle my fingers in his hair and my arm complained about the movement. "I'm alive and almost well. I couldn't ask for more. Thank you." I pointed at the pitcher. "Can I…?"

Narvi filled the cup again and watched me drink another cup. I could have drunk an ocean and it wouldn't have been enough, but I let it be and gave the bed a pat. "Come lie down with me?"

A sweet smile graced his lips and he came around the other side of the bed. Narvi was careful crawling in, like I was a priceless vase and any overexuberant movement would shatter me. Once he was under the covers, he curled up into my side, his head nestled gently on my shoulder. It pulled a little, but I could bear it for another moment like this with the son I had lost.

I ran my fingers down the length of his scalp. "Tell me what I've missed."

Narvi closed his eyes, settling into the old comforts of a childhood long gone. "The city is repairing. The dead have been put to rest, the market is running at a bare minimum capacity, and the council seems to have thought of everything. I've helped where I could. I spend the mornings in the infirmary and the evenings helping whoever needs healing. The afternoons are for you." He paused a moment, thinking. "Oh, Váli told me there was a raven from Hel. The gods of Asgard have all arrived in Helheim. She's kept her part of the bargain and Eyvindr, Idunn, and Bragi are being escorted to the Nornir for a new fate."

I drew in a breath. There was a tightness in my chest—something aside from the injury—that I didn't want to let spill over. "That's good news. Hod must be beside himself."

Narvi tilted his head up to look at me. "He is. Tomorrow I have to help him find new things for Eyvindr's return. Clothes, quills, ink, wool. He wants to knit a new blanket for him before he gets back." His eyes were glistening. "I don't think I've ever seen him allow himself to be this happy."

I kept playing with his hair, pushing back a grin. "We're not all smart enough or lucky enough to love people as boldly as we want to. We can't go wasting second chances."

Snuggling his face into my shoulder, Narvi let out a contented sigh. "That, I can understand."

I tapped my fingers gently on his head. "And what about you? Are you alright? Are you fitting in?"

His silence spoke volumes. I waited, feigning patience as he mulled over whatever he was planning to say to me. I remembered his reluctance to tell me anything while I was in Helheim, but what I was met with instead was vulnerability.

"I shouldn't complain. I'm healthy and I have new opportunities, but I'm afraid of what all this means. I know who I used to be, and I'm not quite him anymore. I used to think that everyone wanted to do the right thing; all they needed was a nudge. Now I know that's not true. I don't know how to go back to being someone who doesn't know that."

"You don't have to. Who do *you* want to be?"

He took in a deep breath. Sighed. "I don't know. I still want to do the right thing, to help build something good. I just don't know what that looks like, and I'm not sure how I'm supposed to know, not when I walk out those doors and I know no one and nothing and the people I know remember what the insides of me look like and—"

I squeezed my arms around him too tightly, trying to break the torrent of thoughts pouring out of him. He gasped and began to cry into my nightdress.

"I don't know who I am. They took that from me." His breath hitched, the rest of his words coming in broken pieces.

"I know." I kissed the top of his head, breathed in the sweet smell of him. "It's not fair. But you are one of the bravest boys I've ever known and you're going to find your way around this. Your father and I will be here for you every step of the way. And Hod, and your brother."

Narvi nodded against my chest.

"How did he take it? You being back."

Narvi sniffed, trying to compose himself enough to speak. "It was strange at first. But he thanked me for the runes. I think that was hard for him. We spoke a little about…it. But I don't think either of us is ready to relive it yet. We're still trying to learn to be in the same room together."

"Things take time. You have so much of it. There's no rush." I paused, weighing whether I should say what I wanted to. Whether it would help or hurt. "I think you should consider staying here in the city and working with the council."

Narvi looked up at me, his eyes red and his cheeks tear-slicked. "What do you mean?"

"You know what hope feels like. You know how to help people understand each other, and you've always wanted people to listen to each other. This place is a city built for someone like you. It needs so much, but it gives everything back. People *want* to work together. And I think that after you've had time to think it over, you should consider putting those skills to work as a member of council."

"I can't just ask for that."

"I can." I shrugged and gave him a smirk. "Do you really think they'll say no to a woman who just got impaled? Just think about it; that's all."

He nodded and closed his eyes, weary after all those emotions had come flooding out.

I kept running my fingers through his hair as his breath steadied and softened and he fell asleep. My precious baby son, who had suffered so much. He was so tired.

So was I.

I didn't have the heart to tell him I was finished. Not yet, anyway. When all of this was over, when the city was on its feet and functioning in the hands of the council, I was going to get the fuck out of here. After an eternity of fighting and surviving, all I wanted to do was live in some semblance of peace. No more wars, no more preparing for the worst. Just endless days full of warm meals, and good conversation, and late-night reading. I could bring this life to a close, and the two of us, Loki and I…

Except there weren't two of us anymore.

Fuck.

CHAPTER THIRTY-TWO

LOKI

"No one loved who I became. Not even me."

— *Adelia, Volume 54*

The insides of the cliffs that so much of the city revolved around weren't *that much* different than Helheim. More compact, a building carved away instead of built. And I hadn't quite gotten the lay of it yet. I still found myself taking wrong turns and ending up in front of the wrong rooms.

That wasn't the only reason I'd asked Narvi to come with me, though.

"It's good of you to do this, Father." He was walking with his eyes ahead of him, keeping the same hesitant pace as I was. A trudge, really.

"Yes, you can remind me of that after, when I feel like horseshit and wish I hadn't." I'd worried the skin around my nails raw thinking about what needed doing.

"You'll be fine. When it's done, the air will be clear and even if it's not a *good* result, it'll still be a result." He stopped in front of a closed door and lowered his voice. "Are you ready?"

I took a deep breath. I really wasn't, but I was never going to be more ready than this. My guts were in knots and I wasn't entirely sure my stomach would make it through the encounter—a sensation I hadn't strictly missed since vomiting hadn't been on the table for years—but I was going in there anyways.

"No time like the present to make good on a new fate."

Narvi nodded, knocked, and waited. A voice came from the other side, calling us in.

The room was quaint. On one side was a large bed that had been pushed closer to the wall to make room for a study on the opposite side. A bookcase was tucked into the corner and a large desk had been put in front of it. There wasn't much room to move, but Hod had demanded the enormous thing himself, saying that he needed room to work. And now, tucked into a chair between the desk and the wall, his papers and inks sprawled out across the surface, he looked happy in the chaos, his fingers running deftly over rune indents in the parchment.

"It's me," Narvi said, toying with the loose thread on his shirt. "And I brought someone else who would like to speak to you, but if you say no, we'll leave. Loki would like to discuss what's happened in the past and what the future might look like."

Hod looked up for the first time, the passive joy sliding from his features. What sat there was a kind of shock, a will to run and be anywhere but in the situation he was in. His head turned slowly toward us, and though I knew he couldn't see me, I felt like he could see *through* me. Inside me, at every horrible thing I'd ever done.

He didn't speak for a moment and I took a step back, sure I was about to be asked to leave. Then he opened his mouth, and it took a while for the words to come out. "He can stay."

Narvi looked at me, possibly as shocked by the statement as I was. He set a hand on my shoulder and gave me a nod forward, which was well and good since I wasn't sure my feet wanted to move by themselves.

"I'll leave you two to talk. See you in the morning." Narvi slipped out the door and closed it behind him.

I knew it was rude to stand there saying nothing, especially when I was in the bedroom of a blind man who didn't trust me, but for one of the rare moments in my life, I didn't quite know where to start.

"There's a chair next to the bed, if you plan to actually say something." Hod's tone was brisk, and he was moving a bunch of his loose parchment into a pile, hands keeping busy as I went to fetch the chair and sat down out of arm's reach. Far enough that I hoped it wouldn't feel hostile or threatening.

I took a deep breath, leaned my elbows on my knees. A joke was easy. Brushing things under the floorboards was easy. I'd learned a long time ago to let nothing stick, to let it slough off me like it didn't matter. Maybe that was why being sincere was so fucking *hard* sometimes.

"I've had a lot of time to think about what happened." I cleared my throat and found the courage to keep saying the thing that I'd rehearsed. "About what I did and why. And I'm not here to ask forgiveness, but I do want to apologize. I'm sorry for the way things happened and for the pain I caused you. I'm sorry for getting you killed. If there's something you need to hear from me, I'll tell you."

Epilogues for Lost Gods

Hod huffed and sat back in his chair. "And what brings on this great act of kindness from Loki, who always did what he wanted, whenever he wanted?"

It stung, coming from him. He'd spent so much time on my side, but betrayal changes a lot. "We're both here again. Alive. We'll be in the same halls. I can live with the guilt of what I've done, but I don't want you to think I'm a danger to you here. Even if we never speak again after today, I don't want that to be a worry you carry."

Hod nodded. "Why did you kill Baldur?"

"I...I was angry. Odin and the rest had taken my children from me and I wanted them to suffer the way I had. It wasn't *fair* that they had just gotten away with it—" My body was tensing as I spoke, the memory of all those horrors filling me. The ink stains under my skin were reacting. I took a breath, tried to come back to the conversation. "I think you understand what it's like to lose people you love and to be held at arm's length. I was already sick of what they'd done to *me* but I could live with that. But no one gets to hurt my children."

Hod had picked up a crystal paperweight and was turning it around in his palm, sliding his fingers over the edges. "You could've done more to stop him. Stop Odin."

"I know." Tears were welling in my eyes. "I loved you like a brother, but Sigyn was there and I couldn't let her get hurt. She wanted to help you...but I used sleep runes on her and pulled her out of the crowd. There were so many of them and...I made a choice that—" I shook my head, irritated with myself. "No. That's true, but it also makes it sound selfless when it wasn't. I had to protect her, but I also didn't want to be caught. I chose her over you, and I chose myself. That's true as well."

"Yes, that sounds more honest. More like Loki." Hod slid the crystal between his hands, back and forth. "Did it make you feel better, saving her over me?"

"No. When Eyvindr spoke about you at your memorial, it was the first time I had to face what I was doing. I felt like the worst being in the nine, and it still wasn't enough to make me stop. If I had quit then, or if I'd just taken my family and run instead of killing Baldur, maybe none of it would've happened. Maybe Ragnarok wouldn't have happened. But that's not what I did. I took countless lives instead." I sunk my head down, slipping my fingers into my hair and staring at the floor.

How long would it be before admitting all these horrors stopped making me feel like I was rotting inside?

Hod didn't ask anything right away. I let him sit in silence, thinking. Maybe he was considering how best to murder me in my sleep, but that was the risk I'd taken in wanting to talk. And if that was what he decided to do, who was I to begrudge him a bit of vengeance? It had been my best-known trait for most of my life.

"And what now?" he asked at length. "Something else you want to say?"

"I don't know." I sat up, determined to look him in the face. "I don't expect anything from you. The only thing I hope is that what's between us won't stop you from having a relationship with Narvi and Sigyn. They've already suffered enough for the things I've done, and it's not fair that people hold my actions against them. That kind of thing has gone on too long."

Hod shrugged. "That won't be an issue. I kept training Narvi long after you'd sealed your own fate in Asgard, and I've been helping Sigyn evade her enemies for years. You never made an impact on those choices."

"Good." I nodded, the slightest well of relief in my belly. "Good."

"There's a difference between penance and forgiveness, Loki." He put the crystal on the table and turned towards me. "What happens if I'm not ready to forgive you?"

"Then you don't, and that's fine. I've done so many unforgivable things." I felt compelled to get up and start pacing the room, but knew I should stay where I was. "When Sigyn bargained for the souls of Idunn and Bragi, she did that knowing they will never, ever speak to us again. I'm trying to be more like her. Use this chance to do the right thing."

"Everyone could stand to be a little more like her, I think." Hod linked his fingers together and dropped them to his lap. "There's one more thing I want to know."

I moved forward in my seat. "Anything, just ask."

"What Odin did to you...how bad is it? Hreidulfr told me what he knew about the cave."

I swallowed hard. I'd put the glamour on to keep others from staring quite so much, but people knew. People would know, eventually. The glamour was a simple thing to let slip off, and Hod wouldn't be able to see it properly. It was just...he was asking for a kind of vulnerability I wasn't sure I wanted to have. I'd already bared my soul in trying to make amends, but this felt different. It was remembering a horror I tried to bury every day.

But he had asked, and I had said anything. "It was bad." I paused. Tried to think of the best ways to describe it. "We tried to keep the damage on the right side of my face. It's like wax dripping down a candle. Some bits are more like molten cheese. And my eye...the scarring took my sight in that eye. It's coming back, what with my deal with the Nornir. A little better every day, but the rest is still there."

Hod gave a huff, his face incredulous. "Why is it so hard to believe you?"

"Because I'm a liar, Hod." It stung. I had lain on a rock, exposed for an eternity while the venom ate away at my skin. Ate away at my essence. I had had nightmare after nightmare in that place, dreaming about the end of my children like an endless loop. My one comfort had been in Sigyn, and it was poisoned by the pain she endured for me, eating me alive with guilt.

That cave had stripped me of everything that I was.

And because of who I'd once been, it was all in question. It probably always would be, and I couldn't fault anyone for it.

Hod stood up. He guided himself away from the desk with his hands and toward me. He stood in front of me, his body casting me in shadow, and I felt small. Helpless, like a boy in the shadow of his parents, waiting for their judgement.

Hod's hand rose and found my cheek, cupping it. The softness of the gesture awoke something in me. It was too much kindness. Violence I would have understood. Vengeance. But Hod was touching me like one might touch a wounded alley cat. The pity was too much to bear. Tears rushed down my face and I tried not to let it show. Not to tremble or hitch my breath. I wanted to hide it from him. I didn't want him to know how broken I was, and how deeply he had torn me open with a touch.

"We all paid a price for trying to live as ourselves," Hod said under his breath. "Vengeance is a cycle, and all it causes is pain. I am tired of it." His hand left my skin. "I do not forgive you, but I don't wish you any more pain. I won't punish you for trying to be a better person. I would rather let this version of you grow, the one who means well. Intent doesn't stop us from hurting people. It doesn't make up for the past. But it's the first step in how we atone for what we've done."

There was no version of this discussion that I had thought would go well. Hod was being more generous than I deserved. *I* knew I deserved so little, and yet he was still hoping for better things from me.

He always had.

Was this what it was like to live without so much spite in your heart?

I curled up into myself and wept.

CHAPTER THIRTY-THREE

SIGYN

*"My choices are my own. I've always tried to follow my heart.
Listen to what I needed, even when everyone else was so
loud."*

— Anborgh, Volume 35

It took another two days before I could get out of bed for any proper length of time. It wasn't the pain that kept me there; it was the exhaustion. And maybe just a tiny bit of fear.

I thought I'd earned the right to cower, honestly, what with Loki and Alyssa finding their way in and out of my room like they were on a perfectly timed schedule each day. I was easy to find, which made it difficult to avoid either of them, but their visits never overlapped, and neither of them ever brought up anything beyond the platonic. A bit odd, considering Loki and I had been married for an immeasurable amount of time and so very little of our time together could be called platonic.

I could have asked. I could have forced them to talk about what had happened and what should happen next, but it seemed too daunting a thing to do. We were all the same, I imagined. Afraid the answer wouldn't be the one we wanted. I couldn't see a choice that wouldn't cut off a piece of my heart. So I let them sit in that chair and tell me about the day's goings-on, letting me win at dice, never daring to touch me. Never showing enough affection to be seen as too bold. And the only thing I wanted in all the realms was for someone to hold me, kiss me, and help me grieve. Because while I was corralled inside this windowless room, I thought about the horrors I'd seen out there, the devastation it had done to my body, and when I was alone, I wept.

The days were *so long*. I begged and pleaded but no one would bring me any work to do. A stack of novels were piled next to my bed and I would crack them open and the words would blend together, one paragraph into the next. I couldn't remember the last time I'd had so much rest. You'd think it would be a good thing, but sitting in a room with nothing to do but think allowed the mind to come up with all-new ways to emotionally devastate the people who love you, which doesn't make for a very good way to pass the time.

A knock came at the door. Strangely, no one had come to visit that morning and it was hard to say if my visitor would be Loki or not. I wasn't sure if I liked the change in predictability, but I called for them to come in anyways.

Loki poked his head out from around the corner, his hair a little more kempt than it had been yesterday. He'd woven in some golden beads, and with the smile on his face, I could almost see the man I'd spent so many blissful days with.

"How are you today?" He closed the door and came to the bed, something cupped in his hands. "I brought you something."

I held my hands out, curious. Whatever it was, he made a big show of keeping it concealed until the last moment. When he pulled his hand away, there was a small, flaking pastry cradled in his palm.

My mouth dropped open. "Loki, where—?"

His face was lit up with the simple excitement he used to wear so often. "They found the supplies in the wreckage of the market. It's the first batch. I thought you'd want it."

I held it up to my nose. It was still just a little bit warm inside, the scent of apple and cinnamon wafting out. I took a hearty bite and the sweet, juicy filling rolled over my tongue. I let out a satisfied moan.

"Eat quickly. You and I have somewhere to be."

I squinted at him and finished chewing. "What do you mean?"

"You'll have to find out." He shrugged. "All I'm allowed to say is that we're expected somewhere."

I shoved the other half of the pastry in my mouth, looking him up and down. He was dressed rather finely in a blue tunic and dark brown trousers that weren't marred with the usual mud or dust. Add in his finely braided hair and the pastry. He was putting in an *effort*.

The old Loki, the one from before things had gotten complicated, had always put in an effort. He'd primped and preened himself more than I had, but I hadn't seen that Loki around here, not since he'd been alive again.

I glared. "You understand how suspicious you're being right now, don't you?"

All I got in return was a shrug. "Aren't I always suspicious?"

I stood from the bed, wiping the crumbs from my clothes. "Fine. Let me get changed at least. I'm not leaving this room in my nightdress."

Loki practically leapt from his seat and had his hand on the door before I could protest. "I'll be just outside. Don't take long or you'll get a lecture for making them wait."

I opened my mouth but he'd already closed the door behind him.

Had he ever actively run away from my naked body before?

As I pulled my nightdress off and dug something clean out of the wardrobe, I found myself eager for all of this to be over. I had avoided problems out of fear several times in my life, delaying things so I could avoid the disastrous result, only to finally face up to it because I was tired of worrying. I could feel myself growing close to that point once again, where the sleepless nights and the guarded conversations were no longer worth it. I still had no answer to the issue, but I needed to find one.

But how do you weigh two people against each other? What they'd given me against what they *could* give? The connections we had against the chance to start over? The dedication to a new life against a simple, painless beginning?

Maybe it would sound simple to someone else, but nothing in the realms could have been more difficult.

I opened the door and found Loki leaning against the stone wall, staring down the corridor. He snapped to attention and held out his arm. "My lady."

"You know I don't need help walking, don't you?" I gave him a chastising look. "I'm tired, not feeble."

"I know that." He took my hand and hooked it around his arm anyways. "Consider it a polite gesture, with the benefit that you might not fall on your ass."

I rolled my eyes, sarcasm dripping off my tongue. "Yes, how I have missed this. You are *so* funny, *so* generous to help an old crone like me."

He tapped my hand and started walking in the direction of the city outside. "You said that, not me."

I really was fine, and I wouldn't readily admit it, but it was nice to be this close to him again. Even if it was a big, dramatic act.

When we reached the doors that separated the city from the inside of the cliffs, Loki stopped. "Are you ready?"

"Loki, are you literally taking me outside? Are you *honestly* making this much fuss over taking me for a walk because you think I need to get out more often?"

Loki threw his head back and cackled. "No, that wasn't the idea at all, but now I'm upset I didn't think of that before you did. The look on your face would've been priceless."

He put his hand on the door leading outside, gave me the most telling look, and pushed it open. The square was more or less intact and unaffected by the battle, but the skyline had changed a little; shapes in the distance had altered or were missing, and I wondered how much of our hard work had been demolished. But that wasn't what I was supposed to be looking at.

In the middle of the square were familiar faces. Narvi, Váli, Hod, Hreidulfr, and Alyssa were gathered around something tall underneath a large brown tablecloth, talking amongst themselves. As I followed Loki towards them, Hreidulfr looked up and pointed. The others stopped their conversations, enormous grins pasted on each of their faces.

"This is even more suspicious," I said to Loki.

"Obviously you're paranoid." He was so pleased with himself that the pride practically dripped off him.

When we were close enough to hear one another, I looked around at them, hands on my hips. "And what's all this about?"

"We thought you could use something to cheer you up." Vali leaned an arm on his brother's shoulder.

"It's from us," Hreidulfr said. "But not just us. We told the rest that we'd be giving it to you privately, but lots of people have been working on this for months. Now seemed like the right time, ma'am."

"No one needs to do anything for me." Tension seized my gut, something both excited and uncomfortable. It was abnormal. I had grown accustomed to doing for others, to holding up the world. And to have someone—many someones—have done something specifically for me...I didn't know what to do with that idea. So few surprises had been pleasant ones.

They were all looking at me expectantly. It was easier to give in than to explain why I would rather they give me nothing. "Well, fine, you may as well go ahead."

Hreidulfr took the worn old tablecloth in his hand and pulled it away.

It was a statue, nearly as tall as I was. It was crafted from a patchwork of metal, melted and welded from scraps of different shades of grey and copper and silver. The top was an empty bowl propped over a round, marble basin. Holding up the bowl was a pillar that opened up into dozens of hands in different colours, their palms reaching to keep the bowl held aloft. Inscribed on a plaque in the front was the phrase *No Burden Borne Alone.*

Alyssa stepped onto a tiny ladder behind it and poured a bucket of water into the bowl. It started to overflow, cascading down into the basin. She poured another, and the bowl kept overflowing, something inside it propelling the water in an endless loop. A fountain.

For me.

No burden borne alone.

What I wouldn't have given for help during those long days and months and years in that cave. I still had nights when I dreamt that I was there, my body aching, my arms quivering to hold up the bowl, my fingers burning as venom sloshed over the sides onto them. Sometimes when I woke up, I couldn't figure out which version of me was real.

If I had had more hands to hold that bowl, maybe, just maybe, a larger part of me would have survived those long days.

Tears rolled down my cheeks.

Hreidulfr cleared his throat. "The first time I met you, I had just run into your kitchen in nothing but my underthings. When you sat me down for breakfast, you told me that this family was about loyalty. That none of us fit in out there, so we may as well fit together. I never forgot that. You took me in and took the weight of myself off my shoulders." He pointed towards the city. "And now we have this new home and you're doing the same thing for all of them. Giving them a place to bear the weight of themselves. I know this isn't a happy memory for you, and we can't change it, but we want you to know we've got your back. We'll carry it with you."

Emotion had been building in me from the moment he ripped the tablecloth away, and his speech intermingled with all the doubt and fear I'd been feeling since I'd first woken from my injuries. His words undid me. A sob broke out of me and my knees gave way. My arm was still hooked in Loki's and he caught me as I went crashing to the ground, softening my fall. I wept into his chest, his arms pulling me against him as I struggled to breathe. A hand settled on my shoulder, another resting on my arm. I glanced up from the folds of Loki's tunic to see the others gathered around. Narvi and Váli sitting on the ground next to us, Hod, Hreidulfr and Alyssa hovering above.

I tried to catch my breath. A smile broke through the sobs. These people, these very kind and possibly stupid people, were doing all this for me. I didn't know what to do with a kindness this big. I had spent my youth dreaming that I might be noticed, that someone might see what I was capable of, what good I had done, and love me for it. I had tried to forget it, tried to move on. But this moment was what I had once longed so deeply for. It sunk into that old scar and soothed it, like a balm overdue.

"It's alright," Loki whispered in my ear. "We won't let this memory destroy us. It's finally over. You can let go now."

I pressed my face into his chest, breathing in the honeyed, ashen smell of him. That familiar, uncompromisingly accepting warmth of him. And I let it go in a long, measured breath.

Maybe not forever. Maybe not in the long cold of night. Maybe not even tomorrow. But for now.

I swallowed, my throat parched. I was shaking, but my head was clear. It took a bit of wriggling to convince Loki to loosen his arms around me, but he did. I wiped my eyes, stood up. Looked at the warm, concerned faces around me. "Thank you. I don't know what else to say."

Narvi threw his arms around me, and Váli was quick to join him.

I cupped their faces, one in each hand. "I love you both so much. I've missed you too many days and we have so much time to make up for."

Váli's eyes were glistening as he pressed a kiss to my temple. Narvi sniffed and withdrew, a second of doubt rushing over his face. But then it was gone.

I squeezed his hand. "I promise."

"Now, now, no hogging her." Hreidulfr nudged his way between my sons, forcing them out of the way. "I need a hug, and so does Hod."

I held my hand out to take Hod's, and he let himself be pulled in for that hug. "I'm sorry I haven't been around all that often," I said.

"I *have* found it rather inappropriate that you were so *unavailable* after you were speared by a loom." Hod squeezed me tighter. "I'm sure you'll make it up to me."

"And you," I said, holding an arm out for Hreidulfr to come closer. "Come here, you sentimental giant."

He wrapped his arms around us both. "Well, I didn't really mean to make you cry, ma'am."

"You damn well did, and we both know it."

"Maybe." His hug tightened and Hod let out a smothered squeak. "Oh, I'm sorry."

"No, that's alright." Hod straightened out as Hreidulfr released us. "If I'm going to die again, it may as well be smothered in the arms of a strong man."

All eyes turned to him in silent shock.

"Hod!" I slapped him playfully on the arm. "What has gotten *into* you?"

He waggled a finger at me. "I have never been allowed to flirt or make all the properly dirty jokes I've been thinking of all these years and I have a lot of catching up to do."

I looked at Loki.

"What?" His eyes went wide. "As if he gets it from *me*! Hardly."

The bright smiles on everyone's faces were the best things I'd seen in years.

"If that's the way you want to play things, I think it's time that we—" Hreidulfr gestured between himself, Narvi, Váli, and Hod. "—go have a drink or six, and let the boring adults go back to sleep."

Loki's neck craned towards Hreidulfr. "I think he just called us old."

"Go on. Go enjoy yourselves." I shooed them away with a gesture. "You'll pay for that comment later. You can count on that."

The little band of laughing men gave us a wave, surrounding Hod like a new recruit, and walking together into the city. Then all that was left was Loki and me.

A clunk of metal caught my attention.

Alyssa was stacking the two metal buckets together and folding up the ladder, looking like she was about to sneak away. Then she caught me staring. Her face was riddled with guilt. "Sorry. I didn't want to interrupt. I know I was invited, but it didn't really feel like something that was meant for me, you know?"

I let out a long sigh and collected myself. "This has gone on long enough. Both of you, to my room, now. This conversation is overdue."

The mirth dropped from Loki's face, replaced by something much more uncomfortable. But he started walking, and Alyssa fell into a silent march behind him, both of them looking like they were on their way to a funeral pyre rather than a conversation.

I didn't exactly want to do it either, but it felt like now was as good a time as any. I was more optimistic than I'd been before, and I was probably all out of tears.

Too bad I still hadn't made up my mind.

I let them into my room. Alyssa went to sit on the foot of the bed, and Loki suddenly became very interested in the wood knots on the dresser, running his fingers nervously along them.

I closed the door and leaned against it, not sure where else to stand. "No one wants to be here, discussing this."

Alyssa pursed her lips and shook her head. Loki kept swirling his fingers on the wood, his face dejected, like he already knew what was coming.

"What happened, the way it happened…it shouldn't have." I tried to keep looking at him, to be sincere even through the pain of the words. "You shouldn't have had to see it, Loki. I'm sorry."

He nodded subtly. "How long?"

I squinted. "How long what?"

"How long have you been together? She told me you weren't, but I want to hear it from you."

"We're not," I said, trying to exude sincerity with every syllable. "It never happened before. We're only friends."

"Friends don't kiss each other in the heat of battle, do they?" Loki's voice was still soft and broken, even under the weight of such an angry sentiment.

"No, they don't." I took a breath. Time to be brave. "Alyssa has been here for me, as a friend, for years. And that's all it was. But it's not just that anymore. She admitted to me before the battle that she felt love for me, and I only recently became aware that I…that I love her too. That I have for a while and didn't realise it. But it's there and I don't want to lie about that."

Loki tapped each of his fingers on the drawer, one after the other. "That settles it then."

I crossed my arms over my chest. "I don't think you get to decide when things are settled."

He looked at me for the first time. "I had my chance and I destroyed it. And I placed my last hopes on this working out, but that was my mistake. I need to live with that."

"What about what I think?" I asked. "You've made up your mind in my place, but you haven't listened to what I actually want."

"What more is there to say?" Loki was getting angry, frustrated, and the swirl of black ink under his skin had worked its way underneath the midbicep sleeves of his tunic. "You said it yourself. It was more than a kiss. She can offer you a blank slate, Sigyn. I can't do that for you. So I surrender. I won't get in the way of your happiness again. I just won't."

"Loki, you can't just—"

"Enough." Alyssa stood up. "We've all had a lot of time to think, obviously. Everyone has thought about the very worst possibilities where one of us gets left behind, but have either of you considered that there's another way to do this?"

We both stared at her blankly.

"I get it." She threw her hands at her sides with a sigh. "You're both used to getting the short end of the stick. Nothing ends happily for you. But at some point, that's a choice you're making. So how much of this conversation is about you protecting yourself, Loki? Making sure you bow out so no one else gets the chance to hurt you?"

Loki looked away, putting an arm around his torso. He said nothing.

"Tell me you don't love her." Alyssa kept her gaze on him, intensity burning in her eyes.

His lips pursed. Forcing it down.

"That's bullshit." Alyssa gestured from me to Loki. "Sigyn?"

"Yes." My voice was quieter than I'd meant it to be. "I love him."

Loki's face softened just a little, the hard shell weakening around the edges.

"Then why is anyone here *choosing*?"

The air went out of the room for just a moment. I looked at her, knowing in the back of my mind what she was saying, but not remotely able to allow that thought room to breathe. "I don't understand."

Alyssa's voice wavered and she began to move more erratically, talking with her hands. "If there's anything I've learned about you, Sigyn, it's that you have the uncanny ability to choose the harder path. I'm sure it wasn't as simple as this, but you stayed in Asgard with Loki and faced your family instead of just *leaving* and being happy somewhere else. You stayed with Loki when things were much more difficult than most people would have allowed them to be. You chose to create a city instead of letting someone else do it around you. And now you're choosing the hard road again, maybe because you're just used to suffering. Maybe you can't imagine a life without pain."

Loki huffed. "I've known you for about five minutes and that seems like a lot of things that aren't your busine—"

"Shut up," Alyssa snapped.

I looked from Loki to Alyssa, shocked. But neither of us spoke.

"I'm sorry. But I need you to pay attention. If you hear this and say no, fine. I'll walk away." Alyssa stood her ground, arms crossed over her chest. "But are you both *honestly* not considering the idea that someone can just have a relationship with two consenting adults and that be fine?"

I just stared at her, comprehending and yet not. Vehemently refusing to.

Loki was the first to break the silence, eyeing Alyssa suspiciously. "You can't be serious."

Alyssa's eyebrows raised, her cheeks flushing. "I assumed you of all people…alright. Maybe this is a mistake, but this is what I'm proposing, as clearly as I can stand to say it, because I am *very* embarrassed right now, but you're both being purposefully obtuse and refusing to take the lead, so—" She reached out and took my hand in hers. "Sigyn, I'm fairly certain I really love you, and I know Loki loves you, and there's so much history between you two—" Her confidence was wavering further by the moment. "—I don't want to get in the way of that. But I think you've been happy with me?"

I nodded. The tears were welling up in my eyes again.

Alyssa looked at Loki, who could only bear to watch out of the corner of his eye. "I don't want to make you choose. I don't want any of us to live with that. So I—I'm—" She took a deep breath. "What if *I* choose you *both?*"

Loki looked at me, but I was barely in the room. Hearing everything, but unable to respond. Unable to vocalise that overwhelming storm raging behind my eyes.

"It's possible you've killed Sigyn and her body just hasn't realised that yet. Regardless, I don't know if you're proposing something that you're prepared for." Loki leaned against the dresser, arms over his chest but brave enough to look at us. He was guarded, but there was something on his face that also read as impressed.

"Then you don't know me." Alyssa turned to him and stood as tall as she could muster. "I fought hard enough in my living days to be recruited to Valhalla. I fought my own body for dominance, day in and day out, until the day I lost. Whatever baggage you're carrying around, it doesn't bother me. Very little you can say would change my mind. I'm offering you a way out of this. A solution that, if it works, means no one walks away with their hearts torn out. I feel like it's the *adult* solution, something that no one else here—" She paused, sighed and let down her guard again. "I don't expect you to want me, Loki. I don't even expect you to like me all that much. I'm not sure what we'd be to each other, but if we're both good to her and we both love her, why not just do that? I don't know, maybe I'm an idiot, head empty, I mean who am I to suggest that not one but *two* gods just come live with me and—"

"I would."

The interruption startled both Alyssa and me. Loki's expression was defensive, protective, but it was like some colour had come back into his face.

He shrugged. "As if either of you can reasonably think this concept is new to me. I lived a long and adventurous life before Sigyn, I'll remind you. I haven't done anything as…*permanent* as you're proposing but…I would try."

And just like that, just like my poor mind had been warning would happen, my world began to spin very precariously on its axis. On one hand, it was a plausible, odd, and perhaps misguided answer. Perhaps Alyssa was getting in far over her head with two damaged gods. And on the other hand, there was no possible way for me to conceive of an ending that didn't involve pain.

I must have started to visibly deteriorate, because both Loki and Alyssa reached for me at the same time, taking on my weight and walking me to the bed. They sat down on either side of me and that gesture alone was more than my mind could bear. It shifted very shallowly over what all these words meant. Ideas. Possibilities. Probabilities. Eventualities.

"Are you alright?" Alyssa put her hand on my knee.

"No, I don't think I am."

Loki's hand rose to meet my cheek, gently turning me to look at him. "Think about it, darling. The boys have found their places. The city is ready to move on. And I would give you up if I had to, if I knew you were happy. Even if it killed me again. But if I *don't* have to? I'd be an idiot to say no."

I shook my head, exasperated. "How could it ever work?"

"Well, like I've been trying to say," Alyssa said, drawing my attention, "it would work because we love you. And we'd figure it out."

Loki chuckled, leaning around me to look at Alyssa. "She's smart, your girlfriend."

"Oh, no." A laugh bubbled up from the deep well of anxiety in my chest. I covered my face with my hands. "This is so odd. It's all—" I took a deep breath. It was so much and there were so many things fighting inside me. And the loudest, oldest one was a voice of doubt. That it would never work. That love was for the lucky. That everyone I loved was inevitably torn away from me. And listening to it, I knew that the voice had guided so many of my mistakes. Was I going to let it guide the rest of my life?

They were waiting for an answer, and the longer I drew out the moment, the more worried their expressions were becoming. If I said no, I would break someone's heart. I would break my own.

I took a breath and said possibly the most frightening thing I'd ever said. "Yes. I—I think I want to try."

I looked from Alyssa to Loki as the words sunk in for each of them. Alyssa leaned forward, her head between her legs while Loki leaned back on his palms, laughing with a lightness that felt like an old friend.

After catching my own breath, I pulled Alyssa back towards us. And then she did something I hadn't calculated for. She leaned over and kissed me. My body jolted, the guilt washing over me. But Loki's arm settled behind my back, his hand on my waist, a gesture of reassurance. The guilt faded. And all that was left was the gentle kiss that melted my doubt.

When Alyssa broke away, I looked up at Loki, pleading with him to say something. A tiny smile was curled up in the corners of his lips.

"I would tear down the realms for you, my love," he whispered into my hair. "This is nothing."

I started crying again. If I could just have one moment that wasn't entirely overwhelming—

Alyssa pushed me back onto the mattress and curled up against me, nuzzling her face into my shoulder. "No more crying for you. Only comfort."

Loki laid back and pressed against me, his nose at my temple. They held me as the tears slowly faded out, and the warmth of them, the slow rise and fall of their chests, their fingers tracing lines on my skin—it felt like the very best version of home.

"This is going to be so strange," I whispered.

"And so much fun." Loki propped himself up on his elbow and reached his hand across my stomach to take Alyssa's hand. He kissed her knuckles. "Loki Laufeyjarson, delighted to be married to your girlfriend."

Alyssa threw her head back in laughter. "Alyssa Harris, delighted to be dating your wife."

"No. Oh, no. What have I done." I laughed behind my hands, mortified and so very, very happy.

CHAPTER THIRTY-FOUR

LOKI

*"If you keep getting in the same longship with the same idiots,
nothing's going to change. You have to find other comrades
and new shores. It's not everything, but it's a start."*

— Dvalinn, Volume 102

The city had been simply striving to survive for weeks, and it was strange to stand in the middle of the market square while everyone buzzed from one task to the next, smiles and laughter everywhere. Váli had said the city needed one bright moment, and he had been right. What better excuse than a wedding?

A platform had been erected in the square for the grooms and their more directly invited guests. Dozens of mismatched tables and chairs were being set up on top of it, and an archway made of twine branches and twisted cloth pieces was front and centre. Below, the rest of the city was gathering their own supplies, setting up their own makeshift tables and seating. They had wood for fires as the party raged into the night, homemade alcohol, and a mismatch of whatever could be found to sit on.

It was a scrappy event, but so were all the most interesting ones I'd been to.

I set down the pair of wicker seats I'd been hauling with me and glanced over at Alyssa. She was giving directions to one of the other Modernists. She and a few other people from her time had planned this whole thing, jokingly calling it a "Nine Realms Fusion Wedding," which she insisted would be a beautiful surprise for everyone involved. It was evident to me that Váli and Hreidulfr would've been fine with anything so long as they could save their energy for repairing the city, not wedding planning.

Alyssa listened for a moment to whatever her friend was saying, then dramatically ran her hand over her face. She pointed into the distance emphatically, and the man hurried off.

I smirked. Getting to know her was a slow, delicate thing, but I could see what Sigyn loved most about her. She did everything with passion and flair, like she thrived on the excitement of being useful. If the three of us could get through this awkward, fumbling newness, maybe that part of her would draw me in as well…

A large stringed instrument came too close to my face, tearing me out of my thoughts. Other musicians followed behind, some carrying hand drums, others wrestling instruments that had origins from across the nine. They started tapping and plucking, and it was my cue to leave before the uncoordinated noise began.

A tent had been pitched behind the platform for the privacy of the grooms. It would be easy enough to shirk the gruelling duties of arranging chairs if I simply disappeared from view for a little while. Besides, what if there was something to *eat* inside? I was still in the throes of the joy of eating again, and I would never miss a chance to find a snack.

I peeked through the front flap. "Hello?"

Váli was sitting cross-legged on top of a small table. He was dressed in a fine tunic of royal purple that had been painstakingly embroidered with silver thread, but his grey trousers had seen better days. Finding perfectly intact ceremonial clothing after the end of the realms proved somewhat difficult, it turned out.

He was staring down at a paper clasped in both hands. He looked up, a confused mix of emotions on his face. "Oh. It's you."

"Am I interrupting something?" With all the shadows inside the tent, it wasn't immediately apparent *what* was wrong, but something certainly was.

Váli sniffed and wiped the back of his hand across his nose. "No. Not interrupting, just…well, I guess I have news."

I arched an eyebrow. "Do I have to kill anyone on your behalf? Not a groom, I hope."

He looked up with a smirk. "No. Hreidulfr gave me this as we were getting dressed." He held it out.

I took the paper delicately. Most of my vision had come back, and I could mostly read the thing without extra effort. The top half was littered with signatures, initials, and piecemeal information. I skipped to the bottom. "*The Family branch of the council of Fólkheim finds this household suitable for adoption, and formally charges you with the care and upbringing of the aforementioned child.*" I looked up at him, careful to contain the joy that was welling up in my chest. "Is this it? Is it finally done?"

Váli nodded, a tear spilling over onto his cheek. "He's known for days. Wanted to give it to me before the wedding. I'm going to be a father."

I pulled him into my arms, careful not to damage the paper, and held him as tightly as I could manage—and he let me. "It's about time. You're going to be an excellent family, the three of you, I just know it."

"Thanks." Váli didn't look at me as I let him go, just stared at the ground, a smile bursting up through all that manly bravado he always wore.

"It's appropriate, really."

He looked up. "What is?"

"That you'd be given a child on your wedding day. Your mother and I found out about you and we were married two days later." It was easy to sift through the memory, and I found that even the most complicated pieces of it brought a smile to my face. "We didn't plan for you, but you were the greatest gift we've ever gotten."

A blush rose in Váli's cheeks as he took the paper back from me. "I remember that story. Mother told us it was one of the strangest moments of her life. She was so happy to be with you and so nervous to go against Odin's wishes. But sometimes you have to do what's right for you, and the rest be damned."

I couldn't recall her telling that story to the boys, not at all. I huffed a laugh. "Your mother always had more common sense than I did, so I'll never know why she didn't just turn and run."

"That makes two of us." The tone in his voice was casual, like he'd said it without even knowing he had, still staring in disbelief at the paper in his hands.

I very nearly opened my mouth to say something cruel in return. What I'd said had been self-deprecating but I hadn't counted on him agreeing with me so easily. I should have. It burned a little, and I had heard it from him for so long that it felt a little like he still meant it. Maybe not quite the way he used to, but still. It was salt in a wound that might never truly heal and I wanted to bite back. But I didn't. Whatever would slip off my tongue would be needlessly cruel and defensive, and we were getting better, he and I. Better at this.

Instead, I just smiled and gave him a pat on the shoulder. "You're going to be everything I never was and more. I'm so proud of you."

Maybe it was the vulnerability of the moment, but he looked me in the eyes and seemed just…happy. I couldn't remember a day where he had ever looked at me with such warmth, not since he was small enough to carry on my back.

This. I could bite back my bitterness if it meant my son would look at me with love for even a fraction of the rest of my days.

The sound of crunching dirt rose up from behind me. Hreidulfr had returned, his hair woven intricately with beads, bound up behind his head. Like Váli, he was wearing a clean, mostly well-preserved outfit, and he was grinning from ear to ear.

"You must've heard then," Hreidulfr said, arms outstretched for an embrace.

I gave him a squeeze, slapping him on the back. "Congratulations. I can't wait to meet my grandchild." What a thought. What a beautiful, heart-wrenching thought. I hadn't let myself think too hard on the subject, but now—I pulled away as my own eyes began to water and swiftly ducked around Hreidulfr. "I'm afraid I need to get back to work. Can't have Alyssa noticing I've shirked my duties as Chair Fetcher."

Váli gave me a sly smile and nodded towards the tent flap. "Go on, before she gets you in trouble with Mother."

I scrunched up my nose disapprovingly at him and ducked out before they could read the emotion on my face, or in the ink running up my arms.

When it was finally time for the wedding to begin, I took my place near the front. One of the councillors—there were too many for me to get their names straight quite yet— was speaking quietly to Váli and Hreidulfr as the rest took their places. Narvi stood with Hod and the freshly returned Eyvindr, the three of them back to acting as thick as thieves. The people of the city were sprawled out in front of us, waiting in small, chattering groups for the ceremony to begin.

I wasn't precisely in love with all the eyes on us. On me. It had been a long time since that kind of attention had meant anything but danger, but I tried to push that feeling down. It was just a feeling, not a fact. What was it that therapist woman had told me? *Your thoughts are not reality. Worrying that something is true does not make it so.*

I was many things, but I would not be the one who ruined his son's wedding by having one of his *moments* and hiding in a corner.

An elbow poked into my ribs. Sigyn had appeared next to me. "Are you ready for this?"

"Am *I?*" I scoffed. "I'm not the one who has to make a *speech*."

She waved a hand. "I used to make all kinds of motivational speeches as a child, just for fun. How different could this really be?"

I squinted at her, sniffing the air. "You've already been into the wine, haven't you?"

Sigyn scowled. "Tell no one."

I pulled her against me and pressed a kiss into her forehead. "At least I won't be the one embarrassing anyone today. I happily pass that mantle to you."

Before she could scold me, Alyssa approached. "They're ready for you, Sigyn."

Sigyn pulled herself upright and straightened her dress, walking towards the front of the platform. She was as regal as anything ever was these days, draped in a tattered gown of midnight blue, clusters of white embroidered stars hiding some of the damage. It made me homesick for our old wardrobe of flowing dresses and soft furs.

"She looks stunning, doesn't she?" Alyssa stayed shoulder to shoulder with me, her eyes on Sigyn.

Epilogues for Lost Gods

"She does." I kept Alyssa in the corner of my eye, looking at her but not. Her face was soft, her expression one of pure adoration. "Has she been alright today?"

"Mostly," she said just loud enough for me to hear. "I think she still struggles to believe good things are real."

That made two of us, then.

"My son has asked me to say something today." Sigyn's voice was loud and confident as she announced herself, and she paused to let the crowd quiet. "We are gathered here to celebrate the love of Váli and Hreidulfr, and for the city to share in a moment of unbridled joy. After such struggle and loss, it's sorely needed. But this moment also stands as the beginning of a new era.

"Not far from here, not all that long ago, a marriage like this wouldn't be possible. Váli, Hreidulfr, Loki, myself, and so many of you, lived through a time where being different was unthinkable. Where loving someone could leave you misunderstood at best, and duelling to the death at worst. I watched people I loved dearly hide in the shadows because they knew living authentically would destroy their lives in every capacity. All because of who we loved or the people that we were."

My breathing had quickened as she spoke, and I had only just taken notice. I inhaled deeply, trying to cut off my mind's dramatics before it sunk its claws in me. I'd known what she was planning to say, but hearing it aloud in front of so many people was bringing up things I couldn't afford to focus on.

Fingers slipped between mine.

I looked down. Alyssa had taken my hand and was gazing up at me with kind eyes.

"It's alright." That was all she said, and turned her attention back to Sigyn.

The black in my skin stopped churning.

"This is not what we want for you," Sigyn continued. "This is not the future our city will strive for. We will work tirelessly for a place where all people are celebrated, where no one has to hide. Where the people of the nine realms can make this journey together, regardless of their bloodline, or the grudges we used to hold, or who they lie next to at night. And I know not everyone in this city will like this plan of ours. But rest assured, you are the last remnants of old, broken traditions that will not be tolerated in the walls of this place. I do not expect you to like it, but you will learn to accept it and, in time, perhaps to celebrate it with us."

She took a cup offered to her by the councillor and lifted it. "To my son and his love, and to a better future for all!"

A cheer rose among the crowd, along with a hearty number of cups. If there was going to be dissent about this future she had laid out for them, it wouldn't be now. Wouldn't be today.

It felt bittersweet, if I was being honest. Yes, the future looked bright, but what I wouldn't have given for someone to have said the same to a room of my peers when I was old enough to start knowing myself. What I wouldn't have traded to feel safe as a woman among the people I respected, and not to have simply used that part of myself as a tool of spycraft. How different things could've been, if only I hadn't learned to lick knives in search of love, and lie to make it through another day, one after the other.

I couldn't turn back time and change any of that. I would have to learn to live with it and be content that it would be the last time.

Sigyn came back to Alyssa and me, her gaze glancing to the white-knuckled grip I had on Alyssa's hand. She gave me a knowing, appreciative look and came to stand between us, tucked between our arms.

The councillor took his place under the twine arch, Váli and Hreidulfr in front of him. He had a faded-golden apple in one hand and a small knife in the other. It had been a long time since I'd seen a wedding, but this one looked familiar.

"Today," said the councillor, "the city is gathered to bear witness as these two bind their lives together. We stand here, all of us, united in gratitude for the efforts of Váli and Hreidulfr as they have strived for years to protect us and uphold the laws that make us a fair and just community."

Váli blushed, looking down at his hands, but by the proud look on Hreidulfr's face, he seemed to know how true those words were.

The councillor just grinned, clearly happy to get such a reaction from them in front of their friends and family. "Before we proceed, is there anything you'd like to say to one another?"

Hreidulfr moved to speak, but Váli interrupted him. "No, I am not going last. You're going to be sweeter than I know how to be, and I want people to remember what you said, not whatever fumbling nonsense I manage."

A scattering of laughter came up from the crowd, and Sigyn leaned her head gently on my side.

Váli took Hreidulfr's hands and looked up at him. "I didn't want to love you at first, but I couldn't help it. And when we were apart for all those years, I wished I had never met you, because missing you was the worst thing I'd ever felt. I want to be with you every day for the rest of my life, no matter how complicated things get. You kept my head on my shoulders all these years, and I don't know what I'd do without you. There's no life worth putting back together if you're not in it."

It was Hreidulfr's turn to have his emotions written all over his face. He blinked and rubbed at his eye, sniffing. "It's strange, being this sentimental in front of so many people. I spent most of my time making sure no one knew I loved you more than anything else in the nine. But I do. I'm going to raise a kid with you and build a house with you, and teach our kid to use a sword like you do and—" Hreidulfr tripped on his words, getting more emotional than he meant to. "And I get to do it with you, in front of everyone else, and I get to love every minute of it. Gods, I feel so lucky."

Váli pulled him into his arms and kissed him, whispering things to him too low for us to hear. A small noise drew my attention downwards. Sigyn was quietly sobbing into her hand, a tremble in her body. That, more than anything else, brought tears to my own eyes.

Well, we were all going to cry apparently, weren't we? We might as well.

Váli and Hriedulfr parted, hands still grasped together, their eyes misty.

The councillor cleared his throat, blinking rapidly. "If you're ready?"

They nodded.

The blade bit deep into the apple and the councillor carved it in half. One piece he passed to Váli and the other to Hreidulfr. Juice dripped from the blade and into the councillor's palm. "This apple, which grew from the Sister Tree, plucked from the stolen grafted branches of Yggdrasil that was, symbolises the sharing of a life. By eating from it, you promise to walk together into the future, no matter what bliss or hardship it may bring, and to strive for love in all things."

They both took a bite of their own halves, and the crowd burst into applause.

"The rings?" the councillor suggested, holding out his hand to take the apple pieces.

Hreidulfr slipped a ring from around his thumb and put it onto Váli's hand. Váli did the same, and with the rings exchanged, they fell into a long, joyous kiss.

The drums swelled to life, signalling the beginning of the festivities, and I exhaled for the first time in a while. I had too much emotion swirling inside me and was in serious need of a drink.

"Are you alright?" I bent my head down to sneak a look at Sigyn, who had buried her face in me to keep out of sight.

"I'm fine," she said, sniffing. When she looked up, her eyes were red and she'd left a wet spot in my tunic.

"Yes, you look absolutely fine." I pushed her hair out of her face, starting to pick and preen to make her more presentable.

"He's my first baby, Loki." Her lip started to quiver again. "I just—"

"Hey now." Alyssa put her arm around Sigyn's waist, pinning her between us. "You've got two minutes to feel *all* those feelings, because I'm going to get us all something to drink, and when I get back, we're going to put on a happy face for your son, alright?"

Sigyn nodded, still pouting.

241

Alyssa raced off and I pulled Sigyn against me, hoping to still whatever was bothering her. "What's wrong, my love?"

"Nothing. Everything. My baby is married and it doesn't really change anything, but it *does*. We never got to celebrate like this, and I'm so happy he can. But he's just my little baby, and he's so *grown up*." She pressed her nose into me and groaned. "It's just so *much*, Loki."

"I know." I ran my fingers through her hair, holding her tight. "I understand perfectly. And we're both going to pretend to be just fine until no one is looking, alright? You and I will sort all of this out tomorrow. Let them have their happy day."

She nodded against my chest, and just as quickly as she'd promised, Alyssa was back with a bottle of wine and an armful of cups.

"Time to get *drunkkk!*" she sang, passing each of us a cup.

"Yes, please." Sigyn held hers out greedily. "How do I look? Will they know I was crying?"

"Everyone was crying. You're fine." Alyssa managed to split the entire bottle into all three cups, leaving them full to the brim in a way that certainly wouldn't have been considered socially acceptable in Alfheim. "Drink a bit so it doesn't spill. We're being summoned."

We did as we were told and went together to where Váli and Hreidulfr had stopped. They were standing with Hod, Eyvindr, and Narvi.

"Oh, shit, hold this." Alyssa jammed her cup into my hand and rushed off. She reminded me a little of a squirrel, always darting off in one direction or another. She came back with a fistful of beautiful, freshly picked flowers. She put the bouquet in Váli's waiting hands.

"There's one more thing we need to do." Váli took a step towards Hod and Eyvindr. "When Alyssa was helping us plan the ceremony, she mentioned a tradition on Midgard that we wanted to include. Apparently, the bride would throw flowers towards a bunch of unmarried women, and whoever caught the flowers would be fated to marry next. It's a bit childish, but Hreidulfr and I wanted to give these to you."

Eyvindr's eyes grew wide as the meaning sunk in. He took the flowers delicately from Váli and held them as Hod ran his fingers gently between the stems.

"We don't want to tell you what to do." Hreidulfr sounded nervous and was clearly unsure what to do with his hands. "If you're ever ready, you have our support."

"You..." Hod's voice was low, almost too low to be heard over the music. "You want us to get married?"

"We wanted to pass the torch, I guess. You've waited much longer than we did. It's...I don't know, symbolic, I guess." Váli's voice was soft, like he was afraid of stepping out of line.

A little hitch rose from Sigyn's direction and she was tearing up again, clasping her hand around Narvi's arm. She waved away the attention. "I'm sorry. Keep going."

"I—we never really discussed it..." Eyvindr tucked a loose length of his long black hair behind his ear sheepishly. "It hurt more to dream things we could never have. I don't know if..." He tucked his arm in Hod's and Hod leaned in to him, smelling the bouquet.

"There's no reason not to now..." Hod's voice trailed off, and it was clear this was a very private, long-overdue discussion.

"How about we leave them alone for a bit, hmm?" I put my arm around Hreidulfr's shoulder, gently pulling him away and hoping Váli would follow. "You've made a very beautiful gesture but there'll be plenty of others waiting to talk to you." It was a flimsy excuse but at least it was plausible.

As I was steering them away, Hod cleared his throat and we turned back. "Thank you. Whatever we decide, this means everything to us."

"Of course," Váli said, his face welling up with emotion. He leaned on Hreidulfr and the two of them walked away, hand in hand.

Alyssa stole her drink back and started stepping slowly away from the deeply occupied couple. "This is too much for one day. I'm going to die of dehydration from all the bawling."

"I thought I was the sensitive one in the family." Narvi had a little smirk on his face, staring at his mother as she used him to both emotionally and physically steady herself.

"I'm sorry but I've had a lot of pent-up emotions in the last few years. I might as well get them all out now," Sigyn teasingly scolded him. "Look, aren't those friends of yours? Why don't you go play with them or something instead of harassing your mother?"

Narvi raised an eyebrow. "Play? Mother, I'm so old I don't know my actual age anymore. I'm not going to *play*."

"I've been thirty for literally *centuries*. Don't act like you're the only ageless one in this family." She shooed him away, receiving a sour but affectionate look in return.

Alyssa snagged Sigyn's hand. "I promised you some fun. Let's dance."

A smile spread across Sigyn's face and I could see how eager she was to be off. She looked up at me. "Come with us?"

I shook my head. "I'm going to stay right here for a little while with my drink. I'll join you later."

And with that, they were off, joining a few others near the musicians, dancing like they were young and time had never done them wrong.

I took a breath. Took a long drink. Took stock of what was going on under the surface. Introspection was important, I was told. Noticing was half the battle. And so with all of these things happening around me, what was going on inside Loki?

Anger that I had missed out on so much. A pinprick of envy. Sadness that there hadn't been more days like this with the people I'd loved. Regret that I wasn't the person I'd been before, as horrible as I sometimes was in the past. I wanted to have fun the way I used to, and it hurt that I no longer knew how.

That was one side of things.

But I was also proud. I was thankful to be here, to be trying to repair all the things I'd lost or broken or neglected. I was surrounded by so much happiness, so much hope for the future, and once I stopped being selfish about what I couldn't have, I was left with something light and fulfilling.

Contentedness.

It might not last long. It might not last all day. But for now, here at the edge of a new, brighter life, I had another choice. Another chance. Every day I'd have to choose again, and I hoped I would choose to be a better Loki more often than not.

And after this drink—and maybe another—I would work up the courage to go dance with the others. Because at some point, I needed to stop choosing the dark.

EPILOGUE

SIGYN

Four Months Later

"Here lie the words of those who have lived and died, and died again. Their stories were recorded to unburden their shoulders. The contents are not all happy, but I hope their words help to heal your own scars, so that we all may move forward together."

— Hod - Epigraph, The Book of The Dead Volume 1

"Aren't you going to take a break long enough to eat?"

Loki was flitting around the kitchen preparing lunch while I finished up with a pile of ledgers that were due back in the city. The boys were coming today and they needed to be finished before they returned.

"Leave the city, she said. I'll work less, she said." Alyssa came into the room from behind the sheet that hung between us and a half-built bedroom. She was covered in dust, and when she pulled her homemade goggles and the thick scarf off, her face was the only thing about her that was the colour of skin.

"I work less," I protested. "No one wakes me in the middle of the night for anything anymore, so that's an improvement."

Loki passed behind me and pressed a kiss onto the top of my head. "I wouldn't say that's true, but at least now it's for more pleasurable pursuits."

I blushed. All this time and he was still as big a flirt as ever.

"And you." Loki tilted Alyssa's chin up with a finger and used a damp cloth to wash the dirt from around her mouth. "You look like you crawled out of a mineshaft."

245

He smirked and gave her a gentle, lingering kiss before dropping the cloth into her open hands.

"I see how it is." She made her way to the waiting bucket of water and soap and began to scrub, a grin plastered on her face. "I pull this house together board by board and you just make fun of me while I do it. I see."

"If anyone here gets to complain about their role in the new order, it's me." Loki set a large bowl of greens on the table near me and followed it up with a thick bowl of something that Alyssa had taught him to make. Chilly, she called it, which was actually hot and made no sense. "While the two of you are busy fixing the house and the entire nine, I'm stuck in the kitchen all day." He put a hand over his heart, acting deeply wounded. "I ended the realms once, you realize? And this is the pinnacle of my career?"

"Call it retribution." I got up and helped him set the table, leaving my tiny workspace intact. "It's going to be a few more centuries of breakfasts before you make that up to me."

"Oh, is it?" Loki set down a handful of forks and wrapped his arms around my waist. "I'm sure I could knock a few more years off the tally if you'd like…"

I laughed and slapped his hand away. "You get off. The boys will be here any moment and that's a scar they don't need to carry around with them."

As Loki set the table, I glanced at his arms. The jet black of his skin only went up to his wrists today, little wisps of darkness straining up towards his elbows. Some days it seemed to take him over, reaching as high as his shoulders and filling him with panic. Very rarely, it became explosive, Valravn taking over until the only way forward was to let the darkness out. He woke in a sweat on plenty of nights, crying out until we held him tight enough to calm him.

He'd tried to hide it for a while. He'd get overwhelmed by dreams and thoughts, and suddenly he'd be pulling out long-sleeved tunics and gloves in the middle of summer. But neither Alyssa nor I were fooled, and off he'd go, back to Fólkheim to see about sorting out his mind.

If only we'd had therapists in Asgard when I was growing up. Perhaps a lot of things would have gone differently for a lot of people.

By the time the table was set and Alyssa was washed up and changed, a small ruckus had arrived by horseback outside. Alyssa got there first, swung the door open with an exuberant *hello!*, and rushed outside to meet them.

Three horses and four riders had arrived in front of the house, each of them a sight for sore eyes. They'd already hitched the animals to the posts outside. The weather was good for riding, and I had to hold my hand over my eyes to protect them from the sun. This far from the city, everything was a rainbow of wildflowers, golden fields, and fresh, babbling brooks.

Váli approached first and was immediately accosted by Alyssa. He gave her a one-armed hug, a heavy bag in his other hand. "Alyssa, you're clean for once!"

"Not you too. I just got done hearing about it from your parents." She squeezed him and then let him come to me. I took the bag from him (likely more work from the council), set it aside, and gave him a longer hug than he probably wanted.

Hreidulfr came to join us, his arms full. A young girl of six was tucked against his chest, dressed in a makeshift Valkyrie costume. Her skin was Elven Black, her eyes silver, and her tiny frame wriggled with excitement.

I squealed and stole her from his arms. "You are so beautiful and ferocious today!" I pressed my face into her hair and snorted like a pig, earning me a fit of giggles. "I missed you so much!"

Hreidulfr ruffled her hair and gave me a meaningful look, the kind that said *I'm about to say something serious.* "Remember how we told you she needed to pick a new name to better express herself?"

I nodded.

"Tell Grandma your new name."

"Aurora," she squeaked. "I'm a Valkyrie now!"

"Oh, you picked the very best name!" I squeezed her tighter but she was quickly scooped out of my arms by Loki, who had shifted into a more feminine form while I wasn't looking.

"I'm so proud of you!" Loki lifted Aurora up into the air and spun her, the two of them giggling.

"You're Grandma today!" Aurora said, patting Loki's head with her open palms.

Loki tucked her against her chest and started towards the house. "I am, just for you. Just two fearsome ladies ready for a good lunch, yes? Let's go finish setting the table."

Hreidulfr waited until they were out of earshot before expanding on the previous hint. "People are still getting used to calling her Aurora, and it's been hard explaining why people need to call her 'she', but they're comin' around. We'd be lost without Alyssa explaining it so well, but we're trying."

"That's all you can do." I gave his arm a squeeze. "She's lucky to have you."

"Having Loki around helps. Someone for her to look up to and ask the hard questions that I haven't got answers for. Well, as long as she doesn't catch a habit for trying to destroy the nine." The grin on his face as he started towards the door was contagious.

Váli watched as his husband disappeared inside. His bittersweet expression said so very much. He caught me staring and his lip quivered. "My shrink says forgiveness comes with time. I'm deciding to be happy for her today. Aurora deserves someone who loves her the way Loki does, and I shouldn't be jealous that my kid will get what I didn't from her." He visibly swallowed back his feelings. "It's better than it was, and that's something."

I pressed a kiss onto his cheek. "I love you."

Váli nodded, said nothing, and went inside.

Narvi had already been hovering quietly. He gave a small wave. "Didn't want to interrupt the moment."

I smothered him in a hug. "You're never interrupting anything. How was the trip? Are you sleeping alright? Is your work satisfying? Do—?"

"Mother!" He laughed and pulled away, letting me guide him into the house. "Everything is fine. I'm good. Better. I promise."

As we all sat down to eat, the stories began. Váli and Hreidulfr had their hands full between the city and their child. The need for an army had dwindled, and though they were still training recruits, the city needed their skills in other facets. Things that didn't centre around war.

Narvi had settled into a position on the council as well, with Hod. Narvi told us conspiratorially that Hod and Eyvindr had gotten into the habit of occasionally shirking their duties in order to make up for lost time, which left Narvi with plenty to keep him busy.

The city was thriving. A helping hand had been extended to whoever still lived in Asgard, and they'd needed three trips with three wagons to transport the people willing to try our way of life. Not everyone had agreed, of course. Such a thing is impossible in any realm.

Ravens arrived frequently from Hel. She'd recently let us know that Angrboda had found herself a new pastime: guiding hopeful souls to the Nornir in exchange for an exorbitant price. It was a smart choice, really. They got their chance at a new life, and if they were given a new fate or died trying, she kept everything to their name in Helheim. While I couldn't say I *approved*, I couldn't fault her logic.

She also passed on the news that Idunn and Bragi had left Helheim. They'd been escorted to Alfheim for their own safety, and had been left with enough supplies to start them on their way. Sometimes, I wondered where they were, or if they were alright, but that wasn't for me to know. If she wanted me, I wasn't that hard to find.

We ate heartily. Plates filled and emptied and filled again until the food ran out. Jokes were lobbed across the table at one another until we were breathless. Aurora took to running around the house fighting off invisible foes as Alyssa started to fashion a pair of child-sized false swan wings from nothing but the junk around the house. Váli and Loki stood shoulder to shoulder at the sink, washing the dishes and speaking in whispers. Narvi had gone off on a tangent about runes that Hreidulfr clearly couldn't understand but was too polite to interrupt.

As I looked down the table, laughter filling the room, an old feeling rose in my chest. A warning. That everything I saw now, every person around my table, could be stripped away at any moment. That nothing ever lasts. My chest tightened, a humming building under my skin. I was happy now, but I wasn't meant to *be* happy. I could have it for a little while, but never for long.

A figure knelt next to my chair and found my hand under the table. I turned my head and Alyssa gave me a gentle smile. I must have been showing too many of the horrible, routine thoughts on my face.

"It's alright," she said, leaning into my ear. She pressed my palm to her heart so I could focus on the steady rhythm instead of on my thoughts. Her eyes were clear and loving as they looked into mine. The conviction in them took my breath away.

"Sigyn, no one is going anywhere."

Reviews are critical for the success of indie books. Please consider leaving an honest review of this book and any other you read via whichever review platforms you use. You'll make a lot of indie authors very happy.

If you want the latest news about upcoming books by Cat Rector, including any upcoming books, join the mailing list at catrector.com

Thank you.

MY SUPPORTERS

A while ago, I invited the people who had been supporting my work since the beginning to submit their names for a few perks, meant as a thank you for being the people who helped me build a career. Each of the people on this list has shown love for Epilogues and for its predecessor The Goddess of Nothing At All, and that love has translated into my book sitting on e-readers and bookshelves across the world. Some of these people have been here from the beginning as writing partners, beta readers, and other helpers who have shaped the words in these books. Others arrived after, and they showed overwhelming passion and enthusiasm for my work, helping to tell the world about it. Thank you, every single one of you, for helping me make this dream a reality.

Rowan Liddell
Kaea Branch
LotteH
Carballo
Gabriela Florea
Jolien Nijns
Cheyenne Brammah
Allie B
Casey
A.J. Torres
Lisa H.
Aleksander E Petit
Alex Rae
Tanushka
Fem Lippens (loonieslibrary)
Erin Kinsella

Tanni
Amanda Diegan
DC Guevara
Michaela
Dina B.
Mireya
Vanessa R.
Brinley
Audrey
Matías Ruelas
Analiza
Becca Leigh
E. L. Pagès
fi
Suzanne Fraser-Martin
Nox T.
Lien drst
Esther
Elisabeth
Hannah Decock
Jules
Aiden
Cath
Alice
Rachel Kasparek

ACKNOWLEDGEMENTS

This is the second thank-you page I've had the privilege of writing, and I'm still in shock that I get to do this.

Fortunately, I have a lot of the same people to thank as book one.

Without Erin Kinsella, I wouldn't be writing a book 2. Erin has always been enthusiastic about my work, sometimes more enthusiastic than I am myself. She's always pushed me to reach for more, and insisted there was an audience for my dark little books. Thank you for everything you've done. I can't imagine what would have happened if you weren't here to egg me into writing the weirdest stuff XD

Thank you to Lyra Wolf, who has been a huge cheerleader of my work in the last year. I had no idea when they reached out that we would turn out to be two sides of the same coin. They've been an incredible resource for me, from ranting about the next Tiktok trend, to publishing woes, to how to move from one continent to the other with only four suitcases and some willpower. I've loved getting to partner on so many things, and I'm so thankful to call you a friend and colleague.

After 20 years of friendship, I have more to thank Jessica Brown for than I could ever list here. However this year she and her husband Corey went above and beyond, letting us bunk with them for our move back to Canada. They've learned to handle our quirks, but also been the backbone of our community since we've been back. Living with them has been one of the most emotionally fulfilling experiences of my life, and I'm grateful for the generosity they've shown us. Thank you both for everything, you mean the world to me.

My spouse Vincent has had one hell of a year just because he's attached to me. He braved my first year as a published author (which was nothing short of a rollercoaster) while also moving to Canada. I know from experience how disorienting it can be to live in another culture, and I am thankful for the bravery and/or blind stupidity he's shown in doing this with me. Even though his life to date has been nothing like what we're doing now, he's taken to it like a fish to water. And it doesn't hurt that he's supported my writing career without a second thought. Thank you.

To my family, better days are ahead. We have so much left to do together, and so much time to make up for. I'm excited to see where our paths lead us.

A book is nothing without its readers. The outpouring of love and support for The Goddess of Nothing At All was heartwarming and motivating. I had hoped that people would vibe with a tired, overwhelmed woman who just wanted to get what she'd earned, and many more people understood her than I ever anticipated. Thank you to everyone who read, reviewed, and told someone about the book. There isn't a single thing I can do to promote my book that is more powerful than your recommendation to a friend. Thank you, from the bottom of my heart. It's because of you that Book 2 exists and that I get to keep working on new projects.

If you just read this book and it hit home for you, I hope that part of the message you take from it is that shit is hard, but it's not the end. That getting better is a lot of work, and you might never truly recover from whatever has happened, but it can be better than it was. Have the courage to reach out for help, and don't let go of hope. Change takes time and roads are long, and you should do it anyway.

FURTHER READING

If Norse Mythology intrigues you but you're not sure where to go next, please check out some of these titles. There's also plenty of information online or at your local library. Some more expensive or rare texts might be in your local university catalogue.

Source Books:
The Prose Edda
The Poetic Edda
Gesta Danorum
The Sagas of Icelanders - Penguins Classics Deluxe Edition

Research:
The Norse Myths - Carolyne Larrington
Trickster Makes the World - Lewis Hyde
Vaesen - Johan Egerkrans
The Viking Way: Magic and Mind in Late Iron Age Scandinavia - Neil Price
Seidr: Het Noordse Pad - Linda Wormhoudt
Gods and Myths of Northern Europe - H.R. Ellis Davidson

Retellings:
Norse Mythology - Neil Gaiman
Tales of Norse Mythology (Leather Bound Edition) - Helen A. Guerber
Norse Myths: Tales of Odin, Thor and Loki - Kevin Crossley-Holland
Vikings: The Battle at the End of Time - Tony Allan

Fiction:
Please check out the blog on my website, CatRector.com, or my
Goodreads lists for recommendations

CONTRIBUTORS

Edited and Proofread by Ivy L. James
authorivyljames.com
Twitter.com/AuthorIvyLJames
Instagram.com/authorivyljames

Manuscript Critique by Erin Kinsella
erinkinsella.com/manuscript-critiques/

Sensitivity Read by Dal Cecil Runo
ko-fi.com/dalcecilruno
withkoji.com/@DalCecilRuno

Cover Art by Grace Zhu
gracezhuart.com
twitter.com/gracezhuart
instagram.com/gracezhuart/

Character Art on Website/Socials by LilithSaur
instagram.com/lilith_saur
twitter.com/lilithsaur

Viking Era Ornaments by Jonas Lau Markussen
jonaslaumarkussen.com/graphics-sets/vikingornaments

Cover Text, Interior Formatting and Design by Cat Rector

GLOSSARY OF TERMS

This glossary is a general guide for readers who are unfamiliar with the terms used in this story, however, many of these terms have nuance and history that can't be expressed in a blurb. I encourage you to go search out your own information, either using the internet or with the reference page I've added.

Aesir: One of the two tribes of Gods, referring to those whose home was Asgard. See the Pantheon Tree for details.

Alfheim: One of the nine realms, home of the elves.

Asgard: One of the nine realms, home of the Aesir Gods, and the main location of our story.

Bifrost: The rainbow bridge that connects Asgard and Midgard.

Einherjar: The chosen warriors of Odin. It was believed that when someone died in battle, they might be chosen to Valhalla, where they would dine in Odin's halls and become a part of his army of Einherjar. They would train every day and their wounds would heal every night, and at Ragnarok, the end of the realms, they would fight against the enemies of Asgard.

Ergi/Argr: Old Norse term. In the Viking Age, ergi was used to accuse someone of being unmanly or to insinuate effeminate behaviour. Being unmanly or cowardly was one of the worst things a man could be known for. Insults were taken very seriously in the Viking Age. Calling another man ergi was so insulting that it could result in a holmgang, or duel, in order for the accused to regain his honour.

Fólkheim: The city that Sigyn and her council have founded in the ruins of Vanaheim.

Ginnungagap: Before the existence of the realms, Ginnungagap was the void that sat between Musphelheim and Niflhiem. When the two realms drew close together, the fire and ice mixed to create the giant Ymir, whose body was used to create Midgard.

Gladsheim: One of Odin's halls. Used as a meeting hall, it contains thirteen seats for the Gods. In some texts, only the male Gods had seats in this hall, while in others it's nonspecific.

Gruvrå: A mine spirit from the north that was said to hold dominion over mines, quarries, and ore deposits in mountains. She often warned of disaster and could be convinced to help miners discover new ore deposits if she was given a proper offering. Sometimes benevolent, sometimes territorial, the gruvrå demanded respect, and when it wasn't given, it could result in death and disaster.

Helheim: One of the nine realms. Home of the dead who aren't placed in Freya's halls at Sessrúmnir or in Odin's halls in Valhalla. Sometimes believed to be the resting place of those who died dishonourable deaths of disease or old age, but this may be a view influenced by the introduction of Christianity.

Jotun: The term for the people of Jotunheim. Some sources refer to them as giants but this is technically false according to many sources. They were more likely just another tribe of people apart from the Aesir and Vanir.

Jotunheim: One of the nine realms. Home of the Jotun.

Midgard: Known to us simply as Earth, the land of humans.

Musphelheim: One of the nine realms. A mostly uninhabitable land of fire and volcanoes. Home of the fire giant Surt.

Niflheim: One of the nine realms. A realm of ice and snow. Some sources consider Niflheim and Helheim to be the same realm, while others disagree.

Norns, the: Can refer to many female beings who alter fate, but in this story it refers to the three most well known. The fates are seen in many mythologies as three women of different age groups, and in Norse mythology, they are Urd (the past), Skuld (the future), and Verdandi (the present). They have control over the fates of Gods and men, and can be called on when looking for answers, as Odin often did.

Ragnarok: The final battle prophesied at the end of Norse mythology. A series of events will herald a battle between the Gods and their enemies. At the end of the battle, the realms will fall, ending life as we know it. One version of Ragnarok ends in rebirth, while many skeptics think that this is due to the influence of Christianity and the presence of Jesus during the time of the oldest recorded source.

Seidr: Seiðr. One of the many words used to describe viking age magic. The practitioners believed, among other things, that seidr could be used to alter fate, effect the decisions of others, and bring good fortune. There are many books available on both modern and viking age magic which I highly encourage you to look into.

Sjörå: A water sprite from northern folklore that held dominion over mountain pools, lakes, and lake systems. She often appeared as a beautiful woman who could be won over with gifts and was much less prone to drowning humans as her cousin, the Neck.

Svartalfheim: One of the nine realms. Translates roughly to 'black elf home' and is the home of the dwarves, which are sometimes called black elves in ancient texts.

Valaskjalf: One of Odin's halls. His high tower is a part of this hall, but not much else is known. For the purposes of this story, it's used to house guests, Gods without halls of their own, or Gods who just need a place to sleep for the night.

Valhalla: One of Odin's halls and by far the most known. When someone was killed in battle during the Viking age, Valhalla was one of the places where the fallen dead could go for an afterlife.

Valkyrie: A powerful female warrior with swan wings on her back. She was able to take the shape of a swan and did so in several Germanic tales. They were said to attend battles on earth take the souls of the worthy dead up to Asgard. Their duties also included serving the Einherjar food and drink in Valhalla.

Valravn: A carrion creature of folklore that was known for eating the hearts of the battle-slain (especially kings) in order to gain a gruesome human-like body. Not someone you want to meet in a dark alley.

Vanaheim: One of the nine realms. Home of the Vanir.

Vanir: One of two tribes of Gods, referring to those whose home was Vanaheim. See the Pantheon Tree for details.

Völva/ Völur: One of the many names for a practitioner of seidr in the viking age. Usually women, they were said to have ability to see fate, contact the dead, or speak to the Gods, among other things. There are attestations of male völur, but it was less common, in part because it was looked down upon as an unmanly profession. For the purposes of this story, not all facts known about the völur on Midgard are applied to the people of the other nine realms.

Yggdrasil: The World Tree. This massive ash tree connects the nine realms by its roots and is home to a variety of animals. For the purposes of this story, Idunn's golden apples grow on its branches and it has nine roots instead of the three attested to in the Eddas.

Ymir: The giant that was created at the dawn of the realms, and from which all things descend.

BONUS STORY

Aunts, turn back now. I know you're reading. TURN BACK

Trigger warnings:
Explicit vanilla sexual content, polyamory, moments of existential crisis

HAPPILY EVER AFTER

LOKI

As much as we'd tried to pretend all of it was normal, it wasn't. I'd already spent days watching my hands, trying not to be too up front with the way that I was with Sigyn. It was bad enough that we'd spent so much time apart and hadn't quite figured out marraige out, let alone how to we were supposed to act with each other now that she was in love with someone else.

And we'd agreed to this. I'd agreed to it. I wasn't *mad* about it. I just didn't know what the fuck to do *with it*.

Sigyn and I had already settled down on the pillows in front of the fire, a book for each of us. She was leaning against my side, engrossed in a newly written text from the herbalist in the city. Mine was a less noble pursuit; there was still pursuing, it's just that someone was *pursuing* a good fuck with their starcrossed lover. It was no masterpiece, but it passed the time.

Alyssa came back from the cellar, her skirt pulling along the floor behind her, and she set down a plate of cheese, bread, and fresh fruit in front of us. A moment later she was back with three cups and a pitcher of wine. I looked up from the page and she smiled back at me, and I wondered if she felt as awkward as I did.

She sat down on the other side of Sigyn and let her string her legs over her lap. Her book was a study on Dwarven language. Two scholars and I was here reading smut.

Well, at least I knew myself.

I tried to keep reading, but over the top of my book, I caught sight of Alyssa's fingers running absent-mindedly over Sigyn's bare leg. Her skirt had travelled up,

265

revealing her calf and a good bit of her thigh.

I drew in a breath, trying to press that thought down. So far as I was aware, neither of us had made a move yet. No one knew what move to make.

Scolding myself, I tried to move back to the book, to not pay attention. Then Sigyn made the slightest noise and I knew that noise. My body stirred and there wasn't a godsdamn thing I could do about it.

Alyssa had looked up too, just a little. Trying to be subtle. And I couldn't see Sigyn's face, but her book had fallen and I knew they were looking at each other.

Fuck sakes. All this fucking tension and I was going to end up in a corner alone, tugging my prick like some adolescent boy.

Alyssa's fingers grew more bold, sliding up Sigyn's calve delicately, purposefully, and Sigyn's body tensed against mine, her chest rising and falling in one deep breath.

What the fuck was I supposed to do? Should I move? Leave? Surely that ruins whatever is about to happen here. But then that means staying and is it weird to watch? This wasn't my first trip down this particular alley, but there was something different about it being your *wife*.

I froze as Alyssa put down her book and leaned over Sigyn, kissing her. I was at such an odd angle that I could only see the tops of their heads, hear the slow, languid sound of their lips. I couldn't see a damned thing, but it was so fucking hot.

My prick was pressing uncomfortably against my trousers but there was no way I was going to move. Sure, I didn't want to be noticed, but I didn't want them to stop either. Maybe it was perverted, watching like that, but *they* were the ones making out against *me*.

Like she could read fucking minds, Alyssa raised up her head and looked right at me. Her lips were soft and pouty, the blue in her eyes intense. And without a word, she leaned forward and kissed me.

She'd never so much as touched me as more than a passing gesture, but her lips brushed mine like a question and everything in my body screamed yes. It was an invitation and I was so very happy to accept.

I cupped her cheek in my hand, tasting the newness of her, the familiarness of Sigyn, felt the flick of her tongue against my lip. I shivered.

Yes.

She backed away, bending to give Sigyn another kiss. Sigyn sat up, taking her weight off of me, and I just watched. Watched their hands run over each other, Alyssa's working at the straps on Sigyn's nightgown, pushing one down to expose her shoulder. Her lips trailed the skin there and it was all I could do not to reach into my pants to find some of my own pleasure.

Sigyn's head lolled to the side, eyes fluttering. She caught me watching and reached out pulling me towards her. The kiss she gave me was so wanting and I was beyond wanting. I needed her.

Then Alyssa's lips were on my shoulder and it was so much to take in. A deep moan escaped me and I could feel Sigyn smiling against my lips.

"Let's go to bed," she whispered.

Gods.

Alyssa stood first, holding her hand out to Sigyn, who took it, then took a kiss from her. Even from the floor I could see Sigyn's tongue slide into Alyssa's mouth. I pushed myself off the floor and approached, trying to be careful to understand my role in all this. If I didn't play my cards right, this could all disappear and I would *never* forgive myself.

Taking Sigyn's hand, Alyssa led us to the bedroom. We'd all been sleeping in one bed, sure, but this was new. As she walked, she loosened the tie on her wrap skirt and it cascaded to the floor, leaving only a pair of silken black panties. I tried not to stare, tried to find some way to make these two things line up in my mind; think about fucking your wife, don't stare at other bodies, but she's taking your wife to bed and she's kissing her and *she* invited you to bed too.

The hesitation must have been so very obvious. Alyssa pulled my hand and pushed me to the bed, crawling over top of me, straddling my hips. She flicked her tongue against my ear and my body arched to meet hers. She took my hand and cupped it onto her still-covered breast.

"I would've expected you to be bolder, Loki," she said into my ear. "Don't you want me?"

Something about it still felt like a fucking trap.

The bed moved and Sigyn crawled across the mattress toward us. She'd taken off every stitch of clothing, and when she got close enough, she kissed Alyssa again, sliding her own hand on top of mine so that we were *both* cupping her tit.

Well alright.

Alyssa leaned Sigyn onto the bed, away from me, and started travelling kisses across her bare skin, stopping to lick at her nipples, down the curve of her tit, and I knew where she was going. I got to my knees and moved behind Alyssa, pulling her back up. I pressed her back against my chest, licking the length of her neck. I wasn't going to stop her, no. But that was enough of all this *clothing*.

I pulled Alyssa's shirt over her head, the silk sliding off her pale rose skin to reveal everything underneath. I reached up to squeeze one of her tits, sliding the other hand down her hip, under the edge of her panties, inching them off.

When I looked down, Sigyn was biting her lips, her fingers working at her clit. This. This was what paradise looked like.

I nipped at Alyssa's ear and she moaned, and Sigyn's back arched. Like they were connected, like we could just pass this pleasure around. And we hadn't even gotten started.

I took a breath and spoke into Alyssa's neck. "If you want me to stop, tell me to stop."

She pressed her ass into my prick, grinding against me. "I won't want you to."

Fuck me.

I bent her forward, sliding my hand down her bare back as she resumed kissing Sigyn's skin. When she was low enough, Alyssa took Sigyn's fingers away from where they'd been buried between her legs and put them in her mouth. She licked them clean, then bent her head between Sigyn's legs.

I couldn't see a thing. I didn't want to *imagine* what it was like to watch another woman go down on my wife, I'd done that enough already. I had to see it. I laid down beside them at the best angle I could find and lavished in it as Alyssa nuzzled her lips into Sigyn's and licked at her, drawing out elicit moans.

I'd already started stroking myself, unable to resist, but it wouldn't do. No, I wasn't going to just lie there. So I sat up behind Alyssa, and I considered my options, but we weren't there quite yet. So I licked my fingers and slid them gently between her legs, in search of her own clit.

Alyssa tensed, not having seen it coming, but she didn't move away as I stroked her, trying to figure out what it was she liked. After a moment, she moaned into Sigyn's pussy and I knew I was on the right track. So I slid my fingers inside her.

That was enough to pull her head up and draw a real moan from her. Sigyn opened her eyes as Alyssa straightened out against my body, letting me push my fingers in and out of her. Her fingers were in my hair and my dick was throbbing.

I whispered in her ear again. "Would you mind if I fuck my wife?"

"Only if you forget about me."

"Oh? You want to get fucked too?" I wiggled my fingers in what I assumed were the right places and she all but cried out.

"Yes. Yes, you have to fuck me."

And maybe it was for show, but it was fucking working.

I gently pulled my fingers out of her and let her crawl to the side so that I could lean over Sigyn and kiss her. On my elbows, I looked into her eyes. "And you're sure this is what you want?"

Sigyn licked her lips. "I want you and I want her, and watching you with her turns me on. Keep going."

"Not yet," I said, fumbling to untie my trousers with one hand. "I have you to attend to."

Then Alyssa's hands were around me, untying the string herself, pulling them down and off me. She took my cock in her hand and my mouth dropped open, her hands so *good* on me that I- the words- fuck.

"Don't tease me, Loki." Sigyn reached down and they were both stroking me and my eyes rolled back into my head-

"If you don't stop-" I breathed- "you're both going to be very disappointed.

Sigyn pouted and let go, opting to just kiss me for a moment. Alyssa let go as well, her hands running across my ass. I composed myself, pushed the pleasure down, and slid my cock inside Sigyn. She moaned in my ear and it was almost enough on its own to undo me, but there was still too much to do, too much left to feel. I wanted to know what Alyssa felt like, what we could all do to each other. I kept thrusting into Sigyn and her pussy was so tight around me, and it felt so very good.

And after a moment that felt like forever and only seconds, Alyssa was back, pulling me away. "It's my turn," she moaned. And it fucking was.

I let her push me back onto my ass and she crawled on top of me, pressing down on my cock, still wet from Sigyn's pussy and she rode me like a stallion, grinding herself into me until all I could do was groan and hold her hips, driving my fingers into her. Sigyn's hands were on my back, in my hair, her lips all over my skin and the pressure was building and

And I came inside Alyssa, my wife's arms around my shoulders, holding me still as my body shuddered and the pleasure wracked through me like lightning.

This was going to be one hel of an afterlife.

But neither of the women had come and that was absolutely unacceptable. Alyssa peeled herself off of me, white slipping out of her cunt. And before I could make a move, Sigyn was on top of her, licking her pussy clean.

Gods, I'd never seen anything more beautiful in my life.

When I was collected enough to move, I went to the edge of the bed and knelt down. Sigyn's ass was in the air as she licked Alyssa, giving me a stunning view of everything. So I slid underneath her, pulled her hips to my face, and drove my tongue in her cunt.

Sigyn moaned so deeply that I nearly felt it all the way in her nethers. I kept going, licking at her, using my fingers inside her in all the ways I knew she liked, And Alyssa's moans were growing louder, faster, and then she was coming too, hips bucking against Sigyn's mouth. Once Alyssa was finished, Sigyn sat up, keeping my tongue between her legs, and licked her wet lips. I wanted so badly to know what Alyssa tasted like. But we had time.

Instead I focused on Sigyn, watching as her face relaxed, her head fell back, and then listened to the beautiful sound of her moaning as I pushed her over the edge. My face was soaked with her, and when she fell to the side, lying down to catch her breath, Alyssa leaned in and kissed me, tasting her as well.

The three of us spent, we crawled up to the middle of the bed. Sigyn was already sprawled out in the middle, and we curled up to either side of her, tucked against her slick skin.

"Well, that was something," I breathed, heart still racing in my chest.

"It was fucking amazing." Alyssa rolled onto her back before looking at us again, a bit more fear in her eyes. "I'm sorry if I was too forward. I just- we were all being so strange this week and I think you're both really hot, and I don't want this to be weird, I-"

"Alyssa." I reached out and took her hand. "The only way I would hate this is if you said we could never do it again."

She laughed. "Alright. Good. It was so…"

"Intense." Sigyn filled in, her hand on her heart. "I love you. Both of you."

"I love you too, Sig." I looked over at Alyssa. "And I'm well on my way with you."

She smiled. "Yeah. Same." She yawned. "Can we nap now? I think I'd like to do this again later."

Sigyn shook her head, smiling from ear to ear. "I don't know why we didn't do this sooner."

Alyssa had tucked herself into the crook of Sigyn's arm. "Hadn't found me yet, silly."

ABOUT THE AUTHOR

Cat Rector grew up in a small Nova Scotian town and could often be found simultaneously reading a book and fighting off muskrats while walking home from school. She devours stories in all their forms, loves messy, morally grey characters, and writes about the horrors that we inflict on each other. After spending nearly a decade living abroad, she returned to Canada with her spouse to resume her war against the muskrats. When she's not writing, you can find her playing video games, spending time with loved ones, or staring at her To Be Read pile like it's going to read itself.

Epilogues for Lost Gods is the sequel to her debut novel,
The Goddess of Nothing At All.

Find her on Twitter, Tiktok, and Instagram at Cat_Rector
Or visit her website, CatRector.com

9 781778 076312